ANOTHER YEAR at The FARM on MUDDYPUDDLE LANE

Heart-warming, uplifting romance

Etti Summers

DAYDREAMS

CHAPTER ONE

The bus pulled into the pretty village of Picklewick and drew to a halt. Maisie Fairfax clicked up the handle of her suitcase, tied the belt of her jacket more firmly around her waist, and got to her feet. Bumping her suitcase down the steps of the bus, she rolled it to the side of the pavement and reviewed her options.

She had two: walk the three kilometres from the village to the farm on Muddypuddle Lane, or phone her sister and beg a lift. Neither held much appeal. Getting a lift would be preferable to pulling her suitcase all that way, but she wasn't sure she could face Dulcie's ire. Which was why Maisie hadn't informed Dulcie that she was coming. If Dulcie had known beforehand, she probably wouldn't have let Maisie come.

In some ways, Maisie wouldn't have blamed her. Maisie knew she could be unreliable, but that was only because she hadn't yet discovered what she wanted to do with her life. Dulcie didn't understand her, that was all. Unfortunately, neither did their mother, which was why Maisie was turning up at Dulcie's farm unannounced on this chilly afternoon at the beginning of March.

Dulcie wouldn't be amused, but neither would she send her packing. At least, Maisie *hoped* she wouldn't.

No, Dulcie couldn't — there wasn't another bus back to Thornbury today (Maisie had checked) and even if Dulcie drove her to the train station herself, Maisie doubted whether they would get there in time for her to catch the train back to Birmingham.

She gazed around the high street. Many of the shops had already closed for the day, although a small convenience store was still open, and a fish and chip shop had several customers waiting in line. The thought of battered fish and hot, fluffy chips made her mouth water, but despite having only had a latte and a chocolate chip cookie since she'd left Birmingham this morning, Maisie knew she had to save her money until she managed to find another job.

Lights were on in The Wild Side she noticed, but she guessed that Otto, Dulcie's other half, would be too busy getting the restaurant ready for its first customers of the evening to spare the time to ferry her up to the farm. Besides, Maisie knew that asking Otto to give her a lift would irritate Dulcie even more, and her sister would be irritated enough already.

There was always the option of phoning Nikki, who lived just off the main street, but Maisie's eldest sister would be even more annoyed than Dulcie. Maisie did consider asking Nikki if she could stay with her, but Nikki's cottage only had two bedrooms and both were occupied, so unless Maisie wanted to sleep on the floor, she had no choice other than to go to the farm.

Sod it, she would just have to call Dulcie and get the lecture over with. She would have to face her sister's wrath at some point, so she may as well do it whilst being chauffeured to the farm, rather than when she got there. At least she would have saved herself the walk and spared her arms from being yanked out of their sockets if she had to drag her case up the steep hill.

With a resigned sigh, Maisie took her phone out of the back pocket of her jeans.

Her sister answered after a couple of rings.

'Hi, Dulcie, it's me.'

'Maisie! Hi!' Dulcie sounded surprised. 'Is everything okay?'

'Er, not really.'

'What's wrong? Is it Mum?'

'Mum is fine.' And Mum would probably continue to be fine until she realised her youngest child had done a runner rather than face her disappointment when she learnt that Maisie had lost yet another job.

'Thank goodness for that,' Dulcie was saying. 'You had me worried for a minute.' There was a pause. 'If it's not Mum, what is it?'

'I need a favour,' Maisie said. 'I'm in Picklewick – can I have a lift?'

There was a stunned silence, then, 'Why are you in *Picklewick?*'

'I'll tell you when I see you. Can you come fetch me?'

Maisie could almost sense Dulcie's eyes narrowing as her sister asked, 'Does Mum know you're here?'

'Not exactly.'

'Oh, Maisie! Have you been sacked again?'

Maisie heard Dulcie's exasperation and resented it. It was alright for her: Dulcie had landed on her feet when she'd won the farm on Muddypuddle Lane. She'd had it handed to her on a plate. Plus Dulcie had never had to do a job she loathed for minimum wage. *And* she had lucked out when she'd met Otto. He loved her to the moon and back and treated her like a princess. None of Maisie's boyfriends had ever treated *her* like that, which was why they were *ex*-boyfriends. In her twenty-five years she had kissed an awful lot of frogs, and she was beginning to fear that she would never find a prince.

Maisie lifted her chin. 'I walked out,' she said. 'A customer groped my bum and the manager didn't like it when I objected.'

Dulcie sighed. 'How did you object? No, don't tell me – you slapped his face. Or did you pour a cup of coffee over his head?'

'In his lap, actually. And it was an iced coffee, not a hot one. I thought it might cool him down.' Maisie sniggered. 'He looked like he had wet himself. I got a round of applause from the women at the next table.'

'So now you want to stay here, on the farm?'

'Can I? Please?' Maisie hated begging, but she couldn't face going home. She would have to go eventually of course, but not just yet.

Another sigh from Dulcie. 'Give me ten minutes. And Maisie? You'd better tell Mum where you are – I don't want her calling me in a panic.'

Mindful that she didn't want to get her sister's back up any more than she already had, Maisie sent Mum a quick message.

Gone to visit Dulcie for a few days. Wanted to see the goats. Arrived safe xxx

Her mum's reply was short. *Nice of you to let me know.*

At least Mum knew where she was, so she wouldn't worry. No more than usual, that is.

Maisie spied Dulcie's car and waved, wincing when it screeched to a halt. From the way Dulcie was driving, Maisie gathered that her sister wasn't in the best of moods.

'Get in,' Dulcie ordered, making no move to get out and help Maisie heave her case into the hatchback's small boot. 'Planning on staying long?' she asked when Maisie slipped into the passenger seat.

Maisie shrugged.

'Is that a yes shrug, or a no shrug?'

'Dunno.'

Before Dulcie pulled away from the kerb, she uttered a loud sigh. 'Out with it – why are you here?'

To her dismay, Maisie's eyes filled with tears. 'I'm sorry, I should have asked first.'

'Yes, you should have.'

Maisie brushed her tears away. 'Don't worry, I'll leave tomorrow.'

Dulcie softened. 'You don't have to, but I'm warning you, if you intend to stay more than a day or two, I expect you to pull your weight.'

'I will,' Maisie agreed with relief.

'There are the goats to see to for a start, and maybe Otto could use a hand in the restaurant.'

'I'll do anything,' Maisie said, even though she didn't like working in restaurants, pubs or bars. Her previous two jobs had been in pubs. Neither of them had ended well.

Maisie suspected she wasn't cut out to be customer-facing. She was, however, looking forward to helping with the goats. They were so darned cute, especially the pygmy ones.

'Have any of them had their babies yet?' she asked as Dulcie eased the car into the road.

'They are due any day now.'

Maisie clapped her hands and let out a squeal. 'I can't wait to cuddle a goatling.'

A smile spread across her sister's face. 'Neither can I. If my goat milk business takes off, there will be plenty more baby goats on the farm. Eventually I'm hoping to be able to give up the day job.'

Oh, yes; Maisie had forgotten that Dulcie had a job, besides running the farm. She worked from home though, so it couldn't be too bad. Maisie would love to be able to work from home, but although she had applied for a couple of jobs where that was an option, she had never even got as far as the interview stage.

'I've got a chap coming tomorrow to give me a quote for converting one of the outbuildings into a pasteurisation shed,' Dulcie was saying. 'I managed to buy the equipment second hand, but I've got to get someone to install it.'

As Dulcie chattered away, Maisie relaxed into her seat. It seemed that her sister had forgiven her for turning up out of the blue. Now all Maisie had to do was make herself useful, so Dulcie didn't send her back home before she was ready to go.

Adam straightened up, wiping his filthy hands on an oily rag, and surveyed the tractor's engine.

'Is it fixed?' the ruddy-faced man in his fifties asked.

'Try it.'

The farmer hoisted his sturdy frame into the cab, grinning when the engine started first time. 'You've done a tidy job.'

Adam dipped his head in acknowledgement; he always did a tidy job and because of that his reputation of being able to fix things was growing. It wasn't just tractors he repaired – he was happy to turn his hand to anything mechanical.

'How much do I owe you?' the farmer asked.

Adam gave him a figure, then as the man went to fetch the money, he began stowing his tools in the van.

'Here you go.' The farmer pressed the money into his hand and Adam wrote out a receipt.

'You've got my number if she gives you any more trouble,' he said, jerking his head at the old tractor. It had seen better days, but with a little TLC and some careful handling, it would last a few more years.

Adam was thankful that this was his last job of the day. He needed a shower, some food, and maybe a pint or two if he could summon the energy to pop along to The Black Horse.

Or he could slump on the sofa with a cup of tea and do his monthly trawl of the internet for properties for sale.

There was nothing wrong with where he currently lived, but he was fast outgrowing the workshop beneath the flat. It was bursting at the seams, and even if it hadn't been, he was ready for a change. He was looking for a place to take his business to the next level. And by buying a more substantial property, he was hoping to make his parents realise that he was serious about it.

His parents didn't like what he did for a living, but that was fine: they didn't need to. What they *did* need to do, was to stop giving him grief about it.

As soon as he arrived home, Adam stripped off and hopped in the shower. Turning the dial up so the water was as hot as he could stand it, he freed his hair from the topknot he wore when he was working, and dug his fingers into his scalp. He had a tendency to wear it too tight and the relief when he took it out was blissful.

A good soaping later and with the water in the bottom of the tray finally running clear, Adam stepped out and towelled himself down before taking a clean pair of joggers out of the drawer, along with a fresh tee shirt.

As well as disapproving of what he did for a living, his parents weren't keen on his flat, either. Or the way he looked. When he had started to wear his hair longer at uni, they had put it down to teenage rebellion. The tattoos (of which he had several) and the eyebrow piercing, they had put down to him wanting to fit in and the influence of the other students. But after he'd finished his course and had continued to refuse to cut his shoulder-length hair or take the silver ring out of his eyebrow, they had come to the conclusion that he was simply being bloody-minded. And the pointed scowls when his tattoos were on display, seriously tried his patience.

It didn't stop him loving his mum and dad though, even if they did exasperate the hell out of him.

As he fried his steak and chopped some salad, he realised it had been a couple of weeks since he'd last seen them, and he vowed to call in soon, before his mum phoned and demanded his presence. Maybe he would drop in tomorrow. Which reminded him, he had promised to pop up to the farm on Muddypuddle Lane in the morning to give the owner, Dulcie Fairfax, a quote for installing a pasteurisation unit.

It wasn't something he had done before, but he was confident that he would be able to work it out. For some inexplicable reason he had an affinity with anything mechanical: god knows where he got it from, but it certainly wasn't from his dad.

Deciding he was too tired to go to the pub, after he had eaten Adam settled down on the sofa with his laptop on his knees and a cup of tea on the table next to him. Perhaps he would go to the pub tomorrow evening, instead...

Maisie couldn't sleep. It was too quiet. She was used to the noise of the city, even if she did live in the suburbs. The silence here was unnerving, and she had forgotten that it had taken her a few nights to get used to it when she and Mum had visited the farm the previous Christmas.

Maisie wished the inside of her head was as quiet as the outside. Her thoughts were whirling, the events of the past few days praying on her mind. She had been determined not to lose her latest job, but who in their right mind would put up with that kind of behaviour from the punters? She could have had the bloke done for assault, but she hadn't wanted the hassle. It had been easier to take matters into her own hands. The downside was that she had thought it best to resign before she was sacked.

In a moment of indecision, she wondered what she hoped to achieve by coming to the farm. It was safe to say that her job prospects would be seriously curtailed in a small village like Picklewick. She would have been better off staying in Birmingham. But she'd had to get away, unable to face her mother's continued dismay.

Despite Mum fighting Maisie's corner if anyone criticised her, Maisie could tell that she was a disappointment, and she knew Mum must be comparing her to Maisie's siblings. Dulcie had the farm (the lucky cow), Nikki was a teacher, and Jay used to travel all over the world with his job until he'd settled in New Zealand. Also, all three were in steady relationships.

Maisie's defence was that she was still young. At twenty-five, she had plenty of time to decide what she wanted to be when she grew up. And so what if she played the field? Better that, than get hitched to the wrong guy. The problem was, she was beginning to think there weren't any *right* guys out there.

The quiet of the night was broken by the sound of a vehicle coming up the lane and she heard the engine noise change as it putted into the farmyard. Guessing Otto was home and that Dulcie had waited up for him, Maisie thought she'd give her sister a few minutes to tell him they had a houseguest, before going to say hello. She would have a glass of milk while she was at it, and maybe Otto had brought some goodies back with him from the restaurant. She could do with a snack.

After watching a couple of YouTube videos on her phone, she decided enough time had elapsed, so she stuffed her feet into fluffy slippers, wrapped herself up in her dressing gown and padded across the landing. Treading carefully down the steep narrow staircase, Maisie had just reached the bottom step when she heard voices coming from the kitchen.

Hearing her name mentioned, she paused.

Dulcie was saying, 'I don't think Maisie will ever grow up. She drifts through life without a care in the world, taking no responsibility for her actions. I was never like that when I was her age.'

Otto chuckled. 'You're not that much older than her. There are only three years between you.'

'Exactly! That's what I'm saying! Look, you don't have to give her any shifts in the restaurant; I shouldn't have asked. She's likely to do something silly, or decide it's too much like hard work, or whatever reason she gives for packing a job in. And even if she doesn't walk out, employers soon let her go. She's had more jobs than I've had hot dinners. I think she's waiting for the perfect job to land in her lap, but that's not likely to happen. Nikki calls her Maisie Daydream.'

Maisie bit her lip and her eyes filled with tears. That was so unfair. She wasn't *waiting* for the perfect job – she was *trying to find it*. There was a difference.

Otto said, 'I don't mind giving her a chance, if you don't. She can have a couple of shifts and we'll see how she goes.'

'If she tips coffee in any of your customer's laps, she'll have me to answer to,' Dulcie growled.

Otto's laugh sounded too close for comfort and Maisie had the awful suspicion he was immediately on the other side of the door. It was confirmed when he said, 'I'll just get changed, then we'll have a cup of tea before bed, eh? Maybe, with Maisie here, she could see to the animals in the mornings, so you don't have to get up early. We could have a lie-in, for a change.'

The doorknob twisted and Maisie panicked. Instead of pretending to have just this second come downstairs in order for Otto not to realise she had been eavesdropping, she darted towards the front door and was through it in a trice.

Closing it behind her as softly as she could, she tiptoed around the back of the farmhouse and made her way to the barn. Hopefully the goats wouldn't be as judgemental as her sister.

Adam checked the time and realised he had fifty minutes before he needed to be at the farm on Muddypuddle Lane; enough time to stop off in the village for a brunch panini and a coffee.

He eyed the sit-on lawnmower with satisfaction. It was now running as sweet as a nut, and he had even sharpened the cutting blades. It hadn't been part of the repair, but it hadn't taken long with the grinder, and being willing to go that extra mile was helping to build his reputation because the vast majority of work that came his way was by word of mouth.

He lived on the outskirts of Picklewick, in a flat above what had once been an MOT garage, and the farm was in the opposite direction, so he drove through the village, found a parking space on the high street and hopped out, aiming for the cafe a short distance up the road.

'Adam, what can I get you?' Lou asked. She had owned the cafe for years and, in Adam's opinion, served the best coffee for miles.

'I've just about got time for a ham and cheese panini and an Americano, please.'

She flicked a cloth over the counter. 'Find a table and I'll bring it over. Can I tempt you with a slice of strawberry and vanilla sponge?'

Adam's mouth watered. He was a sucker for cakes. 'Go on, but if I can't fit into my jeans, I'll blame you.'

'Pah! It'll take more than one slice of cake! You haven't got an ounce of fat on you. If I was ten years younger...'

Adam sat down, grinning. Lou was an outrageous flirt, but she was like that with all the men, not just him.

'Here, get that inside you,' she instructed, putting his food and a coffee on the table. He noticed she had given him a generous slice of cake, and he reminded himself to leave her an equally generous tip.

As he ate, he scrolled through his emails, glad to see that a part he had ordered for a trailer had been dispatched, and he highlighted it. As soon as it arrived, he would let his customer know and hopefully he would be able to crack on with the job.

Finishing his food, he drank the last of the coffee and settled the bill.

'See you soon,' Lou called, and Adam waved as he stepped into the street. He was a regular at the cafe, calling in two to three times a week. It was more convenient than making his own sandwiches, and it forced him to take a proper break, otherwise he would be eating his lunch on the run.

Suitably fuelled up, he returned to the van. It was time to take a look at Dulcie Fairfax's pasteurisation unit.

The farm was roughly a five-minute drive out of Picklewick, at the top of a steep lane. He used to go up that way a lot when he was a kid, because halfway up the hill was a riding stable, where his mum used to take him for lessons. He quite liked horses, although he hadn't ridden in years. At the time, the farm had been owned by an old chap called Walter York, but he'd moved into a cottage further down the lane, and Dulcie Fairfax lived at the farm now, along with Walter's son, Otto, who had recently opened a restaurant in the village.

Adam had heard that the food in The Wild Side was good, although he hadn't tried it himself and he probably wouldn't any time soon. It was the kind of place you went to for a special occasion, or if you wanted to impress a date. As far as Adam was aware, there were no special occasions on the horizon and he hadn't had a date in ages. Nor did he want one: he wanted to concentrate on growing his business before he allowed himself to become distracted by a girlfriend.

He was still thinking about the stables and wondering whether the place had changed, when he made the right-hand turn on the lane. Over the tops of the hedges he could glimpse horses grazing in the fields to either side, and out of the corner of his eye Adam thought he could see a donkey. There was something incredibly cute about donkeys, he mused.

Easing around a bend in the lane, he changed down a gear as the incline steepened, but as he came out of it, he swore loudly.

Tearing down the road at break-neck speed was a bloody goat!

Adam slammed on the brakes and came to a standstill just as the goat swerved into the verge to avoid his van, and as he did so he realised a woman was racing headlong after it, her arms windmilling as she fought to maintain her balance and not let her feet run away with her.

'What the hell?' he shouted, throwing his hands up in the air. What on earth was she thinking? He had almost ploughed into her. Thank goodness he had been doing no more than twenty miles per hour, if that.

Her horrified expression as she skidded past the van, told him she realised how close she had come to being flattened. But she didn't stop, and his last sight of her was in his side mirror as she carried on running down the lane in hot pursuit of the goat.

Shaken, Adam sat there for a minute, adrenalin from the near miss making his fingers tingle and his heart pound. His good mood gone, he finally pulled himself together and carried on up the hill to the farm, muttering darkly.

Maisie's heart was in her mouth as she spotted Princess, and she slowed to a walk, not wanting to spook her. The goat was calmly munching on something in the hedgerow, but she was perilously close to where the lane met the main road. It wasn't a particularly busy road, but all it took was one vehicle... A van coming up the lane had nearly taken the goat out as it was, but thankfully it had been travelling quite slowly. Traffic on the main road would be going considerably faster.

'There's a good girl,' Maisie crooned breathlessly, as she drew closer to the animal.

Princess carried on munching, but one eye was on Maisie who fully expected the goat to bolt at any second.

Changing tactics, Maisie calmly sidled to the opposite side of the lane, hoping she was conveying total disinterest in the naughty creature.

Whistling tunelessly (it was more of a wheeze than a whistle because she was still out of breath from her mad run down the lane), Maisie put her hands behind her back, lifted her chin, and pretended to be interested in the sky as she strolled nonchalantly past.

Still chewing, a bunch of greenery protruding from one side of her mouth, Princess kept tabs on her progress, and when Maisie reached the point where she was between the goat and the road, Maisie heaved a sigh of relief. Then she let the daft creature have it with both barrels.

Shrieking at the top of her voice, Maisie leapt up and down, waving her arms.

Spooked, Princess uttered a loud bleat, spun to the left and began to gallop back up the lane, her short fluffy tail held aloft.

Maisie, hopeful that the goat would keep heading in the right direction and praying that she wouldn't double back and try to slip past her, followed at a more sedate pace. Now that the immediate crisis had been averted, she felt a bit wobbly. How could she have told Dulcie that one of the goats – and not even *her* goat, because it belonged to Petra at the stables –

had escaped? And even worse, that it had been flattened by a car.

Oh, gosh, the look on that van driver's face! All Maisie could remember was a pair of horrified eyes and a wide-open mouth. He had yelled something, but the window had been up, so she hadn't caught what he'd said. Which was probably a good thing, because she had a feeling it wasn't complementary. He had waved his hands in the air, too. He hadn't been very happy with her, and she hoped she wouldn't see him again.

Praying he had business at the stables or Walter's cottage, Maisie was dismayed when she didn't see his van outside either property. She did, however, see Princess, who had paused to continue her lunch and had her furry head buried in the hedge next to the entrance to the farm.

Maisie caught up with her, and with another shriek and more arm-waving, she managed to herd the goat into the farmyard.

Thank god for that, she thought, as she watched the errant creature trot calmly into the barn. But Maisie's relief was short-lived when she noticed the white van parked in the middle of the yard, and saw that its driver was deep in conversation with Dulcie.

Oh, dear, now she was for it!

CHAPTER TWO

As one, Dulcie and the stranger turned to look at Maisie. Dulcie's expression was one of mild bewilderment. The man's expression was furious.

'I could have killed you!' he yelled.

Maisie blinked at his anger. 'There's no need to exaggerate,' she said, walking towards him. Dulcie was staring at her, a frown marring her brow.

'You came tearing down the lane too damned fast,' he cried.

'You shouldn't have been driving up it so fast,' she countered.

'What's going on?' Dulcie's gaze flickered between Maisie and the annoying van driver.

Even as she was arguing with him, Maisie could see how hot he was. Dark hair in a bun on the top of his head, a piercing, tattoos, buff, and the sort of face that belonged on a film star, not a bloody delivery driver.

'I almost ran her over,' he said, just as Maisie cried, 'He nearly mowed me down.'

'What were you—?' Dulcie began, then her frown cleared. 'Princess?'

'Yes, I found her in the barn this morning when I went to feed the goats. I think she expected to be fed, too.'

Dulcie rolled her eyes. 'That goat should have been called Houdini.' She turned to the van driver. 'She's forever getting out.'

'You should take better care to ensure she doesn't,' he retorted. 'This one,' he jerked his chin at Maisie, 'almost got herself killed chasing after it.'

Dulcie's eyes widened and she opened her mouth to say something, but Maisie got in first. 'It's not *her* goat,' she snapped, 'so stop it with the lecturing. Princess belongs to the stables.'

She scowled at him, her hands on her hips, and satisfaction stole through her when his face blanched.

He rallied quickly. 'I don't care who the goat belongs to, you still nearly got yourself killed.'

Dulcie asked, 'Was it really that bad?'

'No!' Maisie cried.

'Yes,' van-man snapped.

'Which is it?' Dulcie's lips were twitching.

'He's being a drama queen.' Maisie pulled a face at him.

He pulled one back.

Goodness knows how long the standoff would have gone on, if it hadn't been for Dulcie, who lost patience with the pair of them. 'Maisie, please tie Princess up before she does another runner. Adam, shall I show you where I want the unit to go?'

He seemed to shake himself. 'Er, yes, please. Sorry about the misunderstanding.'

'I do take good care of my goats, you know,' Dulcie said, her tone frosty.

Adam winced, and Maisie almost felt sorry for him. But not quite. There had been no need to make a mountain out of a molehill.

Dulcie softened. 'It was an easy mistake to make. After all, you are here to give me a quote on installing my goat milk pasteurisation unit, so it was natural to assume the escaped goat would belong to me.'

Ah, so he wasn't a delivery driver.

Maisie's interest was piqued. If he got the job, he would be working here for a day or so, or however long it took.

She tracked his progress as he followed her sister into the single storey stone-built shed attached to the side of the barn, and sighed when the two of them disappeared from sight. She had better go do as she was asked and tie the blimmin' goat up before it got up to any more mischief, then she would let the others out into the meadow. Even though they were all close to giving birth, Dulcie reckoned that a few hours in the early spring sunshine would do them good.

Adam stifled a groan of embarrassment as he entered a shed next to the barn, close on Dulcie's heels. He had just made a total prat of himself in front of a potential new client. Not only had he shouted at the woman who had been chasing the goats, he had also accused Dulcie of not taking proper care of her animals. He was surprised she hadn't ordered him off her property.

Deciding to take the bull (goat?!) by the horns, he said, 'I'm sorry about...' He jerked his head towards the yard. 'It gave me a bit of a scare, that's all. I hope I didn't get her into any trouble.'

'No more than she's in already. I'm in two minds to send her home.'

Damn it, now he felt awful. 'Please don't sack her because of me. I should have driven a bit slower.' He had been driving slowly enough, but if he had to shoulder the blame so Maisie kept her job, he would.

To his surprise, Dulcie burst out laughing. 'Maisie isn't an employee: she's my sister.'

Oh, great. Could this get any worse? He had yelled at his client's *sister*? Then he had to remind himself that Dulcie wasn't his client yet, and probably wouldn't be after this fiasco.

'What do you think?' Dulcie asked, and Adam scrambled to put his lack of professionalism behind him.

He'd been genning up on the milking and pasteurisation process, and he hoped he sounded knowledgeable when he asked, 'Where are you planning on doing the milking?'

'Next door.' She placed a hand on the rough-hewn stone wall to her right.

'Good, not too much pipework.' He knew enough to understand that the area where the goats were milked should be separate from where the pasteurisation took place. 'Can you show me the unit? And next door?'

'Of course.' Dulcie ushered him back outside and headed for another door.

Adam followed, but as he did so, he scanned the yard.

Maisie was nowhere to be seen.

The twinge of disappointment he felt caught him off-guard.

Ignoring it, he focused on the job at hand, making notes in the leather-bound notepad he carried with him when he was working.

'How soon can you get the quote to me?' Dulcie asked.

'This evening?'

'Brill! I thought I'd have to wait a few days.'

'Do you mind if I take some measurements?'

'The unit will definitely fit,' she said, a small line appearing between her brows.

'I can see that, but I'll need to factor in some additional pipework. When will it be ready for me to install?'

'Um...' Dulcie wrinkled her nose. 'I've got to get someone to board the shed out first, and lay a concrete floor.' Her expression was apologetic. 'I've gone about this all wrong, haven't I? I should have got the place ready first before I called you in, and I also need an electrician and a plumber.'

'I can give you a quote for the building work as well, if you like, but I can't do the electrics.'

'Would you? That would be great. So, if the quote is acceptable, when could you start?'

In his mind Adam ran through the jobs that were already booked in. 'The week after next?' He would have to rearrange some things, but it was doable.

Dulcie seemed pleased. 'In that case, I'll leave you to your tape measure. Right, I'd better take Princess back to the stables.' She gave him a grin. 'Try not to run me over when you go down the lane, eh?'

Adam winced. 'I had better apologise to your sister before I leave. She must think me a right numpty.'

'I doubt it. Knowing her, she had her head in the clouds and wasn't looking where she was going.'

Adam was fairly sure she *had* been looking, but that was a discussion he had no intention of getting into. Whatever the tension was between the sisters, he didn't want any part of it.

He made a few more notes, then popped back to his van for a tape measure and his phone. He would give the builder's merchant in Thornbury a call to price up the battening, the lengths of wood and the other materials he would need if he landed the job, so he would have all the information at his fingertips ready for when he came to price up the quote this evening.

As he passed by the barn, he caught sight of Maisie. She was stroking a tiny goat and didn't see him, and of their own volition his feet slowed as he took a moment to study her.

Her lips were moving and he assumed she was speaking to the goat, who kept nudging her hand with its head; for food, he presumed. The scene was reminiscent of an old painting of a rural idyll, apart from Maisie's modern clothes.

Adam only realised he was staring, and had been doing so for several seconds, when Maisie glanced up and caught him.

Briefly he thought how pretty she was, now that he could see her face full-on without it being all angry and shouty; then her eyes narrowed and her mouth tightened, and he guessed he was about to be shouted at all over again.

Adam got his apology in first. 'I'm sorry, I overreacted,' he began, taking a few steps towards her.

Maisie scrambled to her feet, dusting the straw from her jeans with little swipes of her palms. She tilted her head.

'You did,' she agreed, 'but apology accepted.' She moved closer, studying him. 'At least you cared. Some drivers wouldn't have given a monkey's butt.'

'There is that,' he agreed. 'Is the goat okay?'

Maisie tutted. '*She* is, *I'm* not. I've never run so fast in my life. Dulcie has taken her home. Are you all done?'

'Not yet.' He pointed at the van. 'I need my tape measure. I've got some measuring up to do.' As he said it, he wanted to kick himself. Why else would he want a tape measure, if not to measure something?

Her lips twitched.

'I'd better go fetch it,' he said.

'And I'd better take this little one to the meadow to join her friends. She doesn't seem keen to go, though. It was only after I had put the others in the field, that I realised she was missing.' She sucked in a breath. 'Please don't tell Dulcie. Princess running off wasn't my fault, but losing Cloud would be.'

'Cloud? Is that what the goat is called? Do they all have names?'

'Of course they do! Goats are people, too.' A blush crept into her cheeks. 'Obviously, they're not *people*, but...' She shook her head. 'Shall we start again? Hi, I'm Maisie, I'm Dulcie's sister.'

Adam grinned. 'Hi, Maisie, I'm Adam and I'm not anyone's brother.'

Eyes twinkling, she said, 'I've got another sister beside Dulcie, and a brother. What's it like being an only child?'

'Challenging. What's it like being one of four?'

'Annoying.'

She paused and seemed to be waiting for him to say something more, but his mind was blank. He couldn't think of a single thing, and when she coughed politely, he realised he was loitering.

'Tape measure,' he muttered to himself. 'I, er, hope to see you again, Maisie.' And with that he hurried to his van, grabbed the tape measure and dashed back to the shed.

Hopefully, he wouldn't see Maisie again before he left – he had made enough of a fool of himself for one day.

'Come on, Cloud, you can't loll around in here all day,' Maisie told the little creature. The goat had found a pile of straw to lie down on and was studiously ignoring her. 'Cloud, stop being so lazy.'

The rotund animal let out a small bleat and stretched out her neck as she lifted her tail, her whole body tensing.

'Aw, big stretch,' Maisie said, expecting the goat to clamber to its feet. Instead, Cloud subsided and seemed to settle down again.

Maisie wondered whether she should fetch a halter and a lead rope, and try to get her to shift that way. Dulcie had warned her that goats had minds of their own. As well as being intelligent, they could also be stubborn.

Cloud uttered another odd little bleat, and once again she stretched out her neck, her torso tensing as she strained.

Abruptly Maisie realised what was happening and she clapped a hand to her mouth to hold in a shriek.

Cloud was in labour! Not only was she in labour, but the birth was imminent. Two tiny hooves could be seen at the animal's rear end, and the rest of the goatling was about to follow.

'Dulcie?' she called, trying not to shout too loud for fear of startling the mum-to-be.

There was no answer, and Maisie guessed Dulcie must be in the house.

With a last look at the goat, Maisie ran out of the barn and across the yard, her voice growing louder as she yelled for her sister. Bursting into the kitchen, she shot through the empty dining room and skidded to a halt at the bottom of the stairs.

'Dulcie!' she screeched. 'Cloud is giving birth. Help!'

The house was still and silent, apart from the ticking of the grandmother clock in the corner.

Drat! Dulcie must still be down at the stables.

Maisie thundered upstairs to grab her phone, her fingers shaking as she stabbed at her sister's number. A ringing coming from the kitchen told her that Dulcie hadn't taken her phone with her, which shouldn't be a surprise considering mobile reception on Muddypuddle Lane was so dire.

She resorted to the landline instead and, after looking up the number for the stables, she waited impatiently for an answer. 'Hello? Is that you, Amos? Is Dulcie there? It's Maisie.'

'Hello, Maisie; how are you? Dulcie's just been telling us that you're visiting for a few days. How—?'

'Sorry to interrupt, Amos. I need Dulcie urgently. One of the goats is in labour.'

'Ah, I see. She's gone down to the bottom field with Petra. I'll send someone to fetch her.'

'Thanks. I've got to go; I might need to boil a kettle and find some towels!'

Maisie high-tailed it back across the yard – and ran straight into Adam, who was coming out of the shed. His chest was a solid wall of muscle and it felt like hitting a brick wall.

His arms came around her as she bounced back and staggered.

'Help,' she panted. 'I need help. Cloud is in labour and I don't know what to do. Dulcie's still at the stables and I'm here on my own and I've never given birth to a baby goat before.' She knew she wasn't making much sense, but she was scared, damn it! Dulcie would never forgive her if something happened to Cloud or her baby, and Maisie wouldn't be able to forgive herself either.

'It's okay,' Adam said, steadying her before letting go.

'It's *not* okay. I haven't got a clue what I'm doing and—' She stopped as a faint high-pitched bleat reached her ears.

'It's lucky the mama goat knows what she's doing then, isn't it?' Adam said and stepped aside.

Cloud was on her feet, busily licking the tiniest, cutest baby goat in the whole world. It was lying in the straw, shaking its little head and bleating, and even as Maisie watched, it attempted to stand, heaving itself up on knobbly legs, to wobble for a precarious second before collapsing back into the straw.

Maisie's eyes filled with tears and she brushed them away, her relief acute.

'Who's a clever girl?' Maisie whispered as she crept closer, not wanting to scare the baby, but itching to cuddle it. Then she froze. Cloud's back was hunched once more, and her neck stretched out. 'Oh God, she's doing it again!' Maisie hissed. 'There's another baby in there. What do I do?'

'The same as you did the first time,' he said.

'But I didn't—' she began, then realised what he meant.

'Cloud seems to be managing just fine on her own.'

'What if she doesn't?'

'We'll deal with that if it happens.' Adam's voice was calm, his tone soothing, and gradually Maisie's heart rate slowed.

He was right. Cloud had coped on her own so far, and the odds were that the goat wouldn't need any help at all. But there was something Maisie wanted to know before she allowed herself to calm down fully. 'Do you know anything about goats?'

'Not much.'

'How about sheep?'

'Can't say that I do.'

'Have you seen a baby animal being born before?'

Adam wrinkled his brow. 'Don't think so.'

Maisie sighed in exasperation. 'So if something *does* go wrong this time, how are you going to deal with it?'

'Me?' He blinked. '*You're* the one in charge of the goats.'

'But you said *we'll deal with it if it happens!*'

'I meant *you.*'

Maisie ignored him. She was too focused on the little feet and the tiny nose emerging into the world.

With a final push from Cloud, the newest member of the farm's herd slithered onto the straw, and Cloud turned around to dry it with her tongue. The baby was very much alive, bleating and shaking its head, its little ears twitching.

Maisie shot Adam a delighted look. His smile was as wide as her own, and she clapped her hands and did a jig.

'Aren't they adorable?' she cried. 'Do you think I can pick that one up?'

The first goatling was balancing on legs that it had little control over, and looking confused, as though it was trying to work out what had just happened. Its mum was busy looking after its sibling, and Maisie felt quite sorry for it.

She moved to within touching distance and knelt down, holding out a hand. The baby goat took a wobbly step and butted its nose against her finger. Carefully, so as not to frighten it, she picked it up and held it against her chest. It was solid and warm, and incredibly soft.

Her heart melted. *If this is what it's like to be in love,* she thought, *then I'm head over heels.*

She had adored the goats from the first time she'd set eyes on them. It had been a few days before Christmas when the breeder had delivered eight of the gorgeous creatures to the farm. They were to form the beginning of Dulcie's herd of dairy goats and Maisie hadn't been able to tear herself away, much to her family's amusement. Her brother's partner, who was an artist, had even painted Maisie with the very same goat who had just given birth, and had given it to her as a Christmas present. It was one of Maisie's most treasured possessions.

Footsteps hurrying across the yard alerted her that Dulcie was back, and Maisie turned to face her sister with a huge smile.

Dulcie wore a worried expression as she entered the barn, but when she spied Cloud and the baby healthy and well, her face lit up. And it positively shone when she saw a second goatling in Maisie's arms.

'Two babies!' she cried. 'How wonderful!' She held her arms out and Maisie placed the tiny goat in them. Dulcie checked it over, then put it down and examined the other. 'They're both girls,' she said happily, then she sat on a bale of straw to watch them take their first, vital drink of milk.

Maisie looked on in wonder, only tearing her gaze away when she felt Adam's eyes on her.

The smile they shared felt almost as special as witnessing the birth of two new lives, and she was glad that he had been by her side and she hadn't had to go it alone – despite his dire lack of knowledge about goats.

Later that evening Adam should have been working out some costings ahead of emailing the quote to Dulcie, but his mind wasn't on his task. Whenever he tried to concentrate, his thoughts would wander, and an image of Maisie's blissful expression as she cuddled the baby goat would hover in front of the screen.

He really had made a prat of himself, hadn't he? But he hoped he had redeemed himself a bit when the goatlings were born. There had been that moment when he and Maisie had shared a look. He wasn't sure what it had meant, but it had felt intimate. Or had he read too much into it? He had a feeling it was wishful thinking on his part, which baffled him as he wasn't interested in getting intimate with her (well, he *was*, because he was a man after all, with a healthy sexual appetite) but considering he didn't want to get involved with anyone right now, getting intimate with Maisie Fairfax wasn't an option.

A thought occurred to him: was her surname Fairfax or was she married? He hadn't noticed a wedding ring, and he scoured his memory for one for several minutes until he gave up. Even if she wasn't wearing a ring on the third finger of her left hand, it didn't mean she wasn't in a relationship.

Crossly, he focused on the spreadsheet, telling himself that none of it mattered because he wasn't interested anyway. A girlfriend would be too much of a distraction right now. When his business was more established, he would start dating again (he didn't intend to remain single forever) but not yet. Unfortunately, the downside of not having a girlfriend was that it increased his mother's efforts to set him up with the daughter of one of her close friends. Mum constantly hoped he would change his mind about Verity.

His father similarly hoped Adam would change his mind about joining the firm.

Both of them continued to be disappointed.

So he told himself to stop thinking about the woman he had met at the farm, and think about the job he was hoping to land. But telling himself that was easier than doing it, and her face continued to dominate his thoughts for the rest of the evening.

A white blouse and black trousers or a skirt seemed to be a staple uniform of restaurants everywhere, Maisie mused, as she checked that her blouse was tucked in and that her hair wasn't escaping its ponytail.

She was standing in The Wild Side's kitchen, along with the rest of the serving staff, being briefed ahead of the first diners' arrival this evening. Although Otto owned the restaurant and was the guy with the Michelin star, he didn't do all the cooking. He had underlings for that, and she eyed the white-coated kitchen staff with trepidation, knowing that as the tension ramped up, there was a fair chance someone would get tetchy. She just hoped they didn't get tetchy with *her*. She had walked out of more than one job because someone had lost their rag.

Whilst Otto explained the menu to the front-of-house staff, the kitchen staff were busy cooking, and the most delicious smells permeated the air.

Maisie had first-hand experience of just how good a chef Otto was, and she hoped she would get a taste of the dishes on the menu at some point. The Wild Side's unique selling point was that it served only locally grown and foraged ingredients, and flowers featured heavily, and not just because they looked pretty. Otto expected his waiting staff to be able to identify the various blooms, in case anyone asked, as well as to be able to explain what the foraged ingredients were.

Maisie was facing a steep learning curve, but one that she was determined to get to grips with, because being allowed to stay on the farm might depend on it.

Thinking of the farm brought an image of the adorable little goat babies into her mind, and she couldn't wait for her shift to end so she could cuddle them. Dulcie had been thrilled with the new additions, and Maisie hoped her sister's good mood would continue when she saw the quote for the pasteurisation shed that the guy, Adam, was supposed to email to her this evening.

Maisie was keeping her fingers crossed that her sister would decide to go with Adam's quote – not because Maisie wanted to see him again, but because she knew that when work started on the shed, Dulcie would need all the help she could get. And Maisie intended to provide that help.

She had only been on the farm a fraction over twenty-four hours, but already she felt less tense and she didn't know whether it was the fresh country air that was responsible for the optimism flaring in her chest, or whether it was something else. All she knew was that she didn't want to go back to Birmingham. She wanted a fresh start, and hopefully the farm was where she could make that happen.

CHAPTER THREE

It was Sunday morning and Otto looked exhausted. Maisie had total respect for how hard he worked and the amount of time and effort he had put into getting the restaurant off the ground. No wonder Dulcie needed help around the farm if Otto was putting all his time and energy into his business

As the three of them tucked into a full English breakfast that Maisie and Dulcie had cooked between them, Maisie wondered if there was anything more she could do to help.

Her opportunity came when Dulcie said to Otto, 'I think we should go with that first bloke who gave us a quote. It was very reasonable and he can start next Monday, which gives us a full week to clear everything out and give it a good clean.'

Otto, who had a mouthful of bacon, nodded, but Maisie noticed his slightly pained expression. Dulcie was focused on her plate and didn't see his dismay. Maisie guessed what was causing it: Otto was playing mentor to a visiting chef from London next week, who would be here to gain experience in sourcing and cooking with foraged ingredients, so Otto would be even more pushed for time than he was currently.

'I can do that,' she offered. Over the past few days she had been trying to make herself as useful as possible, cleaning, doing the laundry, feeding the animals, playing midwife to another set of twin goat babies, as well as doing shifts in the restaurant if Otto needed her. Thankfully, she wasn't working today, so she could devote the whole day to doing whatever Dulcie wanted her to do.

'It's mucky work,' Dulcie told her.

'So? I don't mind getting my hands dirty.'

Dulcie cocked her head to the side. 'No, you don't.' She sounded surprised, which Maisie resented, although she didn't show it.

Maisie had never shied away from hard work. What she *did* shy away from was dumb managers and customers with no manners. She also wasn't particularly keen on being stuck behind a desk, and had managed to lose more than one job because sitting in front of a computer all day had driven her mad with boredom. Then there were those jobs on the factory floors that had been equally as boring but with the addition of loud machinery and not being able to have a wee when she needed one. But her main problem was that she wasn't qualified to do anything in particular – mainly because she didn't know what she wanted to qualify *in*.

In the years since she'd left college with three A-levels and a vague idea that something would present itself, she had tried being a junior in a hairdressing salon, a receptionist in a hotel, a chambermaid (different hotel, she hadn't been able to return to the other one), a care assistant in a nursing home (she had been so upset when one of the residents had passed away that she hadn't been able to face going back), a cleaner (in both an office and a school), a sales assistant in a variety of shops selling everything from shoes (ugh – smelly feet) to jewellery (she hated cleaning silver with a passion), and more pub, bar and restaurant jobs than she could shake a stick at. So, no, hard work didn't scare her. Not being happy or fulfilled, *did*.

'I'll get started after I wash up, shall I?' she suggested, so after she had finished stacking the dishwasher, the pair of them donned old clothes and headed outside.

Maisie wanted to check on the new arrivals on the way.

'You're taking your role as goat herder very seriously,' Dulcie teased, as Maisie picked each new bundle up and checked him or her over.

All four were happy and thriving as far as Maisie could tell, and her heart filled with warmth at the sight of them. 'I'm enjoying it,' she told her sister truthfully. It was the best part of being on the farm.

An hour or so later, Maisie was busy shovelling decades' worth of accumulated rubbish into a wheelbarrow, when Dulcie said, 'Have you decided when you're going back to Birmingham?'

Her spirits sank. 'I was hoping I could stay a bit longer.' She hadn't been here a week yet and already her sister was hinting that it was time she left.

'You can,' Dulcie said cheerfully. 'It's just... Mum was on the phone yesterday evening. I think she's lonely.'

Maisie began to feel guilty at leaving their mum on her own in the house, until Dulcie added, 'I dunno why, because you were hardly ever in.'

'I was!'

'Only at mealtimes and to change your clothes.'

Maisie propped the shovel against the bare stone wall and put her hands on her hips. 'I know you and Nikki think I treat Mum like a skivvy and the house like a hotel, but *you* try living with her. She wasn't as bad when you were at home and Nikki was just around the corner, but since you left and both of you moved to Picklewick, she's been a nightmare.'

'She's worried about you,'

'Well, she needn't be. I'm fine.'

'Are you?'

Maisie softened. 'I'm okay,' she said. 'But I need some time away to think about what I want to do with my life.'

'Have you come up with anything?'

'Not really, although I do like working with animals.'

Dulcie smiled. 'I can see that.'

'Maybe I could train to be a veterinary nurse or a dog groomer.'

'Two rather different professions. But at least you're narrowing it down.'

'How about if I work in a kennels? Or a cattery? A wildlife sanctuary?'

'I'm sure there are plenty of jobs in those areas if you look.'

'In the centre of Birmingham?'

'Probably not.'

'Are there any around here?'

'I'm not sure.' Dulcie sounded hesitant, and Maisie assumed it was because if she did manage to get a job locally, Dulcie would never be rid of her.

'I could open one of my own,' Maisie said.

'A *wildlife sanctuary*?' Her sister's face was incredulous. 'You don't know the first thing about wildlife.'

'I could learn,' Maisie retorted. 'Okay then, what about a boarding kennel?'

'Have you ever looked after a dog? Taken one for a walk?'

Maisie knew she was trying to run before she could walk, but wasn't that where ambition began? People had a dream, then moved heaven and earth to make it come true, and although the dream might be big, the start was small. In order for her to start her career journey, Maisie had to know the final destination.

'Anyway,' Dulcie was saying, 'you need loads of money to set up something like a boarding kennel. You've got to have a property, for a start. You can hardly start one in Mum's garden – it's only big enough for a couple of planters and a patio table. Besides, the neighbours would complain.'

'I know *that*, I'm not stupid.' Maisie gave an exasperated sigh. She wished her family would stop treating her like a kid. 'I would need somewhere like the old farmhouse on the mountain. You know the one, where Jay and Eliza met.' She paused, thinking furiously. 'Doesn't that belong to the farm?'

'Yes, but not for much longer, so you can get that idea out of your head. I'm selling it.'

'Why? It's lovely.'

'It's derelict.'

'It's romantic.' So what if it lacked a roof and had a tree growing in the middle? It would take a bit of work to restore it, but it would look lovely when it was done.

'I have to sell it to pay for this lot,' Dulcie said, gesturing around the shed.

'I thought you said Adam's quote was good?'

'It is, but even so, it's not cheap. Some of the money from selling the old farmhouse will replenish the savings I'll have to dip into to get the pasteurisation shed up and running.'

Maisie experienced a flash of disappointment. She knew it was a pie-in-the-sky idea, but for a minute she had got carried away with thoughts of living there herself and opening a boarding kennel. Or a cattery, or herding goats, or *something*.

The longer Maisie spent at the farm, the more certain she became that she didn't want to return to her old life in the city. The problem was, she didn't have a clue what she was going to do instead.

Whenever Adam drove through the gates separating his parents' property from the secluded lane leading to it, his heart sank, quickly followed by shame that he felt this way. Most people would give their right arm to have grown up in a place like this, with all the privileges that went with being able to afford a house of this size. It was equivalent to a small mansion, complete with winding gravelled drive, sprawling grounds and several outbuildings, one of which housed his dad's impressive collection of eleven classic cars.

Adam drew his van up alongside his dad's Bentley, well aware that it would annoy the pants off his old man. His mum would also wince when she saw it, but as her request to park it around the back had fallen on deaf ears up to now, she probably wouldn't say anything since it would only be the three of them for lunch – as far as he knew. He hoped no one else had been invited. Adam didn't think he could face it.

Although Cedar Trees was his childhood home, he had no emotional attachment to the place. Maybe because it was more like a show house than a home. It was beautifully decorated, tastefully furnished and, as far as Adam was concerned, totally lacking in warmth.

He didn't bother to knock or ring the bell, instead walking straight in and calling, 'Mum? Dad?'

'In here,' his mother shouted from the kitchen, and when he followed her voice he found her basting a substantial leg of lamb with its own juices. The aroma of rosemary hung in the air to accompany the smell of roast meat.

She tilted her cheek for a kiss, and he dutifully gave her a peck.

'When will it be ready?' he asked.

His mum tutted. 'Half an hour. Can you wait that long?' Her sharp comment was justified: he had a habit of eating, then dashing off.

But perhaps he wouldn't if his father wasn't so intent on dissing his lifestyle choices and trying to shove his own in Adam's face. Maybe Dad hoped to wear him down, and that Adam would give in eventually. If that was the case, Dad was wasting his time and his breath.

Adam didn't rise to his mum's comment. Instead, he asked, 'Where's Dad?'

'Take a guess – he's in his study, working as usual. He has to, since everything is on his shoulders.'

See, they've started already, Adam said to himself, the inference being that if Adam hadn't stubbornly refused to join his dad's management accountancy firm, then his dad would have had someone with whom to share the burden.

Adam let it go. He had discovered early on that there was no point taking any notice of the barbed comments. It would only cause an atmosphere and he wanted to enjoy his lunch. His mother was an excellent cook (although she often got caterers in) and she took pride in her dinner parties. Which was lucky, since his parents seemed to throw a lot of them.

She asked, 'So, what have you been up to since we last saw you? How long has it been... two weeks? Three?'

'Two.'

'It seems longer. Well, do you have any news?'

He did, but his mum wouldn't be too keen on hearing it. 'I'm doing a renovation on a feed shed up at the farm on Muddypuddle Lane.'

'A renovation? But you're not a builder.'

'No, but it's part and parcel of installing a pasteurisation unit. Goat's milk,' he added, in case she was interested.

She wasn't. She was staring at his hands. No matter how thoroughly he scrubbed them, traces of oil lingered in the creases and under his nails.

'I wish you would—' she began, then stopped and clamped her lips firmly shut.

Adam held back a sigh with difficulty. He must be such a disappointment to them. This life wasn't the one they had envisaged for him, and neither did he look like an accountant. He wondered if they still explained away his hair, piercing and tattoos as youthful exuberance, or had decided he was too old for such an excuse.

He caught his mother staring at his feet, her face full of disapproval. 'Did you have to wear your work boots?' she asked, her brow creasing in displeasure.

'They're not work boots, they're hiking boots. I'm going for a walk after lunch.'

'On your own?'

'Yes, as it happens.'

'You might ask Verity if she would like to accompany you.'

'Not today. Maybe another time.'

Maybe never. Not only did he think that Verity wouldn't be keen on marching to the top of a mountain, he wanted to take a look at the derelict building on his own. He had spotted the listing online yesterday as he had been checking properties for sale. And because he knew where it was and knew he could look around it without involving the estate agent, he thought he would take a gander later this afternoon.

On paper, it seemed to be exactly what he was looking for, and despite telling himself not to get his hopes up, a quiet excitement bubbled in his chest.

Mild irritation had transformed into downright annoyance by the time Adam drove away from his parents' house, and he hoped a brisk walk in the spring sunshine would blow it away.

How much longer would they keep this up? As his mother constantly told him, she couldn't understand why he lived in a (her word) *hovel*, when he could live in luxury at home. Failing that, his parents had offered to buy him a 'nice' house, instead of the 'horrid' flat he currently lived in.

Obviously, Dad would be able to offset it against tax, but that didn't negate the generosity of the offer.

Unfortunately, the offer came with strings, ones which Adam wasn't prepared to have attached to him. He was managing just fine without their help – more than managing, he was doing well. And it was all down to his own hard work and effort. The situation might have been different if he enjoyed number crunching, as he probably would have gone into his father's business. But he hated it. He had only done an accountancy degree because he had felt pressured into it.

At eighteen, he hadn't felt able to escape his father's expectations.

At twenty-one, he had.

His father had railed and ranted for a while, but Mum had convinced Dad that Adam was just going through a rebellious phase, and that he would soon grow out of it.

Seven years later, they were still waiting and their patience was wearing thin. But they failed to see that the more they pressured him, the more determined he was to make a go of his business.

Adam parked the van at the top of Muddypuddle Lane, just above the entrance to the farmyard where the rough tarmacked road turned into an even rougher dirt track.

He got out and stretched, taking a deep breath of clean fresh air as he scanned his surroundings. Properties didn't often come up for sale in

Picklewick, and commercial or agricultural ones even less so, which was why he was considering the old farmhouse. It wasn't ideal: from what he could recall, it was more ruin than house and would probably need to be pulled down, despite the best efforts of the estate agent to make the online photos look rustic and charming.

As he strode up the track, which was a public right of way onto the mountain, Adam realised that the surface would have to be re-laid if he wanted to be able to drive his van up it. A tractor could manage it, or an SUV, but not his poor old van. The abandoned farmhouse was also further up the mountain than he remembered, and he was breathing heavily by the time he had tramped up the steep hill and the incline finally levelled off.

Pausing for a moment, he turned around to take in the view.

Waking up to this every morning might be worth the expense of making the old farmhouse habitable. If he was Dulcie, there was no way he would want to sell it. But then again, she already had a similar view.

As he resumed his walk, his thoughts remained on the farm. But it wasn't Dulcie he was thinking of now – it was her sister. Her pretty, vivacious, captivating sister.

Was that Adam's van? Maisie pulled the bedroom curtain aside and craned her neck.

It looked like it, but without a logo or any writing all white vans looked the same. And if it *was* Adam's, surely he would have parked it in the yard and not at the top of the lane?

It probably belonged to a hiker she decided, and her gaze drifted up the hillside, following the path. A solitary man was plodding up the hill and her heart gave a leap. It looked like Adam. Possibly. It was difficult to tell from the back, and he was quite far away too.

But when the figure stopped and turned around, she was sure. It *was* him. She was certain of it. And he appeared to be looking directly at her.

Maisie shrank back, hiding behind the curtain. What was he doing up there? It couldn't possibly have anything to do with the pasteurisation shed, could it?

She decided to find out.

After taking the stairs two at a time, she raced through the dining room, into the kitchen, and shot into the utility room. Stuffing her feet into her sturdy boots, she tied the laces, grabbed her jacket off the hook by the door and dashed outside.

And soon realised her mistake.

At the rate she was walking up the track, she would never catch up with Adam. She might, however, meet him as he was coming back down, but if she didn't want to look silly, she would have to carry on going up the hill. Therefore, she reasoned, it would be better to wait for him to return to his van. If she loitered around the barn, she hopefully wouldn't miss him.

So loiter she did; although it was a good hour and a half before she spotted him coming down the track.

Maisie had her story prepared, and just as he reached his van she sauntered out of the yard and into the lane. Feigning surprise, she did a double-take. 'Hello! Have you come to see Dulcie?'

Adam paused, his keys in his hand. 'I've been for a walk.' He jerked his head towards the track.

'Oh, right. Did you go far?'

'To the ruined farmhouse. I'd forgotten how lovely it is up there.'

'You're local, then?'

He nodded. 'I live in the village. The outskirts, actually – above the old MOT garage on the road to Thornbury.'

'Sorry, I'm not from around here.'

'I guessed as much. Your sister's only been at the farm a year, hasn't she?'

'Yes, she has,' Dulcie said, walking across the yard. 'There you are, Maisie! I wondered where you'd got to, then I heard voices. Hi, Adam.' Dulcie sent him a questioning look.

'I hope you don't mind,' he said, 'but I've been for a walk.'

'Not at all,' Dulcie replied. 'It's a public right of way, and even if it wasn't, you're welcome to go for a stroll. I'm glad you're here, so I can tell you in person that you've got the job. Are you still able to start next Monday?'

'Absolutely.' He was beaming and Maisie felt a rush of pleasure, before immediately tamping it down.

She wasn't here to find a boyfriend – she'd had enough of those in the past. She was here to find *herself*.

Dulcie smiled back. 'Brill. See you next week. Maisie, can you round up the chickens? It'll be dark soon and I want them in their coop so we can eat dinner and settle down. Oh, and the goats need fetching in, too.'

Maisie watched her sister amble back to the house.

Adam hadn't moved, but when Dulcie was out of sight, he jangled his keys.

'I'd better go see to the goats,' Maisie said. 'Congratulations, by the way.'

'Thanks. How are the twins doing?'

'Which ones? We've got two sets now, and a single.'

'You have been busy. I'll need to pull my finger out and get that shed done.'

'How long will it take?'

'About a week, give or take. I'm not honestly sure, as I've never done this kind of thing before.'

Maisie was confused. 'I thought installing equipment was your thing?'

'Not really, although I can turn my hand to most things.'

'So if you don't play with pasteurisation units for a living, what do you do?'

'This and that.'

'You sound like a cowboy.' Adam stiffened and Maisie guessed she had offended him. 'Sorry, I didn't mean that the way it sounded,' she backtracked hastily. It was lucky that she wasn't eyeing him up as a potential boyfriend, because after a comment like that she would have blown her chances.

'That's okay. Apology accepted.' He hesitated and Maisie wondered what he was about to say.

Her surprise when he asked her out for a drink, was almost matched by the delight she felt when she accepted.

CHAPTER FOUR

'I can't speak for long, Mum, I'm getting ready to go to work.'

Maisie's mobile was on speaker phone, sitting on the old oak dressing table. She was peering into the age-spotted oval mirror above it and wishing her lashes were longer. It wasn't fair that a man had longer lashes than her. She was referring to Adam: his were thick and dark, a look Maisie's lashes only achieved with the application of two coats of mascara and a lot of wishful thinking.

'Work? What do you mean *work?*'

Maisie pulled a face at the phone, thankful that this wasn't a video call. 'The restaurant. I'm working there.' It was Wednesday evening and her third shift this week was about to begin.

'*Otto's* restaurant? '

'Yes, Mum, Otto's restaurant.'

'Oh, a mercy job! That's kind of him. But you're not being fair to him, are you?'

Maisie ground her teeth together. 'It's not a mercy job. And what do you mean, 'I'm not being fair to him'?'

'You're taking advantage.'

'I am not!'

'What else do you call it? I doubt whether he had a vacancy just as you rocked up. He feels sorry for you.'

'It was Dulcie's idea,' Maisie retorted, then realised she had probably made things worse.

'Your sister isn't doing you any favours. Enabling, that's what it's called. She's enabling you to run away from your problems.'

Maisie's hand jerked and she narrowly missed poking herself in the eye with the mascara wand. 'Bugger!'

'Just because you know I'm right, there's no need to swear at me.'

'I wasn't swearing at you. I was— Never mind.' She took a deep breath. 'I don't have any problems.' Apart from you, she thought. 'My life is just fine, thanks. Actually, it's not *just fine*, it's pretty good.'

'You can't sponge off your sister forever.'

Oh, good grief! 'I'm not sponging. For your information, I'm pulling my weight.'

'Hmm.' There was a brief pause, then Beth changed tack. 'Have you considered Dulcie and Otto in all this? Have you thought about them at all? They've got enough on their plates without babysitting you.'

Maisie slapped the tube of mascara down so hard that it rattled the mirror. 'I do *not* need babysitting. I am perfectly capable of taking care of myself.'

Yet another change of tack. 'And they certainly don't need you hanging around like a spinster at a party.'

'What?' Maisie rolled her eyes. Her mother came out with some odd sayings on times.

Beth carried on, 'They need time alone together, to be a couple. You're bound to be cramping their style.

They can't be doing with entertaining you all the time.'

'They don't have to. I can find my own entertainment.'

'What's his name?' It was said with a sigh, and Maisie easily imagined the eyeroll that went with it.

'Adam,' she snapped, without thinking.

Beth let out a snort. 'I might have known there would be a man involved. What does he do?'

'Why the interest?' Her mum had stopped enquiring about Maisie's boyfriends a long time ago. She decided to leave it there. 'Sorry, I've got to go, Mum. My shift starts in half an hour.'

Her mother made one final effort. 'I'm only asking because I care about you and...' She sniffed loudly. 'I miss you. The house is too quiet.'

Maisie relented. She had assumed Mum would appreciate a bit of me-time, and she had also thought that her mum would have been glad not to have to tidy up after her.

Shame stole over her. Since coming to stay with Dulcie, Maisie had made a real effort to behave responsibly: why couldn't she do that at home?

In a flash of clarity, she understood the reason Dulcie and Nikki were often so exasperated with her. When she returned to Birmingham, she vowed to be more responsible. If she could do it here, she could do it there.

But despite her mother's thinly veiled attempt to get her to go back home, Maisie wasn't ready to leave just yet.

And she didn't know when she would be.

The following evening Maisie skipped downstairs, excitement fluttering in her tummy. Adam would be calling for her any minute and she was looking forward to it.

She found Dulcie in the sitting room, curled on the sofa, watching TV.

Maisie announced, 'I've got the hens in, and the goats are in the barn. I've also emptied the dishwasher and folded the laundry. I'll iron it in the morning.'

'Thanks, Maisie, I—' Dulcie stopped. 'You're all dressed up. Are you going somewhere?'

'I'm having a drink with Adam. That's okay, isn't it?'

Dulcie frowned. 'I suppose. When was this arranged?'

'Sunday,' Maisie mumbled.

'Why haven't you said anything before now?'

Maisie wasn't entirely sure, although she suspected it might be because she guessed that her sister wouldn't approve. When Nikki had spent a couple of weeks on the farm last summer, she had bagged herself a fella and was now living with him in his cottage in Picklewick. Maybe Dulcie thought that if Maisie got her feet even further under the farm's table, she wouldn't want to leave either.

Her mother's words from yesterday flashed into her head, and she realised that she should have told Dulcie about her date sooner; so much for her resolution to behave more responsibly.

'I wasn't sure whether it would go ahead,' she said, aware that her answer was flimsy. Dulcie opened her mouth to reply, but the rumble of an engine saved Maisie's bacon. 'Gotta go. I won't be late!' she cried. 'Bye!' Then she was out of the door and hurrying across the yard.

The van rolled to a halt, and as it came to a stop she opened the passenger door and jumped in. Her heart was thumping and her mouth was dry, but Maisie wasn't sure whether that was due to Dulcie's obvious disapproval, or because she had forgotten just how good-looking Adam was and how much she was attracted to him.

'Hi.' His voice was soft.

'Hi.' Maisie felt unaccountably shy.

'You look lovely.'

'Thank you.'

'I thought we'd go to The Black Horse. Is that okay with you?'

She nodded; she had a suspicion that anywhere with Adam would be okay with her, and as they drove into the village Maisie wondered why she had agreed to go on a date with him, aside from the obvious – his good looks – and that he seemed to be a nice guy. She was flattered he had asked her out, but was going on a date with him a knee-jerk reaction? Although she didn't go out with *every* guy who asked, she often said yes rather than no. Which was probably why few of them tempted her into going on a second one.

She used to be more picky, but after being swayed by a handsome face or a smooth-talking personality and discovering that more often than not there was little substance behind the polished exterior, she had been casting her net a little wider recently. Unfortunately, she still only managed to catch frogs. Either her taste in men was appalling, or there was a distinct lack of 'good ones' out there. Or they were already spoken for.

She had yet to decide whether Adam was a frog or not, but she was dismayed with herself for going out for a drink with the first man who asked her since she had decided to give dating a miss for a while.

Maisie Fairfax, she scolded silently, *you've got no self-control.* But he was gorgeous, and she defied any woman to say otherwise. Anyway, one date was hardly the same as going steady, was it?

Maisie hoped none of these thoughts were reflected in her face, but she worried that they might be, because he didn't say another word to her until he edged the van into a space in the pub's car park.

However, once they were seated and the drinks had been bought, the conversation began to flow.

'Do you still want to know what I do?' he asked when he had taken a sip of his pint.

'Only if you want to tell me. Or I can carry on imagining you lassoing cows.'

'I've never lassoed a cow. A horse yes, but not a cow.'

Maisie raised an eyebrow, encouraging him to expand on the comment.

'I used to go riding at the stables near your sister's farm.'

'Ah, so you know Petra?'

'Not really. She began working there after I'd knocked horse riding on the head.'

'Why did you stop?'

'It wasn't for me. I was more interested in the tractors than the ponies.'

'When you said *this and that...*?'

'If it's got an engine, I'll give it a go.'

'So you're a mechanic?'

'Not as such. I don't just repair vehicles – I like any kind of machines, from a diesel engine to a lathe.'

'Or a pasteurisation unit,' Maisie chuckled. 'How does it work?' Dulcie had explained how goats were milked, and that unlike dairy cows and their calves, baby goats could stay with their mothers and continue to suckle, so Dulcie would still get the milk she needed.

Maisie was fascinated by the whole process, up to and including the products that Dulcie intended to make out of it, and she couldn't wait to give soap-making a go. She couldn't wait to milk her first goat, either. She had a romantic vision of sitting on a low three-legged stool with her head against the goat's flank as creamy milk squirted into a shiny metal pail.

Unfortunately, Adam's description of the milking process, which involved things like vacuum pumps and regulators, blew her vision to smithereens.

'You've done your research,' she observed.

'Did Dulcie send you to test me? Are you going to hold up a scorecard or give me marks out of a hundred?'

'I might, if I knew more than you. I haven't got a clue how you use one of those things.'

'You'll soon get the hang of it.' He sounded confident.

Maisie wished *she* was: not because she didn't think she could operate it, but because she wasn't sure she would still be here when it was ready to use. Dulcie hadn't indicated that she wanted Maisie to leave, but Mum's comments yesterday had sunk their hooks into her and weren't letting go. Was she in danger of outstaying her welcome?

Pushing the worry aside, Maisie made a conscious effort to enjoy this evening. This was the first time she had been off the farm for fun since she'd arrived. All the other times had been for work.

'Have you lived in Picklewick all your life?' she asked, keen to get to know Adam better.

'Kind of. My parents' house is about two miles outside the village. How about you?'

'Birmingham.'

'Do you miss it?'

'I've only been here just over a week.'

He looked surprised. 'I assumed you were a permanent fixture.'

'I'd like to be.' Her reply was wistful. She knew she wouldn't be able to stay on the farm forever, but she wasn't ready to go back home just yet. And that was mostly because of the goats. She simply adored being around them.

'What do you do – aside from delivering baby goats?' he asked.

'I didn't deliver them, if you remember. Cloud did that all by herself.'

'You supervised,' he said. He was regarding her expectantly.

'This and that,' she replied, a twinkle in her eye.

'Cowgirl?'

Maisie chuckled. 'That's probably one of the few jobs I *haven't* tried.' He arched his brows, so she continued, somewhat defensively, 'I haven't decided what I want to be when I grow up.'

'Goat herder?'

'I wish!' Her reply surprised her, and she blinked. 'Actually,' she said thoughtfully, 'that's not a bad idea.

But that would mean staying on the farm, and I don't think Dulcie would go for it.'

'Why not?'

Maisie sighed, debating how much she should share with him, because she didn't want to put herself in a bad light. She resorted to, 'It's complicated.'

'Things often are.' His expression was pensive, and she wondered what *he* didn't want to share on a first date.

When he asked her what bands she liked, she realised he was deliberately changing the subject, which suited her fine, and by the end of the evening she knew his tastes in music (wide and varied), his foodie likes and dislikes, and that he preferred psychological thrillers to action films, although he didn't often go to the cinema.

They had many things in common, and by the time Adam drove the van into the yard, Maisie thought that they had really gelled. Not only was he attractive physically, he also had a friendly, likeable personality, especially when he'd had her in fits of giggles at some of the stories he had told.

One in particular (an incident with a mechanical gazebo and a naked matronly woman in a hot tub) had made her cry with laughter. In turn, Adam had appeared to be amused by her anecdotes of downright rude customers, unreasonable line managers, and some of the unexpected tasks she had been asked to perform.

The one that had amused him the most, was being asked to stand on the loo seats in a male toilet to see if there were any hidden drugs above the ceiling tiles. His reaction when she'd told him she had been working in a school at the time and that the toilet in question was for staff only, had been priceless.

The floodlights in the yard came on as the van bumped across the cobbles. Adam left the engine running and she guessed he wasn't expecting an invitation to come inside the house.

'Thanks for this evening, it was fun,' she said, unclipping her seatbelt.

'Do you want to go out again sometime?'

'Yeah, I'd like that.'

'When do you return to Birmingham?'

'I'm not sure. It depends on how long Dulcie lets me stay.'

Adam studied her. 'Do you think she'll send you packing any time soon?'

'I hope not.'

'Me, too.'

She stiffened as he leant across the seat. In the darkness, his eyes glittered with a question and Maisie answered it by leaning towards him and lifting her chin.

The touch of his lips on hers was electrifying. Her pulse soared as a jolt surged through her and her eyes drifted shut as her lips parted.

Aside from his mouth, he didn't touch her, and when he gently ended it, the disembodied kiss left her breathless with longing. She wanted more of where that came from.

'Friday?' His voice was low and gravelly.

'Pardon?' Hers was higher pitched than usual, and breathy.

' I thought we could go to the cinema.'

'I'm working at the restaurant on Friday.'

'Another time?'

'Saturday afternoon? We could see a matinee. I've got a shift in the evening.'

'I haven't been to a matinee since I was a kid.' He was grinning. 'You'd better pick the film, so you can make sure you're back in time for work. There's a cinema in Thornbury.'

'Good idea. I'll message you.' This time when he kissed her, his arms came around her drawing her towards him.

It was awkward and she felt unbalanced, although she didn't want it to end quite as soon as it did.

'Saturday,' he said, releasing her.

She licked her lips, her mouth tingling. 'Saturday,' she echoed.

As she watched him turn the van around, she wondered whether she might have found another reason to stay in Picklewick.

'You're back, then,' Dulcie said, stating the obvious. She was in the kitchen wiping the counters down, when Maisie entered the farmhouse.

'Looks like it.' Maisie managed to refrain from rolling her eyes.

Had Dulcie expected her not to come home this evening? If so, her sister didn't have a very high opinion of Maisie's morals. She may have had a fair few boyfriends over the years, but that didn't mean she had leapt into bed with all of them: she'd only ever had a handful of lovers.

And neither had she kissed all the men she had dated. Many hadn't even made it to the end of the evening before she had made up her mind that it wasn't working.

'How did it go?' Dulcie asked.

'It was good. Adam is a nice guy.'

'I'm sure he is, but...'

'But what?'

'Are you seeing him again?' Dulcie's expression was disapproving, and Maisie immediately went on the defensive.

'What if I am?'

'I don't think you should.'

'Why? Is it because he has got long hair and tattoos? You're such a goody two-shoes.'

Dulcie's boyfriends had always been vanilla and rather boring. Until she'd met Otto. But Otto was in a league of his own, being a celebrity chef, 'n' all.

Dulcie huffed. 'Just because he's got a couple of tattoos and a pierced eyebrow doesn't mean he's a 'bad boy.' Tattoos are ten a penny these days; no one bats an eyelid.'

'If not that, what is it? Because he's an odd-job man? You're channelling Mum.'

'I am not! I'm nothing like Mum.' Dulcie snorted and flung the dishcloth at the sink. It caught on the tap, hanging there.

'That's the sort of thing Mum would say,' Maisie insisted.

'If you'd let me finish... I don't care if Adam has green hair, a tattoo on the end of his nose, and is covered in oil from head to toe. What I care about is that he's starting work on the pasteurisation shed on Monday and I don't want you messing it up.'

'How the hell can I mess it up? He's hardly going to ask me for advice on how to plaster a wall, is he?'

'No, but I know what you're like. You'll flirt and tease, and lead him on, and then when you've had enough you'll dump him and bugger off back to Birmingham, leaving me to sort out your mess. And I could do without him being distracted, thank you very much!'

'So, basically, you're telling me to back off because I'm so irresistible that he'll do a crap job.' Maisie put her hands on her hips and glared at her sister.

Her sister glared back.

Then Dulcie's lips twitched. 'You do know that you're not all that, don't you?'

Maisie's anger melted away. 'You seem to think I am.'

Dulcie sagged against the sink. 'You've got to look at it from my point of view, Maisie. You get through boyfriends faster than Princess escapes from her pen.'

'That's because they all turn out to be frogs.'

'Frogs, eh? Does Adam have froggie tendencies?'

'Not so far.'

'Which means you will be seeing him again.' It was a statement, not a question, and despite her humour of a moment ago, Dulcie didn't sound happy about it.

'Saturday.'

Dulcie pressed her lips together. 'You've got a shift in the restaurant on Saturday, remember?'

'I haven't forgotten. We're going to the cinema in the afternoon.'

'Hmm. Just make sure you're not late for work.'

'I won't be, I promise. And I also promise not to dump him until your shed is finished.'

'That means you'll be staying here for at least another week.'

Maisie's heart sank. 'Is that a problem?' She had been hoping to stay longer than a week: a lot longer.

'Actually, it isn't. You've been very helpful.' Dulcie sounded surprised, which got Maisie's back up a bit, although she did her best to hide it.

'I've tried to be,' she replied mildly.

'Cocoa?' It was a peace offering.

'Hell, no! I'm not eighty. A glass of wine would be nice.' Then she heard Otto's car in the farmyard. 'Or maybe not. I think I'll go to bed.'

Dulcie gave her a knowing look. 'You don't have to.'

Remembering what their mother had said, Maisie shrugged. 'Otto could do without me hanging around. He sees enough of me at the restaurant. I'll just grab that glass of wine and go upstairs. There's a film I want to watch anyway.'

Maisie was heading up the stairs when she heard Otto come in, and she smiled. With Dulcie admitting that Maisie was useful around the farm, and Maisie making herself scarce so Dulcie and Otto could have some time to themselves, Maisie had put two of Mum's arguments to bed. All that was needed now was for Maisie to try to be the best server Otto ever had, and Mum would have no more objections to Maisie being at the farm.

There was still the matter of being guilt-tripped though, but Maisie couldn't do anything about her mum missing her. Maisie was bound to move out of the family home at some point. She couldn't live with her mum forever, and neither did she want to. It was time Maisie grew up, and she was hoping that the farm on Muddypuddle Lane was the place she would do it.

CHAPTER FIVE

Maisie hurried through her chores on Saturday morning. Not that Dulcie had given her any explicit instructions – Maisie had taken it upon herself to do things, such as collecting the freshly laid eggs from the chicken coop and checking the goats over before ushering them into the paddock.

This morning she also cleaned out the coop, in addition to collecting eggs and feeding the hens their daily grain. Mucking out was a stinky job, and she hoped a hot shower would successfully wash away the whiff of chicken poop. Any romantic notions she'd had about farming had gone the same way as her idea of goat milking. Farming was a mucky, smelly business, but she loved it. Although, when Adam arrived to pick her up just before midday on Saturday, she was still surreptitiously sniffing her hands in case there was a vague hint of hen lingering on them.

Maisie climbed into the van with a smile and a 'Hi,' and as soon as she was settled into the passenger seat Adam stretched across and brushed his lips lightly against hers, before putting the van into gear and pulling out of the yard.

'Hi, to you, too,' he said. 'I hope you didn't mind me suggesting a quick bite to eat first, but I thought you mightn't have time to grab anything before you had to go to work.'

Maisie didn't mind at all. She had been pleasantly surprised at his thoughtfulness. In her experience it was a rare commodity. 'Where were you thinking of?'

'Will Mexmax do you? It's next door to the cinema.'

Maisie loved the spicy chicken and huge burgers that the restaurant chain was renowned for, so she was more than happy, and half an hour later the pair of them were seated in a corner booth, perusing the menu.

'Are you sure you want to see a rom com?' she asked, deciding to have a hot and spicy burger with fries, and an ice cream sundae to follow. The film she was referring to was the latest hilarious blockbuster, and although she wanted to see it, she guessed Adam mightn't be as keen. However, her choices had been limited due to the start times and film length, as she had to ensure she was back in Picklewick by six-thirty.

'It sounds like fun,' he replied gallantly, and if she hadn't liked him before, Maisie seriously liked him now.

'Your choice, next time,' she said, then winced as she realised she was assuming a lot.

'Deal. How do you like working at The Wild Side?'

'It's good as far as waitressing goes. I can't see myself doing it long term though, even if Otto is practically family.'

'Ah, yes, goat herding,' Adam teased gently.

'Not just goats. I've also grown quite attached to the chickens, especially Kevin.'

'Kevin?'

'That's my nephew's chicken. She's female but Sammy has named her Kevin. She's incredibly tame. And so is Flossie, the sheep. She was hand-reared by Otto's dad, Walter. He owned the farm before Dulcie.'

'I know.'

Maisie blushed. 'Of course you do, what with you being a local. I keep forgetting that everyone knows everyone else in Picklewick.'

'I don't know everyone *personally*,' he said. 'But I usually know *of* them. When Walter and Otto put the farm into a lottery, it was the talk of the village. I even bought a ticket.'

'You didn't!'

He nodded, smiling his thanks as a server delivered their meals to the table.

'I can't see you owning a farm,' Maisie said, tucking into her burger.

'Neither can I, but I can see me owning all those barns and outbuildings.'

'Why? What would you do with them?'

'Expand my business. I'm quite limited at the moment. I've been looking for something bigger, but there's not much about, especially on my budget.'

He looked wistful, and Maisie felt for him. She would like a place of her own too, but that wasn't going to happen anytime soon.

After the meal was finished, they strolled over to the cinema.

'Where would you like to sit?' Adam asked as they entered the theatre. There were two tiers, one nearer to the screen, which was almost flat, and the other up some shallow, wide steps.

'Not right at the front. We'll get cricked necks.'

'The back row?'

'Like a couple of teenagers?'

'It depends on whether you want to watch the film, or make out.'

Maisie giggled. 'How old are you? Sixteen? How about this one?'

'I'm happy if you are,' he said, and she sidled into the row, aiming for the middle.

By mutual agreement, they had decided not to buy any snacks, both of them still full from the meal, so they settled down to watch the film.

Maisie was soon immersed in the story, however she was also very conscious of the man sitting next to her, and every so often she stole a glance at him out of the corner of her eye.

When his hand reached for hers, a tingle shot through her which made it difficult to concentrate on the film after that. She kept hoping he would kiss her, but he seemed content just to hold her hand.

It wasn't until he was dropping her off at the farm, that he finally made a move. This time, the kiss lasted longer and was far more satisfying, although it did leave her wanting more.

It was Maisie who ended it, but only because she had to get ready for work. 'I've got to run,' she said. 'I have to be at The Wild Side in forty-five minutes.'

'I can drop you off, if you like. I'll be driving past it on my way home.'

'That's great – if you don't mind. It'll save me walking or asking Dulcie for a lift.' She'd only had to do that once so far, as she usually either went into the village with Otto or she walked along the path through the fields. The one time she'd asked Dulcie for a lift was because it had been raining.

It occurred to Maisie that if she did persuade Dulcie to let her stay for any length of time, she would have to buy herself a little run around; constantly begging Dulcie for lifts would be a sure-fire way of outstaying her welcome. Maisie just about had enough money in her savings account to buy an old banger, and at least she could ask Adam to take a look at it if it packed up.

'Would you like to come in and wait?' she offered, her fingers on the door handle. Adam hesitated. 'Or maybe not, if it will make you feel uncomfortable,' she added.

'I'm starting work on Dulcie's shed on Monday,' he reminded her. 'It mightn't be appropriate.'

'I understand.' Impulsively she leant across to give him a swift kiss. 'I'll be as quick as I can.'

Dulcie, who was in the dining room staring at her laptop when Maisie dashed inside, glanced up with a frown. 'You're cutting it fine. I suppose you want a lift?'

'It's okay, Adam will drop me off at the restaurant.'

'Hmph.'

Irritated, Maisie shot upstairs to change into her work clothes. From her reaction, Dulcie hadn't come around to the idea of Maisie dating Adam, and Maisie felt as though her sister was judging her and finding her wanting.

Even if this afternoon's date had been a disaster, Maisie wouldn't have done or said anything to jeopardise Adam starting work on the pasteurisation shed on Monday. She wasn't that stupid, no matter what her family thought.

'See you later,' she said, as she breezed through the dining room, and she was out of the door before Dulcie had a chance to reply.

'Ready?' Adam asked as she climbed into the van.

Maisie nodded. 'Thanks for this – and for lunch and the cinema.'

'My pleasure. Will you be around on Monday morning?'

'Absolutely! I've got chores to do.'

His smile was warm. 'I'll see you on Monday, then. Maybe we can do something later in the week?'

'I'd like that,' she said, meaning it. And when she gave him a quick kiss in the van outside the restaurant, she knew that Monday wouldn't come quickly enough.

Maisie was up extra early on Monday morning: not because she intended to take greater care with her appearance (there wasn't any point when she would soon have straw in her hair and muck over her clothes) but simply because she was excited to see Adam.

Having managed to spend an inordinate amount of time thinking about him yesterday, she was now restless and on edge at the prospect of seeing him again this morning. By the time he turned up, she was a bundle of nerves and she was forced to give herself a stern talking-to.

Maisie Fairfax, she said to herself, *what on earth has got into you? You are never normally like this with a guy.* Then, as she watched Adam get out of his van from her observation point in the kitchen as she stood near the sink and peered out of the window, it struck her – she was falling for him.

Her startled gasp made Dulcie shoot her a concerned look. 'Are you okay?'

'I'm fine. I stubbed my toe, that's all.'

Dulcie walked over to the sink to rinse out a mug. 'Is that Adam, I see?'

Maisie pretended she hadn't noticed his arrival. 'So it is. He's early.' It was only seven forty-five.

'I'm not complaining,' her sister said. 'The sooner he starts, the sooner I can begin milking the goats. In fact, I think I had better have a go at milking Cloud and Bramble by hand, to get them used to the idea. Want to help?'

'Yes please!' Maisie couldn't think of anything she'd like more.

Can't you? an inner voice piped up, as the memory of Adam's kiss burst into her mind.

Shoving it away – she wasn't here to kiss frogs (or princes) – Maisie followed her sister outside, eager to have a go at milking her very first goat.

Adam was unloading an assortment of tools from his van, but he stopped what he was doing when he noticed her and Dulcie.

'Morning.' He directed the greeting at Dulcie, but his gaze flickered towards Maisie.

'Can I get you a coffee before you start?' Dulcie asked.

'I'm good, thanks. I always bring a flask with me.'

'Okay, but let Maisie know if you need anything, because I'm starting work in an hour. Before that though, we've got a goat to milk. Wish us luck.'

Maisie hoped she wouldn't need any luck; she hoped she would be a natural.

From the ruckus that had been coming from the barn every morning for the past couple of days, Adam assumed that milking goats must take a bit of practice. He was halfway through the renovations to the pasteurisation shed and every day so far this week he'd heard irritated bleating, buckets being overturned and some choice swear words.

He hadn't mentioned anything until now, but this third date with Maisie seemed an ideal opportunity to bring it up. It was Wednesday evening, and they were having a meal in The Black Horse.

'How is the milking going?' he asked.

'Ugh! It's not.' Maisie shuddered.

'I did hear some swearing,' he admitted, 'so I guessed as much.'

'Petra has promised to show Dulcie how it's done tomorrow. Surely it can't be that difficult? And what will happen when we try to milk them mechanically?'

Adam smirked. 'I'm glad it's not my problem. I'll stick to engines, thanks.'

'When will you be finished?'

'Friday, if I don't hit any snags.' He would be sorry the job was ending: seeing Maisie every day had been the highlight. He was hoping to continue to see her after it was over, but he supposed that depended on how much longer she would be in Picklewick. She didn't appear to be in any hurry to return to

Birmingham, and she had even indicated that she would like to make the village her permanent home.

The sound of tinny music had Maisie scrabbling around in her bag, and when she saw who was calling, her face fell. 'It's my mum,' she said. 'I'd better take this, sorry.'

Adam didn't mind in the slightest. He was curious about her family, and although he tried not to look as though he was ear-wigging, it was impossible not to hear, considering she was holding the conversion less than a metre away.

'Hi, Mum... No, not tonight, I'm out for a meal... The Black Horse... With Adam... *Adam*. He's installing the past— Not yet... I don't know... I would have thought you'd enjoy not having to tidy up after me. Look, Mum, I've got to go... Love you, too.'

She made sure the call had ended, then sent him an apologetic look. 'Sorry. I wasn't expecting her to phone. I only spoke to her yesterday. She's missing me. I don't know why – she spends most of the time grumbling that I treat the house like a hotel.' Maisie's expression was sheepish. 'She's right: I do. I think the problem is that I've never left home. Why is it that I revert to about sixteen when I'm with her?'

Adam's parents were the same; they didn't seem able to trust his judgement when it came to what he wanted to do with his life.

Maisie continued, 'It doesn't help that I'm the baby of the family. I don't think she likes the idea of her last chick flying the nest.' She sighed. 'She's nagging me to go home, but the longer I'm here, the more like home it's beginning to feel. Except it's not *my* home, it's Dulcie's, and I don't know if she'll put up with me for more than another couple of weeks.'

'Is it Picklewick itself you like, or the farm?'

'Both, but the farm especially. I like working with animals.'

'Aren't there any animal-related jobs in Birmingham?'

'Possibly. Why? Are you trying to get rid of me?'

'Absolutely not.' His reply was emphatic. The thought of her returning to her hometown made him feel rather sad.

'I'm glad.' Her gaze captured his and he was momentarily lost in her eyes.

She broke the spell. 'Fancy another?' Their glasses were empty, as were their plates.

'I'd better have a soft drink,' he said, having already enjoyed a pint with his meal.

'If you want another, I don't mind walking back to the farm,' she offered.

'I am not letting you walk home on your own; it's nearly dark.' He had a thought. 'Would you like to come back to mine for an hour?' And when he noticed her hesitation, he hastily added, 'Just for a coffee, I promise. I might even be able to stretch to a Jaffa cake or a chocolate Hobnob.'

'Now you're talking! Who can resist a chocolate Hobnob?'

Adam smirked. 'I know the way to a woman's heart.'

It struck him as he said it, that he wished he *did* know the way to Maisie's heart, because he abruptly realised that she was beginning to worm her way into his.

Maisie assumed she must have passed Adam's place on the way into and out of the village on several occasions, but she had never given it a second glance. It was a stand-alone building, three stories high, with a set of large garage-type wooden doors dominating the ground floor. They were painted sky-blue, but had seen better days. As had the door next to it, which she assumed led to the living area upstairs. The brickwork was a dingy cream render, and there was a concreted area at the front daubed with oil stains. An old sign above the garage doors said *MOTs HERE* and the outside looked run-down and unloved.

Maisie hoped, for Adam's sake, that the flat was in better nick, and she could understand why he wanted to move but at the same time she was envious that he was able to rent a place of his own. She wished she could afford to.

Far from being dingy, the tiny hall and the stairs leading to the living accommodation above, were clean and bright, with white walls and a wooden staircase. And when Adam showed her into the flat, she was delighted.

It was a bit blokey for her taste, being sparse and lacking in soft furnishings, but it was as neat as a pin (as her mum would say) and was spotlessly clean.

An L-shaped black leather sofa dominated the living room, and a TV hung on the wall opposite. An old-fashioned LP player sat on a rack of industrial-looking shelves, along with a selection of books and a potted plant. A staircase led to the top floor and, she assumed, the bedroom.

The flat was bigger than she had expected, and another twinge of envy twisted in her stomach. Maisie would give her right arm to live in a place like this – even if it did have a dirty garage-cum-workshop underneath.

'Coffee or tea? Or I've got a bottle of pale ale if you're interested.'

'Coffee, please.' She dropped her bag and jacket on the arm of the sofa and followed him out to the kitchen. This, too, was immaculate: not a dirty mug or a used spoon in sight. 'Are you always this tidy?' she asked.

'Yeah.' He fired up an impressive-looking coffee machine. 'Just because I'm a guy living on my own, doesn't mean I'm a slob.' His wry smile took the sting out of his words.

'I need to take a leaf out of your book,' Maisie muttered. 'I'm the slobby one in my family.'

'I'm sure you're not as bad as that.'

'Oh, I am, believe me. Although, I seem to have turned over a new leaf since coming to Picklewick.'

'Trying to impress Dulcie?'

'You could say that.'

When the drinks were ready they took them into the lounge, but Maisie hadn't managed to take a single sip of hers before Adam slid across the sofa and kissed her.

This was no brief flutter of the lips; this was a passionate, toe-curling, breath-stopping kiss.

The shock of it went right through her before settling deep inside, leaving her trembling with desire. She slowly slid down onto the sofa until she lay on her back, Adam above, holding his weight on one arm until she pulled him down. His body covering hers, her fingers crept underneath his shirt to caress his back, and at her touch he shifted position with a groan and continued to kiss her deeply for several deliciously long minutes.

Maisie wasn't sure how far she would have allowed things to go, but she didn't get the chance to find out.

'Stop, stop,' Adam moaned, dragging his mouth away from hers.

He pushed himself upright and sat back. His hair was tousled, his shirt raised on one side, and he was breathing hard. He looked delectable, and Maisie wanted to eat him whole.

'I'm sorry,' he said, his voice hoarse. 'I got carried away for a moment.'

Maisie adjusted her top and shifted into a sitting position. 'So did I.'

'It was only supposed to be coffee.'

Her smile was small. 'We both knew it was going to be more than that.'

'But I don't want you to think I lured you here under false pretences.'

'I don't. Anyway, I could have stopped you sooner, but I didn't want to.'

He opened his mouth, but whatever he was about to say was lost by the ringing of his phone. 'Dear god,' he muttered. 'I sure know how to kill the mood, don't I?'

'Are you going to answer it?'

He checked the screen. 'It's my mother.'

They exchanged sympathetic glances as he accepted the call.

'Hi, Mum.'

Maisie strained to listen as his mother spoke, but she couldn't hear a thing.

'No, I wasn't in bed,' he said, catching her eye again.

Maisie blushed and Adam quickly looked away. Feeling awkward, she was about to ask where the loo was, when he lowered his phone and mouthed, 'Are you working on Saturday evening?' As she nodded to tell him that she was, Maisie could hear a faint tinny, 'Adam? Adam!' coming from the speaker.

'Hang on, Mum, yes, Saturday is fine, I'll see you then.' Then he did what Maisie herself had done less than an hour previously, and stabbed at the phone, making sure the call had disconnected. 'It looks like I'm going to my parents on Saturday for dinner,' he said. 'At least it'll save me having to cook. I would have preferred to see you, though. When are you free next?'

'Sunday.'

'Fancy doing something?'

Maisie certainly did, but what she *fancied* doing wasn't what she *should* be doing. It was a long time since a man had gotten under her skin the way Adam had, and she knew she had to take it easy.

'We could go into Thornbury and check out a pub or two,' he suggested, and Maisie breathed a sigh of relief.

She wanted to get to know him better first, and even then she mightn't take things to the next level – not if it looked like she would definitely be returning to Birmingham.

Until she knew what was happening, she needed to guard her heart. The last thing she wanted was for it to be broken.

CHAPTER SIX

Adam was in the middle of flushing out the pasteurisation unit ready for its first use, and was currently running his hands along the pipes to check for leaks, paying particular attention to the joints and the valves. Dulcie was hovering anxiously, Maisie by her side. The two of them wore worried expressions.

He sidled past them and went next door to the milking parlour, where he did the same thing. Maisie and Dulcie followed him.

'I need a goat to check it properly,' he said.

He hadn't heard quite as much swearing during these last two days, so he was hoping that the animals were getting used to being milked. However, how they would react to having the business end of the milking machine attached to their udders was a totally different pot of yoghurt.

Maisie said, 'I'll fetch Cloud. She's the most patient.'

Adam also knew that Cloud was one of the pygmy goats and would therefore be easier to handle if the critter decided to take exception.

Maisie was back in a trice, Cloud and her two goatlings in tow.

'Do you want to do the honours?' he asked Dulcie, hoping she didn't expect *him* to try to milk the goat. As far as he was concerned, his job was done as long as the damned thing worked – and he couldn't see any reason why it wouldn't.

He could barely bring himself to watch as Dulcie manoeuvred the goat into position on the raised platform and presented the animal with a hay net filled with vegetable treats to keep it occupied whilst she fiddled around with attaching the suction cups.

Apart from an occasional annoyed stamp of a hoof when Dulcie was too clumsy, the goat didn't seem particularly bothered.

Adam held his breath, almost sagging with relief when creamy milk finally began flowing along the clear tubes. Not that he had thought for one second that he wasn't capable of installing such equipment, but no matter what job he did, there was always an element of worry that something might go wrong.

'Result!' Maisie cried, clapping her hands, and he gave her a triumphant grin. She got her phone out. 'This calls for a selfie,' she said, and she draped an arm around his shoulders and pulled him close, holding her phone aloft.

Their cheeks touching, Maisie took a snap with the goats in the background. Then she insisted on taking a photo of him with Dulcie.

Adam, conscious that his relationship with Dulcie was considerably more formal than his relationship with Maisie, made sure to keep a respectable distance, and he moved out of the way entirely when Maisie started snapping the goat.

Abruptly remembering that he was supposed to be checking the machinery, Adam hurried into the other shed, following the milk's progress, and was relieved to find everything working as it should.

A few minutes later Dulcie joined him, the goat having been successfully milked.

'You've done a good job,' she said. 'I'm really pleased. Come into the house and I'll get your payment sorted.'

'There's no rush.'

'I want to get it out of the way, and I expect you could do with the money.'

He shrugged, not knowing what to say to that. He wasn't exactly destitute, so it could wait a few days, but if Dulcie wanted to settle the debt now, he wouldn't say no.

Maisie was leading a bemused goat out of the milking shed as he emerged into the yard.

'This is a momentous occasion,' she declared, beaming widely. 'We should have an opening ceremony.' The goat bleated, as though in agreement.

'We should have something,' Dulcie agreed. 'But I was thinking more like a goat-petting experience. With the addition of some rabbits and a few chicks, we might encourage visitors to the farm. It's something I thought about last autumn, but I haven't had time to organise it.'

'I'll do it.' Maisie's face was alight. 'Let me, please.'

Dulcie said, 'You just want to get your hands on some fluffy chicks.'

'Yep.' Maisie was totally unashamed.

'We can have a chat about it tomorrow,' Dulcie said. 'Otto will be around in the morning, and I think Sammy wants to see Kevin, so we can pick Nikki's brains at the same time.'

Cloud bleated and tugged on the lead rope, reminding Maisie she was there. 'I'll take her back to the meadow,' she said, then turned to Adam. 'I expect you'll be gone by the time I get back.'

'Probably. Are you still up for Sunday?'

'Absolutely. See ya.'

Adam took a moment to watch her skip across the yard, the goats close behind. Then he realised Dulcie was staring at him and he looked away.

'Come on.' She gestured for him to follow as she went into the house. 'Will a bank transfer do you?'

'It certainly will. Um, Dulcie, I noticed that the old farmhouse on the top of the hill is up for sale. Have you had much interest?'

'None at all, unfortunately. I suspect it's too remote and too much work needs doing, especially since the access road is so poor.' She pulled a face. 'You can't actually call it a road, it's more like a dirt track. Why? Are you interested?'

'I might be.'

'What would you do with it?'

'Live in it. And put up some outbuildings.'

'What's wrong with where you are now?'

'Too small. Anyway, it was only ever meant to be a stop gap.'

'Do you want to have a look around?'

'I've been up there already. I agree, it will need a tremendous amount of work. But it'll be lovely when it's done.'

Dulcie studied him. 'You'll need deep pockets.'

She was right. Plus he would have to sell his place first to raise the necessary funds. Which meant he would be homeless for a while – unless he moved back in with his mum and dad.

The thought filled him with unease. It had taken a lot of effort to escape from his parents' house and the last thing he wanted was to move back in and have his mum looking over his shoulder every five minutes, telling him what to do and how he should do it. Maybe he could buy a cheap caravan, put it on the site and live there for the duration?

'The payment has gone through,' Dulcie said. 'It should hit your bank account in a few minutes.' She straightened up. 'If you're serious about the old farmhouse, let me know.'

'I will,' he promised. 'But can you keep it just between you and me, for the time being?'

'Of course.' She glanced out of the window and Adam guessed she must be thinking that he didn't want Maisie to know. Which he didn't, but only because he wanted to get everything straight in his head first, before he mentioned it to her. However, the main reason he didn't want anyone to know his business was because if his parents got to hear about it, they would do their utmost to talk him out of it, and he could do without the grief.

The following morning Maisie and Dulcie did the milking between them. It took them fifty minutes to milk five goats.

Maisie said, 'It'll get easier as the goats get used to it.'

Dulcie was looking rather despondent. 'I hope so! I can't do this every morning, I haven't got the time.

Thank goodness today is Saturday, otherwise I'd be late starting work.'

'I'll do it,' Maisie promised, adding, 'For as long as you need me to.'

'That could be a couple of weeks,' her sister warned.

Maisie didn't take it as a warning, she took it as a promise. It meant she would have another two weeks on the farm before she was forced to re-evaluate her life. 'That's okay, I'm not in any hurry to go back to Birmingham.'

Maisie realised she had said 'Birmingham' and not 'home' and she wondered whether Dulcie had noticed.

It seemed not, as her sister said, 'Nikki and Sammy will be here soon. Let's put this milk in the fridge, then we can crack on with brainstorming some ideas.'

When they returned to the house they were met by the delicious aroma of baking, and found Otto taking a batch of croissants out of the oven. He'd no sooner done that, than Nikki rocked up with Sammy with his young Border collie at his heels.

'Mum said you've got more baby goats!' he cried. 'Can I go and see them?'

'Of course you can,' his mum said, and four pairs of eyes watched him indulgently as he shot out of the door with a loud whoop, the dog in hot pursuit.

'Let's take a look at this new set-up, then,' Nikki said, just as Walter arrived. He had also brought his dog with him. Peg was a Border collie too, but considerably older and a lot calmer than Sammy's pup.

Maisie held out her hand for the dog to sniff, then fondled Peg's ears. That was what the farm lacked, she thought: a dog. There was an old ginger tom cat who came and went when the mood took him, but the animal belonged to Walter and wasn't the friendliest of creatures.

Whilst Dulcie showed Nikki and Walter the new milking parlour, Maisie stayed put and played with the dog until they breezed back in.

'Adam is a bit of a hottie,' Nikki declared, as Otto placed the croissants in the centre of the table. She took one and bit into it, cupping her hand underneath her chin to catch the crumbs. 'Mmm, this is lovely,' she mumbled around a mouthful of pastry.

'He is,' Maisie acknowledged. She had sent Nikki, Jay and their mum the photos she had taken yesterday.

Nikki furrowed her brow. 'Dulcie mentioned that you two are an item. How long before you dump this one?'

'Who says I'm going to dump him?'

'You always do. Anyway, you'll have to when you go back home.'

Maisie pressed her lips together. She didn't want to think about that right now. Besides, she still had a couple of weeks' grace.

'Good job really,' Nikki carried on. 'Mum wouldn't approve. She hates piercings.'

'And long hair,' Dulcie added.

'She isn't too keen on tattoos either,' Nikki said.

'I've got a tattoo of a sheep,' Walter announced, rolling up his shirt sleeve to show them. Maisie was bemused. If she were to have a tattoo, it certainly wouldn't be a *sheep*.

'Can I have a tattoo?' Sammy piped up. He had returned to the kitchen, catching the tail end of the conversation.

Five adults said in unison, 'No, you can't.'

'I'll have one when I'm grown up,' he said. 'I want a tattoo of a chicken.'

Otto said to his father, 'If Sammy ends up having a chicken on his arm, you know who Beth will blame.'

Walter waved a hand in the air. 'As if I care. It'll be just one more thing that Beth and I don't see eye-to-eye on.'

Maisie recalled how her mum and Walter had squabbled like a pair of kids when the family had spent Christmas at the farm. It had been quite entertaining, with the added bonus that whenever Mum's attention had been on Walter, it hadn't been on her.

Dulcie accepted a cup of coffee from Otto with a smile, then raised her voice. 'Can we get on with ideas for the petting-zoo-spring-event thingy, because Otto has to leave soon.'

'You could have koalas,' Sammy suggested. 'People like koalas.'

'You mean, *you* like koalas,' Nikki pointed out. 'I don't think Aunty Dulcie will be keeping koalas.'

'Uncle Jay could send her some.'

His mother said, 'Koalas are native to Australia, not New Zealand.'

Dulcie sipped her coffee. 'We've got the goats, and three of them have yet to give birth. But that will be soon, so I want to hold the spring event thingy in the next couple of weeks ideally, so the babies are still tiny.'

Otto grinned. 'Spring event thingy? Catchy title.'

'I'm not sure what else to call it,' she said.

'How about Spring on the Farm, or you could hold it at the Easter weekend and call it an Easter Fayre?' Maisie suggested.

'I like that idea! Good thinking, Maisie. Now, how about if we—' Dulcie began, but was interrupted by her phone ringing. 'It's Mum,' she said, accepting the call. 'Hi, Mum. Hang on, let me put you on speakerphone. Just so you know, Maisie, Otto, Nikki, Sammy and Walter are here, so no swearing.'

'Hi, Mum,' Maisie and Nikki chorused in unison, as the others said hello.

'What are you all doing at Dulcie's at this time on a Saturday morning?' Beth wanted to know.

Dulcie said, 'They're helping me plan the Easter Fayre.'

'What Easter Fayre?'

'The one I intend holding to try to bring in some revenue.'

'I thought that's what the goats were for? And who was that man you were draped over, Maisie? Was that the chap who Dulcie got to do all the work?'

'His name is Adam,' Maisie said.

'He looks a bit of a sort,' Beth replied. 'Is he the one you've been seeing?'

'Yes, he is.' Maisie shook her head in irritation, catching an I-told-you-so look from Nikki.

'You can do better than him,' Beth continued. 'But then, I doubt he'll last long. Your boyfriends never do.' It was said with an equal measure of satisfaction and disapproval. 'I don't know why you can't find yourself a nice chap like Otto. Or Giovanni.'

Nikki rolled her eyes as she muttered, 'It's nice of her to include Gio.'

Maisie smirked at her eldest sister and Nikki stuck out her tongue, making Maisie blink in surprise.

Dulcie frowned at them and held up a hand. 'Mum, is there anything in particular you want? I don't like to be rude, but Otto has to go to work in a minute and I want to get on with the meeting while he's still here.'

There was a telling silence, followed by, 'I know when I'm not wanted, so I'll say goodbye. Clearly Walter's opinion is more important than mine.'

'Don't be silly, Mum. Your opinion is equally valid. I know, why don't you stay on the line? It'll be as if you are actually here.'

'But I'm not, am I? I'm here on my own. Maisie, when are you coming home?'

Dulcie tutted, 'Mum, can we get on, please? Do you want to stay on the phone or not?'

'I suppose I'll have to, if I want to be part of the family.'

Maisie wrinkled her nose as her sisters pulled equally irritated faces.

'Okay, then,' Dulcie said, not rising to the bait.

Maisie admired her sister's self-control; their mother was the guilt-trip queen. Thankfully, nothing more was mentioned about Adam, or Maisie's possible return to Birmingham and the family home, and the ad hoc meeting went ahead without further ado.

And with the date now set for the fayre and lots of ideas, Maisie couldn't wait to get stuck in.

This spring was shaping up to be the best one ever.

Adam's spirits sank as he spotted two strange cars parked on his parents' drive. He had stupidly assumed that dinner would be a family affair – just him, his mum and his dad – but it looked as though there were going to be at least two additional guests.

Then he recognised one of the cars and his spirits dropped another couple of fathoms.

The Bentley belonged to Linda and Karl Spencer, long-standing friends of his parents. They were nice enough people, he supposed, but not his cup of tea. Linda and his mum enjoyed nothing more than gossiping about various friends and acquaintances or their latest holidays, while Karl and Dad either played the one-upmanship game or talked shop. Dad usually tried to draw Adam into the conversation, but Adam didn't have anything to be one-up about (and if he had, he certainly wouldn't boast about it) and neither was he interested in his dad's accountancy firm.

It looked like he was in for a boring evening, because he suspected the owners of the other car would be equally as— Damn! He had a horrid suspicion he knew who it might be. His mother was a stickler for symmetry and there was no way she would have invited two other couples plus him, because that would mean seven at the table. He would be the odd-man-out, and in his mother's eyes, that would never do.

Which meant that the driver of the Lotus was probably Linda and Karl's daughter, Verity.

Like him, Verity was single. Like him, Verity's parents would be delighted if he and Verity were an item. Although he suspected Verity's parents would only be happy with that unlikely situation if Adam were to join his dad's firm.

Despite Adam being the sole beneficiary when his parents (god forbid) passed on, and would therefore be a wealthy guy, Linda and Karl didn't approve of what he did for a living. A blue-collar worker wasn't what they had in mind as a suitable husband for their only daughter.

Adam had hoped that they would have knocked the idea of him and Verity getting together on the head by now, but if his suspicion was correct and this was indeed Verity's car, then they clearly hadn't given up yet.

In a petty act of defiance, Adam took a second to gather his hair into a man-bun on the top of his head. In his father's eyes, long hair could be kind of forgiven if one pretended that the owner of the hair hadn't had time to visit the barber for a while, but a topknot was a deliberate style (or lack of it) statement.

Adam also unbuttoned the cuffs of this shirt and rolled up the sleeves, displaying several tattoos, and undid the neck of his shirt another notch. Then he moved the van so it was parked immediately next to the gleaming Bentley. It was childish of him, but with the prospect of an awkward and boring evening ahead, he had to take his fun where he could find it.

Adam didn't bother ringing the bell, sauntering in to find everyone in the sitting room.

Dad and Karl were standing by the mantlepiece, pre-dinner drinks in hand, and Mum was perched elegantly on the edge of one of the armchairs, her legs neatly crossed at the ankle. Linda and Verity were sitting at either end of one of the sofas.

All of them stopped talking and turned to look when he walked into the room.

'Adam, darling.' His mum rose to her feet in a fluid practised move and greeted him with a kiss on the cheek. Only he could hear her as she hissed, 'You could have made more of an effort.'

'Linda, Karl.' He nodded at his parents' friends. 'This is a surprise. I wasn't expecting anyone else to be here.'

He shook Karl's hand and pecked Linda on the cheek. Then he turned to Verity and gave her an even briefer peck than he had given her mother.

'I see they've roped you in too,' he said. His smile was sympathetic. Verity was an attractive woman. A year younger than him, she was pretty, self-assured, and polished to an inch of her life from the top of her shiny, expensively cut hair, to the manicured toenails that peeped out from gold high-heeled sandals.

'Drink?' his mum asked. He could tell she was gritting her teeth.

'No, thanks. I'm driving. I'll have a glass of water with the meal.'

'You could always stay the night,' she suggested. 'Then you can let your hair down.' Her wince when she realised that she had drawn attention to his bun, was quickly concealed.

'My, that's an interesting hairstyle, isn't it, Karl?' Linda's face was full of disapproval.

'I think it looks good,' Verity said. 'It suits you. You've got a rock star vibe going on.'

Linda's gaze shot to his hands and the oil that he could never seem to fully wash off, no matter what product he used or how many times he scrubbed them. He sincerely doubted a rockstar would have such workaday hands as his.

Dinner was as cringe-worthy as Adam suspected it would be. The main topic of conversation centred around the proposed merger between his father's and Karl's companies. Karl, it appeared, wanted to take more of a back seat and would be content for Martin to run it. Even Adam, who had zero interest in his dad's company, could see how lucrative it would be for both parties.

He quietly tipped a glass to his father. Good luck to him, he thought, if that was what he wanted. As long as Dad didn't try to rope him in, Adam was happy for him.

As usual when she was hosting a dinner party, his mum had brought in outside caterers and serving staff, so when the meal was over and brandy and coffee were being poured, Adam took the opportunity to slip into the hall and send a quick message to Maisie.

How is your evening?

She was at work, so he didn't expect an answer straight away and was surprised when she sent an immediate response. *Busy. Yours?*

Boring. Dad talking shop. Looking forward to tomorrow evening.

Me too. But I might bore you by talking goat.

You'll never bore me. Adam hesitated, wondering whether he should send it. Would she think it a bit OTT? Then again, he had to say something… He decided to send it, and had just heard the ping of an outgoing message when his mother stepped into the hall.

'There you are! We wondered where you were.' She saw the phone in his hand and her mouth tightened. 'Do you have to play with that constantly?'

'This is the first time this evening.'

'I'm sure your friends could have done without hearing from you until tomorrow.'

'I wasn't on the phone to my friends.'

Her eyes narrowed. 'Please don't tell me it was to do with your so-called job.'

Adam kept his temper with difficulty. 'It's not a *so-called* job. It's a real job. One that pays my bills.'

'One that impinges on your private life,' she snapped.

He almost retorted that at least *he* hadn't been discussing business all evening, but he held his tongue. 'It was nothing to do with work.'

'What was it, then? Are we so boring that you simply had to check your social media page?' She paused and her cross expression lifted. 'Or were you searching for somewhere to take Verity? There's this lovely little restaurant in—'

'I was on the phone to my girlfriend,' he interrupted, aware he was putting the cat amongst the pigeons by mentioning a girlfriend right now, but since Mum clearly wasn't getting the message that he wasn't interested in Verity...

'You have a girlfriend? You never said. Who is she? Do I know her?'

'No, you don't.'

'What's her—?'

The click-clack of high heels stopped his mum in her tracks as Linda approached.

Her gaze raked Adam, then zeroed in on his mum. 'Is everything alright, Sue?' she asked. 'You were gone such a long time that Martin sent me to find you.'

'Everything's fine,' his mum said, taking Linda by the elbow and guiding her back to the dining room.

Adam trailed grudgingly behind, his reluctance increasing when his mother shot him a look, warning him that the conversation was far from over. He wasn't looking forward to being grilled by her, but at least she could start to get used to the idea of him having a girlfriend.

And she might even back off and stop shoving Verity in his face!

CHAPTER SEVEN

'How are the plans for the Easter Fayre coming along?' Adam asked.

Maisie beamed at him and snuggled closer. This was date number eight (or was it nine? – she was starting to lose count) and they were spending it on the hillside overlooking the farm.

Adam had suggested going for a nice long walk, and they were currently sitting side-by-side on a rock, gazing out over the valley below and contemplating whether to have a fish and chip supper later. For some reason (nothing to do with fish and chips as far as Maisie could tell) the subject had swung around to goats, which must have prompted Adam to ask about the forthcoming Easter event.

'Walter and Amos – you remember Amos from the stables?' Maisie asked, and Adam nodded. 'They've been making bunny runs and hutches, and a pen for the chicks. And Petra is lending us Gerald the donkey, and two Shetland ponies for the weekend. Nikki and Sammy have designed posters and I'll be putting them up around the village tomorrow. And—' She paused for breath. 'Dulcie will be wearing a Peter Rabbit costume.'

'That I've got to see.'

'I hope you will. I'll be disappointed if you don't come.'

'Of course I'll come, and I'm happy to help, if you need me.'

'That would be wonderful,' she said cheerfully. 'We've got face-painting planned, an Easter egg hunt, egg decorating, and Otto and Amos will be manning the BBQ. Dulcie is even planning to offer goat milk ice cream. It should be a fun day – fingers crossed.'

'You're enjoying this, aren't you?'

'I am.' Maisie's mood deflated a little as she thought how quickly Easter would arrive. It would soon be here, then the fayre would be over and her help would no longer be needed on the farm.

'What's wrong?' Adam asked. He was so attuned to her moods that she found it hard to hide her feelings from him. Although, so far, she had managed to conceal the fact that she was falling for him more each day. It would be one hell of a wrench to leave him, the farm and Picklewick behind. So much so, that she was seriously contemplating staying permanently.

Not on the farm obviously, because as Mum had pointed out, it wasn't fair on Dulcie and Otto. Otto, bless him, worked so hard that Dulcie hardly ever saw him; but he was hoping that would change when he hired a second chef. So Maisie wanted to get out of their hair when that happened.

Her problem was, where would she live if not at the farm, and how would she support herself? Her shifts at The Wild Side weren't enough to pay rent on a place of her own.

'I'm thinking about what happens after the Easter Fayre,' she said. 'I expect I'll have to go back to Birmingham, but I don't want to.'

'Why can't you stay here?' He took her hands in his as he turned to face her.

'It was only ever meant to be a temporary visit,' she explained. 'I just needed to get away for a while, to clear my head and work out what I want to do with the rest of my life.'

'And have you?'

'Unfortunately, yes. I say *unfortunately* because I love working on the farm and I don't think there are many of those kinds of jobs in Birmingham city centre.'

'True.'

'Besides, I'm working for bed and board here, and I doubt if I would be able to find the same arrangement anywhere else.'

Adam squeezed her hands. 'What would you do if you went home?'

'Be miserable,' she shot back.

'Then it's a no-brainer. You have to stay here. You have to do what makes you happy.' Adam sounded as though he was speaking from experience. But before she could delve any further, he said, 'How can we make that happen?' and her heart melted that he had said *we*, not *you*.

'Find me a job and a place to live that I can afford?' she joked. 'Oh, and break the news to my mother for me. She won't be happy with me staying in Picklewick. In fact, she'll have a fit.'

'Why?'

'She's been guilting me to go back ever since I got here. She reckons she misses me and she's lonely, but

I don't believe it for a minute; she hardly ever saw me when I *was* there. She's been rattling around that house for years. I don't know why she doesn't rent somewhere smaller. When I'm gone for good, it'll be too big for her to live in on her own.'

Maisie shuddered. The thought of having to go back to the city and not see Adam again made her chest ache. She would talk it over with Dulcie, she decided. If she explained how conflicted she was and how desperately she wanted to stay in Picklewick and on the farm, maybe her sister would take pity on her…

Adam had stopped listening. He was squinting into the distance, the beautiful patchwork of fields and copses of trees in the valley below ignored as he thought about what Maisie had just said. He was finding it harder and harder to imagine his life without her in it. She had crept under his skin and burrowed into his heart; he would do anything not to lose her – she *had* to stay.

Slowly an idea began to form. He had a spare room: maybe she could move in with him?

It was a thought… but maybe not a practical or sensible one.

He wasn't sure how she would feel about the suggestion. Heck, he wasn't sure how he felt about it himself. Would she move in as his girlfriend, sharing the same room? Or would he suggest she move into the box room? Both scenarios were fraught with pitfalls. The first meant that they would be living together as a couple and considering they'd not known each other long, moving in *together* seemed rather premature. On the other hand, offering his spare room may suggest a distance he didn't feel.

Either way, he wouldn't expect her to pay anything, so it would give her a chance to get on her feet.

His gaze flickered towards her, then darted away again as something else occurred to him. What if they fell out? Split up? Hated the sight of each other after a couple of months?

He decided not to say anything for now. Maybe Maisie would be able to sort something out for herself. There would be time enough to share his idea with her if – when – she told him she had to return to Birmingham.

'Shall we grab a chippie supper and go to mine?' he said, to break the silence, and she agreed readily.

She had spent a couple of evenings in Adam's flat since that first night when they had come close to making love, although she had yet to stay the night, and having her there felt natural. How she felt about being at his place, he had yet to discover. She seemed at ease though, so maybe moving in (however they decided to play it) wouldn't come as too much of a shock.

It would be strange to have someone else in the flat on a permanent basis, Adam thought, as they drove the short distance to the village to pick up their fish and chips on the way. Although he had lived in shared accommodation when he was in uni, he'd had his little flat all to himself ever since he'd bought the place.

Would he feel awkward having Maisie there? Would it sour their relationship?

Even if it did, he felt compelled to try. If she was in danger of outstaying her welcome at the farm, he would lose her anyway because she would return to Birmingham and that would be the end of it. But if she stayed, their relationship would have a fighting chance.

Out of the blue, another idea occurred to him: *he* didn't have to remain in the flat. He could always move back in with his parents and give Maisie her own space. He would hate living with Mum and Dad, but it would be worth it if it meant that Maisie would stay in Picklewick.

However, it would also mean putting his plans of potentially purchasing Dulcie's derelict farmhouse on hold, but something else would come up sooner or later. He didn't have to put all his eggs in that particular basket.

Adam decided not to mention any of this to either Maisie or his parents just yet. He would wait to see if Maisie was able to persuade Dulcie to let her stay first. That would be his preferred option, because it meant they could carry on as they were and not force their relationship into a direction it wasn't ready to go in just yet.

But despite not wanting to rush things, he was acutely aware that Maisie had crept into his heart and had taken up residence there. For the first time in his life, Adam Haines suspected he might be in love.

The next few days sped past. Maisie was so busy, she didn't have a minute to herself, although she did manage to fit in a few more dates with Adam, and she felt that they were growing closer. So close, that it wouldn't be long before they made love.

Gosh, she was blushing just thinking about it. She had almost given in to her desire on a couple of occasions, but she'd held back, scared of making the commitment, realising that once she gave herself to him completely, her heart would be well and truly lost.

She hadn't spoken to Dulcie yet about the possibility of staying on the farm indefinitely, so that was also preying on her mind. The timing hadn't seemed right, so whilst she waited, she made herself as useful as she possibly could. And so far, it appeared to be working. Dulcie hadn't said anything, but Maisie could see that her sister was relieved to have the routine jobs around the farm done without having to ask, freeing her up to do things such as soap making and organising the Easter Fayre.

Making soap was what Dulcie and Maisie were doing when the farm's landline phone rang in the hall that afternoon, and Dulcie made a face. She was in the kitchen, mixing cubes of frozen goats milk with a lye solution, and the disturbance wasn't welcome.

'Can you see who that is?' she asked Maisie, and Maisie hastily removed the rubber gloves and safety goggles she was wearing (lye was horrid stuff!) and went to answer it.

'Dulcie?' Beth shouted.

'Hi, Mum, it's Maisie.'

'Is Dulcie there?'

'She is, but she's up to her elbows making soap. Can I help?'

'No, I just wanted to ask— On second thoughts, it doesn't matter.' And with that, her mum ended the call.

'Who was that?' Dulcie asked when she returned to the kitchen.

'Mum. She said she wanted to ask you something then she hung up.'

'Strange. I dare say she'll call back if it's important. She's probably got a bee in her bonnet about the woman next door again.'

'I try to ignore it,' Maisie said. 'They've been feuding ever since her neighbours moved in.'

'Talking about moving, I'm surprised Mum hasn't thought about renting somewhere smaller,' Dulcie said, echoing what Maisie had said to Adam a few days ago.

Now's my chance, she thought, but as she was considering the best way to phrase things, a small red car chugged into the yard.

'Who is that?' asked Dulcie, peering out of the window through her safety goggles. 'Thank goodness I've almost finished. I've just got to pour it into the mould and— Good grief, is that *Mum?*'

Maisie couldn't believe her eyes either. Their mother was clambering out of the driver's side of the car in a rather ungainly fashion. Her face was almost as red as its paintwork, and her lips were pressed into a thin line.

'What is *she* doing here?' Dulcie demanded. 'I thought you'd just spoken to her?'

'I did.'

'Did you know she was coming?'

Maisie shook her head vehemently. 'Absolutely not.'

They watched Beth stomp across the yard, then turned to each other with wide, disbelieving eyes as the door to the utility room opened.

'Dulcie? Dulcie! I need a hand with—' Beth stopped when she caught sight of her middle daughter. 'What the hell are you wearing?'

'Safety goggles.'

'Why?'

'Because I'm making soap. Mum, what are you doing here?'

'That's a fine welcome, I must say. I've come all this way to see you, and all you can ask is what am I doing here?' She huffed loudly, pulled out one of the kitchen chairs and plopped down onto it.

Maisie winced. Dulcie looked far from happy as she took a deep breath. Maisie could almost see her counting to ten.

'What I meant was,' her sister said after a pause, 'We weren't expecting you. Why didn't you tell me you were coming?'

Their mum's eyes briefly flickered to Maisie, and Maisie guessed she was thinking that if turning up unannounced was good enough for Maisie, then it was good enough for her. Maisie also guessed that if Mum had asked Dulcie whether she could pay her a visit, Dulcie would have tried to talk her out of it.

Maisie felt quite sorry for her sister.

Beth's expression grew sly. 'I thought I would surprise you.'

'You've done that alright,' Dulcie muttered, then she said in a louder voice, 'Why did you phone just now?'

'I couldn't remember where the turn-off to Muddypuddle Lane was, but then I saw it.' She licked her lips. 'Aren't you going to offer your old mum a cup of tea? Oh, and fetch my case from the car, will you?'

Dulcie held up her gloved hands. 'I'm in the middle of something. If you want tea, you'll have to make it yourself.'

'Charming.'

'Mum, this isn't a hotel. If you'd told me you were coming...' She shook her head, her exasperation obvious.

'I'll put the kettle on,' Maisie offered, hoping to diffuse the situation. 'And while it's coming to the boil, I'll fetch your case, Mum.'

Hurrying out to the car, Maisie wondered who it belonged to. Mum had learnt to drive a long time ago, but she didn't own a car. She must have rented it for the journey.

When Maisie caught sight of the size of the case, her eyes bulged. This wasn't an overnight bag; this was an on-holiday-for-a-fortnight jobbie. It was blimmin' heavy, too.

Huffing and puffing, she heaved the case out of the boot and trundled it across the yard and into the house.

'Bloody hell, Mum!' Dulcie exclaimed when she saw it. 'Is the kitchen sink in there? I thought you said you were only staying for a few days.'

Beth sniffed and gazed up at the ceiling. 'A few days, a week – whatever.' She brought her attention back to Dulcie. 'I thought you could do with some help with this Easter thing.'

Dulcie turned back to her soap mixture. 'It's all under control,' she said.

'Another pair of hands is always useful,' Beth insisted. 'Anyway, it'll be nice for us to spend Easter together. It's just a pity Jay can't be with us.'

'The way it's going, I wouldn't be surprised if he turns up out of the blue as well,' Dulcie grumbled.

'Aw, wouldn't that be nice!' Beth crowed.

Maisie was only half listening: she was too busy worrying about how their mum's unexpected arrival would impact on her own hopes to remain on the farm. And she wished she had found an opportunity to speak to Dulcie about it before Mum had turned up, because she definitely couldn't now.

'Anyway,' their mother was saying, 'I'll be here if you need me, and as soon as Easter is out of the way, Maisie and I can travel home together in my brand-new car. Won't that be nice, Maisie?'

Maisie's heart dropped to her feet. That was the last thing she wanted.

Adam was a few minutes early to pick up Maisie this evening. It was either that or be unacceptably late. The job he had been working on had overrun, and he hadn't had time to go home for a shower and a change of clothes, so he'd decided to pick Maisie up on time, then go to his. Considering they were spending the evening snuggling on the sofa with a takeaway and a film, it made sense.

Maisie must have heard him arrive, because her bedroom window opened and she stuck her head out.

When she held her hand up, he nodded to show he understood that she would be there in five minutes.

Adam got out and stretched, feeling incredibly stiff. He had been contorting himself into odd shapes to be able to get at an exhaust, and he was extremely grubby to boot. A shower was long overdue.

When the back door opened a minute or so later, he expected to see Maisie, but instead it was Dulcie who walked across the yard towards him. She was followed a second later by an older woman with the same high cheekbones and green-blue eyes, and he guessed she might be Maisie and Dulcie's mother.

'Hiya,' Dulcie said. 'I wondered whether you've had a chance to think about the old farmhouse?'

Adam wasn't sure how to reply. He wanted to put in an offer but he was waiting to see what Maisie intended to do. 'Um, I'm not sure I'm in a position to—' he began, but the woman who had followed Dulcie out of the house interrupted him, saying, 'Aren't you the chap who did the work on the milking whatnot?'

Dulcie's eyes widened and she whirled around. 'Mum, I thought you were supposed to be keeping an eye on the potatoes.'

'They're fine,' the woman said. 'Your name is Adam, isn't it?' She was looking at him with disdain, her nose wrinkled.

He didn't blame her for being less than impressed. He wasn't exactly looking his best right now. Abruptly he wished he had taken the time to go home first. Maisie wouldn't have minded.

Ah, there she was. His heart lifted when he saw her. As usual, she looked gorgeous: her face was glowing and she wore a beaming smile.

It faded when she caught sight of her mother's sour expression. 'I see you've met Adam,' she said.

He held out his hand, glanced at it, saw how dirty and oily it was, had second thoughts and let it drop. 'Nice to meet you, Mrs Fairfax.'

Maisie's mum pressed her lips together.

'Call her Beth,' Maisie said, earning herself a scowl from her mother. Adam thought he had better stick with Mrs Fairfax for the time being. He nodded to her and smiled.

Her gaze swept over him from the top of his bun to the toes of his worn, muddy work boots and her scowl deepened.

Adam was dismayed: he clearly hadn't made the best of impressions, but hopefully he would be able to rectify that when she got to know him better. *If* she had the opportunity to get to know him better.

He hoped with all his heart that she would, because that meant Maisie would be staying in Picklewick. And the way Adam felt about her, he wanted Maisie to stay more than he had wanted anything else in his life.

Maisie was furious and embarrassed. Her mother's rudeness and obvious dislike of Adam were inexcusable, especially since she had only just met him and knew absolutely nothing about him.

'I'm sorry,' she said stiffly as he drove out of the farmyard. 'My mother can be a bit judgemental at times.'

'It's fine. I'm not exactly looking my best. I should be the one apologising – I came straight from a job to pick you up. If I'd known I was going to meet her, I'd have gone home to shower first.'

Maisie knew it wasn't just Adam's lack of a shower that was responsible for her mum's reaction. And she also heard the faint recrimination in Adam's tone.

'I wish *I* had known you were going to meet her,' she said. 'She just turned up out of the blue this afternoon. Dulcie wasn't happy.' Neither was Maisie, but she didn't want to go into that right now. 'She's staying until after the Easter Fayre; she says she's here to help, but I reckon she thinks she's missing out, what with Dulcie, Nikki and now me in Picklewick. And since she retired, I think she's bored and lonely.'

'She doesn't look old enough to be retired. What did she do?'

'She used to be a supervisor in a supermarket down the road from where we live. It was handy, because she could walk to work, and when I was younger I used to pop in on my way home from school to beg a couple of pounds for a bag of chips and a can of pop if she was on a late shift.'

'She must miss you.'

'Yeah, she does.' Maisie pulled a face. 'The thing is, I can't live at home forever just to keep her company. I've got my own life to lead.' And she was growing more convinced that she wanted to spend it here in Picklewick.

Her mum turning up and expecting Maisie to travel back with her in less than two weeks, was making her anxious, and she had a feeling that after the Easter Fayre, Dulcie would be glad to see the back of both of them. Maisie didn't blame her: she wouldn't want anyone invading her space if she was all loved-up. And it wasn't as though Dulcie and Otto were an old married couple: they'd got together less than a year ago and their relationship hadn't been plain sailing either. So that meant that if Maisie intended to remain in Picklewick, she needed to find herself another job and somewhere to live a bit sharpish.

A thought occurred to her – did she want to stay here because it was a fresh new start, or did she want to stay because of Adam?

Pushing it to the back of her mind to think about later, she suggested they go to the flat so Adam could get cleaned up, and order a takeaway to be delivered rather than pick one up on the way and risk it going cold whilst he showered.

Maisie wasn't overly hungry, her mother having killed her appetite somewhat, but she guessed Adam would be starving, so as soon as they stepped inside the flat she asked, 'What do you fancy?'

'You.' His eyes widened. 'Sorry, that just slipped out. I don't mind… Whatever you fancy. I'll, er, just go jump in the shower.'

He hurried upstairs, leaving her standing in the living room with a thudding heart and a dry mouth. Maisie heard footsteps above her head, then the sound of the shower running.

Imagining Adam underneath the jet of hot water as it cascaded over his body made her feel faint, and she knew what she wanted to do…

Tingling with a mixture of excitement, fear and desire, Maisie slowly went upstairs, her pulse throbbing at her throat. She was trembling, her palms were damp, and she almost decided to forget the whole thing. And she might well have done, if Adam hadn't stepped out of the bathroom just as she reached the top of the stairs.

He was naked, water droplets glistening on his skin, his modesty only preserved by the towel he was holding to his face which draped over his chest and stomach to his thighs.

Gosh, he's got nice legs, she thought, as her eyes slid down his body.

He froze.

So did she.

His gaze locked onto hers and she couldn't tear herself away. Slowly, deliberately, her fingers crept to the neck of her blouse and she undid the first button. He stared at the exposed flesh and she saw him swallow as she undid another.

When she loosened a third button and the fabric fell open to reveal the lace of her bra, his eyes caught hers again and she inhaled sharply when she saw the raw desire burning in them, a conflagration that threatened to sear her from the inside out.

And when he dropped the towel and opened his arms, she stepped into them with a flame that more than matched his.

CHAPTER EIGHT

'What time do you call this?'

When her mother shouted from the kitchen as Maisie slipped in through the back door of the farmhouse, Maisie had to suppress a shriek of alarm.

Her heart thudding, she put a hand to her chest. 'You nearly gave me a heart attack.'

'I've been worried sick.' Beth was sitting at the kitchen table, bundled up in a thick dressing gown, and with socks and fluffy slippers on her feet. Her hands were wrapped around a mug, and she had an aggrieved expression on her face.

'I didn't expect anyone to be up this early,' Maisie said, her heart rate returning to normal as she switched the kettle on. She was gasping for a coffee. After the glorious night she'd had, she needed all the caffeine she could lay her hands on if she didn't want to risk falling asleep in the chicken coop.

'I can see that.' Her mother was positively glowering. 'You stayed out all night.'

'Yes, I did.' Maisie was unable to suppress a smile.

She was glowing inside, and she was so happy she could burst. Last night had been wonderful. *Adam* had been wonderful. Considerate, passionate, loving...

'It's five-thirty in the morning.' Her mother cut into Maisie's blissful thoughts.

'I know.'

'Dirty stop-out. I didn't raise you to—' Beth stopped abruptly.

'To what, Mum?' Maisie was becoming irritated. This was none of her mother's business.

'To throw yourself at the likes of that man.'

'By *that man*, I take it you're referring to Adam.'

'Yes. Him. Did you see the state of him? He was dirty and covered in oil. And that hair…' Beth shuddered.

'He'd just finished work,' Maisie explained, keen to defend him against her mother's unwarranted attack.

'That's as may be, but it doesn't excuse his hair and that thing in his eyebrow.'

'It's a piercing.'

'I don't care what it is – it looks awful. The only good thing I can say about it, is that at least it's not through his nose.'

'*You* don't have to like it,' Maisie said through gritted teeth. She took a mug out of the cupboard and smacked it down on the countertop.

'You might have broken that,' her mum grumbled.

'But I didn't. And if I had, I would have bought Dulcie another.' Dulcie would have totally understood. When she had lived at home, stuff had got broken on a regular basis. Their mother had a wonderful knack of winding her daughters up.

How could Maisie go back to that now that she'd had a taste of freedom?

The thought made her feel like crying and she vowed to try to speak to Dulcie as soon as possible, although with Mum here, Dulcie wouldn't be in the most amenable of moods.

'I wondered what was keeping you here,' Beth said. 'And now I know. I'm disappointed in you, Maisie; you could do so much better than that grease monkey.'

Grease monkey! Maisie's mouth dropped open. 'I'll have you know he's got his own place and his own business.'

'Dulcie says he lives above an old garage, and from what I can gather, he does a few odd jobs.'

Maisie was flabbergasted. She knew her mum could be opinionated and judgemental, but this was taking it to the extreme. 'You're a fine one to talk,' she spat, anger sparking through her. 'You worked in a shop, and you might live in a house but you don't own it, do you?'

As soon as the words left her lips, Maisie felt awful. Their mum had raised four kids on her own and had done a damned good job of it.

She felt even worse when her mum's chin wobbled as she said, 'That's why I want more for you. Your father was a waste of space – God rest his soul. I don't want you to make the same mistakes I did.'

'I won't, Mum.' Maisie pulled out a chair, sat down, and took her mother's hand. 'Adam's not like that.'

'Nikki has done well for herself, despite that idiot she was married to, and so have Dulcie and Jay. I don't want you to throw your life away on some ne'er-do-well.'

'Adam's not a… whatever you said. He's hard-working and kind, and—' Maisie stopped. 'I think I love him.'

'Huh! How long have you known him?'

'That's irrelevant. Look at Jay and Eliza – within two weeks of them meeting, Jay was jetting off to New Zealand to be with her.'

'That's different,' Beth said, but when Maisie pushed her on it, her mother clammed up and refused to say anything more. 'I'm going back to bed,' she declared. 'I'm too old to be waiting up all night for you to come home.'

'I didn't ask you to,' Maisie muttered.

Beth had the parting shot. 'You kids will be the death of me,' she said, closing the kitchen door firmly behind her and leaving Maisie feeling as though she had been flattened by a ten-tonne truck.

She wasn't sure whether to feel blessed that she had a mother who cared as much as she did, or annoyed that her mum felt it appropriate to interfere in her life, or guilty because she felt she wasn't living up to her mother's aspirations for her.

In the end, annoyance won by a hair when Dulcie came downstairs and told her that far from waiting up all night for Maisie to come home, their mother had slept soundly from ten p.m. until just before Maisie had returned. And the reason Dulcie knew this, was because she had heard Mum snoring when she'd woken to go to the loo. And then Mum had woken *her* up at just gone five to complain that Fred, the cockerel that belonged to the stables, had disturbed her with its crowing.

If Maisie hadn't already vowed to do her utmost not to return to Birmingham and her mum's house, she would definitely have made up her mind after hearing that!

Adam was on cloud ten: cloud nine wasn't high enough. He felt as though he was walking on a fluffy cloud of marshmallows, and his heart felt just as gooey. Last night had blown his mind, and all he could think about was how soon he could see Maisie again.

However, he was working for the rest of the week, jobs coming in thick and fast (which he certainly wasn't complaining about) and at those times when he was free, Maisie was working in the restaurant.

He was very tempted to wait for her shift to finish this evening and drag her back to the flat to make love to her all night, but both of them needed a good night's sleep after their recent antics, and he was already feeling the effects of lack of sleep: his head was woolly and he kept dropping his tools.

And when his phone rang, making him jump, he dropped that too. Thankfully, it landed on an old rag, so it didn't sustain any damage.

'Hiya, Mum. How are you?'

'I've got a favour to ask. Please hear me out before you say no.'

'How do you know I'm going to say no?'

'Because it involves Verity.'

'Ah.'

'See? That's what I mean.'

He uttered a sigh. 'What's the favour?'

'As you know, your father and Karl have been discussing a merger… Oh, I do wish you'd come on board. It would mean the world to him!'

'Mum, we've been over this.'

'I know, but—' She stopped and he guessed she would have been quite happy to go over the same old ground if it wasn't for this favour she wanted to ask. 'Anyway,' she continued, 'We'll come back to that another time. On Saturday your father and I are having Karl, Linda, his board members and their wives or partners over for dinner, and Karl believes they will be far more amenable to the merger if they can see that your father is supported by his family.'

'What's that got to do with it? It's not as though you or I have any say in how the business is run.'

'You could, if you wanted.'

'Mum…'

'Just come, please. Show your support.'

Adam wanted to say no, as he had been hoping to see Maisie on Saturday because she had the day off, but although his mum and dad were often on his back about the way he lived and his career choice, they rarely asked him for anything, and although he wasn't interested in the business per se, he knew how much it meant to his dad. His father lived and breathed it; it was what made him tick

'I'll be there,' he promised reluctantly. He was disappointed not to be spending Saturday evening with Maisie, but maybe they could spend the day together instead. It would be better than not seeing her at all.

For the first time since she'd arrived at the farm, Maisie was at a loose end. She'd had a lovely morning with Adam, pottering around the shops in Thornbury

and having a spot of lunch in a cafe in the town. Then they'd gone back to his flat and— She blushed when she thought about the way they had spent the afternoon.

'I wish I didn't have to go to this thing with my parents this evening,' he said, as he dropped her off at the farm. 'I would much rather be with you.'

'Your family is important. I'm sure you'll have a lovely time.'

'I'm sure I won't. The only upside is that the food will be good. What are you going to do with yourself this evening?'

'Watch telly, I expect. And listen to Mum grizzle that there's nothing on.'

She would also have to listen to her mother going on about Adam, but her mum's dislike of the man she had fallen in love with wasn't something Maisie intended to share with him. There would be a showdown soon when Mum realised that Maisie had no intention of going back to Birmingham, and there would be hell to pay. Although how Maisie was going to remain in Picklewick if her sister wanted her gone from the farm, was a problem Maisie had yet to solve. She had already started looking for rooms to rent, but unsurprisingly there wasn't anything in the village. There were a couple in Thornbury, so one of those might have to do for the time being, and there were also more job opportunities in the town than there were in Picklewick.

None of them were what she wanted to do long term, but in the meantime she could gain more experience of working with animals by volunteering. There was a wildlife sanctuary a few miles outside Thornbury, and a rescue home for dogs.

She didn't kid herself that this was going to be easy, but she was determined to give it her best shot. For the first time in her life, Maisie knew what she wanted to do, and she also knew who she wanted to spend it with. All she hoped was that Adam felt the same way – because if he didn't, she didn't know how she could deal with that.

Forcing the negative thoughts away, she brightened. 'I could always go over Dulcie's to-do list and see if there's anything I can help with,' she said. 'Although I think we've got everything in hand.' She clapped her hands. 'Ooh! I can't wait to see the chicks. Dulcie is picking them up on Wednesday. I've never held a baby chicken before.'

She glanced at the barn. It had already been set up in preparation for the Easter weekend, and currently housed three rather sweet bunnies who were getting used to their new home. The goats would shortly join them this evening because Dulcie didn't like the thought of the goatlings being in the meadow all night.

As soon as Adam left, Maisie would fetch them in and round up the chickens so Mr Fox didn't eat them.

'I need a kiss,' Adam declared, pulling her towards him, and Maisie settled into his embrace with a contented sigh. Being in his arms felt so right. It was where she belonged, and she couldn't think of anywhere else she would rather be.

'Change of plan, we're eating out instead,' Adam's mother announced when he walked into his parents'

house later that evening. She was coming down the stairs and looked as elegant and expensive as usual. A cloud of perfume wafted over him as she reached the bottom step. 'There was a problem with my usual caterers, so I've booked us into a lovely little restaurant. It's quite new, but it's had the most brilliant reviews.'

Adam had been wondering why there was only his mum and dad's cars on the drive as he'd pulled up in the van.

Slipping a diamond stud into her ear as his dad emerged from the lounge with a glass in his hand, she said, 'Ah, here's your father. Martin, please don't have any more, you're driving.'

'I thought Adam could be our chauffeur for the evening. You don't mind, do you, Adam?'

'Where are we going?' he asked.

'The Wild Side in Picklewick. You might have heard of it?' His mum moved to the large mirror in the hall and leant towards it, turning her head from side to side.

'You could have said; I would have met you there.'

'Ah, but then I would have had to drive myself,' his dad pointed out.

Adam raised his eyes to the ceiling and prayed for patience. If he had known his mother had booked The Wild Side, he wouldn't have agreed to go, despite Maisie not working this evening. He ought to message her and tell her—

'Adam, put your phone away. We're ready to go.'

Reluctantly Adam slipped his mobile back into his trouser pocket. He was wearing a suit tonight, but no tie. He drew the line at ties, preferring to leave the top button of his shirt undone. He'd spotted his mum's assessing look and her quick frown of displeasure when she'd noticed his tie-less state, but she hadn't said anything. She knew when to pick her battles.

Adam also knew which battles to pick, and arguing over his phone wasn't one of them. He would message Maisie when they got to the restaurant. He might even take a selfie of his bored face and send it to her. Next time he ate there – if there *was* a next time because, let's face it, The Wild Side wasn't cheap and he was trying to save his pennies – he vowed that Maisie would be with him. Although, thinking about it, she mightn't want to eat at the very place she worked, and if that was the case, he could fully understand.

The restaurant was busy when Adam and his parents arrived. At the far end of the room several tables had been pushed together to make one long one, and Adam spied Verity, Linda and Karl, along with three other couples. They all looked at Adam and his parents as they made their way to the table, and Adam noticed with annoyance that the seat next to Verity was vacant.

Verity beamed at him and patted the chair. 'You're next to me,' she said, offering her face to be kissed. She pouted expectantly, but he avoided her lips, pecking at her cheek instead. The pout intensified.

After the introductions were made (Adam biting his tongue when he was referred to as the 'heir apparent' to his dad's firm) he took out his phone once more, only to feel a sharp kick on his ankle.

His mum, who was sitting opposite, glared at him. Adam put it away again.

'So,' one of Karl's directors said to him, 'You'll be taking over your father's company one day? He tells me you're exploring other avenues and gaining business experience beforehand. It's good to have firsthand experience of how businesses operate, don't you think?'

And so it begins, Adam thought, as he tried to formulate a reply that wasn't a deliberate lie, but wouldn't contradict the image of him that his parents wanted to portray. It was going to be a very long evening.

The money would come in handy and Maisie had nothing better to do, so she hastily changed into tailored black trousers and a crisp white blouse, her uniform for The Wild Side.

At least Otto had called *her* first to ask whether she could cover for the member of staff who had phoned in sick, rather than contacting one of the others. He must think she was good at her job, which boosted her confidence that he hadn't given her the job out of pity or a sense of obligation because she was Dulcie's sister.

The other upside, besides the money, was being able to escape from her mum for a few hours, because as soon as Maisie had walked into the farmhouse after Adam had dropped her off, Mum had started moaning, and all because everyone had been too busy to entertain her. Maisie had been out all day, Otto had been finalising his accounts and had set up camp in the smallest of the four bedrooms, Dulcie had been making more soap, and Nikki and Sammy had spent the day with Gio, as they had promised to visit his parents. Therefore, Beth had been on her own for the most part, and hadn't been happy.

The situation was made worse when Walter, her arch-enemy, had turned up with Amos to make some additions to the goats' play area in the meadow. This time, they were installing a seesaw.

The speed with which Dulcie had offered to drive Maisie into the village for her shift at the restaurant, had led Maisie to believe that Dulcie couldn't wait to get out of the house either.

'What does she expect?' Dulcie moaned as her little car bounced down the pitted lane. 'That I would be able to drop everything to keep her amused? Here to help, indeed! She's here because she's bored. Can't you persuade her to do some voluntary work?'

'Since when did she ever listen to me? I'm the daughter who can't hold down a job, remember? She still thinks of me as a kid.'

Dulcie made a noise and Maisie sent her a sharp look.

'I know,' Maisie acknowledged. 'I deserve it. But I'm doing my best to behave like an adult.'

'I must say I'm impressed with how hard you work and what you're willing to do. Cleaning out the chicken coop isn't pleasant, yet you've done it.'

'Three times,' Maisie said proudly.

'So why can't you keep a job?'

'Because they all involve people.' Maisie's reply came from the heart. She hadn't had to think about it.

Dulcie manoeuvred the car out of Muddypuddle Lane and onto the main road. 'Yet you're doing okay in the restaurant.'

That's because I have to, Maisie thought; being able to stay on the farm depended on it.

Two minutes later the car came to a halt near the restaurant and Maisie got out. 'Thanks for the lift. Enjoy your evening.'

'Wanna swap?'

'No chance!'

'Maybe I'll go for a drive – a long one,' Dulcie grumbled. 'See you later.'

Maisie gave her a wave, then darted up the side street leading to the rear of the restaurant and the staff entrance.

Otto smiled with relief when he saw her. 'It's busy out there. We've got a party of twelve, and every table except for one is booked. Can you do tables one to eight?'

'Sure can,' she said, tying an apron around her waist and stowing her bag in the small back room that also served as an office. She grabbed a pad and pen as Otto told her what was on the specials, finishing with, 'Check with Fleur as to where we are with orders. I don't think table four has ordered yet.'

Table four hadn't, Fleur confirmed when Maisie went into the restaurant area to ask, and she quickly scanned the tables she had been allocated, checking on their drinks status and making sure no one needed her immediate attention.

Satisfied, she was just about to return to the kitchen to see whether any of the starters were ready, when a burst of laughter drew her attention to the large party of diners.

Pleased they were having a good time, her gaze slid away, then snapped back with a jolt.

She could have sworn that was— Yes! *It was! Adam* was a member of the party.

Maisie frowned: she felt certain he'd said he was having a meal at his parents' house, yet here he was, in The Wild Side. He was sitting next to a woman who was half-turned around in her seat and gazing up at him with a love-struck expression on her face. She was also very pretty.

Adam dipped his head towards her and she said something in his ear. It looked incredibly intimate, and when the woman put a hand on his thigh, Maisie gasped in disbelief.

Ignoring the impulse to march over there and demand to know what was going on, she dashed to the ladies' loos. There was probably a perfectly good explanation, but she needed to compose herself before she heard it. She would take a minute, then she would go back out there and casually saunter up to the table and ask whether anyone needed anything. She would try to act normally and wait for Adam to… *What?* Introduce her? Explain? Ignore her?

But as Maisie dithered, wondering what to do for the best, the outer door to the ladies' loos opened, and on hearing voices she scurried into a cubicle, bolted the door and leant her forehead against it. She wasn't ready to face anyone just yet.

Two sets of heels tapped on the tiles, and the doors to the cubicle to either side of her clicked shut.

She would give it a minute before flushing (so she sounded like a proper loo-user and not some saddo lurking in the toilets), then she would leave.

But what if Adam did ignore her? How was she supposed to react to that?

Nah, don't be silly – he wouldn't do that.

But what if—?

'Adam and Verity make a lovely couple, don't they Sue?' a voice to her left said, breaking into her worried thoughts.

Maisie froze. She straightened up slowly, the blood draining from her face. Surely she had heard incorrectly?

'They do,' the woman on her right replied. 'I'm hoping he'll pop the question before too long, but Adam has still got a few wild oats to sow. I don't think he's *quite* ready to settle down yet.' She tutted. 'When he does, I hope Verity can persuade him to do something about his hair and remove that unsightly hoop he's got in his eyebrow.'

'Oh, I don't know, I think it suits him. And it'll be nice to have some young blood in the boardroom, especially one as good-looking as your son. You must be so proud. He is a real credit to you, and Martin must be thrilled to have Adam follow him into the family business. Let me tell you, John very much wants this merger to go ahead. With Karl intending to step down, the atmosphere in the company has been a bit fraught. It will be nice to know it's in safe hands, especially with Adam ready to step into the driving seat when Martin retires. It's given everyone a real confidence boost.'

A toilet flushed and a door opened, quickly followed by a second flush and the sound of taps being run and hands being washed.

Maisie held her breath. An uncomfortable pressure was building in her chest and she was terrified she might be about to sob. Adam and a woman called Verity? About to pop the question?

How could he? He had *made love* to her, for pity's sake! Had she meant nothing to him?

There was the click of a clasp and she assumed the two women were reapplying their makeup and fluffing up their hair. She prayed for them to leave, before she broke down. This couldn't be happening, she wailed silently. She thought he cared for her, that they had something special.

Adam's betrayal stabbed her in the gut and she felt sick. Not only was she just a 'wild oat to be sown', but he clearly had a girlfriend who was soon to be his fiancée. And he had also lied to her about who he was. Mergers? Boardrooms? Family business? What the hell?!

Maisie realised that she knew nothing about the man she had been sleeping with, the man she had given her heart to, the man she loved.

She had to get out of there right now, before she made a fool of herself in public, and she might have managed to escape with her dignity intact if it hadn't been for one final comment.

'It will be nice to keep it in the family, and Verity is such a lovely young woman,' Adam's mother said.

Maisie lost it. With an anguished cry, she snapped the bolt back and yanked the door open, making the women jump. One of them let out a yelp and placed a hand on her chest, the other backed up a pace or two as Maisie burst out of the cubicle.

She caught sight of her wild eyes and red face in the mirror as she ripped off her apron and threw it at the nearest woman.

'She's sodding welcome to him,' Maisie yelled. 'The two-timing, lying ratbag. I refuse to be anyone's wild oats, and you can tell him that from me!'

Whirling on her heel, she stormed out of the ladies' toilets, ignoring the gasps and a cry of 'Well, I never!' which followed her out.

Tears blurring her vision, she dashed into the kitchen, ran to the office and grabbed her coat and bag. On the way out, she brushed past Otto, who was carrying a couple of plates of food.

'Maisie, where——?'

'Gotta go. Sorry.'

'Are you——?'

She didn't hear the rest of the sentence as she rushed out of the restaurant, because she was too busy trying not to break down completely.

So much for Adam being her prince. He had turned out to be the biggest toad of the lot.

CHAPTER NINE

Adam saw Linda give Karl a nudge and point to something, but he didn't take any notice until he heard Linda say, 'I bet Sue is complaining about something. She usually does.'

He glanced around and when he saw that his mum was speaking to Otto, he cringed. *Please don't let her be making a fuss*, he prayed, making a mental note to apologise to Otto later if necessary.

Her expression was hard, and he guessed that something had irritated her, but what could have annoyed her during a brief trip to the loo was beyond him. But neither was he surprised: his mother could be a very demanding and exacting customer.

He saw her thrust a piece of black cloth at Otto and her lips were moving, but it was impossible to make out what she was saying.

The wife of one of Karl's directors was hovering by her side, looking decidedly uncomfortable, and her gaze kept shooting to Adam and away again.

Adam sent her a sympathetic smile, but she refused to meet his eye.

He wished his mother wouldn't make a fuss. No matter where she went, she always had to complain about something. She wasn't usually as blatant though; a quiet word in the ear of one of the serving staff was usually sufficient. Whatever it was this time, must have really irritated her.

But it was only when Otto looked across the room and his gaze alighted on Adam, did Adam feel a twinge of unease that had nothing to do with embarrassment.

Otto didn't look happy. In fact, he seemed annoyed.

Adam's lips twitched in a half smile, and he hoped he looked suitably apologetic as he gave the chef a little wave. All Otto did was frown and briefly shake his head.

'What?' Adam mouthed, but his mother had reclaimed Otto's attention and Adam's spirits sank even further. He would wait to hear his mother's complaint, then he'd nip off to the loo and message Maisie to warn her that Otto might be in a bad mood when he got home.

When his mum returned to the table, Adam was about to ask her what was going on, but his dad got in first.

'What was all that about? The toilet paper not soft enough? The handwash the wrong fragrance?' he quipped.

His mum said, 'You're not going to believe this, but I've just been harangued by a waitress. I think she must have been having some kind of a breakdown, but whatever it was, she yelled at me and then threw her apron in my face.'

'What did you do to upset her?' Martin asked.

Sue glared at him. 'Nothing. We were powdering our noses and she burst out of one of the cubicles, shouting something about how 'she's welcome to him' and that she isn't anyone's 'wild oats'. I mean, honestly! They should have a separate toilet for staff. She was quite deranged.'

The director's wife added, looking straight at Adam, 'What was odd was that she seemed to know *you*.'

Adam was beginning to get a very bad feeling about this. 'How so?'

'She referred to someone as a two-timing, lying ratbag and said that your mother could tell you that. Or words to that effect.'

The bad feeling was getting worse. 'Mum, what did she look like?'

'I don't know. What does it matter?'

'How old was she? Did she have blonde hair?'

His mother shrugged, but the director's wife said, 'Mid-twenties, maybe? And she did have blonde hair, now that I come to think about it. Do you know her?'

Adam had a sinking feeling that he did, and he retrieved his phone from his pocket.

'Adam, not at the table,' his mother scolded.

His phone to his ear, Adam got to his feet and headed towards the door.

His call went unanswered. As did a second one.

Dread creeping through his veins, he grabbed the attention of a waitress. 'Please tell me Maisie isn't working this evening,' he pleaded.

'She wasn't supposed to be, but someone called in sick so Chef asked her to step in.'

'Can you go get her for me?'

'Sorry, she walked out. She had a run-in with one of your party.' The waitress narrowed her eyes.

'Do you know what it was about?'

A shrug. 'No idea, but she was crying when she left.'

Adam didn't bother to return to the table to ask what the run-in was about; he would find out soon enough when he caught up with Maisie. She was his only concern now, as he hurried outside after her, confident that she couldn't have gone far.

Her heart breaking, Maisie pelted along the high street, ignoring the curious stares from the people she passed. She also ignored the phone call from Adam and she turned her phone off, not wanting to hear his excuses. She didn't want to see him, speak to him, or hear his name mentioned ever again.

Tears poured down her face and her breath came in gasping sobs as she fled towards the outskirts of the village and the path that would take her through the fields and up to the farm.

All she could think about was how badly Adam had deceived her. She had only managed a quick glimpse at his girlfriend, but from what Maisie could remember she was gorgeous. And all over him. They were clearly an item. The woman in the loo had said as much. For god's sake, she had said that she was expecting him to propose soon!

And far from being a man who was struggling to grow his business, Adam was loaded. Or his parents were, which amounted to the same thing. Did he get his kicks out of pretending to be poor when he so obviously wasn't?

Maisie paused to catch her breath; the hill was steep and she could hardly breathe for crying. With shaking fingers, she brushed away the tears, then fished in her bag for a tissue to blow her nose. Resuming her journey more slowly, a pang of guilt went through her as she realised she had left Otto in the lurch. He didn't deserve that, but there was no way she could have carried on serving this evening.

And after this, she guessed she wouldn't be serving at The Wild Side on any other evening either.

But that was okay, she didn't intend to. She was going to leave the farm and Picklewick first thing in the morning. Mum could come with her, or not. Maisie honestly didn't care. Even if she hadn't burned her bridges with Dulcie, she couldn't contemplate remaining in the village. The thought of bumping into Adam made her feel sick. There was nothing for her here now.

Maisie wasn't sure there ever had been.

The dream of living in Picklewick and working with animals, had been just that – a dream. And now it had turned into a nightmare.

She would go back to Birmingham where she belonged.

A bitter laugh escaped her. Her mother had been right: Adam *wasn't* good enough for her. But she had been right for all the wrong reasons. Adam wasn't a ne'er-do-well. Adam was an entitled, doing-very-well-for-himself two-timing ratbag.

'What the hell did you say to her?' Adam hissed in his mum's ear. He had searched up and down the high street but Maisie was nowhere in sight, so he had returned to the restaurant to find out what had happened.

Maisie wasn't answering his calls and she hadn't read his messages either, and he was frantic with worry.

'Can we not do this now, please?' His mother's tone was frosty, and she gave him a meaningful glare.

'I want to know,' he insisted.

'Why?'

'Because you must have said something to upset her.'

His mother removed her napkin from her lap and got to her feet. 'Excuse us a moment, won't you? Martin, order some more wine. We won't be long.' She grabbed Adam by the elbow and steered him into the foyer. 'I would appreciate it if you didn't speak to me like that,' she began, but Adam cut her off.

'What did you say to Maisie?'

'Nothing. Not one word. *She* spoke to *me*, and very rude she was, too.'

'You must have said *something*.'

'Are you calling me a liar, Adam?'

'Not at all.' He raised his hand to run his fingers through his hair, before realising it was in a bun, so he scratched his head instead. Taking a deep breath, he tried again. 'Tell me what happened.'

'I already did. We were powdering our noses and chatting about the merger, and saying that you and Verity were a lovely couple, when this woman burst out of a cubicle and started shouting.' His mother stopped, and her eyes widened. 'Oh, my god! Was that woman your girlfriend? I thought you were making it up to annoy me.'

Adam felt sick. He could all too easily imagine the conversation, and Maisie's reaction on hearing it. No wonder she was upset. He had to talk to her and explain.

He turned to leave, just as his mother said, '*A waitress?*' Her tone was scornful.

'Yes.' His anger was beginning to build.

'But what about Verity?'

'What about her? I've told you before, I have zero interest in Verity. Even if I didn't love Maisie, I wouldn't date Verity.'

'*Love?* Adam, please, you don't mean it?'

'I do.' Hearing footsteps, he turned to see his dad approaching and groaned. He could do without a lecture from his father.

His mother was spluttering with indignation. 'Did you hear what Adam just said? He thinks he's in love with that waitress – the one that was so abusive.'

'Nonsense,' his father scoffed. 'He can't be. I won't allow it.'

'That's enough!' Adam shouted, losing his temper. 'What do you mean *you won't allow it?* It's not up to you who I fall in love with. It's none of your business.'

'Your mother and I are fed up with you making a hash of your life. You've got a wonderful future ahead of you, with a young lady who thinks the world of you, yet you're willing to throw it all away to muck about with engines and chase a piece of skirt.'

'I'm throwing nothing away,' Adam retorted.

His father scowled and drew himself up to his full height, anger flashing in his eyes.

Adam wasn't impressed.

He was even less impressed when his father issued an ultimatum. 'Either you get rid of this stupid notion of being in love, or I'll disown you. Your choice.'

Dulcie was incandescent with rage. 'How dare you! I warned you, didn't I? I told you that if you got up to your old tricks in Otto's restaurant, you would be out on your ear. If it wasn't too late to catch a train, I'd drive you to the station this very minute.'

Maisie hung her head. The tirade had begun as soon as she'd entered the farmhouse to find Dulcie and Mum waiting in the kitchen. Dulcie's expression was apoplectic. Their mother's was smug. Beth usually looked resigned and disappointed when Maisie lost a job, but Maisie guessed Mum was happy this time because it meant there was no danger of her staying on the farm now.

'What the hell happened?' Dulcie demanded. 'Otto told me you insulted a diner, then walked out.'

With fresh tears in her eyes, Maisie said, 'Did he tell you that Adam was there with his girlfriend, soon to be his fiancée?'

'What? No! But aren't you two—?'

'Yeah, that's what *I* thought too. Apparently not. He was having dinner with her, his mother and some others. His mother was talking about how she expected him to pop the question any day now.' Maisie put a hand to her mouth to hold back a wail of anguish.

'No, Otto didn't tell me that, but it's beside the point. You shouldn't have insulted her. This is Otto's livelihood, and you're damaging it.'

'I know and I'm sorry, but I couldn't stand there and listen—'

'Yes, you could.' Dulcie was adamant. 'That's what being a grown-up is all about, Maisie. Control.' She shook her head. 'I shouldn't have expected anything different from you. It's not as though you haven't got a track record of walking out of jobs. Or dumping boyfriends, for that matter.'

'I told you he was no good,' Beth chimed in. 'I could tell as soon as I set eyes on him.'

'Yeah, right,' Maisie said bitterly.

'I said he was nothing but a grease monkey.' Beth folded her arms, her satisfaction evident.

Maisie said, 'It's the opposite, in fact, Mum.'

'Eh?'

'It doesn't matter.' Nothing mattered anymore. Maisie just wanted to find a dark corner and curl up in it until she recovered from her misery. If she ever did. 'I'll go and pack. If one of you could give me a lift to Thornbury, I can be out of your hair tonight.'

Dulcie said, 'Don't be silly. You won't get a train at this time of night.'

'Don't care.'

'Grow up!' her sister snapped. 'You can't wait on the platform all night.'

'I'm not planning to. I'll find a hotel.'

A hammering on the door made all three jump. 'Maisie? Maisie! Open up. I need to speak with you.'

'That's Adam,' Dulcie said.

Maisie glowered. 'No shit.'

'Watch your language, Maisie Fairfax,' Beth snapped. 'Leave this to me. I'll give him a piece of my mind.'

'No need. I can give him a piece of my own.' Maisie squared her shoulders. She might be heartbroken and her life, along with her dreams, was falling apart, but she was damned well not going to let Adam see how much she was hurting. 'What do you want?' she demanded, opening the door a crack.

He was out of breath and looked dishevelled. 'To explain.'

'I don't want to hear it. Save your excuses for someone who cares.' She began to close the door and looked down when she met resistance, to find he had his foot in the way. 'If you don't move your foot, I'll break it,' she warned.

'Verity isn't my girlfriend. We are not a couple. We never have been and never will be, despite my mother wishing we were.'

'She was all over you.'

'Was she? I didn't notice.'

'She had her hand on your leg. And the look on her face...'

'What look?'

'Love.'

'I didn't notice that, either. And do you know why? Because I've only got eyes for *you*.'

'Don't listen to him,' Beth shouted from the kitchen.

'I'm not,' Maisie called back. But she didn't close the door.

Adam said, 'Her parents and mine have been friends ever since I can remember. Mum and Linda had this stupid idea that we would get married, despite me telling Mum I don't think of Verity in that way. I thought she'd got the message but since the talk of a merger—'

'Ah yes, let's don't forget *the merger*. You're going to be on the board of directors.'

'No, I'm not. I never wanted to be an accountant and I don't want to join my father's firm. Look, I don't care whether it's a two-bit outfit with an office above the chip shop, or a multi-million-pound company, I'm not interested. I told them that. And I told them again that there'll never be anything between Verity and me. You are my girlfriend and I love *you*, so I don't care about them disowning me.' He stopped and stared at her.

Maisie blinked. Her eyes felt raw and gritty, and she was weary to the bone. But there was a little nugget in that speech that perked her up no end.

'Did you just say you love me?' she demanded.

He hung his head and nodded, then peered at her from underneath those luscious lashes of his.

Maisie's heart began to sing, and she opened the door wider. *He loved her!* He'd just said so!

But she realised he had also said something else: something she couldn't ignore. 'Are your parents really going to disown you if we carry on seeing each other?'

'It's just Dad blowing off steam. He'll come around, and even if he doesn't, it doesn't matter. I don't need them or their money. What I need is *you*.'

'But they are your parents.'

'So? You are my girlfriend. I love you.' He swallowed. 'I know you accused me of being a lying, cheating ratbag—'

'You are!' Beth shouted.

'But I haven't cheated or lied,' he insisted.

Beth yelled, 'You're still a ratbag!'

'Mum! Stop it.'

'Well, he is! He's cost you your job.' Her mum came to stand beside her and tried to elbow her out of the way. Maisie stood her ground.

'Is that true?' Adam asked.

'Yes, it is,' Beth said. 'And she's going home with me tomorrow, as Dulcie is throwing her out.'

Dulcie called, 'Stop exaggerating, Mum. I'm not throwing her out. It's about time she went home.'

Beth said, 'She's outstayed her welcome and so have you. Go on, scoot. I told her you were a wrong 'un, and I was right. She can do better than the likes of you.'

Maisie wanted to tell her mum to bugger off. She wanted to tell Adam that he definitely wasn't a wrong 'un, and that she absolutely couldn't do any better, but she didn't. She recalled how posh his mother's accent was, the way she had spoken, her expensive clothes and the diamonds glinting at her throat and in her ears. Adam's family were clearly wealthy, and because of her, his parents were threatening to disown him.

She couldn't let that happen. He might think he didn't care, but at some point he would. And she had no intention of being the cause of a rift between Adam and his family.

She told him as much, then she closed the door as he tried to convince her he didn't care about his parents. But he *did* care, and she knew she was doing the right thing.

Letting him walk away, shoulders hunched and head bowed after he had declared his love for her and had been rejected, was the hardest thing she had ever done.

As she lay awake all through the night, Maisie vowed never to let anyone else touch her heart the way Adam had. How could she, when it was shattered into hundreds of pieces and strewn across the misery that her life had become.

How do you carry on when the stuffing has been knocked out of you? One day at a time, Adam decided the next morning, after having absolutely no sleep whatsoever.

He hadn't wanted to get out of bed, despite not actually having managed any sleep, but a sense of obligation to his client this morning forced him to move.

Not bothering with breakfast, he had a desultory shower to try to wash away the smell of despair that lingered on his skin, and it was only when he looked for his keys did he remember that he had left the van at his parents' house and had been forced to use the spare key hidden under a pot at the rear of his flat to get in last night.

Damn and blast. He had no choice but to go fetch it. All he hoped was that his dad would have left for the office by the time he got there. In an ideal world, his mum would also be out, but he didn't usually have that kind of luck.

He was debating whether he should phone for a taxi or walk, when movement outside his living room window made him pause. His van had pulled into the area in front of the garage, followed by his father's car. He could see Mum in the driver's seat, which must mean that his father had driven the van.

Oh, well, it saved him a journey, he supposed.

Hoping that his father would simply post the keys through the letter box and be on his way, he was disappointed when there was a knock on the door.

Reluctantly he went downstairs to answer it.

'You look like death warmed up,' his father observed. 'I've brought you the van. I thought you might need it.'

'Thanks.'

'About yesterday evening... I meant what I said.'

Adam stared at him dully. He didn't care whether they disowned him or not: the damage was done. Through his parents' stupid insistence that he would grow out of wanting to mend machines and would come to work in the family business, they had managed to drive away the woman he loved. If his father hadn't issued such a draconian ultimatum, and if Adam hadn't told Maisie, she would still be in Picklewick.

Or would she?

With Dulcie 'throwing her out' and Maisie no longer having a job, she might have insisted on returning to Birmingham anyway. After all, she hadn't said she loved him back, so that meant she probably didn't.

He'd made a right fool of himself, hadn't he?

But that didn't hurt nearly as much as his broken heart. Adam had never known pain like it and he hoped he never would again.

Wordlessly, he held his hand out for the keys to the van, and with a shrug his father dropped them into his open palm.

It looked like his dad was sticking to his guns, but that was okay, because Adam intended to stick to his too. Dad had to learn that he couldn't bully him. All Adam had left now was his business, and there was no way he was giving it up. It was the only light in what was a very long and dark tunnel ahead.

When a sleek black SUV pulled up alongside the van, Adam barely noticed, too wrapped up in his misery.

But he did a double-take when Otto got out of it.

'Mr Haines, Mrs Haines, good morning.' Otto waved at Adam's mum, who was still in the car. 'I hope the meal was to your satisfaction.'

Martin's reply was stiff. 'It was. Eventually.'

'Excellent.'

Adam's mum emerged from the car. 'I hope you're here to apologise to my son.'

'Not at all. I'm here to tell him that Maisie and her mother won't be going anywhere for a while. Car trouble.' Otto had a gleam in his eye. 'They'll need someone to take a look.'

'Phone a garage.' Adam's tone was wooden.

'Beth did. No joy.'

'Breakdown cover?'

'She hasn't got any.'

'Am I being set up?'

'Maybe.'

'What good will it do? Maisie is determined to go home.' Adam noticed that his parents were following the exchange closely.

'She'll regret it. Anyway, her home is here, in Picklewick.'

'Dulcie mightn't agree with you.'

'Dulcie is a romantic at heart.'

'What about Beth?'

'So is she. That's where Dulcie gets it from.'

'You could have fooled me.'

'Ultimately, she wants Maisie to be happy.'

'As do I,' Adam said.

'What about *your* happiness?'

'Mine doesn't matter.'

'I think it does. Don't you agree, Mr Haines?'

'Yes, but—'

'What about you, Mrs Haines? Don't you think Adam's happiness is important?'

His mother didn't reply, but Adam could see the cogs turning.

His dad began to bluster. 'I think I know what's best for my son.'

'Do you, Dad?' Adam's tone was steady, but inside he was seething. His parents clearly didn't give a jot whether he was happy or not, as long as he did what was expected of him. 'I'll come take a look at that car,' he said.

'Is that woman really leaving Picklewick?' his mother demanded.

Otto said, 'She will if Adam doesn't convince her to stay. She told me about you and Mr Haines making Adam choose between the woman he loves and the parents who don't love him enough.'

Martin took a step towards Otto. 'How dare you! I love my son unconditionally.'

Otto raised his eyebrows.

Adam's father subsided, flushing bright red as he realised what he had said.

'Martin, I don't want to lose him,' his mum cried. 'He's my *son*.'

Adam turned to her. 'You don't have to lose me, but you must trust me to know what's best for *me*. You've got to let me live my life the way I want to live it.' He looked at his father. 'I'm sorry Dad, but I hate accounting.'

Martin rolled his eyes. 'Now he tells me.'

'I did try to tell you years ago, but you wouldn't listen.'

'Do you really love this woman?'

'Maisie. Her name is *Maisie*. Yes, I do. With all my heart.'

He waited for his parents to say something – anything – but when they didn't, his heart sank. It looked like they were still intent on disowning him, which made trying to convince Maisie to come back to him almost impossible. She had been willing to end it, rather than cause a rift between him and his parents.

That rift wasn't going to go away, it seemed.

But then his father said, 'What are you waiting for, Adam? Haven't you got an engine to fix?'

And Adam felt a wild surge of hope as he jumped in the van and followed Otto up Muddypuddle Lane towards the farm and the woman who had stolen his heart.

Engines clearly weren't either Maisie's or her mum's strong point and despite opening the bonnet and peering hopefully inside, the car had continued to refuse to start. Turning the engine over repeatedly had resulted in a flat battery, and now the damned thing was completely dead.

'I might know someone,' Otto had said. 'His number is down at the cottage. I'll call him on the way to the restaurant.'

'You're going in early,' Beth had observed.

'Got things to sort out.'

Maisie and Beth had gone back inside.

'Put the kettle on,' Beth had instructed. 'We might as well have a cuppa while we're waiting. Got any biscuits?'

Maisie had grimaced. The thought of food turned her stomach. Otto had tried to tempt her with some homemade scones earlier, but she'd refused. Bless him, he had done his best to make her feel better, saying that he fully understood her reaction last night, but Maisie still felt awful. He had been so kind, and she had repaid that kindness by causing ructions in his restaurant.

He had found her sitting at the table nursing a cold cup of tea at ten to six this morning, and she had ended up telling him all about the overheard conversation, Adam confessing his love for her and that his parents had threatened to disown him, which was why Maisie felt she had no option but to leave. She couldn't have that on her conscience.

Otto had been incredibly sympathetic, which had made her feel even worse.

Dulcie had calmed down too, Maisie discovered, when her sister had rolled out of bed an hour or so later. Dulcie had even chatted to her as Maisie had stuffed the last few items into her case, telling her that she didn't have to leave if she didn't want to. Dulcie had said that Maisie could stay on the farm indefinitely, but Maisie had insisted she was better off going back to Birmingham.

There was no way she could remain in Picklewick now.

Maisie was sitting at the kitchen table with her hands around yet another cup of untouched tea and was deep in thought, when she felt a touch on her shoulder. Expecting it to be Dulcie or Mum, Maisie almost leapt out of her skin when she saw Adam standing by her elbow.

'What are you doing here?' she gasped, her heart pounding uncomfortably fast.

'You needed someone to look at your mother's car.'

Maisie glanced around the kitchen and realised they were alone. Where was everyone, and who had let him in? If her mother knew he was here, she would run him off the farm with a flea in his ear.

'The keys are in the ignition,' she said, her eyes downcast. She didn't want him to see the pain in them.

'Can we talk?'

'What's the point? It's not going to change anything.'

'You're wrong, it will,' he insisted. 'Otto spoke to my parents this morning.'

'Oh, god. How much apologising did he have to do?' She lifted her head, appalled to think she had caused Otto such a problem. He should have told her:

she would have gone with him. *She* was the one who ought to be apologising, not him.

'None. He told them a few home truths.'

Maisie groaned. Instead of making things better, Otto had made it worse.

'Long story short, they are no longer disowning me.' Adam pulled out a chair and sat down opposite. Prising her hands away from the mug, he grasped her fingers. 'Whilst they don't exactly give us their blessing, they're not going to stand in our way. They know I love you.' He squeezed her hands. 'Could you ever feel the same way about me?'

'I can't do this,' she said, snatching them back. 'It's pointless. I've got no job and nowhere to live, so I have to go back with my mum.'

'No, you don't. You can move in with me. If you can't face sharing my bed, or you think it's too soon, you can have the spare room. Hell, I'll move out if I have to, so you can live there on your own.'

'You'd do that for me?'

'In a heartbeat.'

'I don't know what to say.' Maisie was astounded. Her heart was screaming yes, but her head was telling her to slow down and think about it. 'I still don't have a job,' she said, stalling for time. She needed to think. This would be such a big step. There was no doubt that she loved him, but they'd known each other for such a short amount of time…

'You do have a job. Otto isn't going to sack you. He told me so. And you won't have to pay rent or help with the bills, or...' Adam trailed off. '*Please*. I can't bear to lose you. You've got to stay.'

'I've already told her that she can stay here,' Dulcie said, appearing in the doorway. 'I still need help around the farm. Maisie, nothing needs to change. You don't have to go home with Mum and neither do you have to move in with Adam if you're not ready. This can be your home for as long as you want it to be.'

'But what about you and Otto? You need your alone time.'

Dulcie twinkled at her. 'Don't worry about us, we get plenty of *alone time*. Anyway, I get the feeling you'll be spending more time at Adam's place than you will here. There's just one thing...'

'What?' Maisie knew there would be a catch.

'You need to put this guy out of his misery and tell him you love him. You *do* love him, don't you, Maisie?'

'I do!' She clapped her hands together, joy surging through her.

'Then I think you'd better tell him,' Dulcie advised.

Maisie went one better: she threw herself at him and kissed him so soundly that she hoped he was in no doubt how she felt about him. *Then* she told him.

'We need more sausages and more bread rolls,' Maisie announced, dashing into the kitchen. 'Otto sent me to fetch them.'

Nikki reached into the fridge, which was looking decidedly emptier than it had done this morning when it had been crammed full of sausages, burgers and Otto's secret hot sauce.

'Here,' Nikki said, thrusting several packets of sausages into Maisie's hands. 'I'll bring the rolls.' They were stacked on the dining room table, and there was now only half the amount that they'd started with.

Maisie hurried out into the yard, where Amos and Otto were manning the barbeque. The farm was thronging with people, mainly families, and Maisie was delighted for Dulcie. The baby animals were the highlights, although the Easter egg hunt had proved popular, and the egg painting was still in full swing. The Shetland ponies were giving rides around the field, led by Petra and October, who worked at the stables, and Walter had been roped into driving the tractor which pulled a trailer for a different kind of ride around the farm.

And then there was Dulcie, who was dressed in a Peter Rabbit costume. She was the biggest hit with the younger children, and as far as Maisie could tell, her sister was having the time of her life. Even Mum seemed to be enjoying herself, chatting with the visitors and directing them to the various activities.

Overall, the Easter Fayre was a roaring success, and Maisie felt proud that she had helped make it happen. But even as she rushed around, helping out here, there and everywhere, part of her was thinking ahead to the next event in the farm's calendar, which would be the sunflower maze in the summer. The seeds would have to be sown in the next couple of weeks, which meant that the ground would shortly have to be prepared. Not only that, the proposed pumpkin patch also needed to be worked over before sowing those seeds too.

Adam, surprisingly, was doing a goat-milking demonstration, then giving out samples of the pasteurised result for visitors to taste, and Maisie paused for a moment to watch, her heart bursting with love.

Soon she would take Adam up on his offer to move in with him – but not into his spare room. If she was going to live with a man, she was going to do it *properly*. The thought made her tingle all over.

The rest of the day was filled with frantic activity and didn't end until long after the last of the visitors had left and the clean-up operation was complete.

Tired but happy, Maisie joined her family in the dining room for a bowl of the curry that Otto had made, and a glass of wine to celebrate a job well done. She had just done a final check on the animals and was the last to sit down at the table.

Dulcie called for quiet before everyone tucked in. 'We just want to say thank you for all your help,' she announced, taking hold of Otto's hand and gazing around the room. 'We couldn't have done it without you, and I'm already looking forward to the next one,' she added, and everyone groaned good-naturedly. 'Before you start filling your faces with Otto's delicious curry, I also want to tell you that I've sold the old farmhouse, so we've got a bit of extra cash to play with.'

'Who to?' Nikki asked, her fork poised above her bowl. 'I thought you were going to give it to Jay.'

'He didn't want it. However, Adam *did*. We're signing the contracts next week.'

Maisie was stunned. He'd kept that quiet; so had Dulcie, for that matter.

Adam said, 'It's going to take a lot of time and money to make it habitable, but it'll be fantastic when it's done. I'll have room for my workshop, and Maisie will have room for her kennels, or a cattery, or a wildlife sanctuary – or whatever she wants to do.'

Maisie was stunned. 'Do you mean that?'

'I do, but it's going to be hard work,' he warned.

'I don't care!' Maisie cried, throwing her arms around him. 'This is a dream come true.'

She had never been so happy. With a wonderful man by her side and a bright future ahead, she couldn't wait to get started.

Maisie Fairfax had kissed her last frog!

SECOND CHANCES

CHAPTER ONE

Beth peered through her nets and frowned in annoyance. Anita, her next-door neighbour, had put her bins out again. That in itself wasn't an issue. Where she had put them *was*. Why couldn't the bloody woman put them outside her own gate?

Why did she have to butt them up against Beth's? It made it look like Beth had double the number of bins to anyone else in the street. That blimmin' dog of Anita's had also woken her up in the early hours, barking its head off. And don't get her started on the kids. The woman was forever shouting at them, screeching at the top of her voice, day in, day out. And the little sods didn't take a blind bit of notice, so Anita might as well save her breath and save Beth from having to listen to it.

Tightening the belt of her dressing gown, Beth stomped into the hall, yanked open the front door and marched down the short path. Muttering under her breath, she dragged her neighbour's bins back to where they belonged – in front of her neighbour's house. And for good measure, she deposited them right in front of the gate. If the woman wanted to get out, she'd have to shift them.

Beth knew she was being petty, but since she'd retired a few months ago, she didn't have much else to think about, and the issues with the woman next door were gradually taking on bigger and bigger proportions.

'Oi! What do you think you're doing?' Anita yelled through her bedroom window.

Beth smiled sweetly. 'Just putting these back where they belong.'

'They're blocking my gate. Damien will be wanting to go to school in a minute.'

From the amount of yelling the bloody woman had done just to get Damien out of bed, Beth was pretty certain the boy didn't want to go to school at all.

'So, move them,' Beth called back, and turned on her slippered heel to march up the pavement and back inside.

Slamming the door with more force than was strictly necessary, she went into the kitchen to make herself a cup of tea, and whilst the kettle came to the boil, she thought about what she would do today.

The oven could do with a good clean and there was a bit of washing in the laundry basket, but probably not enough for a full load. There was a time when the washing machine was always on the go, but that had been when the kids were little. They were all grown up now, with washing machines of their own. Except for Maisie. There wasn't room for a washing machine in the static that she lived in with her boyfriend Adam, so when she wanted to do any washing, she borrowed Dulcie's.

The kettle's automatic switch knocked off, and Beth wondered why the hell she was thinking about washing machines... Oh yes, half a load. She would wait until the end of the week and see what was in the laundry basket then. If she still didn't have enough for a full load, she would chuck in a few tea towels. They could always do with a freshen-up.

Beth made a cup of tea, mashing the tea bag against the side of the mug with a spoon.

She could pop to the supermarket later. She had a few bits to get, and it meant she would have some fresh air – although how fresh it was, being in the city, was debatable.

Dulcie had fresh air. Loads of it. Well, she would, wouldn't she, being halfway up a hillside in the middle of nowhere. Those goats she kept didn't smell too good though, and the chicken coop reeked.

What was she doing now, Beth wondered. There was one way to find out: she would call her. But after listening to twelve rings, Beth gave up. Her middle daughter was probably outside doing farming stuff.

How about Nikki? But when Beth checked the time, she realised that her eldest child would probably be on her way to work. Jay didn't pick up either, and although Maisie answered after the third ring (one day that girl would have to have her phone surgically removed), she sounded out of breath.

'Am I allowed to ask why you sound like you've just run a marathon?' Beth asked.

'We're moving stones.'

Of course she was. What else did one do on a Thursday morning?

Maisie was obviously busy, so Beth said, 'I'll let you get on, but be careful you don't put your back out. It can ruin the rest of your life, can a bad back.'

'I'll be fine, Mum. Stop fussing.'

Beth hung up, muttering, 'That's what mothers do – fuss.' Not that any of her kids appreciated or cared just how much she worried about them. That was the privilege and arrogance of youth: they thought they were invincible. And the younger they were, the more invincible they thought they were.

Nikki, being the eldest, was starting to have an inkling that life was harsher and less forgiving than she'd assumed, but she wasn't there yet. She would soon change her tune when she was staring middle age in the face and wondering where the grey hair, wrinkles, and saggy boobs had come from.

Where had all the years gone? One minute Beth had been dancing in the Plaz, flares flapping around her legs, a disco ball pixelating her skin and the taste of Snake Bite on her tongue; and the next, she was rubbing her bunions and wondering where she could buy support stockings. The bit in between was a blur of nappies, nits and teenage strops. In those days she had longed for an hour to herself, a bit of peace and quiet where nobody was demanding anything of her.

'Be careful what you wish for,' she grumbled, startled when she realised she'd said it out loud. Flipping heck, she was talking to herself now. Maybe she should get a cat? There was a distinct similarity between cats and daughters: they were both disdainful (scornful, even), they both treated their homes like a hotel, and they both came and went as they pleased at all hours of the day and night, but at least cats didn't answer back.

Beth sighed disconsolately. She would give her right arm to have one of her kids answer her back right now. The house was too big and too silent, except for the echoes as she rattled around in it.

Should she find something smaller? It would certainly be less to clean. Not that there was much cleaning to be done now that her youngest had moved out.

Was it because of *her* that all of them had moved away? Had she been such a bad mother that at the first opportunity to leave Birmingham (and her) they'd leapt at it?

She tried to console herself with the thought that at least her daughters were still in the country, unlike Jay who couldn't have gone any further away if he'd tried.

As long as they were happy, that was all that mattered she told herself, ignoring the inner voice that wanted to know whether *she* was happy. And if she wasn't, didn't she deserve to be?

But how could she be happy when she was so damned lonely?

Annoyed at having such negative thoughts, Beth tried to count her blessings. And she was the first to admit that she had many: she was healthy, her kids were healthy, she had a nice little pension to top up her OAP pension, she had a roof over her head…

It should be enough, but it wasn't. Beth missed her kids, and there was nothing she could do about it.

Or was there?

Walter removed his brown corduroy trousers from the back of the chair in his bedroom, stared at them, then put them back. Even he had to admit that they had seen better days. He was going for tea at the farm, not mucking out a sheep shed, so he had better wear something halfway decent, or Otto would be giving him concerned looks out of the corner of his eye.

The same went for the checked flannel shirt and the khaki-green pullover that he liked to wear over the top.

Walter opened his wardrobe door. Now, where was the nice shirt that Nikki and Gio had given him for Christmas? Ah, there it was, hanging next to his funeral suit.

Slipping the shirt off the hanger, he put it on, stiff fingers struggling with the buttons. He had a bit of arthritis in his hands, and sometimes it played him up.

A tidy pair of trousers later, and he decided he scrubbed up okay. His hair was getting a bit long though, so when he went downstairs he put a note on the calendar as a reminder to make an appointment with the barber.

Having supper at the farmhouse was a rare treat these days. Poor Otto was usually so busy, what with running the restaurant, training new chefs for Alistair (his old boss when he used to live in London), and working on another foraging cookbook, that Walter hardly saw him.

He wished his son didn't work so hard, but Otto had a passion which couldn't be denied. And Dulcie was no better. The girl was holding down a day job as well as running the farm and starting a new business.

Walter reflected sadly that it didn't used to be like that in his day. Farmers were farmers back then; they didn't usually have to go get a second job to make ends meet. He blamed the government. And the supermarket chains for being too greedy. So many farmers today were packing it in, that very soon there wouldn't be any farms left.

Walter continued to fret about the state of British farming all the way up the lane. He didn't envy youngsters today – they always seemed so busy. Mind you, he hadn't sat on his backside twiddling his thumbs. He had worked damned hard. He'd had to. Farming wasn't a nine-to-five, Monday-to-Friday job, with weekends off.

He had bloody loved it though, despite it almost being the death of him. Walter still couldn't bear to think about how he had managed to run up so much debt and how ill he had become as a result, without feeling ashamed. Having to get rid of the farm had been one of the darkest times of his life, but he recognised that it had to be done. It didn't stop him from missing the old place though, and he tried to help out when and where he could. The problem was that Otto continued to fret and fuss if he thought Walter was doing too much. And whilst it was lovely that his son cared about his welfare, Walter was bored rigid.

Now that he felt better in himself (and he had done for a good long while), he missed being busy. And although he hated to admit it, he was lonely. Even Amos at the stables, who was roughly the same age as him (give or take a few years) didn't have enough hours in the day. What with helping out with the holiday lets, looking after his great-nephew, baby Amory, and having found love with Lena, Amos was constantly on the go. Whereas Walter always seemed to be searching around for something to do.

As usual, Walter had Peg with him, and the dog darted ahead into the farmhouse, announcing his arrival. A wall of delicious cooking smells hit him when he stepped inside.

'Hi, Dad.' Otto was at the stove, stirring and tossing, several pans and pots on the go.

Dulcie was in the dining room, laying the table. Walter had never used that room for dining in, preferring to eat his meals at the kitchen table. It was these little changes, probably more than the big ones (such as the farm no longer having a flock of sheep), that made him realise every time he visited that this was no longer his home.

Brushing his sadness aside, he hurried towards Dulcie to give her a kiss. 'Do you need a hand with anything?' he asked, after he had greeted her.

'No thanks, Walter, it's all under control.' Dulcie always said that, even though he could tell that it sometimes wasn't, and he knew the reason was that she and Otto worried he might become ill again if he overdid it.

Fat chance of that! He was more likely to die of boredom these days.

'How is the soap-making coming along?' he asked, over dinner.

Dulcie had recently invested in a small herd of goats and was using their milk to make soap and other lotions and potions, and Otto also made the most wonderful ice cream with it.

'Slow but steady,' she replied, around a mouthful of aromatic beef. 'I've been experimenting with new scents and adding different flowers into the mix.'

Walter had been given a few samples to try in the past, and he must admit that the soaps did smell nice. Dulcie packaged them beautifully, too. Her soap was a quality product.

'Lavender, rose and vanilla are still my best sellers though,' she added. 'I'm thinking of planting some lavender bushes in the orchard, but I'm not sure whether they'll like it there.'

'If you want a hand, give me a shout,' he offered.

'Thanks Walter, but I've got it covered. Maisie likes planting things.'

'How is she getting on at the old farmhouse?' he asked.

Never in a million years did he think that the derelict farmhouse on the mountain above, could be brought back to life. He'd assumed it was too far gone, but from what Dulcie was saying, Maisie and her fella were making a go of it.

'It's going to take time,' Dulcie said, 'because they're concentrating on getting the business side of things up and running first.'

'Have they decided what they're going to do with it?'

'Kennels, I believe. But don't take my word for it – Maisie changes her mind like the wind.'

Walter thought he might go take a look. It was a long time since he had ventured onto the hillside above the farm, and he wondered if they'd managed to improve the track that led onto the mountain. A few weeks back, he had watched with interest as a lorry had hauled an ancient static caravan up Muddypuddle Lane, wincing as it had inched its way up the narrow road.

He hoped the caravan was well insulated because the top of the mountain could be a windswept place, and he didn't envy Maisie and her fella living in it come winter. Still, youngsters didn't feel the cold like old folk did, and Walter couldn't deny that he was old. His aching joints were eager to remind him every morning. But again, that could be due to sitting on his behind for most of the day. Use it or lose it, wasn't that how the saying went?

The way Walter was going, he would seize up before long, so maybe a nice walk to the top of the mountain would do him good, and he could pop in and see Maisie and her caravan at the same time.

Beth parked her little red car in one of Picklewick's side streets, and tried to pretend that she wasn't being furtive. Telling herself that she had every right to be in the village (she did) and that she wasn't obliged to tell her children that she was here (she wasn't), Beth nevertheless scurried along the high street.

When she came to the building she was aiming for, she glanced up and down the road before darting inside.

She was scanning the properties in the 'To Rent' section (there were only a handful) and looking for the one she wanted, when she sensed someone approaching.

'Those are our rental properties,' a young chap said. By 'young' Beth meant that he was in his late twenties.

'I realise that,' she replied.

'Is it a rental property you're after?'

Why would she be looking at rental properties if she wasn't thinking about renting one? She didn't mean to send him a withering look, but his slight recoil made her aware that she must have.

'Is it for yourself?' he battled on.

'Why wouldn't it be?'

'It's just a standard question, madam.'

She pressed her lips together before replying. 'Yes, it's for me.'

'How many beds are you after?'

Beth lost patience. 'Let's cut to the chase. You've got a two up, two down terraced on your website. I would like to take a look at it, please.'

'Hazelnut Road? It has just become available.'

'Can I take a look?' Beth repeated.

'Let me check the diary.'

'I want to see it today. Right now, preferably.'

'I'm not sure that will be possible. We operate an appointment system for viewings and—'

'I've driven all the way from Birmingham this morning, for the sole purpose of taking a look at it.'

'I'm sorry; if you had phoned, we would—'

'I did. I was told I could see it today.'

'Ah, right.' The young man was studying his computer screen. 'Who did you speak to?'

'No idea.'

'There's nothing in the diary.'

'Is everything okay, Zander?' An older gentleman had stepped out of an office and was gazing at Beth with curiosity.

'This lady says she has an appointment to view the new instruction on Hazelnut Road, but there isn't anything in the diary.'

'It's vacant, isn't it?'

'I believe so.'

'In that case, can you hold the fort for half an hour, whilst I take this client to view it?'

Beth breathed a sigh of relief. The organ grinder had come to her rescue, leaving the poor monkey still searching the electronic diary for a non-existent appointment.

Beth felt a smidgen of remorse for fibbing to the young lad, but not enough to come clean. Even if she hadn't been able to wrangle a viewing, she would have peeped in through the windows. It had looked nice in the photographs, so she was quietly hopeful it would be just as nice in real life.

Ten minutes later saw the estate agent unlocking the front door and gesturing for her to step inside.

It wasn't big, but it would do. The front door opened directly into the living room, which probably had enough space for a three-piece suite and a table to eat at. At the rear was the kitchen, leading to a small back garden with a little yard. Upstairs were two good-sized bedrooms and a bathroom. The only thing she wasn't too keen on, was that the stairs were in the lounge. However, it wasn't a deal breaker.

The house had been freshly painted, and was clean and empty of furniture.

'I'll take it,' she announced. 'When can I move in? Monday?'

'It's not that simple, Mrs Fairfax. We have to obtain references, and we'll need to draw up a rental agreement, then there's the deposit to discuss.'

'Well?' she demanded. 'What are you waiting for? Let's get the ball rolling.'

The sooner she moved in, the sooner she would be in the heart of her family again. Her idea to move to Picklewick was a genius one! Wait until she told her girls: they would be thrilled. But she wouldn't tell them just yet. She would tell them when everything was signed and sealed. It would be a lovely surprise.

Walter paused to catch his breath for what felt like the hundredth time, Peg panting by his side. She seemed equally as glad of the momentary rest, but then again, she had covered more ground than him, having dashed around from the second they'd set off.

Surely the hill never used to be this steep? Grudgingly, he supposed that the climb would seem harder – after all, the last time he had been up this way on foot would have been several years ago, and when he had been in better health. The further up the mountain he went, the more frequently he stopped to take in the view. That was his excuse, and he intended to stick with it.

Determined not to let the incline beat him, Walter pushed on, his tread slow and ponderous. By the time the old farmhouse came into view, his breathing was laboured and his legs were in agony, but he felt a spark of pride that he'd done it.

Eighteen months ago his son had been so worried about him that he had quit his marvellous job in London to come home to look after him. And look at him now – able to walk to the top of the mountain and onto the common, completely under his own steam.

But whether he would be able to get out of his chair tomorrow without help, was a different matter entirely.

Now that the gradient had lost its bite, Walter was able to pick up the pace a bit as he made his way to Maisie and Adam's new place. Technically it belonged to Adam, because it was he who had bought it from

Dulcie, but Maisie was his girlfriend (or partner, as she referred to herself) and she lived there too. Not in the farmhouse, because that was just as derelict as the last time he had clapped eyes on it, but in the caravan that he'd watched being hauled up the lane.

It was a miracle they'd managed to get it onto the mountain, but there it was, perched on breeze blocks to keep it off the ground.

He could see two figures labouring over a pile of stones, moving them from one place to another, and a wave of nostalgia swept through him. When he was a boy, this used to be a working farm. He distinctly remembered the elderly couple who used to own it. But the old chap had died, and his wife had followed shortly after, and none of their kids had wanted to take it on. Grown up and with no room for a hill farm in their lives, they had been happy to sell it to Walter's dad for a song.

The outbuildings had been in a bad state of repair even then, but they'd been okay for storing winter feed. Nowadays there was little left of them, aside from a pile of hand-chiselled stone and the footprint of where they used to be.

'Walter!' Maisie had spotted him and came hurrying over. 'What are you doing here? Does Otto know?'

'Why should he? He's my son, not my keeper,' he snapped, then was instantly remorseful. Maisie was only looking out for him. 'I came to see what all the fuss is about,' he said, more kindly. 'I see you're making progress.'

'Slowly,' Maisie said, leading him towards Adam, who was watching him approach.

'Have you come to lend a hand?' Adam asked, shaking hands with him.

'Not on your nelly. That looks like hard work!'

'It is.'

'That's good stone, that is. Are you going to reuse it?'

'You bet we are. But not here. We're going to use it to repair the house and build an extension.'

Walter admired the young man's vision as he talked him through their plans.

'The biggest problem is getting materials on site. The track from Dulcie's farm onto the mountain needs to be tarmacked, and that's going to cost a fortune.' Adam looked so down in the mouth, that Walter's heart went out to him.

He scratched his whiskery chin. 'I've got an idea. There's a forestry track that runs up through the trees over that way.' He pointed to a dark green patch of conifers that had been planted decades ago and had now grown to maturity.

The trees flanked the sides of a hill a fair distance from the old farmhouse, but the logging road running through them was hard-packed gravel and wasn't nearly as steep as the track above Dulcie's farm.

As Walter described it to him, Adam's expression brightened. 'I'll take a look right now,' he said. 'Do you want to come with me?'

'No thanks, lad. I'm knackered. I'll have a quick cuppa with Maisie while she tells me what she's going to do with those sheds once they're built, then I'm off home.'

'I can give you a lift, if you like?'

Walter shook his head. 'You get on and check out that old logging road. I got up here by myself – I'll make it down by myself.'

He had a feeling he would regret not taking Adam up on his offer, but he was nothing if not stubborn. And he probably had more pride than was good for him. But, darn it, he hated being thought of as old and incapable, and he wanted to make himself useful.

Hopefully, he had done that today, and if that was the case having stiff joints and aching muscles tomorrow would be a small price to pay.

CHAPTER TWO

'That's all of it,' Amir announced, holding onto the attic ladder with one hand and balancing a cardboard box on his shoulder with the other. He set it down carefully on the landing, alongside the others, and dusted his hands off.

'Can I make you a cup of tea?' Beth asked hopefully. Anything to delay having to sort them out.

'I'm alright thanks, Mrs Fairfax. I'd better get on. I've got lectures this afternoon.'

Beth tried to press a twenty-pound note into his palm 'for his trouble,' but he refused that as well, so she waved him off, thankful that her neighbour was so kind. She never would have managed to get up the attic on her own.

It was a long time since she'd seen what was up there, but from what she remembered much of it was junk.

As she opened the flap of the nearest box, she couldn't for the life of her work out why she had hung onto an old iron that didn't work, or that vase, considering she had never liked it. Beth anticipated that she would be making several trips to the household waste recycling centre, and she was quite looking forward to it, as she'd never been there before. Not surprising, since she'd only recently bought a car.

She chuckled as she remembered the look on Dulcie and Maisie's faces when she'd rocked up at the farm in it at Easter. Dulcie had feared that she was going to insist on staying longer than the fortnight she'd planned, but her middle daughter needn't have worried; Beth hadn't had any intention of staying. And she had no intention of staying now, not when she would have a home of her own in Picklewick.

A twinge of conscience pricked her: she hadn't told her children what she'd done. She would have to at some point, but not yet, not until it was irreversible. Actually, it was irreversible now, since she had given notice on this place and had taken out a lease on her new one. There was no going back. But she was nevertheless reluctant to tell her kids. Jay, in New Zealand, probably wouldn't mind, but the girls were a different matter.

She honestly didn't know what their reaction would be. She hoped they would understand that she missed them. All three now lived in Picklewick, so was it so wrong for her to want to be near them?

As she settled into her task of sorting out more than three decades of living in this house, Beth prayed they wouldn't be too upset. She knew how irritated they could get with her, and she didn't mean to be annoying, but no matter what she did or said, one or the other of them would get cross.

At times she felt like she was the child and Nikki or Dulcie was the parent. Not so much with Maisie, because her youngest still acted more like a teenager than an adult. Although, to be fair, since Maisie had met Adam, she was less fifteen and more twenty-five, which was her actual age.

Aw, look, Nikki's first pair of proper shoes!

A wave of sadness enveloped Beth, both for the time long gone and for her firstborn who was now a mother herself. And a smidgen of guilt followed quickly in its wake as she realised that she hadn't kept any of her other children's first pairs of shoes. And neither had she filled in their baby books the way she had diligently filled in Nikki's. It didn't seem fair to hang onto Nikki's baby things when she hadn't bothered to keep anything belonging to the others.

Not wanting to lose the shoes completely, she took a photo of them before she added them to the pile meant for the charity shop. She decided she would take photos of anything else that she didn't intend to hang onto but wanted to remember.

Despite looking forward to a new home and a new life in Picklewick, Beth would be sad to leave this house. Her children had been born here. Not in the house itself, of course – they had all been born in hospital – but this was where she had raised them. It held so many memories, some happy, some not so happy, and some downright horrid, but every single one was a piece of the mosaic that made up the picture of her life with her children.

If only they hadn't moved away…

But they had, and she wasn't prepared to rattle around in this house on her own, feeling lonely. She had four kids, one grandchild, and another on the way, and she hardly saw any of them. It simply wouldn't do. Which was why she had taken matters into her own hands and decided to be proactive, rather than sitting here feeling envious because all her friends had family living close by and she had no one.

Having sorted through the first few boxes, Beth took a break, and while she drank her mug of tea, she scrolled through the photos of the little terraced house in Picklewick and knew she was doing the right thing. She would be close enough to babysit Sammy or lend a hand when her daughters needed it, but not so close as to be living in anyone's pocket. She would be independent, yet still part of the family.

It would be perfect.

'Have you heard from Mum lately?' Dulcie asked. She was wiping the counters down as Maisie entered the kitchen. The aroma of freshly made cottage pie hung in the air, and Walter's tummy rumbled. It was nice not to have to cook for himself.

'Not for a few days. Why?' Maisie peered into the oven. 'That looks yummy.'

'I hope it tastes as good as it looks,' Dulcie said. 'Otto didn't make this, I did.'

'I'm sure it'll be delicious. You always were a better cook than me.'

'That's because you had Mum to cook for you.'

'I'm improving,' Maisie replied, 'But maybe I'll ask Otto for some pointers.'

'Best not, unless you want jus with this and jam with that,' Walter chortled. 'And I'm not referring to the kind of jam you can buy in the supermarket either. He was telling me about seaweed jam the other day. It sounded awful.'

Otto had also mentioned bourbon jam, which sounded much better. However, Walter didn't feel inclined to put it on his toast in the morning. How his son came up with these strange food combinations was beyond him.

Dulcie had finished tidying the kitchen and was now checking her phone. 'The last time I heard from Mum was nearly two weeks ago. It's not like her to maintain radio silence. How about you?'

Maisie peered at her mobile. 'About the same.' Her eyes widened. 'Do you think she's okay?'

'There's one way to find out.' Dulcie flicked a finger across the screen and waited for the call to be answered. 'Mum? Thank goodness! Are you alright?'

Walter could hear a tinny voice emanating from the phone, but he couldn't hear what Beth was saying, and neither did he want to. That woman was a damned nuisance.

After a couple of minutes the call ended, and Dulcie looked relieved. 'She hasn't rung because she's busy.'

'She could have messaged one of us,' Maisie said.

'Apparently she's too busy for that, too.'

'Why? What's she doing?'

'De-cluttering.'

Maisie frowned. 'I hope she isn't de-cluttering any of *my* stuff.'

'I thought you had fetched everything you wanted?'

'I did, but there's my old school reports and that project I did for art. Oh, and my cheerleading outfits.'

Dulcie laughed. 'I'd forgotten you used to do cheerleading. I bet Mum didn't keep any of them.'

'I put them in the attic.'

'They are probably still there, in that case. Mum hasn't been up there for years. I used to have to get the Christmas decorations down for her.'

'She won't be needing those again,' Maisie pointed out. 'Not if she spends Christmas here, like she did last year.'

Walter pulled a face. Beth had stayed at the farm for a full two weeks. *And* she'd turned up again at Easter. That visit had been for a couple of weeks, as well. She had every right to be here, considering she was Dulcie's mother, but Walter wished she wasn't so argumentative. Whenever he was in the same room as her, they seemed to butt heads. She was worse than his pet sheep, Flossie. Flossie was a head-butter too, but considerably less prickly. Beth called it, 'being forthright', and 'calling a spade a spade.' Walter called it annoying.

She was a fine-looking woman though, with her good cheekbones and her clear blue eyes, and when he'd first met her, he'd thought she was easy on the eye. It was a pity she wasn't equally as easy on the ear. Or his patience.

Maisie was saying, 'Isn't it daft how you never notice something, but when you do you see them everywhere.'

Dulcie replied, 'What do you mean? Another five minutes and I'll serve up, so do you want to lay the table?'

'Dalmatians,' Maisie said, getting a handful of knives and forks out of a drawer. 'I take it Otto's not eating with us?'

'Good lord, no! Do you think he'd let me cook if he was?'

'True. As I was saying, I saw a Dalmatian dog in the high street the other day, and now I keep seeing them everywhere.'

'Are you sure it's not the same one?'

'Don't say that, because I could have sworn I saw Mum's car in the village the other day too.'

'It's a well-known thing,' Walter said. He'd read about it recently. When the farm was his, he'd barely had time to open a newspaper, but these days he scoured it from end to end. What else did he have to do with his time? He continued, 'It's called 'the frequency illusion' where you see something, like a particular breed of dog or model of car let's say, or hear something like a name, and then you begin to notice it everywhere, so you think it's more common than it is.'

'You learn something new every day.' Dulcie opened the oven door and a waft of fragrant steam billowed out.

Walter's mouth watered. He was looking forward to this – good, simple, honest food, without any frills, just like his wife (God rest her soul) used to make. As so often happened when he thought of her, Walter was filled with sadness. She had died far too young, when Otto was a teenager. It was she who had nurtured Otto's love of cooking.

'I'll put some of this pie aside for Adam to have later, shall I?' Dulcie suggested, ladling out generous portions onto plates.

'That would be lovely, thanks.' Maisie gave her sister a one-armed hug.

It warmed Walter's heart to see how well the sisters got on, because that hadn't always been the case. Maisie had been drifting and rudderless when

175

he'd first met her, flitting from job to job (Nikki used to call her Maisie Daydream), but the girl seemed to have settled down, helping Dulcie on the farm, as well as trying to get the old place on the hill up and running. She was a hard worker, he'd give her that, and so was Adam.

He envied the youngsters their enthusiasm, drive, and energy levels. Just thinking about it made him feel tired, but he supposed feeling tired was par for the course as one got older; and it hadn't helped matters that he had been so unwell. Thankfully, he could feel his energy slowly returning, although he was aware it would never be the same as it was.

He should learn to celebrate the small things, the little wins, such as he and Amos making play equipment for the goats, and him walking to the top of the mountain and back – even though it had laid him up for a couple of days afterwards.

Walter was feeling fine again now though, so maybe it was time to make inroads on all those odd jobs that needed doing around the cottage. If he took it slow and didn't over-exert himself, he was certain he could get them done without having to ask for help. It would give him something to do, and at the same time would prove to Otto and the rest that he wasn't over the hill just yet.

Despite the house looking barer than Beth could ever remember it being, the move to Picklewick still didn't seem real, even though she had given notice to her landlord, arranged for her post to be redirected, informed all the necessary utilities, and had booked the removal company.

It had been difficult to decide what she would take with her and what had to be got rid of (the house in Picklewick was smaller than this one, so about half of her furniture had to go), but afterwards she had felt strangely cleansed. And it hadn't taken as long as she'd anticipated to go through everything, and she was now left with the bare bones of her old home.

She had been quite ruthless and had probably thrown out stuff she could have used in her new place, but she wanted a fresh start; so this morning, with a week left until moving day, she intended to go shopping with Enka, who was probably her oldest friend. She had worked with her for almost twenty years until Enka had packed in her job to help look after her little grandson when his mum went back to work.

'What are you looking for?' Enka asked, as they walked towards the Bullring Shopping Centre, Enka dragging her shopping trolley behind her. Short and dumpy, Enka dressed like a Russian peasant from the nineteenth century and swore worse than a football hooligan. Beth adored her.

She was going to miss her badly, but they were seeing less and less of each other since both ladies had ceased work. Whereas Enka's life was full of her children and her grandchildren, Beth's life lacked both… Hopefully her move to Picklewick would rectify not seeing enough of her kids and Sammy.

Beth patted her handbag. 'Curtains,' she announced. 'I've brought the measurements with me. There are curtains up at the windows already, but they're not to my taste. And I thought I'd buy a couple of cushions to go with.' She beamed. 'I might even treat myself to some new tea towels.'

'I think you should,' Enka said. 'You can never have enough tea towels. Or flannels.'

'Shall we have a cuppa first?' Beth suggested.

If she was honest, she was keener on having a good old chin wag than buying curtains, because she was all too aware that it might be a long time before she saw Enka again. Once Beth was settled in Picklewick, she suspected she would be unlikely to return to Birmingham any time soon.

Cuppas bought, they settled themselves in a corner booth of the retro diner and Beth brought out a packet of Fig Rolls and offered one to Enka.

'I don't think you're allowed to eat your own food in here,' Enka said, taking one, nevertheless.

'I'm not paying those prices for a bit of cake,' Beth said, biting into hers. Fruity sweetness exploded on her tongue. 'Daylight robbery, that's what it is.'

'Will cake be any cheaper where you're going?' Enka asked.

'Doubt it. Nothing is cheap anymore.'

'What's Picklewick like?'

'Pretty, quiet, lots of fields around.'

'It sounds lovely.'

'It is. I'm not sure I'd want to live there if it wasn't for the girls, though.'

'Still, it's a fresh start, isn't it?' Enka helped herself to another Fig Roll and dunked it in her tea. 'You'll soon make new friends.' She arched a heavily pencilled eyebrow and added, '*Man* friends.'

'I don't think so. Not at my age.'

'You're never too old for a bit of how's-your-father,' Enka cackled. 'It puts a spring in your step.'

'I've got enough spring, thank you. Any more and I might as well have pogo sticks strapped to my legs.' Beth paused, her mug halfway to her mouth. 'You don't see many pogo sticks, these days, do you?'

'You don't see many eligible men either – they're either serial bachelors or they're widowers and are looking for someone to wash their smalls.'

Beth chortled. 'You can say that again. I wouldn't have another man if you paid me.' The last one had left her with four kids, but at least he'd had the decency to pop his clogs before the divorce had gone through. Good riddance to bad rubbish, she always said.

But despite Enka's lamentations of there being no eligible men out there, it didn't stop Enka from looking. Beth was going to miss her friend's stories of her disastrous dates. They always made her chuckle. Where Enka found them was a mystery; Beth hadn't had a sniff of a date in years. Mind you, she didn't want to. At her age she was well past all that nonsense.

Love and romance were for the young – and they were welcome to it.

Drip, drip, drip… The damned noise was driving Walter insane. Every time it rained, it was like being tortured by the KGB. It was getting to the point where he began to dread seeing dark clouds gathering, and last night they'd gathered in abundance. Thankfully, the rain had held off until he'd managed to drop off to sleep, but when he'd woken in the middle of the night to use the loo, the incessant dripping had kept him awake.

The rain had stopped at around the same time as the sun had come up, but Walter knew that the dripping would continue for a while yet. Which was why he was at this moment trying to wrestle a set of ladders into position against the back wall of the cottage.

First, he would clear out the guttering, then he would scrape the moss away, before wrapping duct tape around the join between the two lengths.

As he shuffled the ladder slightly to the right, a drip landed on one of the metal rings and splashed into his face. Walter wiped it away with his sleeve, muttering to himself. At his feet, Peg whined anxiously.

'Don't worry, I haven't forgotten breakfast. We'll have tea and toast in a bit. I want to get this sorted first.'

The dog hung back warily, staying a safe distance from the ladder, and her brown eyes gazed worriedly at him. She disliked any change to her routine – unless that change involved a nice walk or an outing in the car. She had enjoyed the walk up to Maisie and Adam's place the other day, but like him, she'd been knackered afterwards. And, like him, the dog wasn't getting any younger.

With the ladder now in position, Walter gave it a little shake. It seemed steady enough. He wasn't keen on ladders, but this wasn't his first jaunt up one. He had done all his own repairs around the farm, apart from when the farmhouse had needed a new roof. About forty years ago, that had been, and he'd left it to a team of roofers because they knew what they were doing better than him. He was pleased that the roof was still going strong. Dulcie would probably get another forty years out of it before it needed replacing.

Taking a deep breath, Walter slid the roll of duct tape over his arm, and with a final check to make sure the ladder's base was level, he began to climb.

He had got about halfway up when his foot slipped, and Walter had a split second to lament the fact that he'd forgotten to change out of his slippers before he hit the ground with a sickening crack.

Walter wondered if he'd fallen asleep in front of the telly again as he struggled to open his eyes.

'Dad, can you hear me?'

Bloody hell, it was bright. Walter squinted, blinking as his eyes watered. Then he realised where he was, and as his memory came flooding back, his wince was equal parts pain and embarrassment.

Otto was peering at him anxiously. Walter struggled to sit up, but Otto put a hand on his shoulder.

'Do you know where you are?' his son asked.

'Of course I bloody know. I'm in hospital. I've broken my leg, not lost my marbles.'

'Just checking.'

'What time is it?'

'Why, have you got somewhere you need to be?'

'I haven't, but I bet you have.'

'I don't need to be anywhere else but here.'

'Liar.' Walter appreciated the sentiment though.

181

Otto sank onto a red plastic chair. 'What were you doing, going up a ladder at your age?'

'Cleaning out the gutters.'

'You should have asked me to do it.'

'Hmph. What's the time?' Walter repeated.

'Eight forty-seven.'

'Have you been here all day?'

'Yes.'

'You need to get off home.'

'I wanted to wait until they found you a bed.'

The ache in Walter's leg was abominable, and he shifted uncomfortably.

'They had to pin it,' Otto said.

'I know; they told me.'

'You'll have a cast for about six weeks.'

'They told me that, too.'

'How are you feeling?' Otto asked. He looked drawn and there were bags under his eyes.

Walter felt awful for worrying him. 'Not so bad.' His reply didn't fool Otto.

'Do you need any pain relief?'

'Aye, I could do with some.'

'I'll fetch a nurse.'

Walter closed his eyes. Not only was he in pain from his broken leg, but he felt sick, probably from the anaesthetic. His head was fuzzy, his memory jumbled. He remembered thinking, 'Oh shit,' followed by a terrible pain in his lower left leg. And he remembered Peg whining and licking his face. Then nothing until the ride in the ambulance and his arrival at hospital. More blurry memories; something about a CT scan and an X-ray, then being told he needed an operation.

He remembered feeling embarrassed because they cut his trousers off, and he recalled being asked to count backwards from ten. He also remembered asking someone to give Peg her toast, and lying flat on his back as he was being wheeled down a corridor, but he wasn't sure which order those memories were supposed to be in. He had a vague recollection of a firm female voice telling him to open his eyes, then more corridors, then being lifted into the bed he was currently in, before sleep reclaimed him.

His eyes must have drifted shut now, because he was startled by someone touching his wrist. 'Mr York, your son tells me you are a bit uncomfortable.' A nurse was peering at his chart and writing something down.

'You could say that,' he agreed.

'We'll get you something for your pain. Otherwise, how are you feeling?'

'Not so bad.'

'Not so good, more like,' Otto muttered. 'The daft sod.'

'Fell off a ladder, I heard,' the nurse said.

'He was wearing slippers.' Otto was shaking his head.

'We won't be doing that again, will we?' the nurse trilled.

'No, he bloody well won't. Will you, Dad?'

Walter pulled a face. 'I'll wear trainers next time. I forgot to—'

'I meant,' Otto broke in stonily, 'you won't be going up a ladder again.'

'But what about my guttering?'

'What about your waterworks?' the nurse asked. 'Do you need the toilet?'

Now that she'd mentioned it, Walter realised that he did need a pee. He also realised that it was going to be fun and games to get from the bed to the bathroom and back.

'Help me up,' he muttered to Otto.

The nurse said, 'No need. I'll get you a bedpan.'

'I'm not peeing into a bedpan. I'm not disabled.'

The nurse gave him a look. 'I think you'll find that is exactly what you are until your leg mends. You, Mr York, are going to need all the help you can get for a while.'

CHAPTER THREE

Beth was a bag of nerves. She should have said something before now. Well before. Like, when she had first thought of moving to Picklewick. Or when she had arranged to view her new house. Or when she'd signed the contract (which was the same day she'd been shown around it). Or any time since then. Even yesterday would have been good – better than today in fact, because today was moving day.

And none of her kids knew.

Her stomach was in knots at the thought of how they would react. Surely they would be pleased to have their old mum living close by? But this was Dulcie and Maisie she was thinking of, and they mightn't be thrilled. Nikki wouldn't mind; Nikki was a different kettle of fish to the other two (Jay was different again, being a boy). Nikki was more like Beth in a lot of ways: straight talking, forthright, didn't suffer fools gladly. If she saw a problem, she'd want to fix it.

Maisie was a dreamer, a butterfly, flitting around without a care in the world. Beth had to hand it to Adam though, he'd grounded her youngest child, so there was hope for her yet. Dulcie sat between the two, personality wise and timewise. She would be the trickiest of the three to convince that Beth had made the right decision. Beth knew, without a modicum of doubt, that Dulcie loved her. But loving someone didn't mean you always got on, and Dulcie and Beth had often been at loggerheads when Dulcie lived at home.

A wave of guilt washed over her at the thought of 'home'. She was about to walk out of her kids' childhood home for the last time, and she hadn't given them the opportunity to say goodbye to it. What kind of mother did that make her?

After the removal men loaded the van, Beth walked around the house one last time. It was strangely upsetting to see it empty, as though its soul had dissipated, leaving a shell of the former happy home. Saying that though, Beth realised the house had lost its soul long before today. The soul had left it when Maisie had gone to Picklewick to live.

Beth set off for the village shortly after the removal van and, as she drove, her thoughts turned away from the house she had moved out of, and towards the one she was about to move into. She was looking forward to this new era in her life, with one exception – at what point did she announce her arrival to her girls?

She couldn't do it now obviously, because she was driving, and neither did she want to have that particular conversation over the phone if she pulled over into a layby. Better to do it face to face.

Or was it? A phone call would mean that she could tell them the news in as few words as possible and then end the call, thereby giving them time to process it before she saw them. Or would that be taking the coward's way out?

Probably, and no doubt Dulcie would hightail it into the village as soon as Beth put the phone down.

Oh dear, she really had got herself into a pickle, hadn't she?

Deciding to wait until her furniture had been unloaded because she couldn't deal with the removal men, Dulcie, and Maisie at the same time (Nikki would be at work, as this was a school day, and Beth didn't think it would be good for the poor pupils if Nikki got the news whilst she was in class), Beth carried on towards the village, mulling it over in her mind.

There was no option, she realised. She would have to tell them over the phone this evening. She would invite them to her new house, and although dealing with them en masse wasn't her preferred option, she knew she wouldn't have any choice, no matter which way she played it. As soon as she told one, the other two would know anyway.

Beth tried to put her dread to the back of her mind and concentrate on driving. The journey to Thornbury was on good A roads, but once past the town, the roads became narrower and twistier, and the chances of meeting a slow-moving tractor were greatly increased. So it was with slightly sweaty palms that she entered the outskirts of Picklewick, relief at arriving safely easing some of her tension.

She hadn't realised how stressful moving house could be, and that was without having to buy or sell a property. But she only had herself to blame for being even more stressed than she should be.

Hazelnut Road was just before the start of the high street proper, so she was hoping to park up without seeing anyone who knew her. Keeping her eyes peeled and feeling like a spy in a low-budget movie, Beth sank lower into the driving seat as she turned into the street where her cottage was situated.

Relief washed over her when she saw that the van had arrived, and she pulled into the kerb a short way beyond it. Clambering somewhat inelegantly out of her little red car, her back stiff and her knees protesting, Beth reached for her handbag.

'Won't be a sec,' she called to the men in the van. 'Just got to collect the keys.'

Beth took off down the road and hurried towards the estate agent, returning with the keys as fast as her legs could carry her. The removal men had opened the back of the van and were already manoeuvring her settee onto the raised platform.

Excitement fluttered in her chest. Beth was hardly able to believe that this lovely terraced cottage was to be her new home. It was considerably smaller than her house in Birmingham, but that was a bonus as far as she was concerned. Now that her last chick had flown the nest, two bedrooms and one reception room were plenty. And she loved the period features in this house. Nikki would probably say that it needed updating (it still had a back boiler behind the gas fire in the living room, and an airing cupboard and hot water tank in one of the bedrooms), but Beth thought it was perfect, and she particularly loved the built-in cupboards either side of the chimney breast. They were probably original, from when the house was first built, she thought happily, as she inserted the key into the lock and opened the front door.

But her happiness quickly evaporated, and she let out a cry of dismay.

The living room ceiling was all over the living room floor, and water was pouring through the hole.

Beth felt like crying and when one of the removal men said, 'Right love, where do you want this sofa?' she began to wail.

'I'm so sorry,' Zander, the young chap from the estate agent's office said, for the fifth time. 'You have my word that we'll get it repaired as soon as possible.'

'How soon?' Beth demanded. She felt sick. She had a van full of furniture, the house was inhabitable, and she was at her wits' end.

'We'll have to contact the landlord, obviously, and see whether they want to organise the repairs, or whether they'll want us to do it. And if so, we'll have to obtain quotes and—'

'So, it could be months?'

'Hopefully not that long. Thank goodness you had the presence of mind to turn off the water at the mains.'

'I didn't; one of the removal men did.'

The two men were currently sitting in the van, twiddling their thumbs. Beth could tell that they weren't amused.

'It prevented even more damage,' Zander said.

'Never mind that!' Beth cried. 'Where am I going to live?'

Zander paled. 'Oh, uh, well, I'll, um, have to check the landlord's insurance policy as to whether there's any contingencies built in for—'

Beth lost her patience. 'Don't bother. I'll stay with my daughter. Keep me updated as to when I can move back in. Not that I've actually moved in at all. And I don't expect you to chase me for rent when I'm not actually living there.'

'Of course not, Mrs Fairfax, although there may be—'

'Whatever you're about to say, don't.' Beth held up her hand. 'You've got a deposit and the first month's rent. You're not getting a penny more out of me until I've moved in.' That was the last word Beth intended to say on the matter.

She accompanied Zander to the door, locked it behind them, then handed him the keys.

'You've got my number,' she said, and marched over to the van.

The driver wound his window down. 'Where to, love?'

'Muddypuddle Lane. It's not far, just the other side of the village. You can follow me.'

Now I'm for it, she thought, as she got in her car and began to drive. She wasn't looking forward to the next couple of hours. Dulcie would be furious, and she had every right to be. Beth's life was going to be hell for a while. She just hoped that the repairs wouldn't take as long as she feared.

With the van tailing her, Beth drove slowly up the steep lane, wincing every time her little car encountered a pothole, and preying that her china wasn't being bounced around too much.

Bracing herself for a serious telling off, she turned into the yard, and didn't know whether to be relieved or disappointed when she saw that neither Dulcie's nor Otto's car were there, and guessed that no one was home.

To make sure, she knocked on the farmhouse door and tried the handle. It was locked. Beth waved to the driver to wait a sec and made her way over to the barn.

Apart from the rabbits, it was empty of animals. Perfect.

'You can unload everything into the barn,' she told the driver.

It was the only logical place for her furniture to go. It was dry, and if Otto could dig out some plastic sheeting or tarpaulin, it should be safe enough until she was able to move it into her new house.

It took less time to unload than to load, and half an hour later Beth was waving them off. Wishing she had a nice cup of tea, she sat herself down on the settee to wait. There was little else she could do.

After the excitement of the day, Beth had fallen asleep. The barn was surprisingly warm and cosy, and her settee had always been comfortable, so she was disorientated when she woke to the sound of an engine pulling into the yard.

Blinking owlishly, she heaved herself off the sofa, feeling stiff and not quite with it, knowing that she needed to sharpen up if she was to survive the next few minutes. Peeping warily around the open barn door, she saw Dulcie get out of Otto's car, and heard her say, 'That's my mother's car. What is she doing here?'

Otto also got out, looking as handsome as ever. Dulcie had done alright for herself, Beth thought with pride. He was a good bloke, was Otto, and Beth was comforted by his presence. He wouldn't let Dulcie get too mad with her. Hopefully.

'Mum? Where are you?'

'In here.' Beth emerged slowly.

'What are you doing in the barn? Why didn't you tell us you were coming?'

Beth didn't move, and Dulcie walked towards her. It was only when Dulcie got near enough to see inside the barn that she stopped, and her eyes widened.

'Mum, what's all that?'

'My furniture.'

'Why is it in my barn?'

'I had nowhere else to put it.'

Dulcie's eyes widened even further. 'Please don't tell me you've been evicted.'

'I haven't been evicted.'

'Thank goodness! For a moment—' Dulcie stopped. 'What's going on?'

'I've got something to tell you, but can I have a wee first? And I'm dying for a cuppa. Got any cake, Otto?'

Wordlessly Dulcie opened the farmhouse door and gestured for Beth to go inside. As she hurried into the downstairs loo, she could hear her daughter and Otto having a hushed conversation, but despite putting her ear to the toilet door, she couldn't make out what was being said.

Nothing good, probably.

She was quite subdued when she entered the kitchen to find a teapot on the table and a slice of cake waiting for her. Despite her bravado, she didn't have much of an appetite.

Dulcie was leaning against the sink, her arms folded. 'Well?'

'I wanted it to be a surprise,' Beth began, 'but there was a leak in the hot water tank and the living room ceiling came down, and I had to go somewhere so I came here. My stuff will be alright in the barn, won't it? I thought if Otto could find some tarpaulin, he could cover it over.'

'Mum, you're not making sense. Are you trying to say that you've had a leak, and the ceiling has come down?'

'I'm not *trying* to say it – I *am* saying it. That's exactly what's happened.' Beth poured tea into a mug and took a grateful sip. She was parched.

'But you've not got a hot water tank. You've had a combi boiler for years.' Dulcie's expression was one of puzzlement.

'My new house has got a back boiler and a hot water tank.'

'Your new house? Have you moved?'

'Not quite. I was supposed to move in today, but when I got there, I found the ceiling on the floor and a great big puddle in the middle of the room.'

'Mum, that's awful! What does your landlord say?'

'It's through an estate agent, and they say they'll fix it, but it could be a while.'

'Have they offered you alternative accommodation?'

'No. I don't believe there is any.'

'Surely, they must have something on their books? They can't leave you homeless.'

'They've got to check the landlord's insurance policy, apparently.'

'How long will that take?'

'No idea. So, can I stay here?' Beth saw Dulcie and Otto exchange glances. Clearly having her stay with them, wasn't at the top of their wish list.

'Of course you can,' Dulcie said.

'My stuff will be okay in the barn, won't it?'

'It will, Beth,' Otto said. 'I'm sure I've got something to cover it over. Do you want a hand bringing anything in?'

'In a minute. I'll eat my cake first.' Her appetite was coming back. Dulcie wasn't as put out as Beth had feared. Mind you, Dulcie didn't know the whole story yet.

'Where are you moving to, Mum? I'm assuming it's somewhere smaller.'

'It definitely is.'

'Good for you. I've been saying for ages that the house is too big for you. Is that why you were having a clear out?'

Beth nodded, her mouth full of cake. She hoped she didn't look as shifty as she felt.

'Is your new house in Bournville?'

Beth inhaled sharply and a crumb went down the wrong way. Coughing until she was all hot and bothered, it took her a moment to catch her breath. When she had, Dulcie was still looking at her expectantly.

'Not exactly. It's in Picklewick,' Beth mumbled.

Dulcie was silent. Eventually she said, *Where?*

'Picklewick.'

'That's what I thought you said. The house you're renting is in *Picklewick?*

'Yes.'

'Why?'

'I would have thought that was obvious. You're all here – except Jay. I miss you.'

'And you were supposed to be moving in today?'

'Yes.'

'When were you planning on telling us?' Dulcie's tone was frostier than the inside of a freezer.

'Today. This evening. When Nikki got home from school. I was going to ask if you'd like to pop in and see me.'

'You didn't think to mention it before now?'

'The time didn't seem right.'

'And you think *now* is the right time?'

'It wasn't supposed to happen like this.'

'I bet it wasn't.'

Beth got to her feet. 'I'll go get my cases.' There wasn't any point in continuing the conversation right now. She'd go to her room, have a lie down for a bit, and let Dulcie share the good news with her sisters. 'Am I in my usual bedroom?' she asked.

It was Dulcie's turn to look shifty. 'Not exactly.'

Beth winced as she heard her own words echoed back at her. 'Oh?'

Were they decorating? Or had Otto moved his office from the small fourth bedroom?

'You're in the bedroom at the back. The other is being used. Or it will be tomorrow.'

'By who?' Beth asked, her imagination running wild. She hoped the room wasn't being used because Maisie was moving back in. Beth had had such high hopes of Maisie and Adam's relationship working out. Such a shame.

'Walter.'

Walter? Wonderful! That was all she bloody needed.

'I can walk to the car,' Walter grumbled, as a nurse produced a wheelchair. He was supposed to sit in it for the journey from his hospital bed to the patient pick-up point outside the main door.

'Humour me,' the nurse said.

Walter inched his way forwards, turned slowly and sank into it with a grunt. He didn't want to admit it, but he was relieved that he wasn't expected to walk – or should he say 'hobble' – out of the hospital. Even with Otto to carry his bag and Dulcie hovering beside him, just going from the bed to the wheelchair had exhausted him. And a trip to the bathroom laid him low for a good couple of hours.

That damned nurse had been right: he *was* going to need some help. Which was why he would be staying with Otto and Dulcie for the duration. He would have someone to cook his meals and do his laundry, and, more importantly, make sure he didn't fall down the stairs. Negotiating them, both up and down, was going to be interesting, and he had a feeling he might be using his bottom for both manoeuvres. It wouldn't be pretty or graceful, but it would be the safest way.

Dulcie had suggested that they bring one of the beds down and put it in the living room, but Walter had flatly refused. As long as he took his time, he would be able to negotiate the stairs twice a day. And the room Dulcie had decided to put him in was the one nearest to the bathroom, so he wouldn't have such a trek if he needed to go to the loo in the middle of the night. At his age if he only got up once for a pee, he considered himself fortunate.

Armed with a printed list of dos and don'ts, a small box of painkillers and an appointment to visit the fracture clinic, Walter left the hospital with a sense of relief.

'Where's Peg?' he asked as Otto went to fetch the car, leaving him and Dulcie to wait by the main doors.

'At the farm.'

'I was hoping you might have brought her with you. I've missed her.'

'She's missed you, too. She hasn't settled at all, bless her.'

'She's never left on her own,' Walter said. The dog had been his constant companion since he had been forced to give up the farm. And when Otto had moved out of the cottage on Muddypuddle Lane and had gone to live with Dulcie at the farm, Walter had been glad of her company.

'She's not on her own,' Dulcie told him. She hesitated, and Walter's heart sank. Don't tell me Maisie and Adam have had a falling out, he prayed silently. It was none of his business and he certainly wouldn't say anything, but they'd seemed so well suited.

'My mum is with her.'

'Eh?'

'My mother. She's come to stay for a while.'

Walter's mouth dropped open. He hadn't been expecting that. No one had mentioned anything about Beth coming for a visit. The last thing he needed when he wasn't feeling himself, was Dulcie's flippin' mother.

197

He tried to keep his tone neutral as he said, 'That's nice. Is she staying long?'

'A few weeks.'

Damn. 'Is everything alright?'

Dulcie rolled her eyes and sighed. 'Where Mum is concerned nothing is ever alright. To cut a long story short, she's decided to downsize and is moving into a smaller house. She was due to move in yesterday, but when she arrived at the property there had been a leak and one of the ceilings had come down. So she's staying with us until the house is repaired.'

Walter prayed it wouldn't take long; hopefully she'd be gone in a week or two and he could spend the rest of the time at the farm in peace, not seeing her again until her Christmas visit, which was a good few months away.

'There's more,' Dulcie said. 'The house she's supposed to be moving into is in Picklewick. My mother is going to be living just down the road.'

Bloody marvellous, Walter thought. If anything was guaranteed to set his recovery back, it was that.

CHAPTER FOUR

Beth had made herself useful whilst Dulcie and Otto had been fetching Walter from the hospital. She had cleaned the kitchen, the downstairs loo, and the upstairs bathroom, and had put all her clothes away.

Eyeing the view from what was usually her bedroom but was now to be Walter's for the duration of his stay, she consoled herself with the knowledge that at least she could see up the mountain from the room she had been allocated. She couldn't see as far as Maisie and Adam's place, but it was a comfort knowing that her youngest child was just over the horizon.

During this time her phone had rung twice. The first call had been from Nikki, whose opening gambit had been a hissed, 'What the hell, Mum?' Apparently she'd heard the news, first from Dulcie who had sent her a message, then from Maisie who had tried to phone her when she had been in class and *then* sent her a message.

It seemed that Nikki wasn't pleased for two reasons. One, that Beth had kept it a secret ('You're as bad as Maisie. Scratch that, you're worse.') and two, because Maisie had phoned her during a lesson observation. Beth hadn't helped matters by telling

Nikki that if she was so concerned about receiving calls, she should have turned her phone off.

The comment hadn't gone down well. Nikki had used her 'teacher voice' and had told Beth that she would see her later. It had sounded like a threat.

Maisie had accused Beth of being unable to cut the apron strings, and that she needed to let Maisie have a life of her own. Trust Maisie to make it all about *her*. Maisie clearly still had some growing up to do. The only person who was pleased that she had moved to Picklewick was her grandson. Sammy had sent her a message with one word in it – 'Wicked'. She briefly wondered what he was doing using his phone during school (she knew it was strictly against the school's policies), but she let it go. She needed all the support she could get, even if it was from an eleven-year-old.

Peg, Walter's gentle Border collie, also seemed pleased to see her and, after Dulcie and Otto had left for the hospital, the dog had followed her from room to room, as though Beth was a rather peculiar sheep that needed rounding up. Beth didn't mind. She appreciated the company, and it was one more 'person' on her side.

After she had done the chores, she made a cup of tea and sat at the kitchen table to await Walter's arrival.

Beth heard him before she saw him. As usual, he was grumbling, but she supposed this time he had good reason. She had never broken a bone in her life (but then, she hadn't been prone to going up ladders), but she could imagine how inconvenient it must be. Painful, too. She shuddered at the thought of the metal pin they'd inserted into Walter's leg, and wondered whether he would beep when he went through airport security, and if so, would the hospital issue him with some kind of letter to explain.

Beth sat up straighter when the kitchen door banged open, and Walter limped in, flanked by Dulcie. She had her hands outstretched, as though expecting to catch him if he toppled over.

Walter didn't say a word when he saw her, but his lips tightened and Beth guessed he was as unhappy to see her as she was to see him. Living in the same house as him was going to be a challenge, she thought, consoling herself with the hope that his stay at the farmhouse would only be for a few days. As soon as they could see that he could cope on his own, Dulcie and Otto would surely send him home.

Moving slowly, Walter headed for one of the kitchen chairs and lowered himself into it with much grunting and face pulling. His leg was sticking out, and Beth hoped no one would trip over it.

Peg, the traitorous creature, had been waiting patiently by the door, and was now nosing her master, asking to be fussed. So much for Beth thinking that Peg was on her side. Maybe she could get a dog of her own...?

Nah, it would need walking come rain or shine, and although Beth would be happy to take a dog for a walk when it was fine, she wouldn't be too keen on having to take it out when it was hammering down. And then there was the hair everywhere, and the dog poo that would need picking up. On second thoughts, maybe she would get a cat. Cats were far less trouble – maximum gain for minimum effort.

Whilst all this was going through her mind, she was studying Walter. He didn't look well. 'Drawn' was the best way to describe him. His cheeks were gaunt and his eyes had sunk, and the skin on his face was almost as grey as his hair.

Beth found herself feeling sorry for him. The fall and the subsequent operation had taken its toll.

'Let me get you a cup of tea,' Dulcie said. 'Here, give me your coat.'

Beth watched her daughter fussing around him and wondered whether she should play nice and offer to help. 'I'll make it,' she said, getting to her feet.

Otto had disappeared upstairs with Walter's bag, but he wasn't up there long and when he came back down Beth asked him if he also wanted a cup of tea.

'Not for me thanks. I'm going to the cottage to pack a few things for Dad. Anything in particular you want me to bring, Dad?'

Walter reeled off a list of things he couldn't live without, and Otto headed off, leaving Beth, Dulcie and Walter to make small talk.

Walter shot the opening volley. 'I can't believe you just turned up here out of the blue.'

Beth narrowed her eyes as she poured boiling water into the teapot. So that's how he was going to play it. 'I can't believe you were up a ladder at your age,' she retorted.

'Anyone hungry?' Dulcie asked.

'No,' Beth said.

'Yes.' That was from Walter. 'The food in that hospital was dire.'

Dulcie said, 'If you want something quick, I could heat up some soup or make you an omelette.'

'I don't want to put you out,' Walter said.

Beth returned fire. 'You should have thought of that before you went up a ladder. And in slippers, too.'

'It was an accident,' he shot back. 'Unlike what you did. You could hardly call moving house and not telling anyone an *accident.*'

'What I do is none of your business.' Beth's voice was sharp. How dare he lecture her on what she should or shouldn't do.

'Ditto.'

'Ooh, get you and your fancy words. Been looking up the crossword answers, have you?'

'Don't be so childish.'

'It's better than being oldish.'

'Oldish?'

'Yeah, too old to go up a ladder, and too stupid to realise it.'

'Mum!' Dulcie was aghast.

'It's true. Anyway, he started it.' Beth glared at Walter.

Walter glared back.

Beth had gained a lot of experience in outglaring teenage daughters, and she smirked when Walter looked away first. When she noticed that Dulcie was glaring at *her,* Beth quickly rearranged her features.

'I'm not standing for this, Mum. Walter needs rest; not you goading him. If you can't behave yourself, you'll have to go.'

Beth gasped. 'Where?' Surely Dulcie wouldn't throw her own mother out.

'Maisie's static has three bedrooms. You can stay there until your new house is repaired.'

'No!' Beth cried. Maisie would never agree. And even if she did, a static caravan would be too cramped for three.

Dulcie was still glaring. 'Promise me you'll behave yourself?' She had her hands on her hips and looked as though she meant it.

Beth forced out a reluctant, 'Yes'

'Good.' Dulcie turned her attention back to Walter, and Beth felt a small degree of satisfaction that Dulcie was going to berate him too.

But she didn't. When Dulcie said, 'What's it to be Walter, soup or omelette?' Beth ground her teeth together to hold her irritation in check.

The next couple of weeks were going to be very long indeed.

Bloody hell, this was going to be worse than he anticipated, and he wasn't referring to his broken leg, either. Walter was referring to Beth. Why, oh why, did she have to rock up at the exact same time he was incapacitated? And it looked like she'd already sharpened her knives and wasn't averse to stabbing him with them. Talk about kicking a man when he was down.

He held the moral high ground though: climbing a ladder to see to his guttering himself because he didn't want to bother Otto, might have been misguided but it had been done with the best of intentions. He couldn't say the same for the stunt that Beth had pulled. Deceitful and underhand, that's what she was. Although he did concede that she had a stroke of bad luck with her ceiling coming down. If she had been able to move into her house in the village today, her actions wouldn't have had such annoying consequences.

Poor Dulcie. Walter felt very sorry for her. Not only did she have him and his broken leg to contend with (which he was deeply sorry about) but she now had her mother to put up with. The woman was a menace.

Abruptly, he felt exhausted. All he wanted was to crawl into his own bed in his cottage and sleep for a week, but his cottage was out of the question. To his chagrin, he was acutely aware that he needed help (the nurse had been right) and the only way he would get it was to stay with Otto and Dulcie for a while. Otto, the poor boy, had too much on his plate with the restaurant to be able to give him a great deal of assistance, but Dulcie worked from home, so she'd be able to keep an eye on him. Walter hoped he wouldn't put her out too much.

'I think I'll go for a lie down,' he said as soon as Otto returned with his things, but as he tried to get up, he didn't know how. He feared putting any weight on his plastered leg, and he couldn't lever himself up using just the one.

Shuffling awkwardly to the edge of the chair, he reached for his crutches and promptly knocked them over. Dismayed and humiliated, he could feel his face flushing, and if he hadn't been so damned cross about the whole thing, he had a horrible suspicion that he might have burst into tears.

Quietly Otto bent to retrieve the crutches, holding them in one hand whilst he offered the other to Walter, who took it gratefully. But even with his son's help, Walter found it a struggle to get to his feet, and he was even more irate and embarrassed by the time he was upright.

Gritting his teeth and looking straight ahead, he limped out of the kitchen. Ungainly and awkward, he realised that using the crutches was going to take some practice. They hurt his arms, and even the short journey from the kitchen to the foot of the stairs left him with aching wrists and hands.

Panting with the effort, Walter gazed upwards in dismay. The thirteen steps might as well be a thousand. The thought of trying to heave his old carcass up them made him want to weep.

'I can't do it,' he muttered, leaning against the wall to try to take some of the weight off his good leg.

'No problem, Dad; if you can't get to the bed, we'll bring the bed to you.'

'I don't want to be a nuisance.'

'You're not a nuisance.' Otto put an arm around his shoulders.

'I'm sorry, son.'

'You've nothing to be sorry for.'

'I'm causing you nothing but trouble. It's not the first time you've had to bail me out.'

'Stop that right now. I'm not going to put up with you feeling sorry for yourself. Accidents happen.'

'I should never have gone up that ladder.'

'Too right you shouldn't, but what's done is done. Look on the bright side – it could have been a lot worse.'

Walter had been trying not to think about that.

Otto continued, 'Anyway, it'll only be for a few weeks. You'll be back on your feet in no time – excuse the pun. Let's get you into the living room, then I'll bring the bed down.'

Walter allowed himself to be guided into the lounge, where he sank gratefully onto the sofa with a grunt. Otto handed him the TV's remote control and gave his shoulder a squeeze before returning to the kitchen. Walter couldn't hear what was being said, but he could guess. Otto and Dulcie would be kind, he had no doubt. But he couldn't say the same for Beth. And even if she didn't say it aloud, she would be thinking it.

For the umpteenth time, Walter lamented that Beth was witnessing his frailty. He was a proud man (stubbornly so, Otto reckoned) and he hated her seeing him so helpless. It made him feel rather vulnerable, and the last person he wanted to show any weakness to was Beth Fairfax. Knowing her, she would take advantage and go for the jugular.

As he sat there, listening to the sound of Otto manoeuvring a bed across the landing, Walter wondered why he and Dulcie's mother didn't get on.

Ah, that was easy – she was annoying. But he didn't look too closely at why he found her annoying because it didn't matter. What mattered was that, aside from the next couple of weeks, he was going to see an awful lot more of her now that she would be living in Picklewick. He wouldn't simply be able to stroll up the lane and pop in to have a cuppa with Dulcie, because *she* might be there. And whenever Dulcie and Otto invited him for lunch or supper, in the interests of fairness they would have to invite her too.

For Walter, with Beth on the scene, life wouldn't be the same again.

What a palaver, Beth grumbled to herself, as she carefully crept down the steep stairs the following morning. It was incredibly early, but she had woken up to go to the loo and hadn't been able to go back to sleep. Typical.

She could have done with a couple hours more, because she'd been awake half the night. And that was Walter's fault. Twice she'd heard Otto go downstairs, presumably to check that the old man hadn't fallen out of bed. Or, worse, fallen over when he went to the bathroom.

The fuss if that had happened, didn't bear thinking about. Yesterday had been bad enough.

As Beth tiptoed through the dining room and into the kitchen (she didn't want to risk waking Walter), she pursed her lips as she remembered how Dulcie had fluffed pillows and smoothed the duvet before Otto had sent everyone out of the room so he could help his father change into his pyjamas to have a nap.

What was wrong with falling asleep in the chair like a normal pensioner, Beth wanted to know. She often napped in a chair, but she didn't feel the need to change into her nightie to do so.

Pouring boiling water into a mug, she mashed the tea bag against the side, then added milk, wincing at the rattle of the glass milk bottles as she closed the fridge door.

When she sat down at the kitchen table, she took a sip and grimaced. Ergh! Goat's milk! She had forgotten that was what Dulcie and Otto drank now, although they must have bought normal milk because she'd had a couple of proper cups of tea yesterday. No doubt the cow's milk would have been bought especially for Walter.

Beth, slightly ashamed of her uncharitable thoughts, tried not to feel bitter. If Dulcie had known she was coming, she was sure that Dulcie would also have stocked up on normal milk for her.

Recognising that some of her negative feelings regarding Walter stemmed from him living so close to the farm whilst she lived so far away, Beth resolved to try harder to be nicer to him. With her now living in the village (or she would be as soon as the repairs were done on her house) she had no reason to feel as resentful.

The remainder of her negative feelings were due to him simply being annoying. She had never met such an irritating man. If she said the sun would come up tomorrow, he'd argue that it wouldn't.

She wondered how he was feeling this morning. Like a right idiot probably. What seventy-something bloke in his right mind would venture up a ladder whilst wearing slippers? He had been an accident waiting to happen.

Beth drank her tea and debated whether to poke her head around the door and ask if he'd like a cup. Then she decided against it, in case he needed the loo. She didn't mind making him a cuppa or fetching him something from the kitchen, but she drew the line at helping him to the bathroom, even if she didn't have to accompany him inside. And Walter seemed to need to go an awful lot. No sooner had he been helped into bed, he'd decided he needed the toilet, so Otto had to help him out of it and help him to get to the loo, then help him get back into bed. For Walter, a simple trip to the toilet involved an awful lot of helping, and right now Beth didn't feel up to it.

She suspected she never would.

However, in the interest of being nice (or *nicer*, at least) Beth vowed to help where she felt able.

Before too long, she heard someone stirring upstairs and shortly afterwards Dulcie appeared, bleary-eyed and yawning.

'I'm not going to ask if you had a good night,' Beth said, 'because I know you didn't. How many times did Walter get Otto out of bed?'

As soon as the words were out of her mouth, Beth could have kicked herself. So much for her vow to be nicer. But how could she be nice when her daughter looked exhausted?

Dulcie didn't reply; instead she asked, 'Do you want another cup of tea?'

Beth leapt to her feet, or as close to leaping as she got at her age. 'I'll make it. You sit down. Can I get you some breakfast?'

Dulcie shuddered. 'No thanks. Too early for me. I'll have something in a bit. Is Walter awake?'

'No idea.'

'I don't think I'll disturb him. We'll let him sleep, shall we? He needs his rest.'

What about me? Beth thought. *Don't I need my rest too?* She'd had a traumatic couple of days, what with the stress of moving and the subsequent disappointment. But when her inner voice told her to stop being so selfish, she had to admit it was justified. She *was* being selfish. Jealous, too, because Dulcie never showed *her* such concern.

It made her feel rather sad.

She didn't expect thanks for anything she'd done for her kids, but a bit of consideration now and again wouldn't go amiss.

Telling herself that things would pick up when she was living in her own house, Beth tried to look on the bright side: she could now see her girls whenever she wanted (within reason, of course), and she hoped to soon make friends in the village.

She could also be involved in the farm, because living in Picklewick meant that she would no longer feel left out. The fact that Walter would also be involved was a cross she would simply have to grin and bear.

'I can manage.' Walter sounded as cross as he felt, despite it being patently obvious that he wasn't able to manage the stairs without help.

Otto regarded him patiently, and Walter felt a stab of remorse. He ought not to be so grumpy, but he couldn't stop himself. He'd had a dreadful night's sleep, partly because his leg was giving him grief, partly because he hadn't been able to settle in a strange bed, and also because he kept fretting that he would need the loo and wouldn't get there in time.

It had taken him ages to heave himself out of bed and walk out the back to the downstairs bathroom, and that was *with* Otto's help. So he'd lain there worrying, until he'd worried himself into needing to go. Getting up once in the night was normal: three times was a damned nuisance. And it hadn't helped that Otto had kept coming downstairs to check on him.

Between one thing and another, Walter had only managed an hour's sleep here and an hour there.

He used his good leg and his arms to haul his backside onto the next step. Then he sat there for a couple of seconds, panting.

'Are you sure you won't have a shower?' Otto asked. 'We can wrap your cast in cling film and pop a bag over it.'

'I can't stand for long enough, can I?'

'I'm sure we can find something for you to sit on. A plastic garden chair perhaps?'

'It won't fit.'

'Something else then…'

'Like what?'

'I don't know. I'll have to have a think.'

'Don't take too long – I want a bath today, not next week,' Walter snapped. He knew he'd gone too far when Otto's eyes narrowed and his jaw clenched. Hastily, Walter attempted some damage control. None of this was Otto's fault, and it wasn't fair to take it out on him, especially since Otto was doing his best.

'I'll have a strip wash in the downstairs bathroom,' he said with a resigned sigh.

'Good idea.'

Walter eased himself down the stair he had hauled himself up just a moment ago, and struggled to his feet. His anger wasn't aimed at Otto; it was aimed at himself. What on earth had made him think he could climb a ladder at his age? Just look at where his idiocy had got him. Not only was he unable to have a bath or sleep in his own bed, he had to put up with Beth

Fairfax to boot. She had a front row seat, and was currently sitting in the kitchen, smirking at his discomfort as he made his slow, awkward way to the loo, Otto hovering behind him, just in case.

Damn and blast her! The only way things could get any worse, was if Beth was the one who was accompanying him.

CHAPTER FIVE

Beth could have predicted Maisie's first words, so when her youngest cried, 'Mum! How could you!' she wasn't surprised.

'I thought you'd be pleased,' she said, knowing she was poking an angry wasp's nest but unable to help the sarcastic reply.

'You're joking, right?' Maisie gave her an incredulous look.

Beth tried not to show how hurt she felt. Maisie could at least pretend. Huffing, she stared out of the kitchen window. The kitchen was a nice enough place, but it wasn't where she would have wanted to spend the day. But with Walter hogging the living room, she didn't want to sit in there and have to listen to his sarcastic sniping. She wondered whether she should phone the estate agent and hurry them along. She hadn't been at the farm a day yet and already she was near the end of her tether. And Maisie wasn't helping.

'I can't believe you were going to move into a house in Picklewick without telling us,' Maisie continued. 'When did you arrange—?' She gasped and clapped a hand to her mouth. 'I *did* see your car in the village a couple of weeks ago! It wasn't the frequency effect, or whatever Walter called it.' She turned to Dulcie. 'I *knew* it was her car.'

Beth continued to stare out of the window, unable to think of anything to say in her defence. She was guilty as charged.

Maisie let out an exasperated sigh. 'Why didn't you discuss it with us first? Or at least, tell us what you were planning?'

'I wanted it to be a surprise.' Beth's voice was small. She really, really should have told them when the idea first came to her, but she had been too scared that they would have talked her out of it.

'It was a surprise alright,' Maisie grumbled. 'No wonder you've been busy *de-cluttering*.' She narrowed her eyes. 'What have you done with all my stuff?'

Beth was confused. 'What stuff? You took everything with you when you moved into the caravan. Your bedroom was empty, apart from three mouldy plates and a bed with broken slats. Did you use it as a trampoline?'

'My cheerleading stuff. It was in the attic.'

'It wasn't.' Beth was positive. 'I got rid of it years ago.'

'You didn't! I wanted to keep it.'

'Is that so? You haven't thought about it in years, have you?'

'No, but that doesn't alter the fact that I wanted to keep it.'

'I sold the whole lot, twirly baton and all, to a woman six doors down. The money I got for it paid for your school trip to Norfolk.'

'Oh, okay.' Maisie visibly deflated.

Beth had always made sure her kids never went without, and if that meant flogging a few bits and pieces, then that's what she did.

Dulcie hadn't said a word from the moment her sister had arrived, but now she said, 'Tea, Maisie? Before you see to the goats?'

Maisie nodded and took a seat at the table. 'Where will you be living?'

Some of Beth's tension eased. 'Hazelnut Road.'

'What's the house like?'

'Two up, two down, small garden. Living room ceiling currently on the living room floor.'

'So I heard. When will it be fixed?'

'Soon, I hope.' Beth hesitated. 'I won't be a nuisance, honest. I won't visit unless I'm invited.' She ignored Dulcie's snort. It wasn't Beth's fault that she felt the only way she would get to see her girls at Easter had been to rock up at the farm unannounced. If she'd waited for an invitation, she would still be waiting.

Dulcie put a fresh pot of tea in the centre of the table and got the milk out of the fridge.

'How's Walter?' Maisie asked, and Dulcie clapped a hand to her mouth.

'Oops, I'd forgotten Walter. Mum, do you mind asking him if he'd like a cuppa? And I don't think he's had any breakfast yet. Could you see what he wants? I've got to get on – I start work at nine, and Otto needs to be at the restaurant soon.'

Beth heaved a resigned sigh. She didn't relish running around after Walter, but if it helped Dulcie she would do it. At least Dulcie and Maisie didn't seem too cross with her now that they'd got over the initial shock. As long as she survived the next few weeks living in the same house as Walter, she had a feeling that moving to Picklewick might be the best thing she'd ever done.

Walter could hear voices coming from the kitchen and realised that Maisie was berating her mother. He didn't blame her. If he was Maisie, he'd be cross with Beth too.

But when his conscience reminded him that he had been no better when he'd hidden the farm's financial problems from Otto, he felt a bit guilty for being so judgemental. He had acted far worse, hiding the situation for months, until the stress had put him in hospital and forced Otto to give up his lucrative job as one of London's top chefs.

So Walter honestly didn't have a leg to stand on. Beth relocating to Picklewick without informing her family was small fry compared to what he had done. Maybe he should cut her some slack.

But cutting her some slack didn't make her any less irritating or abrasive. She rubbed him up the wrong way, and he suspected he did the same for her. Speak of the devil…

Beth's face appeared around the living room door. 'Tea? And Dulcie wants to know what you want for breakfast.'

'I'll have a cup, if there's one in the pot. But tell her not to bother with breakfast. I can make my own.'

'Pft! How are you going to do that without any hands?'

'I've got hands.' He waved them in the air. 'See?' Was she really as daft as she sounded?

'They'll be holding onto your crutches,' she told him.

She had a point. 'Other people manage.' He wasn't sure how, but they must do.

'If you think you can fry yourself an egg, be my guest.'

'I don't want a fried egg.'

'What *do* you want?'

'Toast.'

'One slice or two?'

'Two, but I can do it myself.'

'Dulcie keeps her toaster in the cupboard next to the sink. Good luck with bending down to get that out and don't blame me if you fall over.'

'I won't fall over.'

'Look—' She moved further into the room and put her hands on her hips. 'Stop being such a stubborn old git and let me make you some toast. It's no bother. It'll be more bother if you fall and break your other leg.'

'I won't fall,' he repeated. She was right though; until he got the hang of those crutches, he was a danger to himself. It didn't help that he felt as weak as a kitten and utterly exhausted. 'Not too much butter, and a dab of marmalade wouldn't go amiss,' he relented.

'There, that wasn't so hard, was it?'

Actually, it had been torture admitting, even tacitly, that he needed help from Beth. At least he was out of bed and dressed (thanks to Otto), which made him feel less of a patient and more of a guest.

Beth returned a few minutes later with a plate of hot, buttered toast and a mug of tea. Thankfully she didn't decide to keep him company, so he ate his breakfast in peace whilst watching morning TV. But eventually he needed the loo and the thought of Beth's eyes on him as he made his way through the kitchen, got him cross all over again.

Before that though, he had to get out of the chair. Determined not to call for help, he shuffled his bottom closer to the edge of the seat and positioned his good foot as near to the chair as possible. It took him three goes before he managed to get to his feet, and by the time he was upright sweat was beading his brow and trickling down his back. But he'd done it!

Unfortunately that was where it fell apart. As he reached for his crutches, he managed to knock them over. They fell to the floor with a clatter which brought Dulcie and Beth running.

Dulcie got to him first, bending down to pick them up. She held onto his elbow to steady him, as he slid his arms into them.

'You get back to work,' Beth told Dulcie. 'I'll sort Walter out.'

'I don't need sorting.'

'I think you'll find you do.'

Yeah, he could guess what kind of sorting she would like to do to him.

With the crutches in position, he hopped forwards, his progress slow and hesitant. Despite the rubber ends, Walter was scared they would slip and he'd fall, as Beth had predicted. Now that she'd put the idea in his head, he couldn't shift it. Thanks, Beth.

As he gingerly hopped and swung his way through the dining room, he was all too aware of Beth inches from his elbow, ready to catch him should the worst happen. What use would she be if he did topple over, was anyone's guess. He was more likely to take her down with him and Dulcie would then have two patients on her hands, not one.

'No need to stand so close,' he hissed. Dulcie was on a call, headphones on, her eyes focused on the computer screen.

'There's no point in me being four feet away, is there?'

She was so close Walter could smell her perfume. Or maybe it was her shampoo or the washing powder she used. Whatever it was, he liked it.

Dulcie shot them a look and put her finger to her lips.

'I don't need you to accompany me to the toilet,' Walter insisted.

'Don't be stubborn. Otto had to take you this morning.'

'That's because I wasn't used to the crutches.'

'And you are *now?*' Beth sounded incredulous.

'I'm getting the hang of them,' he insisted.

'Shh!' Dulcie was frowning and shaking her head.

Beth said, 'Get a move on, you're disturbing Dulcie.'

'I'm going as fast as I can. And you're the one who's disturbing her, not me.'

'Excuse me, for a second,' Dulcie said, and removed her headphones. 'Do you mind? I'm trying to deal with a customer complaint here.'

'See?' Walter hissed. 'I told you that you're disturbing her.'

Dulcie huffed. 'It's both of you. Please keep the noise down. If you want to bicker, do it in the living room – quietly.'

'I don't want to bicker,' Beth said. 'He started it.'

'You sound like Sammy,' Walter retorted.

'Better than sounding like a miserable old codger.'

'I'm only miserable because you make me miserable.'

'Mum! Walter! *Stop it.* If you don't keep the noise down, I swear I'll go and work at the restaurant and leave the pair of you to slug it out on your own.'

Walter was immediately contrite. 'Sorry, Dulcie.' He stared at Beth, who glared stonily at him before adding her own apology.

Walter carried on walking (if you could call it walking) and managed to get as far as the bathroom without pausing. Once inside, he bolted the door and leant against it.

His shoulders were sore, his arms were aching, and so was his good leg. Being injured was no joke when you were his age, and he briefly wished he had accepted the hospital's offer to refer him for assessment for a wheelchair. But, then again, he would never get a wheelchair through the farmhouse's narrow doorways.

There was nothing for it, he would have to get used to the crutches. Short dabs, every so often, would give him a bit of practice without overdoing it. But right now, making it to the loo and back was practice enough. Maybe he'd feel a bit stronger tomorrow.

And maybe pigs might fly. He was kidding himself if he thought he would bounce back in a matter of days. It was going to take a couple of weeks. He hated having to admit it, but the fall and the operation had taken it out of him, and he felt he was almost back to where he'd started when he'd suffered the collapse last year.

Almost, but not quite. Mentally, he was much stronger than he had been, and he had Otto and Dulcie to thank for that. His broken leg was a setback, that was all, and once it was mended he would soon be back to his old self. He'd learnt his lesson though – no more climbing ladders.

But if he couldn't keep busy with DIY, he would have to find something else to occupy him, otherwise he would go mad with boredom. And although he had Peg to keep him company, he was often lonely. He just wished he knew what he could do about it.

Beth hated being at a loose end, but with the living room being out of bounds (there was no way Beth was going to join Walter to watch the nonsense that was on daytime telly), and with Dulcie needing peace and quiet in the dining room, Beth didn't know what to do with herself.

If she had been in her own house, she would have run the vacuum cleaner round and done a bit of dusting, but knowing that she mustn't make too much noise, she satisfied herself with giving the kitchen the once over (despite it being spotless) and bleaching the downstairs bathroom. Then she made yet another cup of tea. If she drank any more of the stuff, she'd need to use the loo as much as Walter; although she strongly suspected he was only doing it to wind her up.

Unable to sit still any longer, Beth rinsed out her mug and went outside. She would check on her furniture, then maybe she would go for a stroll.

True to his word, Otto, the dear boy, had found some tarpaulin and a length of plastic, and had covered all her bits and pieces. Thankfully, the barn was dry and there was no rain forecast, so she needn't worry. And with any luck, she would be moving into her own home before too long.

She spent a few minutes watching the rabbits hop around their runs, and even stroked a soft ear or two. Then she wandered over towards the goats' field. But before she got there she bumped into Maisie, who was coming out of the pasteurisation shed. She had Peg with her, and Beth was flattered when the dog greeted her like a long-lost friend.

'She's really taken to you,' Maisie observed. 'I didn't think you liked dogs.'

'Because we never had one when you were a kid?'

'We didn't have any pets.'

'There was a good reason for that. Looking after you lot was enough.'

'I would have helped.'

Beth raised her eyebrows.

'Okay, maybe I wouldn't have helped as much as I thought I would.'

'You wouldn't have helped at all. None of you would. You'd have made all the right noises in the beginning, but after a couple of weeks it would have fallen on me to look after it.'

Maisie gave her an apologetic look. 'You're probably right.'

'I know I am.'

'I'm sorry I gave you such a hard time earlier. But you've got to admit, turning up with all your worldly possessions yesterday was a bit of a shock.'

Beth bit her lip. 'It was more of a shock for Dulcie.'

'And Walter,' Maisie added, with a grin. 'I wasn't expecting him to be here.'

'Neither was he. From what Otto told me, his dad had expected to go home and pick up where he left off. But at his age, a broken leg isn't something you can shake off easily.'

'Don't you mean at *your* age?' Maisie teased. 'He's only a year or so older than you.'

'Four, actually, and thanks for reminding me.'

'You don't look your age,' Maisie said.

'Flatterer. What do you want?'

'Take Peg for a walk for me?'

'I might have known.'

'Please? I promised Walter.'

'Oh, well, if you promised *Walter.*'

'Don't be so mean. He would take her himself if he could.'

Beth knew Maisie was right. Walter worshipped that dog. 'Go on then,' she said. 'I'll take her down the lane for a stroll.'

'Thanks, Mum. It means I can get on with soap making.' She looked hopeful. 'You could always give me a hand with that, if you like?'

'No thanks! I'll stick to taking Peg for a walk.'

Beth called the dog to her and had just turned away when Maisie asked, 'What have you got against Walter, anyway?'

Beth didn't answer, because she didn't honestly know.

Beth looked at the pained expression on Walter's face as he thanked her for taking Peg for a walk.

'You're welcome,' she said sweetly. 'Peg's a poppet.' Unlike her owner, she thought, but didn't say.

'How far did you go?'

'Only down the lane and back.' Beth helped herself to the mashed potato she had cooked for everyone's tea. And by 'everyone' she meant herself, Dulcie and Walter, because Otto was at the restaurant. If he hadn't been, he wouldn't have allowed her anywhere near the stove.

Beth had enjoyed feeling useful though, and seeing the way Dulcie and Walter were devouring their food, she assumed she hadn't done too bad a job. It was rather tasty, she thought; gravy made with the juice from the sausages and from frying onions was a taste sensation. She'd added a bit of swede to the mash, and was serving carrots and peas with it.

'I bumped into Lena. She was asking after you, Walter. She says to tell you that Amos will pop up to see you in a couple of days.' Beth had met Lena, Amos's other half, a couple of times and liked her immensely. It would be nice to have another woman of roughly the same age around, and Beth was hoping that Lena would carry through her suggestion of, 'You must pop in for a coffee when you're settled.'

She fully intended to throw herself into village life and make as many friends as she could.

Walter muttered, 'I don't want him to see me like this.'

'Like what?' Beth asked. She genuinely wanted to know. People broke bones every day – what was so special about Walter's broken leg?

'Helpless,' Walter replied.

'Hopeless, more like,' Beth muttered under her breath, earning herself a sharp look from her daughter.

'You're not helpless,' Dulcie said in a no-nonsense tone.

'What do you call it then?'

'A little less able than usual.'

Walter snorted. 'A lot less.'

'You managed to get out of the chair by yourself a couple of times this afternoon, and you're walking so much better on your crutches.'

'I still can't get upstairs by myself,' he grumbled. 'I want my own bed. I don't like sleeping downstairs; it's not natural.'

'It's unavoidable,' Dulcie soothed. 'And it'll only be for a few weeks.'

'I bet I could manage my own stairs. They're nowhere near as steep as yours. I'd be able to have a bath, too.'

Dulcie put her knife and fork down and looked him square in the eye. 'Walter, you can't go home just yet. You know that.'

'I bet I could.'

'You couldn't even make yourself some toast this morning,' she pointed out.

This is like being at Wimbledon, Beth thought. She'd never been and didn't want to, but she'd seen enough clips on the telly of people swivelling their heads from side to side as they followed the ball, and Beth was doing the same thing. She wondered who would win. Her money was on Dulcie, if only because Walter would need a lift to his cottage: he would never make it down the hill on his own.

A wicked thought entered her head. Perhaps she could offer to take him home? Then she hurriedly dismissed it. Dulcie would never forgive her, and neither would Otto. Besides, if anything bad were to happen to Walter because he'd returned home before he was able to look after himself properly, she wouldn't forgive herself either. He might be a royal pain in the backside, but she didn't want any harm to come to him.

Walter growled, '*She*—' He jabbed his fork in Beth's direction, and Beth flinched. 'Didn't give me the opportunity to find out.'

'Have a go now, why don't you?' Beth glared at him.

'I will, after I've finished my tea.' He jabbed the fork into a piece of sausage and shovelled it into his mouth, then chewed vigorously.

'Look, Walter,' Dulcie said. 'We're not being deliberately awkward. We care about you, and we want to make sure you can cope on your own before we take you home.'

He sighed, pushing his empty plate away. Having a broken leg and being cross about it hadn't affected his appetite, Beth noticed. She was pleased he'd enjoyed her cooking, though.

He said, 'I know you care, but I need to be in my own home.'

'This used to be your home, can't it be your home again for the time being?'

'No. It's yours and Otto's.' His voice was firm. 'It's not mine. There's been too many changes.'

'Oh, Walter, I'm so sorry.' Beth saw that Dulcie had tears in her eyes.

He said, 'You've nothing to be sorry for. It's only natural you wanted to make the place yours.'

'It's yours, too, Walter. It always will be.'

'That's where you're wrong, my lovely girl. My house is the cottage down the lane now. And I want to return to it.'

'Walter, I—'

He slapped his palm down on the table, making Beth jump. 'Damn it, Dulcie, I'm old enough and ugly enough to know what's best for me.'

Beth snorted, disagreeing with both parts of that statement. Old didn't necessarily mean wise, or even sensible. And he certainly wasn't ugly. He wasn't bad looking at all, despite his face being on the rugged side. It must be from all those years working outdoors.

'What you need is a housekeeper,' Beth said.

'Are you offering?'

'Not likely. I couldn't think of anything worse than listening to you carping, like you did today. On and on, grizzle, grizzle, moan, moan.'

Dulcie was staring at her, her gaze intense.

'What?' Beth demanded.

'Mum, you're a genius.'

'I am?'

'Hear me out,' Dulcie began, and Beth's spirits sank. Nothing good ever followed those three little words. Dulcie said, 'Being Walter's housekeeper is a great idea. He would be happier, and you would be doing Otto and me a massive favour.'

Beth was shaking her head. 'No, definitely not. No way!' Could she be any clearer? 'Over my dead body.'

'That could be arranged,' Walter muttered. 'There is no way that woman is staying in my house.'

Dulcie smiled at him. 'Even if it means you can stay there too?'

'Don't I get any say in this?' Beth demanded hotly.

'Of course you do. If you don't feel you can look after Walter in his own house, you can help look after him here. But can you keep the noise down when you're doing it? One of my callers thought there was a domestic going on and asked if they should call the police.'

Beth glowered at her. Hadn't she been helping already? And what thanks had Walter given her? None, that's what. He'd done nothing but complain, and whine, and——

An idea struck her. Walter in his own home would be a less miserable Walter. If he stayed here he would continue to gripe, and she didn't think she could face another day of him carping. And once he was back in his cottage, she would do her utmost to convince Dulcie and Otto that he could manage on his own. Then she could move back into the farmhouse and enjoy some peace and quiet until her house was ready for her.

The surprise on Walter's face when she said, 'Okay, I'll do it,' was the highlight of her day.

CHAPTER SIX

On the one hand, it was a relief to be in his own home. On the other, Walter was in it with Beth. He didn't know whether to laugh or weep, and was hovering on the verge of hysteria despite having been home for only a couple of hours.

Walter had wanted to leave the farmhouse immediately after he'd finished his sausage and mash (he would say that for Beth, she was a decent cook), but Dulcie had refused. In the end, he'd stayed there another night, and Otto had brought him and Beth to the cottage this morning.

His son hadn't been happy about it, but he'd not been able to put up much of an argument considering Beth was going to be staying here with him. How long, remained to be seen. If Walter had his way, she would be gone by the end of the week. All he had to do was to prove that he could make himself a sandwich and wasn't in danger of falling over when he put his trousers on.

Beth would be sleeping in Otto's old room, and he could hear her pottering around in there now. She had brought a case with her, but he hoped she wasn't bothering to unpack it, as she would only have to repack it in a day or so.

Anxious to prove that he didn't need her help, Walter eased himself into the kitchen, Peg close behind.

The collie seemed equally as happy to be home, although the traitorous little madam seemed just as happy to have Beth here. He was sure that Peg would soon change her mind the first time Beth yelled at her – which was bound to happen. Beth didn't strike him as much of a dog lover, and she had yet to experience the joys of picking up poop or bathing a dog who had rolled in something nasty.

Walter leant a crutch against the fridge door and used his free hand to remove the milk. A careful swivel and he was able to put the bottle on the counter. Pleased with his progress so far, he carried on with his tea-making, remembering to retrieve the crutch. So far, so good.

Then he realised he wouldn't be able to carry his mug into the living room, because he hadn't yet mastered being able to walk with just one crutch. Which meant that until he did, he would either have to eat and drink standing in the kitchen, or rely on someone (Beth) to carry it in for him.

Beth came downstairs at the exact moment he decided to give simultaneous tea-carrying and walking on one crutch a go, and managed to slop it everywhere. To his chagrin, she didn't notice the wet floor and stepped in the little puddle. Her foot skidded, her leg went from under her, and she almost fell.

Righting herself, she glared at him, taking everything in with one scornful glance. 'What are you doing?' she demanded. 'I could have broken my neck, you silly man.'

She snatched the mug out of his hand, spilling the rest of the tea, and put it down on the countertop with more force than was necessary.

Walter winced. 'I was making tea.'

'Making a mess, more like.' She tore off a couple of sheets of kitchen roll and bent to mop up the spill.

Walter glared at the top of her head, feeling useless. He couldn't even make a cup of tea without incident, so what hope did he have of preparing a meal?

Then he told himself off for being so negative. He could have drunk it standing in the kitchen, and if he had, he wouldn't have spilt it. However, standing for more than a few minutes made his good leg ache, but the way around that was to ask Beth to bring one of the dining chairs into the kitchen. Problem solved!

Mostly.

Eating his dinner whilst balancing a plate on his knee wouldn't be easy, (the chair wasn't high enough to be able to eat at the worktop), but he was sure there must be a tray around here somewhere. And if not, Beth could pop into the village and buy him one.

Beth straightened up and put the sodden kitchen roll in the bin. 'Go sit down, you daft old sod. I'll fetch you a cup of tea.'

'Can you bring a chair into the kitchen first?'

She didn't move. 'What's the magic word?'

'Eh?'

'Haven't you got *any* manners?'

'Oh, I see. *Please.*' His sarcastic emphasis didn't go unnoticed, but he ignored her arched brow. A momentary standoff ensued, but Beth gave in first and went to fetch the chair.

'Where shall I put it?'

He pointed to a corner. 'There will be good.'

Plonking it down, she said, 'What do you want it for, anyway?'

When he explained and she nodded to show she understood, he knew they were on the same page: she wanted him to be self-sufficient as much as he.

It was lunchtime and Beth was hungry. Walter must be too, but she couldn't work out how to use this blimmin' oven. It had taken her long enough to realise that there wasn't a kettle, and that the curved tap beside the sink dispensed boiling water as well as ice cold.

Otto's doing, she surmised. He liked his gadgets, being a chef, but all she hoped was that she wasn't expected to use any of them.

Giving up on the stove for the time being, she decided to make them both a sandwich, then she'd work out what they could have for their tea, and if she needed to go shopping she could pop into the village.

She also wanted to give the cottage a good clean. On the surface it was tidy and looked clean enough, but it wasn't up to Beth's standards and if she was to live here for a few days, she didn't intend to live in muck.

Well, what could you expect from an old chap who lived on his own, she mused as she bustled to and from the fridge, taking out the makings of a cheese and pickle sandwich. She was pleased to see that he used real butter, not the chemical-infused rubbish that the supermarkets tried to pass off as butter. And he had proper milk too, although the date was up today, so she would have to buy more soon. The bread wasn't as fresh as she liked, either. She would go shopping tomorrow, she decided. Today she would clean.

Sandwiches made, she took them into the living room and placed them on the table. The two of them ate in silence, Walter sneaking Peg the odd morsel, and Beth made a note to remember to turn the telly on in future. Mindless daytime TV would be better than listening to Walter chewing.

He did manage to force out a 'thank you' after he'd finished eating, so that was something. Her sarcastic, 'You're welcome,' earned her a sharp look.

Leaving Walter to his crossword puzzle, she took the empty plates into the kitchen and began to clean up. After about half an hour, during which Beth had run several bowlfuls of hot water and had cleaned out most of the cupboards, she became aware that she was being watched.

Walter looked thunderous. 'What are you doing?' he demanded.

Beth was on her hands and knees, the contents of his saucepan cupboard spread out on the floor around her, scrubbing vigorously at a rusty mark marring the white melamine shelf.

'Ballet dancing. What does it look like I'm doing?'

'Interfering.'

'Somebody has to. This place is a disgrace.'

'I find that offensive.'

'Yeah, so do I – that's why I'm giving everything a good wipe over.'

'Unbelievable. I thought you were here to help. Peg needs a walk and Flossie, Princess and Toffee need checking.'

'I'm not your servant, you know,' Beth retorted. The cheek of the man! She was doing her best to help and he was ordering her around. 'Fine.'

She gathered the pans together and shoved them noisily back into the cupboard. The clatter brought Peg running into the kitchen, barking loudly.

'Now see what you've done,' Walter said. 'You've frightened my dog.'

Peg didn't look frightened, but Beth was instantly repentant. The poor creature had enough to put up with having Walter as her owner; she didn't need Beth scaring the living daylights out of her.

Beth stomped into the hall to fetch her shoes and as she was putting them on, she said, 'What am I supposed to be checking?' Beth had seen Walter's pet sheep and the two goats belonging to the stables, from the window. They looked fine.

'I always checked my flock every morning.'

'Yes, but what did you check *for?*'

'That none were injured or ailing, that one of them hadn't got caught in a fence, that they weren't having difficulty lambing...'

Beth was horrified. '*Lambing?*'

'It was an example. None of them are pregnant. It's the wrong time of year.'

'Why mention it?'

'As I said, it was an example.'

'I don't need to check: they look fine. None of them are caught in a fence.'

'How about limping?'

'The only thing limping around here is you.'

He pursed his lips. 'Very funny. Can you check anyway? They might need their feet looking at.'

Beth put her hands on her hips. 'I am *not* looking at their feet.'

'I don't expect you to. Amos or Petra will see to it.'

'So why don't you ask *them* to check the animals?'

'They're busy.'

'And I'm not?'

'No, you're interfering.'

'We're back to that, are we? Come on Peg, let's go for a walk and leave your ungrateful master to stew in his own juice.'

Honestly, some people! She would have thought he'd be glad to be back in his own house, being waited on hand, foot and finger. But no... all he could do was sit there with a sour expression on his face and berate her for trying to help.

Sod him. If he wanted to live in muck, then so be it. She would do the minimum necessary until he could cope on his own, and then she was out of here.

'Blinkin' heck,' Walter muttered as he opened first one cupboard, and then another. That damned woman had rearranged all of them. Where the hell were the tea bags?

He found them in the same cupboard that the coffee was in, which might seem logical to her, but it was the cupboard furthest away from the magic tap. He knew that wasn't the correct name for the tap that spat out both boiling and freezing water, but he'd joked with Otto that it was magic when Otto had renovated the kitchen prior to Walter and Otto moving in, and the name had stuck.

The tea bags should live on the shelf underneath it. As should the mugs, which were now in the cupboard with the plates.

Hopping awkwardly and cursing as he went, he put his cupboards back the way they were. And if she moved any of his stuff again he wouldn't be accountable for his actions.

As he popped a tea bag in a mug, movement beyond the kitchen window caught his attention.

A woman was sitting on the topmost rung of the gate leading to the paddock. She was swinging her legs, her face turned away as she gazed into the field. For a moment he couldn't place her and he wondered whether she was one of the riding school mums. Then it hit him.

The woman was *Beth*.

His breath lodged in his throat and he feared he was hallucinating because she looked years younger, and he caught a glimpse of how she must have once looked: vibrant, carefree, not yet weighed down by time and age.

Then his focus sharpened, and she was Beth Fairfax again: pensioner, cantankerous, disagreeable.

She must have been striking once though. And as she sat there, her face lifted to the sun, he could see a younger version, one that had echoes of her beautiful daughters etched on her face. Walter, despite his dislike, had to admit (as he had done previously) that she was still a handsome woman. If only she wasn't so difficult and obstinate…

Walter paused, wondering where he was going with that thought, but the destination eluded him.

Whatever fanciful notion she had generated in him, swiftly disappeared when he watched her clamber gracelessly down from the five-bar gate. His heart was in his mouth. If she were to fall… And she had the cheek to accuse him of being silly when he'd gone up the ladder! She was just as bad. One slip of the foot and she could have broken her hip.

Irritated at her carelessness, he hobbled to the back door as fast as his cast would allow and yanked it open. 'What the hell do you think you're doing?' he bellowed, feeling rather satisfied when he saw her startled expression.

'Checking this lot,' she called. 'You asked me to. Don't you remember?' She began walking towards him. 'Or is your memory going?'

'I didn't ask you to climb a bloody gate,' he yelled back. 'And my memory is fine.'

'I was enjoying the sun. Or is that not allowed?'

'Don't be so silly.'

'Who are you calling silly?' She was close enough to see the flash of anger in her eyes.

He said, 'You, obviously. You could have fallen.'

'So says Spider Man. You're the one who fell, not me!'

She was daring him to contradict her. 'Which is why I know what I'm talking about. Breaking a hip is no laughing matter.'

'You didn't break a hip. Are you sure you're not losing your memory?'

'You could have broken yours.'

'But I didn't.'

'Gah! There's no talking to you!'

'Don't, then. See if I care. I'm fed up with you bumping your gums.'

'And I'm fed up of everything about *you!*' Walter yelled.

He liked to think that he whirled on his heel and marched inside, but what actually happened was that he did an awkward shuffling about turn, involved hopping, then limped slowly indoors.

He could feel Peg booping him on the leg in concern, and he guessed that the dog mightn't be getting her walk after all as Beth stomped in behind him and reached for the handbag that she'd looped over the back of one of the dining chairs.

'I'm going out,' she announced.

'Where?'

'Shopping. Your milk is off, and your bread is stale.'

'The milk seemed alright to me.'

'It would,' she growled. 'If I said it was white, you'd argue that it was blue.'

'What are you rabbiting on about?'

'Can I get you anything? A gag? A sedative? Some manners?'

Walter stared at her in shock. She had the cheek to ask him about *his* mental health when *she* was the one who was talking gibberish? He lowered himself in his usual chair. 'Take your time.'

'Don't worry, I will.'

'Good.' Walter had to have a last word. He didn't know why, he just had to.

Listening to her car door slam and Beth gunning the engine, he let out a sigh. So far, this day was an unmitigated disaster. Goodness knows how bad the rest of them would be whilst she was under his roof.

'Nasty, horrible, vile, obnoxious,' Beth muttered under her breath as she tore off down the lane. 'Pig-headed, crabby, bloody-minded…' she added, braking as she rounded the corner, to reach the junction at the bottom of Muddypuddle Lane at a more reasonable speed.

Feeling a sudden urge to see if they'd started work on her house (this was only day three of Hot Water Tank Horror, but she hoped they would have done *something*) she parked outside and got out.

The house was as quiet as the grave and when she peered through the window, her hands cupped around the glass, she was dismayed to see that the living room looked exactly as she had last seen it. Not a single piece of plasterboard had been removed.

Beth felt like crying. But instead of having a weep, she drew on her infuriation with Walter and strode off in the direction of the high street.

'I'm here about my house,' she announced as soon as she stepped inside, ignoring a youngish couple who were sitting at the desk and talking to Zander.

He had frozen in the middle of a sentence, his eyes darting from her face to the office door and back again as he muttered, 'Oh, god.'

'No, just Mrs Fairfax. What are you doing about my house?'

'Um…'

'I've just come from there, and nothing's been done. Not. A. Thing.'

'We're, um, awaiting instructions from the landlord.'

'What's his phone number? I'll give him a ring myself.'

'I'm sorry, Mrs Fairfax, but we're acting as the letting agent so everything needs to be done through us.'

'But that's the problem – nothing *is* being done. I want to know when I can move in. Do you realise the conditions I'm living in at the moment?'

Zander bit his lip. The couple looked like rabbits caught in headlights. Their eyes were out on stalks and they were staring at her as though she'd lost her mind.

Perhaps she had. Walter had the ability to bring out the worst in her.

'Disgraceful, that's what it is,' she cried. 'I can't take much more of it.'

Zander said, 'I'll, um, get onto them right now. In a minute. When I've finished dealing with my current clients.'

'Your *current client* is standing right here and wants you to phone my landlord immediately. I'm not leaving until you do.'

'Go ahead,' the chap said to Zander. 'I think this lady's need is greater than ours.'

Zander nodded, his jaw tense. Beth felt a twinge of remorse, but it didn't last. The chap was right, her need *was* greater.

But Beth wasn't in luck. There was no answer when Zander phoned, and she had to concede defeat. With Zander's promise to keep trying and that he would phone her as soon as he had any news, Beth left his office with a heavy heart.

She really thought she was going to cry, as tears pricked her eyes. Walter was right: she was stupid. She must be, to have thought she could pull this off. She had gone from being comfortable (if somewhat lonely) in her house in Birmingham, to being extremely uncomfortable living in the home of the most obnoxious man on the planet. And she had no one to blame but herself.

Beth felt a touch on her arm as a voice said, 'Hello, Beth. I thought it was you.' Lena was standing in front of her, gazing at her in concern. 'Are you okay?'

Beth shook her head. 'Not really.'

'Is there anything I can do to help?'

'Not unless you can magically repair a collapsed ceiling.'

'Oh, dear. Do you want to talk about it? We could go for a coffee. Things often seem better after a chat.'

Beth didn't think it would be better at all, but a coffee and a chat would be very welcome, nevertheless.

As soon as they were settled in the squishy chairs near the window, cappuccinos in hand, Lena wanted to know what had got Beth so upset.

'It's Walter,' Beth said, and went on to explain.

Lena listened without interruption, until Beth ground to a halt, embarrassed. 'It sounds so daft when I say it out loud,' she muttered. 'He's not a bad person, but he's not the easiest man to get on with, and when the pair of us are together we fight like two rats in a bag.'

Lena said, 'I don't know Walter particularly well, but Amos does. He reckons Walter is a typical farmer: stoic and taciturn, but he's got a heart of gold.'

'He hides it well.'

'I might be wrong, but I think he's had a lot of heartache in his life. His wife died when Otto was a teenager, and Walter raised him whilst trying to keep the farm going. That can't have been easy.'

'No, it can't,' Beth agreed softly. She hadn't realised. She knew all too well how hard it was being a single parent.

'And there was all that trouble before Dulcie took over the farm.'

'What trouble?'

'Don't you know?'

'Dulcie mentioned something about Otto having to raffle the farm off, but I couldn't have been listening.'

Lena studied her. 'What I'm about to tell you is common knowledge, so I'm not speaking out of turn or breaking any confidences, but it might help you understand Walter a bit better. Hang on.' She beckoned the waitress over and ordered two more coffees.

Beth was intrigued. She hadn't really gone into the details of how Dulcie had acquired the farm. All she knew was that her daughter had won it in a lottery and that it used to belong to Walter. Dulcie was forever complaining that the farm was a money pit – hence the drive to make soap, sell goats milk, have open days, and so on – so Beth had assumed that running a sheep farm had got too much for Walter, and he had decided to retire. At around the same time, Otto had come back to Picklewick to live, and the two of them, father and son, had moved into the cottage on Muddypuddle Lane when Dulcie had acquired the farm.

Lena drank some of her coffee and settled back. 'Walter has kept that farm going singlehandedly since Otto left to go to catering college. It's not easy being a farmer, but he was fifteen, maybe twenty years younger then, and he coped. But gradually he stopped coping. Amos feels guilty because he had no idea that Walter was struggling, until the Christmas before last when he collapsed and was rushed into hospital. When Otto came to see him, he realised that not only was Walter mentally and physically exhausted, but he had also run up huge debts trying to keep the farm afloat.

Dealing with all that worry, whilst hiding it from everyone – Otto included – had taken its toll, and Amos told me that Otto had worried that Walter wouldn't recover. I must admit that I was shocked when I saw him; he was all skin and bone, and looked so frail... I didn't recognise him.'

Beth hadn't touched her drink. She was far too caught up in the tale Lena was telling.

Lena continued, 'Amos reckons Walter feels guilty because Otto had to give up his job in London to look after him, even though it has all worked out brilliantly in the end.'

Beth couldn't disagree with that. Dulcie and Otto were perfect for each other, and the move from London hadn't impacted Otto's career. On the contrary, he now had a book deal he wouldn't otherwise have had and owned his own restaurant.

'Walter was devastated, of course,' Lena was saying. 'He'd lived on that farm all his life. It must have been awful to see it raffled off.'

Beth wished she'd known this earlier. It was her own fault for not being more interested, and she felt guilty and ashamed for judging him so harshly. His tale didn't detract from the fact that he was grumpy and argumentative, but she could now understand why – to a certain extent.

Feeling better about returning to the cottage on Muddypuddle Lane and vowing (yet again) to be more sympathetic towards Walter, Beth drank her coffee, glad that Lena had explained. And when the conversation moved away from Walter and onto their respective families and other things, Beth hoped that she had made her first real friend in Picklewick.

CHAPTER SEVEN

Walter hoped that an afternoon of retail therapy would have put Beth in a better mood. He wasn't going to hold his breath, though. He was, however, desperate for a bath.

With Peg at his heels, Walter made his way to the bottom of the stairs and stared up. Feeling stronger than he had felt when he'd attempted the stairs in the farmhouse, and more confident with Beth out of the way, it seemed an ideal opportunity to give them a go. It was going to be a challenge getting up them whilst hanging onto his crutches, but he thought he could do it.

Parking his backside on the second step, he used his good leg and one arm to ease himself onto the next, then repeated the performance. So far, so good. Feeling pleased with himself, he carried on this way until he eventually reached the top. He'd even managed to keep hold of his crutches. Result!

Making sure he was well away from the yawning stairwell, Walter clambered to his feet, using the banister for leverage. It was hard work, and he was hot and out of breath by the time he was fully upright. But the novelty of being upstairs in his own home was worth it, as it meant he could have the bath he so desperately wanted, and he would be able to sleep in his own bed tonight. Ha! That'll show 'em! A couple of days of this, and he would be able to send Beth packing.

Aware that she might return any minute, he gathered some fresh clothes from his bedroom and limped to the bathroom but couldn't resist a quick look in the spare room on his way.

Beth had laid out some things on the chest of drawers, make-up and whatnot, and her case had been placed neatly underneath the window. He refrained from looking inside the wardrobe, guessing that she had probably unpacked. It unnerved him to think that it was *her* clothes hanging in there and not *Otto's*. It gave her presence an air of permanence that her short stay didn't warrant.

Huffing to himself, he locked the bathroom door and lowered his backside onto the closed lid of the toilet, grunting with relief as he took the weight off his good leg. When he'd got his breath back, Walter turned on the hot water tap in the bath, steam gradually filling the room as he undressed.

It wasn't easy trying to ease the jogging bottoms that Otto had lent him over the plaster cast, but he finally managed it. Thankful that when Otto had renovated the cottage, he'd had the foresight to put in a bath with handles (futureproofing, his son had called it), Walter sat on the edge. Then putting his good leg in the bath and keeping his broken one raised and stuck out at an awkward angle so it didn't get wet, he eased himself down into the water.

The splash when his behind hit the bottom of the bath made him wince as a mini tsunami slopped over the side, but the watery mess was immediately forgotten as the lower half of his body was immersed in lovely hot water. It was a bit uncomfortable with one leg stuck over the side, but Walter didn't mind, as he happily soaped himself. This was so much better than trying to stand in the shower (Otto never did manage to find anything for him to sit on) and he even began to hum a little tune.

However, the humming stopped when, some time later and after several attempts, he realised he couldn't get out. Walter was well and truly stuck. Bugger!

He sat there for a while, topping up the hot water when it started to cool and straining to listen to any sounds from downstairs.

When he finally heard the front door open and close he breathed a sigh of relief: rescue was at hand.

'Walter?' Beth called.

'Up here!' He heard her tread on the stairs and recognised the creak on the landing as she reached the top.

'I see you managed the stairs,' she said.

He heard her walk into the spare room, and the sound of the wardrobe door opening.

'Beth?'

'What?'

God, he hated this. 'I'm stuck.'

'Stuck?' Footsteps hurried into his bedroom and hurried back out again. 'Are you in the bathroom?'

'Yes.'

'What do you mean stuck? Please don't tell me you can't get off the toilet.'

'I can't get out of the bath.' He thought he heard a snort of laughter but he couldn't be certain. 'You can't come in,' he added.

'How do you suggest I get you out, if I can't come in?' She tried the handle. The door didn't budge. 'Did you lock it?'

'Yes.'

'Oh, Walter. What were you thinking?'

That he hadn't wanted the worry of her walking in on him whilst he was naked in the tub – that was what he had been thinking. Now though, he would be perfectly happy for her to see him in the altogether if it meant he could get out of this blasted bath.

'Are you any good at picking locks?' he asked.

'Yeah, I'm an expert. I'll just go get my hat pin.'

'No need to be sarcastic.'

'I might be able to break the door down,' she called.

Walter rolled his eyes. 'You're almost seventy; you'll break your shoulder, not the door.'

'I won't if I use a sledgehammer. I bet Dulcie's got one.'

Walter baulked. 'You're *not* using a sledgehammer on my door.'

'How else do you suggest I get you out?' Her tone became sly. 'Perhaps I should phone Otto.'

'Don't you dare!' If Otto knew about this, Walter would end up back at the farmhouse faster than Peg gobbled her dinner.

He thought frantically. They had to do something. He couldn't stay here for much longer – he was starting to look even more prune-like than he was already.

The lock was an old-fashioned one with a key, because both Walter and Otto had wanted to keep as many of the cottage's period features as possible. Apart from the kitchen. Otto had insisted on installing a state-of-the-art kitchen, and Walter didn't have the heart to refuse him. His son had sacrificed so much already…

Walter didn't know if his idea would work, but he wanted to give it a shot. 'Can you go out to the shed?' he called. 'Find a thin screwdriver and bring my newspaper up.'

To be fair to Beth, she didn't waste time asking why. He listened to her trot downstairs and waited impatiently for her to return.

'Got 'em,' she announced. 'Now what?'

'Slide the newspaper under the door, then see if you can poke the screwdriver into the lock and wiggle it until the key falls out.'

'Nice.' She sounded impressed and Walter puffed out his chest.

It was far too soon to give himself a pat on the back though, because his idea mightn't work. He had seen it done in a film once, but what happened on screen probably wouldn't work in real life.

Walter held his breath as he heard scraping noises coming from the direction of the lock, then he let it out in a whoosh as he saw the key begin to wiggle.

'Newspaper!' he yelled, realising that she had forgotten it, and his heart was in his mouth until Beth had shoved it underneath the door.

He hadn't realised until now just how much of a gap there was between the door and the lino; no wonder he could feel a draft when he sat on the loo. It was something that needed to be fixed, but right now he was extremely grateful for it.

His attention was firmly on the door, as the barrel of the key was slowly pushed out of the lock. It hung there for a moment, and once again he held his breath. When it finally dropped directly onto the newspaper, Walter let out a whoop and slapped the water, sending it sloshing over the side.

'The key is out!' he cried. 'Pull the newspaper towards you.' Then he abruptly deflated with the fear that it mightn't fit under the door, especially with there being carpet on the other side.

He couldn't look. Screwing his eyes shut, Walter ground his teeth, praying that Beth would be able to retrieve the key.

When he heard it turn in the lock and the door click open, he could have wept for joy. Until he remembered he was starkers. His eyes flew open and he grabbed a towel off the rail to cover his embarrassment.

Beth was standing in the doorway. He fully expected her to smirk, but she wore an odd expression, one that he couldn't decode.

Walter flushed under her gaze, even though his modesty was preserved by the towel. 'Good job,' he said.

Seeming to snap out of whatever had got hold of her, Beth snatched up another towel and stepped towards him. He appreciated that she kept her eyes averted, as she held out a hand. Grasping it, Walter got his good leg into what he hoped was the correct position to bear his weight.

'One, two, three,' Beth chanted, and on 'three' she leant back and heaved.

Walter emerged from the bath like Neptune rising from the waves, only with considerably less grandeur. Water cascaded over the floor, but he was upright and that was all he was concerned about.

Feeling more foolish than he had ever felt in his life, he perched his scrawny backside on the edge of the bath and swung his legs to the floor. Beth, he noticed, had her head turned away and was steadfastly gazing at the ceiling.

Without looking at him, she handed him the dry towel. 'Can you take it from here, or do you need me to help you get dressed?'

'I can manage.' His voice was hoarse. 'Thanks'

A smile teased the corners of her mouth. She looked so much nicer when she smiled. She should do it more often, he thought.

She said, 'You're welcome. I'll be downstairs. Shout when you need me.'

When. Not *if*. It seemed that Beth was just as aware as Walter that he needed far more help than he cared to admit.

The last thing Beth had expected to see when she returned to the cottage was a naked man stuck in a bath. She had to admit that she had felt acutely embarrassed, but probably not as embarrassed as Walter! His face had been a picture, she thought, as she basted the pork chops she was cooking for their tea. But his face was the only thing she had looked at. The rest of him had been strictly out of bounds.

However, she had caught a glimpse of his chest and the smattering of grizzled grey hairs covering it. The sight had given her a bit of a pang. It was a long time – many years – since she had been within touching distance of a bare male chest

She had quickly looked away. Such pangs belonged in her past, when she had been young enough to have done something about them. These days she didn't have the energy nor the inclination.

Companionship wouldn't go amiss though. That was what she had missed when the kids were growing up: someone to share her worries with at the end of a difficult day, or to share the joys when good things happened. She even missed washing up whilst someone else dried. Not that her husband (God rest his soul) had wielded a tea towel very often. Or listened when she needed a good grizzle. He'd not been there for many of the good times either, now that she came to think of it. So what was it exactly, that she missed? How could you miss something that you'd never had?

Beth shook her head to clear it of such fanciful thoughts. It wasn't surprising that she was out-of-sorts, considering the stressful few days she'd had. And there were likely to be more stressful days to come.

Beth suppressed a snort: her day hadn't been half as stressful as Walter's. He'd had a right old time of it. At one point she had honestly feared she wasn't going to be able to get the door open by herself – unless she used the sledgehammer.

But try explaining a smashed door to Otto. He was bound to notice, although maybe they could have kept it from him long enough to convince him that Walter didn't need looking after. Beth hadn't wanted to take the risk though, and neither had Walter. He wanted her gone almost as much as she wanted to leave. Although he might change his mind when she plonked a nice pork chop with roast potatoes and veg in front of him. She bet he wouldn't manage to cook a meal like that whilst balancing on one leg!

The evening meal wasn't as uncomfortable as lunch had been, despite the events of earlier, and Beth began to relax.

When Walter asked, 'Did you get what you needed in the village?' she didn't go looking for a hidden meaning or disguised sarcasm, and took the question at face value.

'Yes and no. I called into the estate agent because I checked on the house and noticed they hadn't started on the repairs. I didn't get much joy.' She spooned out a portion of apple sauce and popped it on her plate, before offering the bowl to Walter.

He tasted the sauce and his eyes widened. 'Did you make this yourself?'

'I did. And the stuffing and the Yorkshire puds.'

'Very tasty.' Beth inclined her head in acknowledgement.

She had always been a dab hand in the kitchen, and it was a pleasure to see someone enjoy her cooking again. These past couple of years, Maisie, although still living at home until recently, had been out more often than she'd been in, and Beth had stopped cooking tea for her because she'd hated wasting food. This meal definitely wasn't going to waste, she was pleased to see, as Walter tucked in with enthusiasm.

'That's the no bit,' he said. 'What's the yes?'

'You're eating it. I also bumped into Lena, and we had a coffee.'

'Lovely woman, Lena. Amos has got a good 'un there. Mind you, she hasn't done too badly herself; Amos is the salt of the earth. He'd do anything for you, would Amos. Gotta take it easy though – angina. We're a couple of old crocs. Although at the moment I'd say I'm more croc than he is.' He gestured to his broken leg with his fork. 'Just you wait until I get this cast off – I'll give him a run for his money. Talking about casts, I've got an appointment at the fracture clinic the day after tomorrow. Can you… Do you think…?'

'Yes, I'll drive you there.'

'Thank you.'

Beth wondered if it had hurt him to ask. She knew how much he hated being reliant on her, but Dulcie and Otto were busy; she wasn't. It felt rather good to be needed again, even if it was Walter who was the one needing it.

Surprisingly, he hadn't needed help getting dressed after his bath, and neither had he needed her assistance in getting down the stairs. He'd inched down on his bottom, although Beth had held his crutches. It would be handy if he had a pair for upstairs use, she'd mused, and she'd made a mental note to ask Lena if she knew where she could get hold of a spare pair.

After Beth had stacked the dishwasher (she'd never had one of those and had needed to pick Walter's brains on how to work it, the same as she'd had to ask him about the stove), the two of them settled down in front of the telly with a cup of tea and a custard cream or two.

Despite being on her own with Walter and not having Dulcie or Otto as a buffer, Beth felt more relaxed in the cottage than she had in the farmhouse. Probably because Walter wasn't being so tetchy, she surmised. By unspoken mutual agreement neither of them had mentioned the bathroom incident when Dulcie had phoned to check that they hadn't killed each other yet, nor when Otto had popped in on his way to the restaurant to see how they were getting on (i.e. no fatalities) and ask whether they needed anything.

Having a secret seemed to have broken a barrier between them, and even though Beth didn't want to be here and Walter didn't want her here, there appeared to be a ceasefire for the moment. How long it would last was anyone's guess, but Beth wasn't going to look a gift horse in the mouth.

As she got ready for her first night under Walter's roof, she wondered how much her new-found reluctance to wind him up was due to what Lena had told her, and she could feel herself softening towards him.

If this evening was anything to go by, maybe looking after him for a few days wouldn't be such a strain after all.

Walter didn't know what the technical word was for the gadget that enabled him to pick things up off the floor (he called it the 'grabby thing'), but it didn't half come in handy this morning to retrieve his dropped sock.

He was currently sitting on his bed, getting dressed for his hospital appointment and feeling rather nervous. He hoped everything was okay under the cast.

Eventually dressed (everything took three times as long with a broken leg, he had discovered), he lowered himself cautiously down the stairs and limped into the kitchen. The delicious aroma of bacon had made his tummy rumble in anticipation whilst he was upstairs, and he was eager to tuck into his breakfast.

Beth was standing by the stove, wielding a frying pan. 'Pancakes, and bacon with syrup for breakfast,' she announced. 'Go sit down, it's almost ready.'

She joined him at the table, her own plate piled just as high as his, and he reckoned that both of them needed to keep their strength up for the ordeal ahead. Him, because he hated hospitals and wasn't relishing having his leg poked and prodded, and Beth because she had confessed to him that she was fearful of driving on strange roads.

Her admission had surprised him: he'd been under the impression that nothing fazed her. Over the past couple of days, since *Bathgate*, he had begun to notice chinks in her armour. Beth Fairfax wasn't as indomitable as she appeared. She was still grouchy though, and they'd had a couple of spats, but nothing like it had been.

Walter was quietly hopeful that things were settling down.

He was also quietly hopeful that he might have his house to himself again shortly. Maybe this hospital visit would help move things on. If he had a good report from the fracture clinic, it might give him more leverage in persuading Otto that he could manage without Beth's help.

Although, Walter had to admit, having Beth around did make life easier. She cooked a mean breakfast, for one, and she took Peg out for her daily constitutional for another. Maybe he should keep her around for a while longer.

He was still mulling it over on the drive to Thornbury and the hospital, and he continued to think about it after the doctor had announced that she was pleased with his progress and would see him again in four weeks.

Realistically, he knew that he still needed help with many things and having Beth here was the easiest option. Besides, he was getting rather used to her.

'Do you fancy stopping off somewhere for a spot of lunch?' Beth asked, as she drove out of the hospital's congested car park.

'What about my leg?'

'You can bring it with you,' she replied, deadpan.

Walter rolled his eyes. 'I meant, should I be out and about with it?'

'I don't see why not. It's not as though you're ill, or contagious. You see people with broken legs all the time.'

Walter didn't like to admit that he was worried someone might bump it, or that he wouldn't be able to make it from the car to wherever it was they were going. It had been difficult enough walking from the patient drop-off area to the fracture clinic's waiting room.

'Breakfast filled me up,' he said by way of an excuse, even though he didn't want to go home just yet. He was quite enjoying being out of the house.

Beth was staring straight ahead, her attention on the road as she negotiated the traffic through the busy town. But Walter could have sworn that there was a disappointed set to her shoulders.

Relenting, he said, 'There's a pub called The Dancing Pheasant halfway between here and Picklewick. It used to have a good reputation, but I don't know what it's like now. We could give it a go, if you want.' Then he decided to be honest with her; after all, she had shared her concern about driving on unfamiliar roads with him. 'I'm worried about knocking my leg, or not being able to walk far,' he confessed. 'The pub has got its own car park.'

Beth shot him a glance before hurriedly looking at the road again. 'Sorry, Walter, I didn't think.'

Wow! Beth had apologised?! That didn't happen very often.

'I'm surprised I'm hungry at all after bacon and pancakes,' he said. 'But I am.'

'Me, too. Shall we give it a go?'

So they did. And very pleasant it was.

To Walter's surprise they had quite a lot to chat about, and he found himself enjoying her company. Lunch was bitter-sweet though, because the last time he'd been out for a meal with a woman it had been with his wife, when she was alive. Not that they'd gone out for meals much: that had been reserved for special occasions.

Still, this was very nice and as they waited for dessert and coffee, he sat back with a contented sigh.

'This is a real treat,' Beth said. 'I don't eat out very often – unless you call having a cuppa in a cafe and smuggling in a packet of Fig Rolls, eating out.'

'I don't eat out at all,' Walter said. 'Except for going to Dulcie's.'

'What about the pub? Do you ever go to the Black Horse?'

'Now and again, but not for a meal. I used to play darts.' He hadn't played for a long time. Now that he came to think about it there were lots of things he hadn't done for a long time, and he realised how insular he had become over the years.

'Is there much to do in Picklewick?' Beth asked.

Walter's mind went blank. 'I've no idea.'

'I wondered what was on at the community centre.' She got out her phone, the tip of her tongue poking out as she scrolled, and Walter could imagine her doing the same thing in school when she was a girl, as she worked on her sums or concentrated on her spellings. The image made him smile.

'Yoga, mother and toddler group, photography club, bingo, knit and natter… And The Black Horse has a quiz night and karaoke. Can you sing?' she asked.

'Er, no.'

'Me, neither. I sound like a scalded cat. Knit?'

Walter shook his head.

'Do you like quizzes?'

'I don't mind Tipping Point on TV, and I quite like The Chase.'

'Wanna give it a go?'

'Oh, I don't think so. I can't see myself being on TV, can you?'

Beth chortled. 'Not on the telly! Down the pub.'

Walter blinked. 'Maybe.'

Beth carried on, 'There's a gardening club.' She wrinkled her nose. 'Nah, if I feel the urge to get my hands dirty, I'll ask Dulcie if I can grub about in her veggie patch.' Beth fell silent for a moment, her eyes on the screen, then she yelled, 'Kite flying!' and Walter almost leapt out of his skin.

'Where?' His gaze shot to the window.

'There's a kite flying club,' Beth explained. 'I quite fancy flying a kite again. I haven't done that since I was a kid. Pendine Sands in West Wales. We had a caravan for a week.' She looked wistful.

Their desserts arrived, along with their coffee, but Beth didn't begin to eat hers straight away; she was busily typing one-fingered into her phone.

Walter was tempted to tell her off, the way he'd heard her reprimand Maisie for playing with her phone at the table, but he held his tongue.

Then he wished he hadn't when Beth made an announcement. 'Righty-ho, I've just signed us up for Half Board on Thursday afternoon.' And when Walter stared at her in confusion, she explained, 'It's an afternoon of board games. And on the following Monday we're going to bingo.'

'I don't like bingo.'

'Have you ever been?'

'No, but—'

'Don't knock it until you try it,' she said, around a mouthful of apple crumble and custard. 'If you give it a go and still don't like it, we can try something else.'

'What if I don't want to?'

'I'll go on my own, and you can be Mr Boring all by yourself.'

'I'm not boring,' he protested.

'Prove it!'

Walter pulled a face. He didn't think he could. In fact, he was fairly certain that he *was* boring. Maybe playing board games and so on was the sort of thing that might help alleviate the loneliness he had been feeling…

It looked like he would be going to bingo after all!

CHAPTER EIGHT

Beth had never seen a cribbage board before, and she gazed at it with a mixture of puzzlement and disbelief. The block of wood was about a foot long and had a succession of tiny holes drilled into it, running along its length in two parallel rows of two. Four small brass pegs had been set in the board.

Walter moved all the pegs to the one end of the board, saying, 'The winner is the first to reach 121 points.'

Beth didn't have a clue how points were gained, and she was even more bemused when Walter produced a pack of cards and began to explain the rules.

They sounded rather complicated.

When Beth had booked them into Half Board (so called, she found out, because the session was only ever half a day) she had imagined Scrabble, or Monopoly. But Walter's eyes had lit up when he had spied the crib board, and she didn't have the heart to refuse him when he'd suggested a game.

He even seemed enthusiastic about teaching her to play, although she suspected he might change his mind when he realised that the rules were going over her head. Blankly she stared at the hand he'd dealt her, wondering what she was supposed to do with it.

His explanation of her having to decide which two cards to discard, had passed her by.

'Walter?' someone said, and Beth glanced up to see a dapper chap in his seventies, with salt-and-pepper hair and a moustache beaming down at them.

'Remember me? Stanley Childs?' the old fella asked, holding out his hand. Walter began to struggle to his feet, but the man gently pushed him back down. 'Don't get up,' Stanley said. 'I heard you'd broken your leg.' He turned his attention to Beth. 'Aren't you going to introduce me to your lady friend?'

Beth snorted. Lady friend, indeed. And she didn't need 'introducing'; she was perfectly capable of introducing herself.

'Beth Fairfax,' she said, before Walter could open his mouth.

Stanley shook her hand, holding onto it for longer than was strictly necessary. His gaze locked onto hers. 'Charmed,' he said. 'Fairfax... Now where have I...? Oh, yes! Otto's better half, Dulcie. You must be her sister.'

Beth rolled her eyes and giggled, despite herself. Walter shot her a cross look.

Stanley didn't appear to notice. 'How long are you in Picklewick?' Stanley asked.

'Permanently,' Beth replied.

'Are you living at the farm?'

'No, she's living with me,' Walter interjected.

'I see.' Stanley's eyebrows shot up.

'It's a temporary arrangement,' Beth leapt in before Stanley got the wrong end of the stick. She didn't want him to think that she and Walter were an item, not when Stanley was so handsome and suave.

She wasn't too keen on his moustache, which was a bit too handlebar-ish for her liking, but the rest of him was easy on the eye, and she bet he was a hit with Picklewick's female contingent – the older ones, that is. Such as herself.

She was so glad she hadn't had to twist Walter's arm to persuade him to come with her today. If she'd had to come on her own, she probably wouldn't have bothered. Or rather, she wouldn't have had the courage. Walking into a roomful of strangers terrified her, especially when they undoubtedly knew each other. She would have felt like the new girl in school, and probably would have turned tail and run. Now, though, she knew Stanley, so if she did come on her own next time, she mightn't be quite as nervous.

'I'll leave you to it,' Stanley was saying.

Beth didn't want him to go. And the reason was that she really didn't want to learn how to play cribbage – or any other card game, for that matter. She had her eye on a group of ladies who were setting up a game of Cluedo, which was more to her liking.

She said to Stanley, 'Do you know how to play cribbage?'

'I do. Why, would you like to challenge me to a game? I warn you, I like to win.'

'Good. So does Walter.' She got to her feet. 'Take my place. I'm sure Walter would prefer to play against someone who knows what they're doing.'

Stanley looked startled. 'Three can play crib, you know.'

Beth sent Walter an apologetic smile. 'I haven't played board games for ages. Let me ease myself in slowly with a nice game of Cluedo – if those ladies will have me – and I promise I'll give cribbage a go next time.'

And with that, she shot off, feeling Walter and Stanley's gaze following her.

But when she neared the table where the ladies were about to begin their game, her courage failed her and she swerved off in the direction of the loos that she'd noticed on the way into the community centre (at her age it was always wise to know where the nearest toilet was), and she hurriedly inside.

When she emerged, the first thing she noticed was that Walter was sitting on his own. The second was that the cribbage board had disappeared and in its place was another game. *Cluedo.*

'Stanley's gone to fetch us some tea,' Walter said. 'When he comes back, how about a nice game of Cluedo?'

Beth could have kissed him.

Bingo. Ugh. Walter surveyed the community hall with suspicion. Roughly fifteen tables were laid out with four or so chairs at each. At the far end of the room, on the stage, was another table with a round black basket containing a number of white balls, and a microphone. Behind it, and off to the side, was a second table displaying a variety of objects. It reminded him of a raffle table.

Walter had never played bingo in his life and, seeing the avaricious faces of the people gathered there, he wasn't sure he wanted to start now.

'Ooh, you can win a fish and chip supper, or a bottle of sherry,' Beth said, spying the table of prizes. 'I'm partial to a glass of sherry.' She smacked her lips.

Walter preferred beer, or whisky, if he was forced to choose something stronger.

Lowering himself into a chair, he studied the bingo card.

What he didn't like about bingo was the element of luck. There appeared to be no skill involved whatsoever, but remembering Beth telling him not to knock it until he tried it, he decided to keep an open mind. After all, he had enjoyed playing Cluedo the other day – although, he hadn't enjoyed Stanley being part of the game. Stanley was too suave for Walter's liking. Or would *smarmy* be a better description?

Stanley thought he was the bee's knees. He had always been the same. Walter remembered him from school, and the girls had fallen over him then. The man had had two wives, one deceased and one divorced, and Walter suspected he was on the lookout for number three. Walter hoped Stanley hadn't set his sights on Beth. She was too good for the likes of Stanley Childs.

As the thought went through Walter's head, he was pulled up short.

A week ago, he would have been happy for Stanley to go gunning after Beth. He probably would have thought they deserved each other.

But not now. When it came to Beth, Walter had undergone a seismic shift. And it had taken another man's interest in her to make him realise that he actually liked her. *Liked* not *tolerated*.

Well, well, well… That was a turn-up for the books, he thought. In fact, he felt quite proprietorial over her, and he didn't want to see her get hurt. Stanley was a user, a player, a ladies' man. Beth deserved better.

Beth heard the sound of the shower going and she smiled. The little plastic stool she had found in the charity shop in the village had been perfect for Walter to sit in in the cubicle. It was a bit on the low side, but she'd made him practice getting up from it before he'd given it a go in the shower. He still needed help waterproofing his cast though, because he couldn't quite reach to put a plastic bag over it. Unlike Beth, who was quite flexible for her age, Walter was as stiff as a board.

However, Beth had a plan to do something about that, and as soon as he was dressed and downstairs, she would put that plan into action.

They were going to Dulcie's for Sunday lunch (Beth was looking forward to seeing everyone), but they had a couple of hours before they needed to leave and she intended to use the time wisely.

'Armchair yoga,' she announced, when Walter appeared in the living room.

'Is this another one of your hare-brained activities?' Walter was smiling, so she didn't take offence.

'This one is for your benefit, not mine,' she retorted. 'I'm bendy enough. See?' She bent over, touching the carpet with her fingers. There was a time when she used to be able to put her palms flat on the floor, but that had been before she'd had the kids.

Nowadays, her tummy got in the way and her boobs threatened to unbalance her.

When she straightened up, Walter's eyes were on stalks. 'Please tell me you're not expecting me to touch my toes,' he begged.

'Not straight away, but eventually you should be able to. And when your cast is off, you'll find it much easier to bend and stretch.'

Walter stared at her, and she realised she wouldn't be living here when the cast was removed. That's what they were working towards, wasn't it – him managing on his own and her moving back in with Dulcie (or into her own house, if the repairs were completed). But, oddly enough, that goal no longer seemed as imperative as it had when she had agreed to move into the cottage on Muddypuddle Lane.

Aside from those first few days when she had wished she was anywhere but here, Beth had settled into life in Walter's house surprisingly well. She thought they muddled along together quite nicely now. They still bickered a bit, but nowhere near as badly as they used to. She would miss the place when she left. Without her realising it, the cottage had gradually come to feel like home. But what was even more surprising (disturbing, actually) was that she would miss Walter. Unbeknownst to him, he had provided the company she craved and, on occasion, she felt as though they were an old married couple – without the obvious; they didn't share a bedroom.

As Beth watched Walter expertly manoeuvre himself into his seat, something about that last thought niggled at her, but she couldn't put her finger on it.

Then she let out a gasp as it came to her: her and Walter *in the same bed.*

A flush spread up her chest into her neck and her face, and she felt a flutter in her tummy.

'Did you sprain something?' Walter asked. 'All that bending and stretching is bound to put your back out.'

'I'm fine,' she retorted. 'Hot flush.' Beth fanned herself vigorously with her hands, flapping them in front of her face and hoping that any mention of the menopause would have him changing the subject rapidly. She also hoped that he didn't realise she was too old for a hot flush. She was thankfully past all that, although she had heard of some poor women who continued to have them into their seventies.

True enough, Walter looked petrified at the thought that she might feel tempted to expand further and he seemed more than happy when she returned to the subject of armchair yoga.

'Sit up straight,' she commanded. 'Hands on your knees. Close your eyes and breathe.'

'I always breathe.'

Beth sat down in the adjacent chair, her back ramrod straight. 'You need to do it mindfully,' she said, remembering the online tutorial she had watched earlier.

'How do you mean *mindfully?*'

'Breathe from the stomach and think about it as you're doing it. In through the nose, hold it for a second, then out through the mouth.'

'It's a load of old cod's wallop, if you ask me. People have been breathing for thousands of years and they didn't need anyone to tell them how to do it.' He opened one eye and squinted at her.

Beth glared at him. With a resigned shake of his head, he closed it again.

Beth watched him carefully, telling herself that it was to make sure he didn't cheat, but in reality she was enjoying gazing at him. He was relaxed, the lines in his face not as prominent, and he looked considerably better than the day Dulcie and Otto had brought him home from hospital, and although Beth couldn't take all the credit, she took some. Hearty, regular meals, someone to do his laundry and cleaning, someone to make sure he was okay... It made a difference.

'Can I stop breathing now?' he asked.

'Better not,' Beth chortled. 'You'll keel over.'

'You know what I mean.'

'You can open your eyes,' she conceded. 'We're going to do thoracic rotations next.'

'Eh?'

'Put your hands behind your head, like when you were in school, then twist to face that way—' She twisted her head and torso to the left. 'Then this way.' She twisted to the right. 'We do this ten times each side. One, two...'

Walter copied her, but they were twisting in opposite directions, so with every second twist they found themselves staring each other in the eye. Beth was glad when they'd finished that exercise.

'Are we done?' he asked.

'No. Next, we drop our heads to our chests.' She demonstrated. Walter followed suit. 'Can you feel the stretch in your neck?'

'I can feel something. I think I've done myself a mischief.'

Beth ignored his grumbling. 'Sit up and look straight ahead, arching your back slightly. And repeat,' she sang.

Ten of those and she was starting to feel a little dizzy from all the bending and stretching. Determined to plough on and convinced that it was doing them some good (it might take a while for the benefits to become apparent), Beth showed him how to flop forwards so that his head was between his knees.

It was called the rag doll position, but Walter looked more like a broken doll by the time he had attempted ten of those. Beth wasn't feeling much better. She thought of herself as fairly fit for her age (there was that phrase again, *for her age*) but clearly she wasn't, because the deep breathing she had been trying to do had become more of a pant and a grunt.

Poor Walter's face was slowly turning purple with the effort. 'This is supposed to be good for you?' he puffed as he straightened up.

'Shall we do some arm exercises now?'

'Goodie. I can't wait.'

Beth rolled her eyes and tried not to tut. The ungrateful so-and-so. However, she had to admit that it was harder work than the man in the video had led her to believe.

After windmilling their arms around and trying (unsuccessfully) to grab their hands behind their backs, Beth called it a day.

'The rest of them involve standing next to your chair,' she explained, 'but I don't think you're up for that.' A giggle escaped her. 'There is one exercise you've already mastered though…'

'What's that?' Walter winced as he rubbed his shoulder.

'Standing on one leg,' she laughed. 'It's called *the stork*, but you're supposed to alternate which leg you stand on.'

'Very funny.' He didn't appear amused.

'We'll have another go tomorrow,' she promised. 'Ten minutes every day and you'll be a new man.'

'I'm quite partial to the old one,' he said.

Funnily enough, so was Beth...

Painting and drawing weren't Walter's forte. He hardly knew one end of a pencil from another, and the only time he had held a paintbrush was when he'd been nagged into redecorating. But here was Beth, insisting that they give an art class a go.

She said, 'You enjoyed Half Board.'

They'd been twice now, and Walter did enjoy it, especially since Stanley hadn't shown his face last time. 'I didn't like bingo,' he argued.

'But at least you tried it. And you won a powder puff and mirror set.'

'You may have noticed that I didn't bring it home with me.'

'You could have regifted it.'

'I think it had been regifted too many times already.'

'You're probably right.'

Walter glared at her suspiciously. He wasn't often right, and he wondered whether she was being sarcastic.

Once again, they headed for the heart of the village and the community centre. Walter was quietly impressed at how much went on inside the unassuming red-brick building. It was nothing to look at on the outside, being shabby and unappealing, but inside was an Aladdin's cave of clubs and activities, this morning's being an art class.

Walter wasn't surprised to see some familiar faces as many of the same people tended to frequent the same clubs and classes. It seemed that the village had an active troop of enthusiastic pensioners, and it looked like he was going to be one of them if Beth had her way.

Several easels had been placed in a circle, around something that Walter could only describe as a chaise longue. He eyed it doubtfully, hoping he wasn't expected to draw it, because it wasn't particularly inspiring. He had been expecting a bowl of fruit, if he was honest. It was a nice shade of red though, so maybe the class was doing the colour red this week…? He wasn't sure how these things worked.

A plump woman wearing a multi-coloured kaftan and lots of chunky jewellery spotted him and Beth hovering in the doorway, and she hurried forward.

'Hello, hello, come on in, we don't bite – not unless we're drawing teeth, ha, ha! Welcome to Art for Art's Sake. I'm Melanie, your teacher. Have you done much drawing or painting? Never mind if you haven't – everyone has to start somewhere, and we're a non-judgemental lot. Would you like to sit next to each other? Of course you would. What's your name?'

'Walter,' he mumbled, wondering when the woman was going to draw breath.

'Walter, you can sit here, and—?'

'Beth,' Beth supplied.

'You can sit here. Did you bring an overall or a pinny? No? Not a problem, I've always got spares.' She pointed to a box in the corner. 'We'll be working with pencil or charcoal today, whichever you prefer. The paper is already on your easel and so are the pencils. Any questions?'

Walter had one. 'Are they red?'

Melanie blinked. 'Er, no, they're HB pencils. We're not using coloured pencils today. Enjoy the session and shout out if you need any help. I'll be doing the rounds anyway, to see how you're getting on.'

'I thought they'd be red,' he muttered as he hobbled to his chair, thankful that he wasn't expected to stand. He'd had visions of people pacing around in front of their easels and using the ends of their brushes to check angles and whatnot.

Beth hung her handbag over the back of her chair. 'Why red?'

'That chaise longue thing is red.' He pursed his lips and lowered his voice. 'It's not very interesting, is it? I don't know anything about drawing, but even I can see that with a couple of lines and a squiggle, it'll be done. How long did you say the class was?'

'Two hours, with half an hour in the middle for refreshments.'

'I reckon it'll take me about ten minutes,' he murmured, eyeing up the other artists.

There were about fifteen in all, and the low buzz of conversation filled the air. When Melanie clapped her hands and called for quiet, the room fell silent, the chatter replaced by excited expectation – although what was exciting about a wannabe settee, Walter couldn't imagine.

Melanie said, 'I told you I would have a treat for you, and I know speculation has been rife.' She smiled widely. 'I think many of you have guessed what we're going to be drawing today, so before I bring our model in, I just want to say please don't be embarrassed. The naked human form is the most natural and beautiful thing there is, no matter the age, the shape, or the gender. My advice is to forget that you're drawing a person and concentrate on capturing the essence and the form. Are we ready?'

A chorus of agreement filled the room, but Walter didn't join in. He was starting to get a bad feeling about this.

His fears were confirmed when Melanie opened a door, and cried, 'Artists, here is your model for today – Stanley!'

Walter's horror when Stanley Childs strode into the room, was only exceeded when Stanley removed his robe with a flourish and stood before them with a big grin on his face.

Stanley was naked.

Beth wasn't normally a blusher but when she had caught sight of Stanley in all his proud nakedness, she had felt a whoosh of heat flooding her cheeks. Maybe if she had been more prepared, she wouldn't have reacted as strongly. Walter had let out a gasp along with the other artists, but whilst there had been a flutter of giggles from the rest, he had scowled.

Afterwards, the two of them had immediately fled to The Black Horse for a restorative pint.

Despite having downed half of his ale, Walter looked haunted. Beth might have felt the same if she had spent two hours staring at Stanley's spread-eagled figure, legs akimbo, giving Walter a first-class view of the man's tackle.

'Brazen,' Walter muttered, reaching for his pint and taking a gulp.

Thankfully, Beth's easel had given her a slightly less graphic view, although she had a feeling she might think twice about buying sausages again. Beth suspected that even Melanie, who was probably more used to seeing random naked strangers, had been taken aback by the glee with which Stanley displayed himself. She'd also had a bit of a to-do trying to persuade him to cover up during the interval. It had been enough to put Beth off the Ginger Nuts (an unfortunate choice of biscuit, under the circumstances) although she did rally enough to manage a plain digestive.

'No more art classes,' Walter declared. He had a wild look about his eyes, and Beth could swear his hand was shaking.

'I thought your drawing was rather good.' He shot her a disbelieving look, so she added, 'You captured his expression perfectly. Melanie said it was an interesting caricature.'

Walter had drawn a disembodied head, with an exaggerated Cheshire cat smile and jug ears. Despite it being cartoon-like, it was clearly recognisable as Stanley. Stanley hadn't been amused when he'd seen it, despite Melanie advising him not to look at any of the drawings, and Walter had been on the receiving end of a venomous look.

Stanley hadn't been too enamoured of Beth's attempt either. Despite being able to see Stanley's proudest assets (although she had thought his pride somewhat misplaced), Beth had given him an Action Man anatomy where it counted.

'I need another,' Walter said, draining his glass.

'I think I'll join you.'

'You're driving,' he pointed out.

'We'll get a taxi.'

Drinking brandy this early in the day (it was not quite six o'clock) soon began to take its toll, and after her third, Beth was tipsy, bordering on drunk. She knew she was heading for inebriation because her nose was going numb. It was a sure sign she should stop. But she was having too much fun. She hadn't let her hair down like this in ages. Walter had recovered from his ordeal and was regaling her with stories about when he used to own the farm. Many of them made her laugh, but a few were rather poignant, and when he talked about his wife, Beth could hear the pain in his voice and her heart went out to him.

'I still miss her,' he said, his eyes damp. 'Do you miss your husband?'

Beth shook her head. 'I'd just started divorce proceedings when he died. He was a waste of space – although I'd never tell the kids that. He spent most of his life, and most of his money, in the bookies. The irony was, he'd had a bit of luck on the horses the day he was killed. He'd watched the race in the pub over the road and was on his way to collect his winnings, when he stepped into the street without looking. His winnings paid for his funeral.'

Walter put a hand on hers. 'You must have had it tough, bringing up four kids on your own.'

'I coped.' It had been hard, but her children had never gone without.

Walter squeezed her hand. 'They're a credit to you.'

Yes, she thought, they were. Even Maisie, whom she had lain awake night after night worrying about, had settled down. Adam was a good man. Although Nikki's first husband had been useless and Beth had fretted that her eldest girl had married a wrong 'un, Nikki had eventually seen sense and had got shot of him. Beth thoroughly approved of Gio, her new partner. She approved of Otto, too.

'And Otto is a credit to *you*,' she told Walter. 'He's done incredibly well for himself.'

'Despite having me for a father,' Walter lamented.

'Don't say that. You did the best you could.'

'I lost the farm.'

'He's got it back. I wonder if we'll hear the sound of wedding bells soon?'

'I hope so. I think the world of Dulcie.' Walter paused to take a sip of his drink. He had moved on to Guinness, and it left a foam moustache on his upper lip.

Beth leant across the table and wiped it away.

Walter caught her hand mid-wipe and brought it to his lips. When he kissed her fingers, a thrill tingled right through her.

He said, 'Thank you for all your help. I couldn't have managed without you. I can't believe I'm saying this, but I've enjoyed your stay in the cottage and I'll miss you when you leave.'

Beth's eyes filled up. She would miss him too.

Who'd have thought it!

CHAPTER NINE

Beth raised her face to the sun and closed her eyes, feeling the welcome warmth on her skin. It was peaceful in Walter's garden, just the drone of insects and the occasional bleat from Flossie, who was missing her little goaty friends. Petra had taken them to the stables to have their hooves trimmed, leaving the sheep on her own for the morning. Flossie wasn't happy and was letting everyone know.

Walter was in the garden with Beth, reading his newspaper and huffing now and again when he came across an article he didn't like. Since the weather had become warmer, they'd taken to coming into the garden for an hour after breakfast if they didn't have anywhere to be.

Today was a quiet day. Beth had chores to do in the house, and later she would take Peg for a walk. She quite fancied going further afield and calling in on Maisie. She would drop her a text later and ask whether she would be in this afternoon.

A few more minutes, then she'd get a move on. It was a perfect day for drying washing and she had a mind to put fresh sheets on both their beds. Beth was quite content sitting here, though. She was quite content, full stop.

Without opening her eyes, she said, 'Do you realise it's exactly a month today since I moved in with you?' Not moved in, as such, because her living here was a temporary arrangement, but Walter would know what she meant.

'A month? It feels like longer.'

Beth's eyes flew open.

'In a good way,' he added hastily.

She closed them again. 'It does,' she agreed.

Yet at the same time, the month had flown by. Soon Walter's cast would be coming off and although he would continue to use crutches for a while, he would become increasingly more mobile and increasingly less dependent on her.

Beth suspected that he could manage most things well enough on his own now anyway, but she hadn't mentioned it and neither had he. Both of them were far too comfortable with their current arrangement to want it to change. Sharing Walter's house was preferable to living with Dulcie – although Beth never thought she'd hear herself say that.

She was about to begin her chores, when her phone rang. She had left it in the kitchen and hurried inside to answer it.

The number on the screen made her pause, and for one ridiculous second she was tempted to ignore it. However, it couldn't be ignored forever. They would call back and eventually she would have to answer.

'Hello?'

'Mrs Fairfax? It's Zander. I thought you'd like to know that all the repairs on the house in Hazelnut Road have been completed. I've just been out to check, and I'm happy to say that you can move in whenever you're ready.'

'Oh, great. Thanks. I'll, um, pop in for the keys.'

Although she had been expecting a phone call at some point, now that she had received it Beth wasn't sure how she felt. She should be delighted. But she wasn't. She felt flat. Sad, almost.

As she thought about the little terraced house, she could no longer imagine herself living there. It wouldn't feel like home. Walter's cottage felt like home. And despite the new friends she had made and the active social life she now had, she feared she would be lonely living on her own.

With a heavy heart she returned to the garden to tell Walter the news.

'Beth doesn't mind taking me,' Walter said to Otto for the third time that morning.

'*I* want to take you, Dad. I'd like to be there when they remove the cast, so we know how best to help you when Beth moves out.'

'I don't need any help.' Walter knew he was being surly and ungrateful, but he couldn't help how he felt. He didn't want Beth to leave. But if she had to (and he knew that she did), he wasn't going to be railroaded into moving into the farmhouse for a few days, or having anyone stay here. It was Beth, or no one.

And he was beginning to think that no one might be preferable to Beth, because since she had given him the news four days ago, they seemed to have reverted to their sniping, carping ways. It was as though the past month had been a dream. The way things were going at the moment, he might actually be glad to see the back of her.

So, maybe her moving out was better for everyone. But, despite trying to convince himself of that, he still didn't want her to go.

Beth, on the other hand, appeared eager. She had arranged a van and a couple of blokes to move her stuff and had spent the last three days cleaning both Walter's cottage and the house in the village. He hadn't realised his place was so dirty.

It had given him a pang to see her cases packed, ready for the move tomorrow. The house would feel empty without her.

'Dad, come on,' Otto urged. 'We're going to be late.'

Walter pressed his lips together grabbed his crutches and followed Otto outside.

As they got in the car Otto said, 'I hear Beth has been stocking your freezer for you.'

'Hmph.'

'That's kind of her, isn't it?'

'Stop being so patronising.'

Otto looked shocked. 'I'm not. I was simply making an observation.'

'You were speaking to me like I'm five years old.'

'I don't know what's got into you lately. Are you worried you won't cope on your own?'

'Grr.' Walter gritted his teeth.

'Dulcie and I will make sure you're okay.'

'I don't need anyone checking up on me. I'll be fine.'

'You're still going to need a bit of help. It'll be a while before you will be able to put much weight on that leg. Then there's the physio and the exercises you'll have to do.'

Walter took a deep breath. He knew Otto's comments were coming from a place of love. He knew Otto worried about him, and he knew he deserved all this fussing because his track record of taking care of himself in the past hadn't been great.

But without the farm to run and the associated money issues, things were different now. Otto didn't need to worry. Walter could take care of himself. And once the cast was off, he would soon be back to his pre-accident self. He would have his house all to himself again, and he wouldn't have to consider anyone else. He could put the kitchen cupboards back the way they were (Beth kept changing them), there wouldn't be any mysterious potions and lotions in the bathroom, and no having to watch Beth's smalls blowing on the line next to his. His house would be nice and peaceful again.

But was that really what he wanted?

'Bye, then.' Beth wondered whether she should give Walter a hug. Maybe not: he didn't come across as a hugger. She settled for a smile and a self-conscious wave instead.

'Good luck in your new home.'

'You'll have to come visit when I've settled in.'

'I will.'

Beth was fairly certain he wouldn't. 'Will I see you at Half Board?' Her gaze flickered to his leg, now free of its cast.

'Maybe.'

'If it's transport that you're worried about, I can fetch you and bring you back.'

'We'll see.'

'And if you need me to take you to your physio appointments, just ask. You've got my number.'

'Thanks.'

'Okay, then, I'll be off. Take care, Walter.'

'You, too.'

The exchange had been stilted and awkward, and by the time Beth had opened her car door, Walter had gone back inside the cottage.

'You're welcome,' she muttered. After everything she had done for him, Walter hadn't even thanked her. He'd waved her off without a second glance.

Irritated and feeling rather flat, Beth drove to her new house in the village. She had been looking forward to this day for such a long time, but now it seemed something of an anticlimax.

With a feeling of deja vu, Beth pulled into the kerb near the house on Hazelnut Road and cut the engine.

'Here we go again,' she said, seeing the van arrive in her rear-view mirror.

She had just unlocked the door and stepped inside, when she sensed someone behind her. Assuming it was one of the removal men, she glanced over her shoulder and was shocked to discover Dulcie and Maisie. And behind them were Otto and Adam.

'We've come to give you a hand, Mum,' Dulcie said.

Maisie added, 'You didn't think we'd let you move house on your own?'

It hadn't occurred to Beth to ask for their help, but it was very welcome nevertheless, and she was touched that her daughters were here.

'Nikki says she'll pop in to see you after school,' Dulcie said.

Beth felt the prick of tears and she swallowed hard. How could she have ever thought that her daughters wouldn't want her living near them?

'Where do you want this, love?' a gruff voice asked, and everyone hurriedly moved out of the way as two burly men manhandled her sofa through the front door.

'Just there, please.' Beth pointed to a spot in front of the fireplace, and when they set it down, she shoved one end until it was at the perfect angle.

After that there wasn't any time to think, as a succession of boxes, white goods and pieces of furniture were ferried into the house. Beth directed proceedings, darting upstairs and downstairs, then back again to ensure everything was placed where she wanted it.

In much less time than she had anticipated, the van had been unloaded and most of her things had been put away.

Adam was on his hands and knees connecting the telly, when Dulcie suggested a break.

'I'll put the kettle on,' Beth said and bustled into the kitchen, wondering which cupboard held the mugs.

She needn't have worried, because no one would be having a hot drink. Otto was opening a bottle of champagne, and the pop of a cork made her jump.

'Here's to your new home,' he said, pouring the sparkling liquid into tall flutes. He handed the first one to her.

Beth took it, her lip wobbling. 'I didn't expect this.'

'I know you didn't,' Dulcie laughed. 'You had hoped to fly in under the radar, and you would have done if the ceiling hadn't come down.'

Everyone looked up at it.

'You'd never know.' Adam said. 'They've done a good job.'

'They took their time,' Beth grumbled.

Otto said, 'I bet my dad is glad they did, otherwise you would have moved in sooner, and he would have ended up back with us.'

Beth said, 'I bet he's not. He couldn't wait to get rid of me this morning.'

'Don't you believe it! He's gutted.' That was from Dulcie.

'Only because he'll have to make his own cups of tea from now on.'

Dulcie was looking at her oddly. 'I thought you two were getting on better.'

Beth had thought so, too. She had been wrong. Now that her services were no longer required, the cease-fire was over.

It was gloves off once more.

Beth sat on the sofa in her new living room, a mug of cocoa on the table next to her, the TV remote in her hand as she flicked through the channels. She was tired, but she was also restless. This would be her first night in her new house, and she guessed it might take her a while to get used to the place. And to being on her own. It was strange how quickly she had become used to someone else's presence.

Or maybe not. After all, Maisie hadn't left home too long ago. But then again, when she had lived there, Maisie hadn't been in much. Always out gallivanting, that one. Gallivanting... Her own mum, the kids' grandmother, used to accuse her of doing the same thing. Beth had always had somewhere to go, and someone to go there with. Those were the days when she had been young, free and single. The only one of those things she could lay claim to now, was the single bit. Her youth had disappeared under the weight of being a wife and a mother, and the decades in between. She had been single after the kids' father had passed away, but it hadn't bothered her then because she had been too busy getting through the days.

It bothered her now, though. The month she had spent with Walter had made her realise that her loneliness hadn't gone away; it was still there, despite having three of her four children on her doorstep. The house had been full when they had helped her unpack, but they couldn't stay forever. They had returned to their own lives, their own homes, and their own loves, leaving her alone and lonely once more.

Turning the telly off in irritation, she wondered what Walter was doing now. Revelling in having his house all to himself? Or wishing she had been there to warm up the casserole she had left him for his supper?

The first, probably.

And with that she finished her cocoa and took herself off to bed.

'How are you coping, Dad?'

'Fine.' Walter was glad that this was a phone call and Otto couldn't see him roll his eyes.

'Is there anything you need?'

'I could do with some milk and bread.'

'I'll drop them in on the way home from the restaurant this evening, if you're still up.'

'I'll be up.'

'Or I could pop in tomorrow?'

'Whatever suits you best, Otto.' Walter didn't mind either way; he would be pleased to see him regardless.

Amos and Lena had called in yesterday and they'd had a nice chat, but in the three days since Beth had left, time had dragged. It would be better when he was able to get out and about, he told himself. At the moment he couldn't walk far because he wasn't able to put much weight on his bad leg and he was still reliant on crutches, and neither could he drive yet. So he was stuck in the house.

Amos had kindly offered to have Peg for a couple of hours, so although Amos hadn't been taking her for an actual walk, she had been able to potter around the stables with Petra's dog Queenie. Walter felt quite envious. It came to something when his dog had more of a social life than he did.

Maybe he should go to Half Board tomorrow? Get out of the house for a bit. He could have a taxi there and back. Beth would probably be there, and the thought of seeing her made his heart leap. How was she getting on in her new house, he wondered. He had offhandedly asked Otto, who had told him that he'd helped her move in, along with Dulcie, Maisie and Adam, and they'd all had a glass of bubbly afterwards to toast her new home.

Walter felt quite put out that he hadn't been invited, despite knowing that he would only have been in the way and would have been as much use as a chocolate teapot.

Remembering her offer to take him to Half Board, he reached for his phone, but chickened out before he made the call. She had probably only offered out of a sense of obligation, considering she had taken him the other times he'd gone. He bet she didn't expect him to take her up on it.

His hand dropped to his side and he let out a despondent sigh. Having his house back wasn't living up to expectations. He had assumed he would enjoy the peace and quiet.

How wrong he had been.

The peace was like a heavy blanket, slowly suffocating him in loneliness, and the quiet was like a precursor to the grave. He was rattling around in the house, each room emptier than the last. It didn't help that he kept expecting Beth to walk through the door, or see her pottering in the kitchen, and he had lost count of the number of times he'd thought he'd heard her tread on the stairs, or smelt her perfume, only to find that his senses had deceived him.

A knock on the door made his heart surge with hope, and although he was pleased to see Amos, who had brought Peg back, a part of him had hoped it might have been Beth. A stupid part, because why would Beth want to visit *him?*

'Are you okay?' Amos was studying him.

'I'm fine.' Walter bent to ruffle Peg's ears. She licked him on the hand and dashed inside. A second later she was back, her tail down. She looked forlorn. 'I think she's missing Beth.'

Amos gave him a keen look. 'She's not the only one, I warrant.'

Walter let out a snort. 'As if.'

'Have it your way, but you were a happier bloke when she was around.'

'Never!'

Amos shooed him inside. 'Put the kettle on. The least you can do is make me a cuppa after I've minded your dog this morning.'

Walter scowled at his old friend but didn't argue.

'Have you heard from Eliza?' Amos asked, and Walter was glad to change the subject.

'I have. She's doing great! Five months pregnant now.' He sobered. 'I wish Emrys was here to see it. He would have been chuffed.' Walter's brother had emigrated to New Zealand thirty-odd years ago, and had died there a couple of years back. Eliza was his daughter. She had visited Picklewick at Christmas, searching for her father's roots, and had found love in the form of Jay, Beth's son.

It was strange to think of the ties that bound Walter and Beth together: Otto and Dulcie, Eliza and Jay... When Dulcie had won Lilac Tree Farm in the lottery, Walter could never have imagined how rich his life would become. He now had a whole new family, Beth included.

But he didn't actually think of Beth as family, though. He thought of her as... The word eluded him.

'It'll be Otto and Dulcie's turn next,' Amos was saying. 'There will be the patter of tiny feet at the farm.'

Walter chuckled. 'The only tiny feet Dulcie is interested in at the moment belong to the goats.'

'Pity. I think you could do with a grandchild to keep you occupied, and to keep you company.'

'I'm fine as I am.' He *would* like a grandchild, though.

'You can't fool me, Walter York; I've known you too long. It's not too late, you know.'

'Too late for what?'

'Love.'

'You're talking out of your backside.'

Amos ignored him. 'Look at me and Lena. Who would have thought we'd ever get together. Yet here we are.'

'I don't think of Beth like that.'

Amos got to his feet. 'You do; you just can't admit it.'

Thankfully Stanley was fully clothed for the art class today, and neither was he posing. He was sitting at an easel, staring at the basket of fruit arrangement that was on a table in the middle of the room.

Beth thought the subject of today's composition was considerably more boring.

She hadn't been back to the art class since that first time with Walter, but boredom and loneliness had driven her out of the house. There was only so much cleaning and baking one could do, and her girls were all at work so she couldn't pop in to see them either. She had considered driving up Muddypuddle Lane to visit Walter, but she didn't know whether she would be welcome.

It was daft to miss him so much, but she couldn't help how she felt. The question she didn't have an answer to though, was did she miss him for himself, or did she miss looking after someone – anyone?

It surprised and dismayed her to realise that she felt lonelier in Picklewick than she had felt in Birmingham. How was that possible? There was an ache in her chest that she couldn't explain, a kind of longing, but she didn't know for what.

'Walter not with you today?' Stanley asked, his eyes lighting up when he saw her.

'Not today.'

'Did I put him off?'

'Pardon?'

He nodded at his crotch. 'Not everyone is as well endowed. Some men feel threatened or inadequate.'

Beth coloured, but she rallied quickly. 'Walter doesn't need to worry on that score,' she replied, with a suggestive wink.

Stanley's face fell. Clearly that wasn't the response he had expected. 'So, are you two an item?'

Beth simpered and smiled coyly. Let him make of that what he would. She had met men like Stanley before; the slightest encouragement and he'd be sniffing around her like a dog searching for leftovers in a bin. But if he thought she was unavailable, he'd look elsewhere for his entertainment.

Stanley nodded slowly, his expression solemn. 'I'm pleased for him. Walter deserves a second chance of happiness.'

Beth's eyes widened. Gosh, that was profound.

'Treat him right, Beth,' Stanley said. He brightened. 'But if you get fed up with his cranky farmer ways, you know where to find me.'

'Right. Thanks.' What else could she say?

'You make a lovely couple, by the way,' he added.

'You do,' Melanie said, making Beth jump. She hadn't realised the art teacher was so close. 'I wish I had a fella who looked at me the way Walter looks at you. That's love for you – makes me go all gooey-eyed. It's a shame he's not here today; I loved his caricature of Stanley.' Stanley scowled as Melanie continued, 'I'd like to see what he could do with a basket of fruit, but I suspect still life isn't his speciality.'

Beth had stopped listening. She was stuck on the word *love*. It couldn't be true. The woman was talking out of her backside. Walter didn't love her. He didn't particularly like her. But for Stanley and Melanie to think the same thing…

Could there be some truth to it? Did Walter have feelings for her?

The thought made her knees go weak and she had to sit down. Shuffling towards the nearest unoccupied easel, she plopped onto the chair. Her pulse was racing and there was an odd sensation in her tummy. Her heart felt full and the ache in her chest was one she hadn't experienced in decades. So it wasn't surprising that it took her a while to understand what it signified.

Beth was in love.

The realisation caught her unawares, and she froze.

Suddenly everything made sense – the loneliness, the restlessness, the longing for something she couldn't name...

And, Beth being Beth, there was only one thing for it – she had to speak to Walter.

Leaping to her feet, she ran out of the room, ignoring the startled looks of her fellow artists, and raced home to fetch her car.

Cursing at the slow-moving traffic in the high street, she put her foot down when she left the village and was soon zooming up Muddypuddle Lane, before coming to an abrupt halt as she slammed on the brakes outside Walter's cottage.

It was then that her courage failed her, and she began to question her impulsive flight. What kind of madness had overtaken her? All it had taken were a few misguided and ill-informed comments, and she was daft enough to believe that Walter might have feelings for her. She was behaving like a schoolgirl with a crush. And she had been about to make a total and utter fool of herself. Thank goodness she had come to her senses in time.

Taking a moment to catch her breath and tame her too-fast heart, she closed her eyes, willing herself to calm down. She would go home, have a nice cup of tea, watch some drivel on the telly, and try to forget that she loved Walter.

Knuckles rapped on the driver's window and Beth's eyes flew open as she uttered a shriek.

Walter was peering in at her. 'Beth?' He made a wind-the-window-down motion.

She wound it down.

'Did you forget something?' he asked.

'No, I…' She trailed off. 'I shouldn't have come. Sorry.'

'Would you like a cup of tea, since you're here? I've got your favourites, pink wafers. And Peg would like to see you. She's missed you.'

'At least someone has,' Beth muttered.

'*I've* missed you too.'

'You have?'

Walter nodded. 'The house is empty without you.'

Beth stared at him, trying not to read too much into it.

'So is my heart,' he added.

Beth blinked. 'Excuse me?'

He froze, his expression closed. 'Never mind. I shouldn't have said anything.' He turned away and she heard him mumble, 'Stupid, so stupid.'

'Walter!' Her voice was sharp, but she couldn't leave it like that. She couldn't leave *him*. She had to know if he meant what he'd said.

He stopped, his back to her.

'Do you love me?' she called, amazed and frightened at her boldness, dreading his reply. If he said no, if she'd got it wrong, she didn't know how she would be able to face him again. She would die of embarrassment. Or possibly a broken heart. Either way, the result wouldn't be pretty.

She saw his shoulders stiffen, read the tension in his back, and feared the answer.

'Yes.' Then a low, almost furious, 'God help me.' She guessed he didn't want to love her but he couldn't help himself. She understood that, because she felt the same way.

'And I love *you*, Walter.'

He didn't turn around, not for a long time, and the silence stretched between them.

Peg broke it. The dog came charging out of the house, thundered past Walter and threw herself at the car door, whimpering ecstatically.

In slow motion, Beth watched Walter topple as the dog unbalanced him.

Beth was out of the car in a second, pushing Peg away as she knelt beside him. 'Are you hurt?' she cried, scouring his face for signs of pain.

'Only my pride. Damned dog. I swear she likes you better than me.' He was on his side, gazing up at her, his expression as grumpy as when she'd first met him.

It made her laugh. 'Thank goodness. For a minute, I thought I'd have to move back in.'

'Would that be so bad?'

'No…'

'I love you, Beth.' He pushed himself into a sitting position, as Beth fended off Peg's enthusiastic licks. 'Peg's a good judge of character,' Walter said. 'She's been pining after you.' He looked deep into her eyes. 'So have I. Can I kiss you?'

'I think you should. But can I get up first? There's a lump of gravel poking me in the bum.'

It took Beth two attempts to get to her feet, and Walter three. She had to help him up.

'Are you sure you're okay?' she asked.

'I am now. How about that kiss?'

'Go on then. And afterwards you can make me the cup of tea you promised, and I'll have two pink wafers, please.'

'You're wish is my command. *I'm* going to look after *you* for a change.'

Beth's hand slipped into his. 'How about we look after each other?' she suggested. 'That's what married folk do.'

'Beth Fairfax, are you proposing to me?'

'Not on your nelly! If there's any proposing to be done, I expect *you* to do it. Anyway, I would probably say no – after all, we can't stand the sight of each other, can we?'

'Nope, that's why I'm going to close my eyes when I kiss you. Now, stop talking woman, and pucker up.

'What's going on, Mum?' Dulcie's gaze roamed over Beth's face, then Walter's. 'Why have you called a *family meeting*?' She did air quotes with her fingers.

It was Sunday morning, and Beth was well aware that everyone in her family were busy people. But they could spare her half an hour. 'I'll tell you when Nikki gets here,' she said.

'I see you picked Walter up on the way,' Maisie observed. 'It's nice that the two of you get on.'

Beth bit back a smile and ignored the hip bump Walter gave her. 'Get the kettle on,' was all she said.

'It's on.' Dulcie rinsed out the teapot. She was adding a couple of fresh teabags when Sammy and his dog burst in through the door, Nikki and Gio following.

'Are we having a party?' he cried.

'No party, Sammy.' Beth gathered him to her, inhaling his little boy smell and swearing that he'd grown since the last time she'd seen him.

'Can we have one?' he persisted.

'Not right now, your nanna has got something to tell us.' Nikki was looking concerned.

'Make the tea and bring it into the living room,' Beth instructed, ushering Walter ahead of her.

'You're enjoying this,' he murmured out of the corner of his mouth. 'They're probably taking bets on what it's about. Do you think any of them have guessed?

'I expect so. But it's nice to make it official. They can gossip amongst themselves after we've left.'

Dulcie appeared with a tray and began to pour. Once or twice, she opened her mouth to speak, but Beth quelled her with a look.

When everyone had a drink in their hands, Beth cleared her throat. 'We've got an announcement,' she said, then paused for dramatic effect. 'I've moved in with Walter. Permanently. We're a couple.'

'A couple of what?'

'Don't be dense, Maisie – a *couple*, couple.'

Maisie's mouth fell open. 'Oh, *that* kind of couple. Bloody hell, Otto, you were right. I thought you were pulling our legs.'

Walter turned to his son. 'You guessed?'

'I *knew*. I've known from the minute you two met. It was just a question of time, wasn't it, Dulcie?'

Beth stared at her middle daughter and everything clicked into place. 'You set us up!' she accused. 'You knew I'd agree to help Walter out, if only to get rid of him. Dulcie Fairfax, you conniving, sneaky—'

A cork popped. Otto was opening a bottle of champagne for the second time in a week. 'I think this calls for a celebration.'

'Hang fire a minute,' Walter said. 'There's more.'

Beth took up the baton. 'As I'm living with Walter now, I'm not going to need my house in the village.'

A chorus of groans erupted, and Dulcie cried, 'Don't tell me we have to help you move again.'

'Not necessarily,' Beth said. She glanced at the faces of her family, settling on Maisie. 'My tenancy agreement was for six months initially, so there's no point in moving all my furniture again if I've got to pay the rent on it for half a year.'

Dulcie said, 'Can't you get out of it? It seems silly to pay rent if you're not living there.'

'Unfortunately, I can't,' Beth replied. 'Anyway, I'm happy to continue paying it, especially if someone else is living there.'

'Who?' Nikki demanded.

Beth focused on Maisie again. 'Maisie, Adam, how much longer until the old farmhouse is ready to live in?'

Maisie shrugged. 'I dunno… Five, six months.' Beth grinned as realisation dawned on her youngest child's face. 'Are you saying that me and Adam can live in your house in the village?'

'I am. I've spoken to the estate agent and it will take a bit of rejigging of the contract, but it can be done. If you want to live there rather than in that cramped and dingy caravan whilst you do your house up, you can.'

Maisie's eyes filled with tears and she leapt up to give Beth a hug. 'That's so kind of you, Mum,' she sobbed. 'We can't thank you enough.'

Beth added, 'I'll take the bits and pieces I want and move them into Walter's cottage, but you can have the rest. They'll do you for the time being, and what you don't want, you can get rid of.'

'Thanks, Mum,' Maisie said, sniffling. 'We'll be able to live in comfort until we can move into our forever home.' Then she let out a gasp. '*That's it! That's the perfect name for our new place – The Forever Home. We've been trying to think what to call it.*'

Everyone began talking at once, and with a meaningful glance at Beth, Walter and he left them to it.

'They seemed happy for us,' Beth said when they were outside. 'I can't believe Dulcie and Otto were so sly.'

Walter took her in his arms. 'I'm so glad they were. We might have got there on our own, but it could have taken a while. Who knows how much time we would have wasted bickering at each other?' He kissed her on the cheek. 'Come on, let's go home to *your* forever home.'

As she drove the short distance to Walter's little cottage, Beth realised that Walter was right; it was her home now. And by coming to Picklewick, both she and Walter had a second chance at love, and this time she knew it would last forever. Even if they did bicker now and again…

LAZY DAYS

CHAPTER ONE

Table booked at a suitably posh and expensive restaurant? *Tick.*

Taxi ordered? *Tick.*

Ring safely in pocket? *Tick*

Ashton shuffled nervously from foot to foot as he checked his appearance in the hall mirror. As usual, his hair was sticking up at the front and he smoothed it down. It immediately sprang back up. He was overdue a haircut, but he'd forgotten to go to the barber. He hadn't forgotten to buy a new shirt for the occasion, though. He'd debated whether he should wear a suit but decided against it – he didn't wear one if he could avoid it.

A car horn alerted him that his taxi had arrived. Checking yet again that the ring was in his pocket, he grabbed his keys and hurried out the door.

'The Wild Side in Picklewick please, but can we pick someone up on the way?' Ashton asked.

After giving the driver Lacey's address, he settled back in his seat and tried to relax. His leg jerked nervously, and he put a hand on his knee to hold it steady. The other began to jerk instead.

'Calm down,' he muttered under his breath, conscious of the taxi driver who kept catching his eye in the rear-view mirror.

'Special occasion, is it?' the chap asked.

You could say that, Ashton thought. 'Anniversary.'

'How many years have you been married?'

'We're not married.' *Not yet.* 'This is the anniversary of our first date.'

He had met Lacey outside a nightclub in Thornbury two years previously. She had broken one of her stiletto heels, and he had helped her limp home. She had been somewhat the worse for wear, so when she'd offered to take him out for a drink to say thanks, he hadn't been expecting to hear from her again especially since she didn't have his phone number. But she did have a fair idea of where he worked, because he had been wearing his Royal Mail uniform at the time. Her night out may have been drawing to a close, but his day had been about to start, as he had been on his way to begin his shift.

He had almost forgotten the incident, but was sharply reminded of it a few days later when he'd found her loitering outside the sorting office in the hope of catching him. She'd caught him alright – hook, line and sinker. They had been going steady ever since.

They didn't live together though, despite Ashton spending more time at her place than his own. At least, in the beginning he did, but that was until the early morning starts had begun to get to her. These days, he tended to return to his own little house when he had to be up at the crack of dawn, to allow Lacey to get a decent night's sleep. She wasn't a happy bunny when she was tired.

The taxi pulled up outside the terraced house she shared with a friend, and the driver beeped the horn.

When there was no sign of her, Ashton got out and rang the bell.

Lacey opened the door after the second ring. 'Sorry, I couldn't find my shoe.' She hopped forward on one shoe-clad foot before catching hold of his arm and bending down to slip a strappy silver sandal onto her other foot.

They shared a smile as she locked up.

'You and shoes,' he said, shaking his head and opening the rear door of the taxi for her.

She got in, and he hurried around to the other side. 'Where are we going?' she asked.

'Somewhere nice.' Ashton caught the driver's eye again and gave a little shake of his head, warning him not to spoil the surprise by telling her.

The restaurant they were about to dine at was owned by celebrity chef Otto York, and Lacey had wanted to try it ever since it had opened. It had a sterling reputation, was always fully booked, and was eye-wateringly expensive.

It was also a fitting place to propose, Ashton thought, as he patted the ring in his pocket yet again before hastily dropping his hand to his side and hoping she didn't notice how nervous he was. He didn't want to spoil *that* surprise, either.

Ashton didn't do cheesy. He wasn't a hide-the-ring-in-the-bottom-of-a-champagne-flute kind of guy, and neither did he like the idea of putting it in the delicately flavoured wild bilberry cheesecake with the lavender biscuit base and rosehip compote drizzled prettily around the plate.

Instead, he waited for the coffee to arrive and topped up Lacey's glass with the sparkling rosé wine before he made his move.

'I've got something to ask you,' he began, his hand edging towards his trouser pocket.

Lacey had been relaxing into her seat, a contented expression on her face, but she seemed to stiffen and there was a guarded look in her eye.

It was now or never. Taking a deep breath, he eased the jewellery box out of his pocket and slid off his chair into a kneeling position. There was a sudden hush and Ashton was aware that every pair of eyes in the restaurant were trained on their table. With trembling fingers, he opened the box to reveal a sparkling square-cut diamond encased in gleaming platinum.

'I love you with all my heart, Lacey. Will you marry me?'

Everyone held their breath. And continued to hold it as the hush stretched into an awkward silence. Ashton watched as the wary expression in Lacey's eyes turned to one of embarrassment.

'Um… Can we, like, talk about this later?' she asked, glancing around and blanching.

Ashton felt the colour drain from his own face, only to return in a whoosh of dismay and mortification as realisation struck.

Lacey was turning him down!

Carla pushed through the crowded pub, craning her neck as she went. The place was hot and noisy, and her nose was assaulted by a hundred different perfumes, the smell of hops, and the lingering aroma of food from the buffet laid out at the rear of the room near the bar.

Carla loved it. She would love it even more if she could spot Yale.

He was the man who was currently making her heart sing and her insides perform somersaults. He was also her line manager, and the company they worked for didn't encourage fraternisation between management and staff, especially those staff whom a manager was responsible for.

Carla fully appreciated why, but it hadn't prevented her and Yale from 'fraternising' at every opportunity. She hoped to be able to get him on his own this evening so they could fraternise some more. It might be difficult though, because the reason she and many of her colleagues were at the pub was because one of their number (and a reasonably senior one at that, hence the good turnout) was retiring.

She and Yale hadn't made any arrangements to see each other after the party, but she was seriously considering inviting him back to hers later. The anticipation of making love to him for the very first time was making her quite giddy. It would take their relationship to the next level, and maybe they wouldn't have to sneak around as much. Or would the increased intimacy mean they'd have to sneak around even more? She bloody hoped not.

There he was!

Her heart lurched at the sight of him. Tall, classically handsome, even with the round spectacles (which Carla suspected he wore more out of vanity than necessity because it made him look intelligent), Yale was the sort of man most women – and many guys – looked at twice.

If (*when*) they took the next step and slept together, Carla wondered whether it might be an idea for her to transfer to a different department. But she loved what she did and loved the department she was in. Besides, any move would probably be a step backwards, as there wasn't an equivalent role to hers at the same level. Still, the insurance company they both worked for was large and new opportunities arose all the time, so it wouldn't hurt to keep an eye open. She had been a fraud investigation officer for a while, so she could even consider applying for a promotion.

Right now, promotion was the furthest thing from her mind. All she could think about was how sexy Yale looked when he laughed. He was currently chuckling at something one of the blokes in the credit department said, and she dearly wanted to go over and join in the banter, but she thought it best not to.

Yale continually impressed upon her the importance of not broadcasting their relationship, so she was careful not to give anyone cause to suspect that the two of them were anything other than colleagues. It made life difficult because she struggled not to let her feelings show when she was at work, but she could appreciate where he was coming from. He did her annual appraisal, checked her performance, and could even discipline her if necessary, so the last thing he needed was to be accused of favouritism. Which someone would no doubt do if they knew about them, despite Yale having never shown her any preferential treatment.

Carla bought a white wine spritzer and mingled for a bit, chatting with various people, yet she was always aware of Yale in her peripheral vision. Now and again he would casually pass by, close enough for her to smell his cologne, and one time his hand even brushed against hers.

A buzzing from her clutch bag made her reach for her phone, and she smiled when she saw who the message was from, smiling even wider after she'd read it. Yale had found an empty function room on the first floor and he wanted her to join him. Carla's pulse fluttered as she anticipated a swift but passionate kiss out of the view of prying eyes. It looked like they *would* be able to grab a couple of minutes together after all.

After she meandered through the throng and stepped into a corridor leading to the loos, the noise level dropped significantly. Spying a staircase at the far end, she headed for it, glancing behind to make sure no one was watching. Gordon from sales was coming out of the men's toilet, but he didn't notice her, so she trotted up the stairs as fast as she could in her too-high heels.

When she reached the top and emerged into an expansive, empty room, Yale was waiting for her. Music, voices, and laughter floated up the stairs, but Carla felt disconnected from it.

His eyes glittered when he saw her and as he reached for her, she sank into him. His mouth found hers and he kissed her hungrily, his hands roving up and down her back, settling on the cheeks of her bum, pulling her close.

'Let's get out of here,' she murmured when they eventually came up for air.

'Can't.' His mouth found hers again.

They kissed for a few minutes more, then Carla broke away. 'Why not?'

'Got a wedding to go to tomorrow. Better not have a late night.'

Late night? Carla had been hoping he would stay *all* night, not merely for part of it.

Yale ran a hand through his hair, his fingers raking it into position, and Carla smoothed her dress, which had ridden up during their embrace.

He said, 'I need to go back to the party before I'm missed.'

'Another kiss?' she begged, hoping she would be able to change his mind about spending the night with her.

His grin was rueful. 'Can't get enough of me, eh?'

'Never,' she murmured seductively as she pushed him back against the wall and pinned him in place with her arms. She pressed herself against him and her eyes closed, as she anticipated another thrilling kiss.

'*Stop!* What the hell do you think you're doing?' he demanded at the same time Carla heard a woman cry, '*Yale?* What's going on?'

He shoved Carla away so violently that she staggered and almost fell. Regaining her balance, she turned her shocked face to the person behind her.

The woman was tall and slender, dressed to the nines, and had shiny, bouncy blonde hair. Even though her mouth was twisted in outrage and her eyes were narrowed into a furious glare, Carla could tell she was pretty.

Yale held out his hands in supplication. 'It's not what you think, Rachel. You've got to believe me.'

'Yale?' Carla was bewildered. Who was this woman? And who cared whether someone on the staff had caught them snogging? The company might take a dim view, but it was hardly a crime. Yale was seriously overreacting.

He turned to her, the sexy smile gone. In its place was disgust and contempt. 'Why can't you take no for an answer? How many times do I have to tell you I'm not interested?' He brushed past her, saying to the woman, 'I came up here to use the gents because someone had been sick in the ones downstairs.'

He jerked his chin, and Carla's confused gaze flickered to a sign at the far end of the room. It said *Toilets* and there was an arrow next to it.

'She must have clocked where I was going and followed me,' he continued, taking hold of the woman's arm and leading her towards the stairs. But before he descended them, he paused, turned to Carla and snarled, 'That's it, I'm done. No more Mr Nice Guy. I'm reporting you to HR for harassment.'

'What?' Carla's voice was faint. This couldn't be happening.

Yale shook his head sadly. 'There's no point in denying it and pretending nothing happened or that it was a misunderstanding. My fiancée witnessed your appalling behaviour.' He put his arm around the woman and ushered her down the steps. 'Come on, darling. I'm sorry you had to see that. What are you doing here, anyway? I thought you were in Walsall for the evening.' His voice faded as they reached the bottom, then disappeared altogether, lost in the laughter and chatter of the party.

Carla couldn't move. She was frozen to the spot, disbelief, horror, and heartbreak rendering her immobile. Then, as the realisation that Yale had a *fiancée* solidified in her brain, she slowly sank to the floor.

He had lied to her, had used her, and had toyed with her emotions. He was nothing but a cheating, slimy scumbag.

So why did her heart feel like it had been torn in two?

'You look awful,' Vicky announced as Carla slunk into the office on Monday.

Carla not only looked awful, she also felt it. After crying herself silly when Yale had left her alone in the empty room, she'd managed to stagger out of the pub, thankfully avoiding eye contact with anyone, and had made her way home to sob in the safety of her bedroom.

She had continued to weep on and off for most of the weekend, and by Sunday evening she had been a total mess, having not eaten or slept for forty-eight hours. Feeling nauseous but knowing she should eat, she had ordered a takeaway, managed to force about a third of it down, and had then collapsed exhausted into bed.

Getting up for work this morning had been hard, and despite her best efforts, she knew she looked hideous.

'You shouldn't be at work if you're not well, hun,' Vicky continued. She stroked her bump protectively.

'What I've got isn't catching.' Carla flung her bag and coat on her desk and dropped into her chair.

'Do you want to talk about it?'

'Yes, but not here.' She glanced around furtively. Yale's door was open, but he wasn't in his office.

She dreaded seeing him. This was going to be so awkward, and she felt the first fluttering of anger as she considered the position he had put her in. No wonder the bloody man didn't want their relationship to become general knowledge. He could hardly have broadcast it, considering he was already *in* a relationship. He had a fiancée, for pity's sake!

Her anger was accompanied by shame and bitterness. She wouldn't have gone near him with a barge pole if she'd had the slightest inkling he was taken, and she wondered whether anyone else knew he was engaged. Yale had only been working in the Birmingham office for a couple of months, having transferred from the Leeds branch, but that was no excuse for hiding a fiancée. There'd been no hint of it on the grapevine either, so she could only assume he had deliberately kept it quiet.

Vicky said, 'Shall we grab an early lunch? You can tell me all about it then.'

Carla guessed that Vicky would be shocked to learn that Yale was a two-timing arsehole. And she would be even more shocked when she knew it was Carla he was two-timing, as she hadn't told anyone, not even her best friend Dulcie, that she had been seeing him.

Deciding to get her head down and do some work (it would be an excuse not to look at Yale or acknowledge him when he appeared) Carla stowed her bag under her desk and started up her computer. She had got as far as logging into her emails when the phone rang.

It was an internal call and the news wasn't good. Mrs Bissett in HR wanted to see her. *Now*.

Carla bit her lip as she felt the remaining colour drain from her already wan cheeks. Had Yale carried through with his threat? She hadn't honestly thought he would. She'd assumed it had been bluff and bluster in the face of almost being caught in the arms of another woman.

Another woman... Carla never imagined that *she* would be the other woman. It made her feel ashamed and immoral.

Standing up abruptly, she sent her chair scooting backwards. 'I've been summoned to HR,' she announced when she caught Vicky's concerned glance. 'Shit and double shit.'

'I take it from your reaction, it isn't going to be good news?'

'No.' Carla scanned the office to make sure no one was listening. 'I've been seeing Yale,' she said.

Vicky's brow furrowed. 'Okay, it's frowned on but it's hardly a reason for HR to get involved.'

'There's more.' Hurriedly she explained what had happened at the party.

'What a rotter!' Vicky looked furious.

'Rotter?'

'I'm trying not to swear. I don't want the baby to hear.'

'No, of course not.' Carla straightened her shoulders. 'Wish me luck.'

'I bet it's about something else and not about that at all,' Vicky replied, trying to reassure her, but her tone lacked conviction.

Carla was expecting to see Yale in Mrs Bissett's office and was thankful when he wasn't. Still, she was nevertheless alarmed when the HR Manager informed her that an assistant would sit in on the meeting to make notes.

After being invited to sit down, Mrs Bissett explained the purpose of the meeting.

Carla struggled to take it in. The words 'allegation', 'misconduct' and 'investigation' lodged in her head, swirling around as she tried to make sense of them.

And when Mrs Bissett said, 'Possible disciplinary action,' Carla felt tears well up and threaten to spill over.

'I can't... It's not... It wasn't like that!' she blurted. 'If he's told you that I threw myself at him, he's lying. We've been seeing each other for the past month. As boyfriend and girlfriend.' As soon as she said it, she knew it wasn't true. How could he be *her* boyfriend when he was committed to another woman?

Hopelessly, not expecting to be believed, she continued, 'He's only saying that because his fiancée caught us together.' Oh, that sounded so bad when she said it out loud, even if it was the truth. Feeling the need to explain, she added, 'I didn't know he was engaged, honestly I didn't. He never told me, otherwise I wouldn't have...' She trailed off.

'May I stop you there, Carla. You'll have the opportunity to put your side of the story at a later date. This is just an informal chat to make you aware there has been a complaint and that you are under investigation. Furthermore, as you work in the same department as the complainant, I'm afraid we'll have to transfer you until matters are resolved one way or another.'

Close to tears, Carla tried to work out what she meant by 'one way or another.' And when she heard that she was being transferred to sales, which she had little experience of and even less enthusiasm for, she was unable to contain her dismay. The tears she had been so valiantly trying to hold back, spilled over and trickled down her cheeks as she began to sob.

It wasn't fair! *She* wasn't the one in the wrong, yet she was being punished for it.

At the sight of her distress, Mrs Bissett showed a modicum of compassion and sent her home for the rest of the day. As far as Carla was concerned, it was the least they could do.

And the way she was feeling right now, they'd be lucky if she showed up tomorrow. Or ever again!

Carla stared at her phone's screen, seeing the concern on her mum's face.

'Have you spoken to anyone? Taken some advice?' her mum asked.

Carla nodded. It was mid-afternoon in Birmingham, seven in the morning in the Caribbean, which was where her mother currently was. She worked as a holiday rep for Silver Sands Getaways and, as the name suggested, she got away a lot. During the summer, Carla hardly ever saw her. She didn't see her all that often in the winter months, either.

The arrangement suited them both, especially since Carla still lived at home. At thirty years of age, she felt that she should have a place of her own, so this was the next best thing. Considering she didn't have a whopping great mortgage around her neck, it was probably better. The benefit for her mum was that the house was occupied whilst she was away.

Right this minute, Carla wished her mum was here, despite her not being able to do anything other than give her a cuddle and some moral support.

'I've spoken to my union rep,' Carla replied. She'd had a long conversation with a lovely man called Charlie, who had basically told her not to panic. But how could she not panic? She could lose her job over this, and the thought of going to work tomorrow, into a different department and doing something she was overqualified for, made her feel ill.

What was worse was that even if her colleagues didn't know what had gone on, rumours would be rife and she didn't think she could face the whispers behind her back and the speculative looks. If she had been allowed to remain at her own desk, she might have been able to ride it out. But not as things currently stood.

Her voice breaking, she said, 'I can't go back there.'

'Then don't.'

'But I *have* to. I can't resign. It would be seen as an admission of guilt.'

'I'm not suggesting you resign,' her mum said. 'I'm suggesting you take a leave of absence until this blows over.'

So that was precisely what she did.

CHAPTER TWO

It was surprising the amount of wildlife which could be found in urban areas, Ashton thought, as he left the house. To be fair though, Thornbury wasn't as urban as some towns he could mention, as it was surrounded by rolling hills and farmland, pretty villages and tiny hamlets.

It also benefitted from having a canal running through it, and that was where he was headed now, his camera around his neck. It was a substantial piece of kit, and he often attracted odd looks from strangers as they wondered why he was carrying such a large camera and what on earth he could be photographing.

This morning, he was hoping to spot a heron. They regularly fished in the canal on the outskirts of the town, especially in the early morning when it was quiet. Only the most resolute of joggers and the occasional dog walker were out and about at this time of day.

Sidling through a swing gate, he stepped onto the towpath and walked along it for a short distance until he found a suitable place to stop. The towpath was well-maintained, but the edges had been allowed to grow wild, and large trees and bushes lined the gravelled path. Wildflowers grew freely, and the hum of busy insects added to the birdsong and the quacking of squabbling ducks.

Slipping his rucksack off, Ashton carefully wriggled between two substantial bushes and took out a small folding stool, making sure it was steady on the uneven ground. He had also brought sandwiches and a flask of tea, but he didn't take those out just yet. He wanted to give the resident wildlife time to forget he was there first. Photographing wildlife took patience, and that was something Ashton had in spades. He could spend hours sitting on a riverbank, in a field, or on the side of a mountain without being bored.

Lacey hadn't understood. With the benefit of hindsight, he finally realised that she hadn't *wanted* to.

With peace settling around him as he blended into the undergrowth, Ashton's mind began to wander. He'd found himself doing that a lot over the past few weeks, which wasn't surprising considering his humiliation in the restaurant.

When Lacey had refused his offer of marriage, she'd said she wanted to talk about it later, but little discussion had been involved after he'd taken her home. She had clearly been embarrassed, and the surprise he had planned had come out of left field. As far as she was concerned, marriage had been the last thing on her mind. In fact, she was contemplating ending their relationship, and this made up her mind. Lacey may have been the love of Ashton's life, but he clearly wasn't the love of hers. And, he had discovered, she wanted more excitement than a mere postman could give her. Apparently, he wasn't ambitious enough, either.

Ashton hadn't been able to argue with that. He *wasn't* ambitious. He had no urge to climb the corporate ladder and no burning desire for greater responsibility because, along with the increase in salary, there would be an increase in stress. He liked his work-life balance just the way it was. Besides, he enjoyed what he did. He was out in the fresh air for a big part of his shift and getting plenty of exercise at the same time. He didn't want to be stuck behind a desk all day. He earned enough to pay his bills, with a bit left over for his hobby plus a meal out now and again and a couple of drinks down the pub.

Thinking of meals out made him cringe as he recalled the events of that night, and he vowed never to set foot in the place again. The staff had been lovely, but he had felt the weight of their pity as he'd paid the bill and left sharpish. And if it wasn't for the fact that Picklewick was on his round, he probably wouldn't have gone anywhere near the village again, either.

A flash of orange and turquoise caught his eye, and Ashton sucked in a breath. It was a kingfisher!

The bird plunged into the water, then flew onto an overhanging branch to eat its catch.

Ashton's camera whirred silently as it captured image after image. He zoomed in, the telephoto lens displaying the bird's gloriously iridescent plumage as it manoeuvred the fish into the right position to swallow it whole. Breakfast finished, it darted off peep-peep-peeping as it disappeared from sight.

Ashton let out a soft, delighted breath. What a treat! He couldn't wait to show Lacey the photos—

Reality threw a bucket of cold water over him as he remembered that he and Lacey were no longer together. And even if they were, she would have shown scant interest in his photography. The only photos she was interested in were those with her in them.

Crossly, he told himself to stop thinking about her. It didn't change anything and only served to make him feel even more sad.

These past few weeks had been awful, filled with misery and hurt, and today was no exception. He didn't think he could face going home just yet. He would stay here a while longer, because although they had spent more time at her place than at his, the house felt far too empty. He could cope with the silence, but the loneliness in his heart was a different matter.

Dulcie was waiting by the door when Carla arrived at the farm, and as she held out her arms, Carla stepped into her embrace. 'Aw, you poor thing,' her friend said, hugging her tight, then called to her partner over her shoulder, 'Thanks for picking her up, Otto.'

'No probs. See you later,' Otto said, getting back in his car and driving out of the yard.

Carla hugged her back fiercely. 'I could have got the bus,' she protested. She had considered using her mum's car, but as she didn't drive often, she didn't feel up to a long journey on unfamiliar rural roads, especially when her head was 'in the shed' as her nan used to say.

'Nonsense! Otto had to go into Thornbury anyway, so it was no bother.'

'Are you sure you don't mind me staying with you for a while?'

'Of course not! You should have come sooner. I did ask you to.' Dulcie released her and slipped an arm through hers, leading her across the cobbled farmyard to the house.

A black cat ran up to them, almost tripping Carla as it wound around her legs.

'That's Magic,' Dulcie said. 'She seems to have adopted us. I think she's a stray.' She bumped the door open with her hip. 'Coffee? Or wine?'

Carla wasn't in the mood for alcohol. 'Coffee, please.' She plonked herself down on a kitchen chair. 'Thank you for having me. I don't think I could have faced another day on my own in that house.'

Dulcie gave her a stern look. 'I'm going to set a few ground rules, and the first one is that you have to stop thanking me. I'm your friend – that's what friends are for.'

Carla smiled sadly at her. 'Everyone descends on you when they've got a problem, don't they? Nikki, Maisie, your mum, and now me.' She barked out a laugh. 'At this rate there won't be anyone left in Birmingham. They'll all be here!'

'Do you blame them?' Dulcie pointed at the view through the window. 'Look at it! This place is gorgeous.'

'It is,' Carla agreed, accepting a mug of fragrant coffee. She had been travelling for ages, and this was very welcome.

Dulcie joined her at the table, cradling her own mug. 'I can't believe the investigation is dragging on for so long, even if that ratbag is out of the country. Surely they can carry on without him?'

'Apparently, he didn't give a statement, or whatever it was that HR wanted him to do before he went on annual leave. He's in Mexico currently.'

Dulcie gave her a shrewd look. 'Was this holiday already planned, or did he decide to flee the country because he didn't want to face the flak at work?'

'I'm not sure he had any flak to face,' Carla replied miserably. 'I'm the bad guy, remember? I'm the one who '*threw herself*' at him.' She did air quotes with her fingers. 'Vicky says everyone knows, despite it supposedly being confidential.'

'He's leaking it,' Dulcie said. 'He's going on the offensive and getting his version in first, so no one believes yours even though it's the truth.'

'I can't go back there. The thought of walking into the office makes me feel sick. Thank goodness HR agreed I could take leave until it's sorted out. Without pay, of course. But I don't care. I would happily live on fresh air if it meant I didn't have to go back there.'

'What will you do? Resign?'

Carla shook her head. 'I want to, but it'll make me look guilty.'

'Can they sack you?'

'Probably. Definitely, if they believe Yale. Which they will.'

Dulcie reached across the table and clasped her hand, saying gently, 'Don't you think it's better to resign, instead of being sacked? Especially if you've no intention of ever going back.'

Carla lowered her head. 'I don't know what to do,' she replied, her voice breaking.

'Whatever you decide, you can stay here for as long as you need.'

'You might regret saying that.' Carla's chin wobbled.

'Nah, the bright lights of Birmingham will lure you back eventually. How many times have you told me that Picklewick is a lovely place to visit, but you wouldn't want to live here?' She finished her coffee. 'Drink up and unpack your case, then I'll introduce you to the goats and show you how you can earn your keep.'

'Please don't tell me you want me to milk them,' Carla begged.

'Better! I'm going to do goat walks.'

'You're joking, right?'

'Not at all. You've heard of llama walks? Well, I'm going to be offering goat walks. Goats are nicer than llamas because they don't spit.'

'You want me to walk *a goat*?'

'Why not? They've got to start their lead training, and getting out in nature will do you good. You'll be the farm's official goat walker from now on.'

Carla almost wished she was back in Birmingham. Almost, but not quite.

Carla had seen goats before. The last time she'd visited the farm, Dulcie had been looking after the two goats belonging to the stables. Now though, Dulcie had eighteen goats of her own. *Eighteen!* She also had a flock of chickens, several cute bunnies, and a cat. How did she cope with all those animals, especially the goats?

Carla found out the following morning after Dulcie had shown her the changes she'd made since her last visit.

'I milk the adults every morning,' Dulcie said, rattling a bucket filled with something she called sheep nuts. It was ridiculously early, but Carla had been awake and heard Dulcie pottering around downstairs, so she'd got up. She was beginning to think she should have stayed in bed.

They were standing next to a gate leading to what Carla could only describe as a kids' play area – but for goats. As she watched the young goatlings jump and prance as they followed their mums, she wished she had half their energy. She felt like she had been steamrollered, picked up, then steamrollered for a second time.

Dulcie rattled the bucket again and opened the gate, careful to keep the treats out of the animals' reach. Tutting, she said, 'You know the rules, girls; you have to wait until you're in the milking parlour.'

Bemused, Carla watched as Dulcie shepherded the goats inside, before attaching the milking equipment to their udders. The goatlings didn't seem at all bothered as they trotted off to the barn for their own breakfast of fresh hay, bleating loudly with excitement.

Organised chaos was the best way to describe it, Carla thought. Dulcie was in her element, and Carla marvelled at how much her friend had changed since she'd won the farm. Once upon a time, Dulcie would have run away screaming if a goat so much as looked at her (in fact, Carla recalled Dulcie doing just that when a hand-reared sheep had demanded to be petted) yet look at her now. She was every inch a farmer.

She was so happy and so in love with what she was doing, that Carla felt a pang of envy. Dulcie was also madly in love with Otto, which gave Carla another pang. Once upon a time, she'd hoped that her relationship with Yale would lead to the kind of happiness Dulcie enjoyed.

Groaning inwardly, she told herself to stop thinking about him, but it was hard not to. If the investigation hadn't been hanging over her, she might have been able to put him out of her mind completely after the way he'd treated her She had initially thought she was heartbroken, but as the days had dragged into a week, and then a second, she'd realised that what she'd felt was infatuation, not love. As someone who dated a lot but rarely allowed a man to touch her heart, it had been a shock to discover how smitten she'd been. But she'd mistaken attraction, lust and the excitement of keeping their relationship quiet, for love.

Carla would never make the same mistake again.

Milking done, the two friends went indoors for a breakfast of scrambled eggs on toast, as the farm had an abundance of free-range eggs, courtesy of a small army of chickens. There was also a glut of juicy, ripe pears from the trees in the orchard, as well as punnets of glossy blackberries in the large fridge where the milk bottling took place. Dulcie had told her some of Otto's dishes in his restaurant featured the fruit. She explained that he obtained much of the produce he used in The Wild Side from the farm and its surroundings, including the spinach and other salad leaves growing in the veggie plot. As Dulcie had shown her around, Carla admired the couple's resourcefulness and ingenuity.

'How do you like the goats?' Dulcie asked, sprinkling salt on her eggs.

Carla swallowed a mouthful before she spoke. 'The little ones are cute.'

'It's their mums who will be walked.'

'Can't I walk the babies instead?'

'They'll play up if they're separated from their mothers. The adults are used to having halters on, so hopefully they shouldn't find going for a walk too stressful.'

'Couldn't you have had dogs instead? They *like* being walked.'

'I'm leaving the dogs to Maisie. Did I tell you she's opening a boarding kennel? Anyway, owning goats was your suggestion, remember?'

'I didn't think you'd do it. I was simply throwing ideas out there.'

'And that one stuck.' Dulcie grinned. 'Go on, why don't you take Cloud for a walk after breakfast? The fresh air will do you good.'

'With the whiff of goat in my nostrils? Hmph!'

'The view from the top is gorgeous.'

'You want me to walk all the way up the mountain?' Carla was incredulous.

'It's hardly a mountain. More like a hill.'

'I thought I was here for some rest and relaxation?'

Dulcie scoffed, 'The only time you relax is when you're sprawled on a sun lounger on a Mediterranean beach with a cocktail in your hand, and even then you're on high alert in case a fit guy walks past.'

Carla pressed her lips together. The thought of ogling any man right now turned her stomach.

Sprawling on a sun lounger sounded good, though. Suddenly, she realised how utterly weary she was and how much the last couple of weeks had taken out of her.

She also realised she had come to the farm for a complete change of scenery, and hiking up the mountain while towing a goat was as complete a change as she could possibly get.

'Okay,' she agreed with a sigh. 'Saddle her up.'

'You can't ride her,' Dulcie warned, looking alarmed.

'I wasn't going to. It was just an expression.'

'I wouldn't put anything past you. You're always up for a laugh. My mum used to call you the wild one. I was the sensible one. Talking about being wild, how about we go out for dinner this evening? Otto suggested we go to the restaurant so he can cook you some proper food. He didn't think much of me shoving a supermarket pizza in the oven last night, although I thought it was a perfectly acceptable meal. We can come back here afterwards and crack open a bottle of wine. What do you say? I know it's not the party lifestyle you're used to, but it's the best I can do – unless you fancy a drink in The Black Horse. I've got to warn you though, it's bingo night.'

Carla wrinkled her nose.

'I didn't think bingo would float your boat,' Dulcie laughed. 'Wine and a natter back at the house, then.'

However, it wasn't the thought of bingo that Carla disliked. It was the thought of going out. She hadn't been out – as in a bar or a pub – since that night. Not only had Yale's deceit given her heart a knock, but her confidence had also taken a battering.

328

It didn't help that she'd had too much time to dwell on what she was doing with her life, and how it had gone so horribly wrong. One minute she had been having fun, enjoying her job, loving her social life, and with the prospect of being in a relationship with someone she really liked, and the next minute, everything had come crashing down around her.

The subsequent thinking and dwelling over the past two weeks had led to the realisation that all her friends were moving on with their lives, whereas hers hadn't changed in almost a decade. She was thirty and what did she have to show for it? She mightn't have a job soon, she didn't have a place of her own, and she didn't have anyone special in her life. Even Maisie, Dulcie's flighty younger sister, had settled down and was making a go of things.

Fed up with herself, Carla followed Dulcie as she went to fetch the goat. She'd read that llama walks were meant to lift the spirits and relieve stress and anxiety, so maybe walking a goat would be just as relaxing.

Somehow she doubted it.

I wonder whether goats are able to find their own way home, Carla mused as she gazed at the heather and bracken-covered hillside. The farm was down there somewhere, but she couldn't see it from here and she prayed she wasn't lost. Hence the hope that goats had similar homing instincts to pigeons.

She had stopped for a breather, one of many because this hill was steep, but Cloud didn't seem bothered that her nice comfy barn was out of sight. The animal was busy gorging itself on the surrounding foliage, as were her babies.

For the first ten minutes, Carla had been concerned that the goatlings would wander off (she really didn't fancy having to explain to Dulcie that she'd lost two of her precious goats), but she needn't have worried as they didn't stray too far from their mum. And while Cloud had tip-tapped obediently behind Carla as she had led her along the narrow dirt path, the babies gambolled and scampered amongst the heather.

They were incredibly cute and funny to watch. However, they soon realised from their mother's contented chewing that there was a smorgasbord of munchable leaves all around, and they quickly settled down to nibble at them.

As she watched them eat, she wondered how much further she needed to go. Would this do as Cloud's first proper walk? The goat had behaved herself, so did she need any more training?

Aside from the contented chewing noises, it was rather peaceful up here with just the wind and a bird call or two. The sun was warm and the springy heather looked quite inviting, so Carla decided to extend her breather into a proper rest and enjoy the solitude and the view.

It was a far cry from the noise of the open-plan office where she should have been this morning. The scenery was better, too.

Keeping a firm hold on the lead rope in case Cloud decided to make a break for it, Carla sank into the heather as her thoughts lingered on work, and she wondered what they were saying about her. She really should give Vicky a call to see how bad the gossip was and to reassure her friend that she was okay. She also wanted to find out whether Yale was back from leave yet.

Carla could feel her anger growing at the thought of that man going about his normal day while she was effectively in exile.

Did she miss work? Did she heck! Given a choice, she would rather be sitting on the side of a hill in the sun and watching goats eat grass, than be at work, but it was the principle of the thing. And also, the small problem of losing her job would mean no income.

Reflexively, she eased her phone out of the back pocket of her jeans and checked to see whether there was anything from HR. There wasn't, and she didn't know whether to feel disappointed or relieved. She desperately wanted to get this over with, but feared what would happen when it was.

Movement caught her eye and she stiffened. Was that a rabbit? Carla held her breath, keeping as still as possible. No, it wasn't a rabbit. It didn't have the ears for it. It looked like a cat, and was bounding and bouncing over the grassy tumps. Unusual markings, she thought, as it came closer – a brown back and white chest. Then suddenly it was gone.

She exhaled slowly.

Having lingered enough, she got to her feet. It was time to go back. She reckoned she'd been out here long enough.

Realising he was whistling, Ashton pressed his lips together to trap in the sound. Lacey had hated whistling. She used to say it 'did her head in,' and that it was tuneless, which he vehemently denied. He didn't for one minute believe his whistling was tuneless. In fact, as he was shoving letters and leaflets through the letterboxes on Hazel Road, he thought he had been giving a fairly decent rendition of *Sittin on the Dock of the Bay*.

Knocking on the door of number twelve and handing the young woman her parcel, it occurred to him that he no longer had any reason to suppress his whistling tendencies. He could whistle to his heart's content, and no one would stop him.

Pursing his lips, he gave an experimental toot.

'Someone's lively this morning,' the woman said.

She looked familiar, but so did most of Picklewick. Then it occurred to him where he'd seen her before. 'You're usually at the farm on Muddypuddle Lane, aren't you?'

'That's right. It belongs to my sister, Dulcie.'

Ashton slapped a palm to his forehead. 'Of course! Maisie, isn't it? I thought I knew you from somewhere. You look like her, too.'

'All us Fairfax kids look the same. Even my brother Jay, although he's more masculine.'

'I'm off up there in a bit,' he said, patting the Royal Mail bag which was slung across his body. Not that he had anything for Muddypuddle Lane in there, as those letters were currently in the back of his van.

'Do you want me to take them for you?' Maisie asked.

'Thanks for the offer, but I'd better not. It's against the rules.' He smiled. 'You could be anyone, and I've also got post for the stables and the cottage. Besides, I quite like driving up there – great views and I sometimes get to see some wildlife.'

'Yeah – Dulcie!' Maisie giggled. 'Don't tell her I said that.'

'I won't.' Ashton gave her a wave as he walked off.

It didn't take him long to finish his route in the village, and then it was time to hop back in the van and head off to Muddypuddle Lane. He had a couple of farms, isolated houses and businesses after that, before moving on to a small hamlet about two miles away. He didn't mind the deliveries being so far apart because he enjoyed the drive through the countryside, especially in the summer. Everything was bursting with life and was so lush and green. The sun was a welcome sight, and he wound down his window to let the breeze play over his face.

Slowing to turn into Muddypuddle Lane, he smiled as he saw the horses in the field. They were galloping, their necks arched and tails held high, and seeing them made his spirits soar. There was nothing quite as beautiful as a horse running free.

As he got out of his van at the stables, he breathed in the scent of horse. It wasn't an unpleasant smell, and when he saw an equine head poking over the top of a stable door, he paused for a moment to give its nose a stroke.

Letters delivered, it was the turn of the farm at the top of the lane next.

After handing Dulcie her post, Ashton was about to get back in his van when he saw a woman walk into the farmyard. She had a goat on a lead, closely followed by a pair of gambolling youngsters.

It wasn't the goats that gave him pause though, it was the woman. She was gorgeous – spiky dark hair, high cheekbones, big hazel eyes and a figure a man could lose himself in for days. Not only that, but he was certain he had seen her before.

'Made it back safe, I see,' Dulcie called to her. She turned to Ashton. 'This is my friend Carla. She's staying with me for a while.'

He took a second to find his voice. 'Hi.'

Carla smiled, instead of replying. It didn't quite reach her eyes.

'This is Ashton, my postie,' Dulcie said to Carla. 'You met him last time you were here, remember?'

Ah, that explained it. It was over a year ago, but he had a good memory for faces.

Carla looked at him, but there wasn't any recognition in her eyes. And why would there be? As Ashton recalled, the meeting had been a very brief one indeed.

He gave her a nod, and as he opened the van door he heard her say, 'I think I saw a stray cat. It definitely wasn't Magic.' She pointed up the hill. 'It was up there.'

Dulcie said, 'It's probably Walter's ginger tomcat. That creature is feral.'

Ashton got into the driver's seat and clipped in his seatbelt.

'It wasn't ginger,' Carla was saying. 'It was chocolate-coloured with white all down its front. It looked like it had lain in a pot of paint. It was really small though, but very bouncy.'

Ashton paused. It didn't sound like a cat. From Carla's description, it sounded remarkably like a stoat or a weasel. He'd only ever caught glimpses of a weasel, and he had never seen a stoat.

Vowing to return after his shift, he drove off down the lane. However, it wasn't the possibility of photographing one of the elusive creatures that caused the buzz of excitement in his chest – it was the possibility of seeing the woman with the troubled eyes.

CHAPTER THREE

'How was the goat walk?' Dulcie asked after the postie had driven off.

'It was good, actually.'

She smiled. 'I knew you'd like it. Can you do me a favour and take them to the field? I've got to get back to work.'

Carla felt awful. She'd descended on Dulcie without warning, so of course Dulcie had to work. As well as the farm, her friend had a 'day job' working for a large energy supplier, dealing with customer complaints, but there was an upside in that Dulcie was able to work from home. Carla didn't know how she managed to do both.

'What else can I do to help?' Carla asked.

'Aw, that's sweet of you, but Maisie will be here in a minute.' Dulcie shot her a meaningful look as she said, 'You won't believe how much she does around the farm. She finally seems to have found something she enjoys. I'm going to miss her when the kennels are up and running.'

'When will that be?'

'Early next year, Adam estimates. Bless him, he's doing most of the work himself, as well as running his business. It's a good thing he's so brilliant at stuff like that. He can turn his hand to anything.'

'What does Maisie do on the farm?' Carla was still wondering how she could help.

'Milking, bottling, soap making, egg collecting, rabbit feeding – anything and everything.'

'Surely there's something I can help with? I can't just sit around doing nothing.'

Dulcie reached out to stroke her arm. 'You don't have to, honestly. You've had a tough time of it lately. Just relax and put your feet up.'

As Carla watched her walk back to the house, tears pricked her eyes. Dulcie was the best friend ever, and Carla wished she still lived in Birmingham. It wasn't the same without her. When Dulcie won the farm, Carla had been convinced Dulcie would soon realise life in the sticks wasn't for her. But to her surprise, Dulcie had taken to it like a duck to water (after an initial blip or two) and was now incredibly happy. She was also madly in love, and Carla couldn't help wishing that she could find a love like that. She had begun to think she might have found it with Yale, but look what a rat he had turned out to be.

Carla returned Cloud and her babies to the field to join the other goats, and watched them for a while, enjoying their antics as the little ones played together. Then she dawdled back to the house.

When she got there, she discovered Maisie had arrived and was about to start making soap.

Maisie greeted her with a hug. 'Long time, no see,' she said.

'It's been a while,' Carla agreed. 'I hear you'll be running a kennel soon.'

'Yeah, who'd have thought it!'

'Not me.' Carla grinned at her. 'Look at you, adulting at last.'

Abruptly, she sobered as she realised that Maisie's lifestyle was now far more adult than her own. Maisie was the one with a house, a business plan, and a partner. Whereas Carla was still living with her mum, her boyfriend had turned out not to be hers at all, and she wasn't sure whether she still had a job.

Maisie gave her a sympathetic look. 'Dulcie told me about your stinker of a boyfriend.'

'But he wasn't *my* boyfriend, was he? He was someone's *fiancée*.'

'Stop beating yourself up. You weren't to know.'

'Is that what I'm doing?'

'Uh-huh.'

'But he could cost me my job.'

'So? Get another.'

'That's easy for you to say,' Carla retorted.

'Because I've had loads of them?' she laughed. 'Doesn't that prove my point?'

'But I like my job.'

Maisie shrugged. 'In that case, you'll have to fight for it.'

Easier said than done, Carla thought. How could she fight when she didn't have a leg to stand on? Yale had made sure of that.

'Why the goggles?' Carla eyed the pair in her hand with mistrust. They weren't exactly fetching.

'Lye is basically sodium hydroxide,' Maisie explained. 'It's horrid stuff. You don't want to get it on your skin, and definitely not in your eyes.' She gave her a pair of black, heavy-duty rubber gloves. 'You'll need to put those on as well.'

'Why use it at all, if it's so horrid?'

'When it's mixed with fats and oils the chemical reaction leaves no residue, so it's perfectly safe. In fact, you can't make soap without it. Well, you *can*, but it's not classed as natural soap.'

Carla frowned. 'Do you mean that the soap I washed my face with this morning contains lye?'

'It does. Plus goat's milk, coconut oil, olive oil and fragrance.'

'You know an awful lot about it.'

'I've been making soap for a couple of months now, but there's still a lot to learn.'

Carla examined the equipment and ingredients laid out on the workbench. She and Maisie were in one of the sheds next to the milking parlour. After being informed that it used to house sheep, Carla was convinced there was still a whiff of the woolly animals in the air. Her eyes roved around the room, noting the fridge and freezer, the racks of shelves with colourful bars of soap on them, and the table with an old bookcase behind which held the finished products, packaged and neatly labelled.

'Where do you sell it?' Carla asked.

'Online, although we do have the occasional customer who buys it direct from us when they pop up to the farm for their milk and cheese.'

'You and Dulcie have a proper production line going on.' Carla was filled with awe.

'We have. In fact, Dulcie's hoping that by the autumn, she'll be able to give up the day job and concentrate on this. She's just started making candles too, as another string to her bow.'

Maisie was interrupted by the sound of a vehicle pulling into the yard, and she went to take a look. When she returned ten minutes later, she said, 'That's another satisfied customer. Dulcie gets people popping in all the time to buy milk and cheese, and when I mentioned we had a glut of pears, she bought a bag of those as well. There's a lot of surplus produce, so it's good she can make few pounds from it.'

'I don't know how she manages to fit it all in. How does she cope with people just turning up out of the blue if she's working?'

'Luckily, she's got me most of the time, but when the kennel is up and running I won't be around much, so I've no idea how she'll manage.' Maisie put her goggles on and slipped her hands into the rubber gloves, indicating that Carla should do the same. 'You won't believe how inconsiderate some people are, though. Last week, she had someone knocking on the door at eleven o'clock at night, wanting to buy milk for their bedtime cocoa.'

'Why doesn't she have a proper shop?'

'Not enough hours in the day, can't afford the rent – to name two reasons. Anyway, when she does give up her job, she'll want to be on the farm, not in the village, and renting a shop would eat into her profits.'

Carla waited a moment before she donned her goggles. 'I wasn't thinking about a shop in the village. I was thinking about her having a shop *here*. I noticed she keeps the milk and cheese in the bottling shed, the soaps in here, and the fruit in the barn. If she had everything in one place, with a proper counter, display units, and set opening times, it would be much easier for her. If customers are already dropping in ad hock, it makes sense to have them arrive when it's convenient for Dulcie, and there's also the likelihood of add-on sales if all the items are together.'

Maisie was staring at her, her eyes huge beneath the goggles. She shook her head slowly. 'Carla Mason, you're a genius! Why didn't we think of that?'

When they eventually began making soap, Carla was smiling. She mightn't be able to sort out her own pathetic life, but at least she could be useful to someone else.

Ashton drove into the yard and tucked his car to one side, out of the way of any farm vehicles which might be trundling back and forth. Then he got out, slung his camera around his neck, feeling the familiar weight of it, and patted his pockets to make sure he had the lenses he might need. He'd attached the telephoto lens before he'd left the house, but he mightn't keep it on the whole time he was out. It depended on what caught his eye and how he was going to photograph it.

Locking his car out of habit, he headed across to the house to speak to Dulcie. But it wasn't Dulcie who answered his rat-a-tat knock, it was her friend, Carla.

On seeing her, Ashton's pulse quickened. She really was gorgeous, and although he wasn't ready to start dating again (it would be quite a while before he put himself out there), at least it proved he might be one day.

'More post?' she asked, then she clocked the camera and her eyebrows rose.

'Hi, is Dulcie in? I need to have a quick word.'

'Yeah. Hang on a minute.'

She turned away, presenting him with her profile, and he tried not to stare at the curve of her cheek or the way her long lashes curled almost to her brow.

She yelled, 'Dulcie, your postman wants a word!'

Ashton heard Dulcie shout that she would be there in a second, which left him and Carla gazing awkwardly at each other.

'You've got a big camera,' she said, then to his amusement she blushed furiously. 'That's not a euphemism, by the way.'

He held back a smile. 'I didn't think it was.' He stroked the long lens absently, then realised what he was doing and snatched his hand away. Oh flip, now *he* was blushing.

Carla smirked. 'What's your speciality? Or shouldn't I ask?'

'What? *No!* I don't—! He sighed. 'Wildlife.'

'You're here because of the cat, so am I right in thinking it wasn't a cat at all?' She studied him, and he felt the weight of her stare on his face.

'Probably not. From your description, I'd say it was a stoat or a weasel.'

She shook her head. 'I doubt it. It was tiny.'

'You'd be surprised how small they are. Squirrel sized.'

Her eyes widened. 'Really?'

Dulcie appeared in the doorway. 'Hi, Ashton. Is anything wrong?'

'Not at all. I wondered whether I could park my car in your yard? I'm off for a walk, you see, and—'

'He thinks the cat I saw this morning might be a stoat or a weasel. He wants to photograph it.' Carla sounded excited.

Dulcie's gaze dropped to his chest and the camera sitting there. 'You're a photographer?'

'In my spare time.'

'Any good?' she asked.

'Not bad. Hardly professional level, though.'

'If you manage to take a couple of snaps of it, will you show me?' Carla asked.

Snaps? He tried not to take offence. 'I will,' he promised. 'But the likelihood of seeing it is small.'

'*I* saw it.'

'Right place, right time,' he replied mildly.

Dulcie suddenly asked, 'Is photography just a hobby, or do you take on paid work?'

'Not as such. I have sold a couple of photos, though.' He tried to gauge why she wanted to know.

'I wonder whether you could take some shots of the farm for our website? I'll happily pay the going rate.'

'I'd be delighted to, but there's really no need to pay me.'

Dulcie scowled at him. 'That's no way to run a business.'

'I'm not running a business. I do this for fun.' He gently tapped the camera.

'I'll pay you in kind, then,' she said, shooting Carla a look when Carla giggled.

Ashton refused to meet Carla's eye. 'There's no need,' he reiterated.

'There absolutely is!' Dulcie was insistent. 'How about some fresh produce? We've got pears, eggs, milk and cheese, and I could add a couple of punnets of blackberries. Oh, and how about soap? Perhaps your girlfriend would like to take a look at our website and choose some. We do candles, too. Better still, how about a nice romantic meal for two in The Wild Side?'

She was gazing at him hopefully, and Ashton tried not to flinch. He had no intention of stepping through The Wild Side's door ever again. Not after the last time.

'I, um, don't have a girlfriend.' He glanced at Carla as he said it, then hastily looked away.

Dulcie said, 'Sorry, I thought you did. My mistake.'

'We split up.'

'That's a shame. Would your mum like something instead?'

'The fresh produce is fine,' he replied, not wanting any but guessing that Dulcie wasn't going to take no for an answer.

'Great! I'll leave a note with my number on under your windscreen wiper, and we can chat about it tomorrow or the day after, if that's okay?'

'That's fine.'

'We could do it now, but we're going out in half an hour and I need to get ready. We're having dinner at The Wild Side.' Her eyes widened. 'You're welcome to join us.'

He caught Carla's surprised expression out of the corner of his eye. Even if he did consider accepting Dulcie's offer, he got the impression that Carla wouldn't appreciate him being there.

'I'm not really dressed for it but thank you anyway.' He glanced over his shoulder at the hillside behind the house. 'Thanks for letting me park my car here, I appreciate it.'

Dulcie said, 'It's no bother. Next time, don't ask. If I see your car in the yard, I'll assume you're off photographing something. And don't forget to give me a call.'

'I won't,' he promised. He was flattered she'd asked. Although, considering she hadn't seen any of his work, she might wish she hadn't. However, as he walked briskly up the path, he realised he was very much looking forward to showing Carla what he was capable of. No, not *Carla*, he amended – *Dulcie*.

Ignoring his mental slip of the tongue, he pushed on up the hill – he had a small, elusive mammal to capture on film.

Carla twiddled the stem of her wine glass, growing a little exasperated.

'You thought Ashton was hot when you visited last time,' Dulcie pressed. It was the second time she'd mentioned it.

'I don't think so now, okay?'

'Why not? He looks the same as he did before. He hasn't changed in the slightest.' Dulcie waved her glass in the air and wine sloshed out. Otto looked bemused.

'Maybe not, but *I* have.'

The three of them were enjoying an early dinner in The Wild Side, Dulcie enjoying it more than Carla and Otto combined, judging by the amount of wine she'd consumed.

Slurring her words, Dulcie said, 'You know what they say – the best way to get over one man is to get underneath another.'

'No thanks.'

'But he's cute!' Dulcie took a slug of her wine, and Otto gently took the glass out of her hand. 'Oi! What are you doing? That's mine.'

'You're tipsy,' he said.

'I know. Isn't it wonderful?'

'You won't think it's wonderful tomorrow morning when you're dealing with shouty, sweary customers.'

Carla said, 'She always was a lightweight.'

Dulcie looked affronted. 'I'm not!' She turned to Otto. 'Tell her I'm not.'

'She is,' he agreed, laughing.

Dulcie scowled and poked her tongue out. 'I'm not speaking to you. Go and do something cheffy and leave us girls to talk about girly stuff.'

Otto stood up, grinning. 'I'll send someone over with a couple of coffees.'

Dulcie tracked his progress to the bar. 'He's lovely,' she sighed.

Envy nibbled at Carla once more. She was delighted to see Dulcie so happy and in love, and would give anything to have that for herself.

'Do you think he's cute?' Dulcie asked.

'What? Otto? Er... I haven't really thought about it.'

'Not Otto, you dipstick – Ashton.'

'Oh, we're back to that, are we? Can we please stop talking about your postman?'

'Okay, but I think he fancies you.'

346

Carla rolled her eyes. 'I don't care if he does. Have you forgotten the reason I'm here?'

Suddenly Dulcie didn't seem quite so tipsy. 'No, I haven't. But I don't believe Yale was the love of your life, and I certainly don't believe you're heartbroken.'

Her comment made Carla pause. 'You're right, he wasn't and I'm not. He could have been, though.'

Dulcie snorted. 'Yeah, if he'd had a personality change. Anyone who behaved the way he did, is a creep.'

Carla had to agree. Admittedly she had been upset at how he'd deceived her, but she was over that now. She was still upset, but not about him – she was far too worried about losing her job. Yale could go to hell, as far as she was concerned. But that didn't mean she wanted another man in her life. It would be a very long time before she would get back on the dating horse again. She had too much going on to even consider it.

You win some, you lose some, Ashton thought as he made his way back down the hillside to his car. Two hours of sitting motionless in the bracken hadn't revealed even a glimpse of a stoat. However, he'd shot some lovely images of skylarks, a vole, the fattest bumblebee in the world, rabbits playing, and a slinking fox in search of his supper. So it hadn't been all bad.

Dusk was now falling and it would be dark soon, so it was time to make a move. He was absolutely starving, and thinking of food reminded him of

Dulcie's offer to dine at The Wild Side this evening. Although his emotions were telling him he had been wise not to take her up on it, his stomach was yelling at him that he should have done. Despite never wanting to set foot in the place again, from what he could remember, the food had been delicious. No wonder, considering Otto York was a Michelin-star chef. Maybe one day he would be able to face going back.

As he neared the farmhouse, Ashton's thoughts turned to the photos Dulcie had asked him to take, and he began to scan his surroundings for suitable subjects.

The sun had almost dipped below the hills on the opposite side of the valley, and the sky was bathed in pink, peach and gold. Directly below him was the field of sunflowers. He had passed the nodding yellow blooms on the way up the hillside, but he'd been focusing on the possibility of spotting the stoat or weasel and hadn't paid them much attention.

He noticed them now, though. With the setting sun highlighting them, the flowers positively shone. Before he knew it, he had lifted the camera. Hopefully, he would get a few good photos for Dulcie.

Then he spotted something and froze.

A stoat was weaving through the long stems, its sinuous body the most gorgeous shades of chocolate: milk chocolate on its head and back, white chocolate on its throat, chest and belly, and the unmistakable dark (almost black) chocolate tip to its tail, which indicated it was a stoat and not a weasel. He was close enough to see that all four paws were also white, and the animal looked as though it was wearing tiny socks.

Praying it wouldn't spot him, Ashton zoomed in. He must have taken fifty photos before it disappeared, and he let out a slow satisfied breath.

This is what he lived for; this was what gave him joy and made him complete – not a job, or money, or things. *This.* Lacey had never understood.

As Ashton returned to his car, his soul filled with the wonders of nature, he made himself a promise that the next woman he gave his heart to, would love this as much as he did.

CHAPTER FOUR

Carla's heart was in her mouth as she eyed the contacts list on her mobile. Would Vicky be at her desk by now? And even if she was, did Carla want to speak to her? What if Vicky told her something she didn't like?

Aw, heck, Vicky was her friend; she absolutely should call her, even if the news from work wasn't the best. Anyway, Carla had hiked halfway up the mountain to get a signal because the mobile reception was so bad at the farm. She'd multi-tasked though, having brought one of the goats with her. She figured she might as well make herself useful, and keeping out of Dulcie's way this morning was also a good idea. Carla was glad she hadn't drunk as much as her friend; the poor girl looked rather green around the gills!

'Can you talk?' was Carla's opening line when Vicky answered the phone.

'Carla?' she whispered. 'Hang on, I'll go to the medical room. There's never anyone in there, and if someone does come in I'll hold my bump and groan a bit.'

Carla heard her friend's muffled voice as she greeted her co-workers, then she heard the lift ping, and knew that Vicky was in the corridor. The sound of a door opening and being firmly closed, was followed by heels clacking over a tiled floor.

'Okay, I can talk now,' she said. 'How are you? What's going on? Have you heard anything from HR?'

'I'm fine. I'm still at Dulcie's.' Carla had messaged Vicky before she'd left Birmingham to tell her that she was staying at the farm for a few days.

'I thought you might be. But how are you really?'

'Okay, I guess. Angry, mostly. I feel so stupid.'

'Don't. It's not your fault. It's Yale's.'

'Is he back from his holiday?'

'Not yet. There's a rumour going around that he needed to take additional time off to recover from the trauma.'

'Trauma? What bloody trauma? *I'm* the one who is traumatised. The—' Carla bit back the rude word she had been about to call him.

Vicky said, 'Don't worry, no one believes it. He's not lying on a psychiatrist's couch, he's lying on a sun lounger on a Mexican beach. With his fiancée, obviously.'

'Obviously.' Carla's reply was pure sarcasm. 'I actually feel sorry for her. She doesn't know what she's letting herself in for.' She hesitated, then asked in a small voice, 'What's everyone saying about me?'

'Nothing bad. Everyone knows you wouldn't throw yourself at a man, especially not one who's already taken.'

Carla was momentarily buoyed up by the news, but it didn't last. 'I don't suppose it matters what they think, it's what HR believes.' It took an effort to rally, but she managed it, saying, 'How about you and Bump? Are you okay?'

'We're doing well.' Carla could hear the smile in Vicky's voice. 'I can't wait to go on maternity leave. Eight working days, then I'm out of here, and one of those is a training day so that doesn't count.'

'Are you still adamant that you're not coming back after you've had the baby?'

'Definitely not! At least, not for long. I'll be damned if I'm going to pay back any maternity pay. I'll have to check out the rules and regulations, so I might have to work for a few weeks. But that's it. After that, I'm done.'

'I don't blame you.' Carla could imagine how hard it would be to leave her baby and go back to work.

Vicky said, 'I'd better get back to my desk before someone comes looking for me. Keep in touch, yeah?'

'I will,' Carla promised, and as she said goodbye she wondered whether Vicky would have already begun her maternity leave when she came back to Birmingham for the hearing. She wished HR would get a move on, as the suspense was killing her. The sooner she knew that she had definitely been sacked, the sooner she could move on.

What she was going to move on *to*, was anyone's guess.

When Carla returned from her walk, Dulcie was sitting at the kitchen table with her head in her hands. Dulcie's mum, Beth, was also there.

Beth got up to give her a hug. 'Men!' she cried. 'There're all bath plugs.'

Carla smiled. 'Bath plugs?'

'You know what I mean. I have to be careful what I say these days, what with our Sammy, and little Amory at the stables. Little pitchers have big ears.' Beth stood back. 'Let me look at you.' The woman's gaze swept her from head to foot, and Carla tried not to cringe under her scrutiny. 'You're too skinny,' she announced. 'And you look worn out.'

'Thanks.' Carla didn't think she looked that bad; a little tired maybe, but that was the stress.

Beth turned to Dulcie. 'She does, doesn't she?'

Dulcie lifted her head. Her eyes were dull, and her normally healthily tanned skin was more of a grey colour. She groaned and dropped her head again.

Beth said, 'Serves her right. She forgets that she's getting older. At eighteen, you can bounce back from a hangover in a matter of hours. At thirty, it takes a day. When you get to my age, it can take a week and there's no bouncing involved. How's your mum keeping?'

Carla blinked at the abrupt change of topic. 'She's good, thanks. In Saint Lucia at the moment.'

'Tell her I said hello.'

'I will.' Carla and her mum messaged each other several times a week. It was often easier than phoning, as there was nearly always a time difference between them.

Beth bustled around making cups of tea and laying out a plate of biscuits, as they caught up on their news. Gradually Dulcie perked up, but there was still some way to go before she was back to her usual self. And when her phone rang, she winced.

Carla smirked, feeling rather virtuous, and left her to it. She'd spotted Maisie through the kitchen window, and went outside to see if she needed a hand. She'd enjoyed the soap making yesterday. It was very different from what she usually did, and had helped take her mind off her problems.

By the time Beth called them in for lunch, Carla had made several blocks of soap on her own (under supervision) and was feeling rather pleased with herself. She was also ravenous, not used to being on her feet as much.

Over a goat's cheese salad with new potatoes that had been slathered with lightly salted butter, the three Fairfax women discussed business while Carla listened.

She was fascinated to see how well Beth and her daughters got on, because the girls had been a bit of a handful when they were younger, and Beth had often been at the end of her tether. Carla supposed it was only to be expected, considering she'd been a single parent with four kids to raise. The eldest, Nikki, lived in the village with her partner and son, Sammy. Jay, the next eldest and only boy, now lived in New Zealand, whilst Maisie had also relocated to Picklewick earlier in the year, Beth following shortly after.

Dulcie said, 'Carla's come up with a brilliant idea. She suggested we open a farm shop.'

'In Picklewick?' Beth asked.

'Here, on the farm. I can't afford to rent a shop in the village and I haven't got the time to man it, either. Not even when I give up the day job.' She glanced at the clock. 'Which reminds me, I start my shift in twenty minutes and Ashton is supposed to be calling in to take some photos of the farm for the website. Mum, do you think you can show him around?'

'Can't, sorry. Walter has an appointment at the hospital, and then we've got a macrame class at the community centre.'

'Maisie, how about you?'

'Adam has a delivery of bricks coming, and I said I'd be there to receive it. If you ask Ashton to come later today or tomorrow—'

'I can show him around,' Carla interjected. 'Tell me what you want him to photograph, and I'll point him in the right direction.' How hard could it be? The farm wasn't that big, and it wasn't as though Dulcie had hundreds of animals or tonnes of produce.

Dulcie pulled a face. 'Sorry about what I said last night. I know you're not ready to jump on the horse again.'

Maisie said, 'I didn't know you could ride?'

'I can't,' Carla replied. 'It was metaphorical.' She held up a hand, anticipating Maisie's next question. 'Don't ask.'

'If you're sure you don't mind,' Dulcie said doubtfully. 'You're supposed to be here for some R and R, not as unpaid labour.'

'I'm sure. Unless there's something else you need me to do?'

'It's all in hand, I think.' Dulcie checked with Maisie, who nodded.

Beth stood up and began collecting the empty bowls. 'I'll just stick these in the dishwasher, then I'll be off.'

Maisie got to her feet. 'I'd better be off, too. You know what delivery drivers are like. They estimate to be there between two and four, but I'd hate for it to be early and miss it.

Dulcie went to prepare for her shift dealing with unhappy customers, leaving Carla wondering what to do with herself until Ashton arrived. It was lovely out – warm and sunny, autumn not yet having made an appearance – so she decided to take a book into the orchard. She had quite enjoyed sitting in the heather yesterday, and hoped the peace and solitude would do her good.

After all, as Dulcie had pointed out, being at the farm was supposed to give her some respite from recent events. If that meant lazing around in the sunshine for an hour or two, that's what she would do.

Carla was fully engrossed in the uplifting romance she was reading (courtesy of the bookshelf in Dulcie's living room) when the sound of a vehicle coming up Muddypuddle Lane jolted her out of the story.

Checking the time, she realised it was probably Ashton, and she hurried to intercept him before he interrupted Dulcie by knocking on the farmhouse door.

He didn't see her at first, and she took a second to study him as he emerged from his car. Dulcie was right – Carla *had* referred to him as hot during her last visit and she could see why. Taller than her five-foot-seven by several inches, he was lean but had muscles in all the right places. His short sandy hair curled a little, and he was clean-shaven, with the loveliest blue eyes. She remembered thinking that he reminded her of a young Robert Redford.

'Hi.' His voice broke into her thoughts, and she realised he had caught her staring. 'Dulcie is expecting me,' he added.

'Er, yeah, she asked me to do the honours.'

'Okay, cool.' He reached into his car and carefully lifted out his camera and a small satchel-type bag which he slung over his shoulder.

'Did you see the stoat?' she asked, and was taken aback by the smile that lit up his face. He had *dimples!*

'I did. Want to see? It's better if we go into the barn,' he said and Carla raised her eyebrows, only relaxing when he explained, 'It's too bright out here to see the screen clearly.'

She followed him into the relative gloom of the barn's interior and waited until he was ready. She assumed he would hand her his camera, but he passed his mobile phone to her instead. 'My camera sends them straight to my phone. Do you think Dulcie might like to see them?' He glanced at the farmhouse, his expression hopeful.

'I'm sure she would, but she's working right now. Which is why you've got me.' Carla pulled a face in self-deprecation.

'No worries,' he said.

But Carla wasn't listening. She was too busy scrolling through the images on his phone. Damn, he was good! He'd captured the essence of the creature she'd seen perfectly. She couldn't believe how clear the picture was. It was like looking at a photo taken by a professional.

She studied each one intently, noticing the animal's whiskers, the play of light and shadow over its fur, and the bright beady eyes. Then she scrolled some more, and when the sunflower meadow came into view, she sucked in a sharp breath.

'Are they okay?' Ashton asked, and she looked up from the screen to see his worried face.

'They're brilliant!' she cried. 'Absolutely flippin' brilliant.' She angled the screen. 'This one is perfect for Dulcie's website. She's going to love it!'

'I hope so.' He looked relieved. 'Where shall we start?'

'In here?' she suggested. The barn was home to several adorable bunnies. 'Or maybe we could take them outside? Dulcie has a pen that can be moved around.'

'Perfect.'

There was a momentary awkward hesitation on both their parts, and it was only when he made no move to catch any of the rabbits that Carla realised he was expecting *her* to catch one.

Oh, crumbs.

The pen was in the orchard, just by the gate, and Carla was thankful that it wasn't far because the rabbit was squirming and wriggling. She popped it into the pen, glad to be relieved of the little creature.

'Do you think we can move the pen?' Ashton asked.

'Why?' She wasn't being awkward; she genuinely wanted to know.

'Because I'd like to get a shot of the rabbit without the pen in the picture. Maybe we could put it over there?' He pointed to an apple tree with lavender growing near the base of the trunk.

Carla could immediately see how the new location would work. The rabbit she had picked was the cutest: lop-eared with black and white fur that would stand out well against the lavender flowers, and the green foliage would hide the metalwork.

She picked the bunny up and held it whilst Ashton moved the pen.

'Make sure it's secure,' she advised, remembering Dulcie telling her that rabbits were excellent escape artists, which was one of the reasons they weren't left on their own outside for long as the naughty little creatures often tried to dig their way out.

The new location seemed to please the rabbit. It immediately settled down to nibble on a dandelion and Ashton wasted no time taking several shots. He was soon done and ready to move on to the next subject.

'Goats,' Carla announced. 'Let me pop this little fella back first.' She caught the rabbit, cradling it in her arms as she planted a little kiss on its fluffy head, then quickly returned it to the barn.

When she came back, she found Ashton busily photographing fruit. The trees in the orchard were laden with ripe pears and plums, although the apples weren't ready for picking just yet. On the other hand, the blackberries were definitely ripe. The shiny black fruit glistened in the sun, and Carla's mouth watered as she thought of blackcurrant crumble with lashings of golden custard.

They reached the goats' field and she was quiet for a while, letting Ashton concentrate, but the silence felt strained (although he didn't seem to notice) and eventually she felt compelled to fill it.

'Have you always been a postman?' she asked.

'Not really. I was a child once.'

'Ha ha, very funny.'

He grinned at her, revealing those dimples. 'Yes, I've worked for the post office since I left school.'

'Do you like it?'

'I do.'

'Why?'

'Dunno, really.' His attention was firmly on the camera, but she noticed his knuckles whitening as he tightened his grip and wondered why her question had caused such a reaction.

Carla persevered. 'Is it because you're outside a lot?'

'Partly.'

'Do the early starts give you more time to do this?'

He paused, holding the camera away from his face. 'I still do a forty-hour week.'

'But not nine to five?'

'No.' He lifted it back to his face. 'How about you? What do you do?'

'I work for an insurance company.'

'Doing what, exactly?'

'I'm a fraud investigation officer.'

'Do you like it?'

'Yes, it's interesting.'

'Are you from Birmingham?'

'I am.'

'Do you like it there?'

'Not as much as I used to. Do you like living in Picklewick?'

'I don't live in Picklewick. I live in Thornbury. It's a town about nine miles away.'

'I know it.'

'Yes, I do like it there. As towns go, it's not too big and it's got everything I need.'

'Like what? Pubs, restaurants, shops?' she guessed.

'A canal and good links to the countryside.'

'Do you live on a boat?'

He chuckled. 'No, I live in a regular house, but the canal is a brilliant place for wildlife.'

'Why photography?'

He put the camera down to his side. 'Why so many questions?'

Carla shrugged. 'Just making conversation.'

'I love photography because I can't paint and I want to capture some of the magic. Most people see a sunset, but few see a kingfisher or an otter in the flesh.'

'You're incredibly good. You've got a real talent.'

'Meh, anyone can take a decent photo.'

'I can't.'

'I bet you can.'

'Seriously, I can't. I've got a pretty good camera on my phone, but the photos usually come out blurry, or I've not noticed a lamp post coming out of someone's head.'

'You can teach yourself how to compose photos.' He pointed to one of the goatlings who was on top of the climbing frame. 'See that little one? If you took a photo of it now, it should be good because most of the animal is visible, and there's grass and sky for the background.' He slipped his hand out of the camera's strap and offered it to her. 'Give it a go.'

'*Me?*' Carla was incredulous. 'What if I drop it?'

'You won't.' He sounded certain, so she took the camera, holding it tightly. Then she relaxed her grip, fearful she'd break something with the strength of it. There were so many dials, buttons, and numbers, and she had no idea what they were for. Was she supposed to do something with them, or could she just point and shoot?

'Go on,' Ashton urged.

'Just like that? I don't have to twiddle or turn anything?'

His smile was indulgent. 'You can, if you want, but let's take one step at a time, eh?' He leant in, and she caught a whiff of his aftershave. He smelt lovely. 'Just look through there, and press this button,' he said.

'That's it?'

'Pretty much.'

Carla glanced around. What should she take a photo of? The goat on the climbing frame had jumped down and she bit her lip uncertainly. One of the animals was lying in the sun, its jaws working from side to side as it chewed. Hesitantly, she brought the camera up to her face and closed one eye to peer through the viewfinder. She gasped as she zoomed in on the goat's nose.

'I can see the colour of its eyes,' she whispered. Taking the camera away from her face, she stared at the creature, marvelling at the detail the telephoto lens revealed. 'It's like magic.'

Ashton chuckled, and Carla realised how daft she sounded. 'I mean, I know what zoom lenses can do – I'm not stupid – it's just… I've never looked through one before. It's nothing like the zoom on my phone.'

'No, it isn't.'

She put the viewfinder to her eye again, closing the other. The goat wore a dreamy blissful expression on its face, one that she envied. She pressed the shutter button.

'Can I see?' He moved closer to her, his chest against her arm. 'You can see the photo you've just taken by looking at the LCD screen.' He pressed a button, and the image appeared. Carla had captured the goat's expression perfectly.

'Not bad,' he said. 'Not bad at all. See, I told you that you could do it.'

'Can I have another go?' she asked.

'Absolutely. What else does Dulcie want me to photograph?'

Dulcie had only given Carla the briefest of briefs, so Carla wasn't entirely sure. She paused, imagining what might capture her interest if she were a customer, and what might persuade her to visit the farm. Natural, organic, and nature were the buzzwords that came to mind.

'Chickens,' she said. 'And eggs. People might like to see where their eggs come from.' She was thinking about the farm shop. 'And then the bottles of milk, the cheese, and the soaps.'

Ashton said, 'What if I take a few, then you can have a go? And as I take each image, I'll explain what I'm doing and why. But I must warn you, not every photo is a great photo. Everyone takes duds, me included, so don't expect it to be perfect every time. And before I shut up, I'll just say one more thing – it takes practice to take a really great shot. Lots and lots of practice.'

Ashton's passion for photography was clear, and it was catching. Carla could certainly appreciate what he saw in it, especially when it came to photographing animals.

She wished she'd thought to whip her phone out yesterday and take one of the stoat, but the creature would probably have disappeared by the time she'd got it out of her pocket. Anyway, her photo wouldn't have been half as good as Ashton's.

She could practice taking photos whilst she was here, she mused, as she led him towards the chicken coop in the hope of finding one of the free-range birds lingering nearby. It would give her something to do when she wasn't helping out on the farm. And it might be nice to dawdle through the fields looking for things to photograph.

She must admit that she'd felt better after sitting in the orchard with her book, so maybe Dulcie was right, and she needed time to recuperate. Finding out that your boyfriend already had a fiancée, being dumped, and that you might be about to lose your job, was enough to fray anyone's nerves.

CHAPTER FIVE

Ashton turned his pillow over, seeking the cooler side, and sighed in frustration. It was strange that when he had been with Lacey, he'd often felt exhausted by nine o'clock if he'd been at work that day. Yet since they'd split up, he spent half the night tossing and turning. If only he could have been this awake, Lacey mightn't have—

It was pointless thinking that way. She'd known he was a postman when they'd started dating, and had been aware his job involved early starts, so she could hardly have expected him to be the life and soul of the party when he had to get up at the crack of dawn.

Ashton checked the time. Twenty-past ten, and he was still wide awake.

Was there any point in lying there getting crosser and crosser because he couldn't fall asleep? Or should he get up and do something useful?

He decided to get up.

Pushing the bed covers aside, he swung his feet to the floor and padded downstairs in his boxers. He may as well look through the photos he'd taken today, and if they were any good, he'd email them to Dulcie.

He had also asked Carla for her email address so he could forward her the images she'd taken. He'd only had the briefest of scans through them when he'd arrived home because he had been more focused on food, so he'd left checking the images for another day. But as he couldn't sleep, he may as well look through them now.

Ashton sat at his makeshift desk (aka the table in the living room) and lifted the lid on the laptop. As he waited for it to start up, he decided to make a coffee.

Quietly, he slipped into the kitchen and filled the kettle, wincing at the sound, before remembering that he could make as much noise as he liked. He had become so accustomed to creeping around so as not to disturb Lacey, that it was now second nature.

He snorted softly – they say opposites attract, but perhaps night owls and early birds were a bit *too* opposite. Then there was her inability to appreciate how important photography was to him, and his bewilderment at her insatiable desire to watch soaps and her fascination with reality programmes. Yeah, total opposites.

After making the coffee, he grabbed a packet of oaty biscuits and returned to the living room, eager to see the photos, and clicked through them slowly, dunking a biscuit as he did so.

When he came to the photo Carla had taken of the goat, he paused. It wasn't bad at all he thought, then carried on looking at the rest.

He became so engrossed in what he was doing, that it wasn't until he'd neared the end of the photos did he realise there had been a couple of occasions where he hadn't been able to tell whether it was he or Carla who had taken an image, and it made him smile. She had been so adamant that she couldn't take a good photo, and he was delighted to be able to prove her wrong.

Ignoring the time (it was getting to the point where it was hardly worth going to bed), Ashton emailed the photos to Carla and Dulcie, adding '*I told you so*' and a smiley face emoji to Carla's. He hoped she would be pleased with her efforts and that seeing them would give her the confidence to take better photos.

Ashton stretched out his back and rolled his shoulders. He'd better get some sleep. But as he was finally drifting off, it wasn't Lacey who was in his thoughts, as she had been every other night since the split – it was Carla and the sweet look on her face as she'd cuddled the rabbit.

To her surprise, Carla found she was enjoying her regular goat walks before breakfast, and after just a few days she wasn't nearly as breathless walking up the hill. She was starting to fit into the slower pace of life at the farm and felt better for it.

When she entered the kitchen, Dulcie was whisking up eggs in a bowl. 'Good, you're back. I'm making scrambled eggs for breakfast. Would you like some?'

'Yes, please.' She was hungry. 'Can I do anything?'

'You could pop a couple of slices of bread in the toaster.'

'On it.'

Soon afterwards, she was sitting opposite Dulcie and tucking into her breakfast. Swallowing a mouthful, she asked, 'Is there anything you want me to do today?'

'Why don't you take a day off?'

'*You* don't.'

'It's my business, my farm. You're here to relax.'

Relaxing sounded good, but Carla knew she would feel guilty. She couldn't just sit around while Dulcie and her sister worked so hard.

'Actually, there *is* something you could do,' Dulcie said after a second. 'You could pop into the village and do some market research for me.'

Intrigued, Carla asked, 'Such as?'

'Have a mooch around the shops and see how they display things. I want to get some ideas.'

Carla felt a surge of excitement. 'Does that mean you're going ahead with the farm shop?'

'Otto and I talked it over, and we both think it's a great idea. It can't hurt to have a dedicated space to display the goods properly, and having set opening times will be a godsend. Eventually, I hope to have an online ordering system, so people can pay and collect.'

'Wow! You really are expanding, aren't you?'

'That's the plan. The farm is almost at the point where it pays for itself, and I'm hoping this will give it the extra push.'

Carla was pleased for her. She remembered how out of her depth Dulcie had felt when she'd first won the farm, and how she had considered selling up and moving back to Birmingham. It was wonderful seeing her so enthusiastic.

A trip into the village would be a welcome change, and she was looking forward to mooching around the shops. She also liked the idea of doing market research, especially as she had a vested interest in the venture, since the farm shop had been her suggestion.

'Can I get you anything while I'm out?' she asked after nipping upstairs to change and checking she had her car keys, purse and phone. As well as looking around the shops she might treat herself to a coffee and a cake.

Dulcie was staring at her computer and smiling. 'Ashton has sent the photos through. They're amazing. Take a look.' She scooted aside so Carla could see the screen.

'Oh, wow. They *are* good.'

Dulcie was grinning. 'In his email, he said that you'd taken a couple of them, and they were just as good as his.'

'He said that?'

Her friend's nod was emphatic. 'He did. And I must admit, I can't tell which ones are yours.'

A glow of pride warmed Carla's insides, and she grinned back. He'd asked for her email address, and she wondered whether he'd sent her anything, so she took her phone out of her bag.

He had! And when she read the 'I told you so' comment, she laughed out loud and showed it to Dulcie.

'To think he's done all this for nothing,' Dulcie said. 'He's definitely one of the good guys. I feel I should thank him in some way, but I don't know how. A dozen eggs and a bag of pears isn't enough. And he didn't seem keen on a meal in The Wild Side.'

Carla thought hard. 'Apart from photography, is there anything else he's into? I'm thinking maybe tickets for a concert or a football match?'

'I've no idea. I don't know anything about him, really. Just his name, what he does for a living, and that he lives in Thornbury. And he's single.'

'Oh no you don't, lady.' Carla gave Dulcie a warning look. 'I'm not going there.'

'Yale didn't break your heart,' Dulcie reminded her.

'No, but he's put me off men for a while.'

'I'm not suggesting you marry Ashton,' Dulcie replied. 'I'm just wondering where my love-them-and-leave-them friend has gone.'

'I'll let you know when I find her,' Carla retorted. The situation with Yale had caused an internal shift, and she had become more wary and less flighty than she'd been, but surely that wasn't a bad thing?

Dulcie's attention returned to the computer screen. 'Maybe I could get Ashton a voucher. I believe there's a photography shop in Thornbury which might do vouchers or gift cards.'

Carla said, 'Why don't I pop into Thornbury instead of Picklewick? If the shop sells them, I can pick one up.'

'That would be great. Thank you.'

It was the least Carla could do, considering Dulcie and Otto's generosity in letting her stay with them. Not that she'd seen a great deal of Otto because he was at the restaurant most of the time. However, Dulcie had assured her the situation would change as soon as he'd trained up a head chef and hopefully he could take a back seat, and he and Dulcie could spend more time together, especially if she gave up the day job.

Right now, Carla was wishing she could give up *her* day job, but unfortunately she had no other strings to her bow. Her bow had one solitary string on it, and she had a feeling it was about to snap.

After another quick scan of her emails to make sure she hadn't missed anything from HR or the union rep, Carla slipped her phone back into her bag, resolving not to think about work until she had to. She much preferred to think about her trip to Thornbury.

InFocus was a serious camera shop with serious equipment in the window, and Carla drew in a sharp breath at the equally serious prices. Good gracious, cameras weren't cheap, were they? If she had realised how expensive they were, she probably would have been too scared to touch Ashton's.

Her eyes roamed over the shelves as she tried to find the one Ashton owned, but they all looked much of a muchness and she was soon confused. And as for the lenses... Blimey, there were so many, and all of them had indecipherable strings of letters and numbers in their descriptions.

A shelf of second-hand equipment caught her attention. The items on it were considerably cheaper. This is the way forward, she thought, then pulled herself up. Anyone would think she was contemplating buying one. How daft would that be, considering she mightn't have a job soon and needed to hoard her pennies.

Realising that work had intruded into her thoughts once more, she walked up to the counter and the middle-aged man standing behind it. He had what appeared to be a camera in front of him, but she wasn't certain because it was in bits.

As he looked up, she said, 'Do you sell vouchers or gift cards?'

'I most certainly do.' He gestured to a small stand next to the till. Each little card had the most exquisite image on it.

She selected one, not caring that it was more than the amount Dulcie had suggested. Carla would cover the additional cost herself. She might need to keep a careful watch on her bank balance, but the boost to her confidence that Ashton had given her by his act of kindness yesterday was worth the expense. Dulcie was right, he *was* one of the good ones. At any other time, she might have been tempted to get to know him better, but not right now. She had too much going on to think about becoming involved with anyone, however brief the involvement might be.

After she'd made her purchase, Carla didn't immediately leave the shop. She wandered around it instead, peering into the locked glass cabinets, trying to recall the make of Ashton's camera.

Nikon, that was it, she remembered, and moved towards the cabinet with a Nikon sign above it.

'Are you looking for something in particular?' the man behind the counter asked.

'I was just curious. I was with a guy yesterday who had one of these. I've no idea which one, though. How do you choose?'

He came out from behind the counter. 'It depends on what you're looking for, how much you want to pay, and what you want to use it for. When people start out, it's normally the price point that has the greatest influence, but not always. What do you currently use?'

'My phone.' Her tone was sheepish.

'But you'd like to get into photography on a more serious level?' he guessed.

'Um, I don't know.' Emboldened by his kind eyes, she scrabbled around in her bag for her phone and clicked on the email Ashton had sent her. 'I took these yesterday,' she said, showing him the screen.

'With your phone?' He sounded incredulous.

'No, on Ashton's camera – he was the guy I was with.'

'Ashton? That wouldn't be Ashton Clarke, would it?'

'Yes. Do you know him?'

The man laughed. 'He's probably my best customer. He's here more than I am, which says a lot considering I own the place.' He pointed to the second shelf down from the top. 'That's his latest camera. It's a mirrorless one.' The man was gazing at her as though she was supposed to know what that meant, so she nodded sagely despite having no clue. 'It's his pride and joy,' he added.

She clocked the price on the ticket and her eyes almost popped out of her head. Bloody hell! If she'd known what it cost, she *definitely* wouldn't have touched it. Had he trusted her that much? Or was money no object and he could afford to replace it if she'd had butterfingers?

The shop's owner provided the answer. 'Ever since that model came out, he's been eyeing it up. You wouldn't believe how pleased he was when he was finally able to buy it. He was like a kid on Christmas Day.'

Carla would like to hear more, but someone entered the shop and from the way the owner greeted them they seemed to be regulars, so she thanked him and left. It was time to complete the second half of her task in Thornbury, and a phone was a better option for this than a camera.

Trying to be circumspect and not make it obvious that she was taking photos, Carla wandered from shop to shop, paying particular attention to a greengrocer, a delicatessen, and a shop that sold bath bombs, lip balms and other fragranced items along the same lines as the things Carla made with her goat's milk. She lingered for a while in each, trying to make it look like she was talking on her phone, and when she thought she'd taken enough, she retreated to the nearest cafe for a well-earned coffee and a sandwich.

It was getting on for lunchtime, and Thornbury was busy. The cafe was no exception, so she was glad when she managed to bag an empty table by the window. She would enjoy people-watching whilst she ate.

She had just finished her prawn sandwich and was debating whether to have a second cup of coffee, when a Royal Mail van pulled into the kerb alongside a post box on the opposite side of the road. Seeing it reminded her sharply of Ashton, so it was a shock when the man himself got out.

Without thinking, Carla leapt to her feet, grabbed her bag and shot outside. Darting between the traffic, she hurried across the road.

Ashton had emptied the post box and was about to return to his van when she said, 'Hi,' somewhat breathlessly.

'Hello.' He smiled at her, dimples out (or should she say 'in'), and she beamed back. 'Retail therapy?'

'I'm running a couple of errands for Dulcie. Thanks for the photos. I can't believe how well they turned out. It must be the camera.'

'Not necessarily, although having good equipment does help. But some people can have all the gear and still have no idea.'

Carla shook her head. 'In my case, it was definitely the camera. I can't take a decent photo on my phone for toffee.' She hoped the ones she had taken today for Dulcie were okay. She should really have a quick flick through them to make sure before she went back to the farm.

She said, 'Dulcie was delighted with the ones you took.'

'I'm glad.'

There was an awkward pause. Carla didn't know what else to say, and she guessed he was probably keen to get back to work. She nodded at the envelopes he was holding. 'Got long left?'

'An hour. A couple more stops, then it's back to the depot. Are you off home now?'

Home, as in the farm on Muddypuddle Lane. Carla briefly wondered what it would be like to actually *live* there, and the thought was rather appealing. Recalling how she'd felt on her first visit when she'd reckoned it was nice for a short getaway, but she wouldn't want to live anywhere so rural, she was quite surprised. Maybe one day, when she had a husband and children, she would seriously consider living the good life in a village like Picklewick, growing vegetables and taking the kids on long walks in the countryside.

Dream on, she snorted to herself. The chances of her finding the love of her life anytime soon were minimal. But something had to give, because her party lifestyle was starting to lose its appeal, even more so since her friends were settling down with mortgages, partners, and babies.

She snapped back into focus as she realised Ashton was waiting for a reply. 'Not yet,' she said. 'I'm going to buy myself a camera.' She hadn't realised that's what she was going to say, until she'd said it.

'You are?' He looked delighted. 'Which one?'

Carla shrugged. 'I've no idea. I'll have to rely on the owner's advice and hope he doesn't fleece me.'

'Were you thinking of buying it from InFocus?'

'I was.'

'Barney won't fleece you. He'll give you good advice.' Ashton hesitated. 'Would you like me to come with you?'

'Yes, please, that would be great. If you can spare the time.'

'I've always got time for anything to do with photography. Do you mind waiting an hour until I finish work, or do you want to go another day?'

'Let's do it today,' she replied, ignoring the inner voice telling her that she was being ridiculously impulsive and she shouldn't be spending money on a luxury item like a camera when she mightn't have a job next week. Because, for the first time since that fateful night when Yale had shown her his true colours, Carla's heart didn't feel quite as heavy, nor her future seem quite so bleak.

Ashton couldn't wait to finish work. He always felt a surge of anticipation when he was about to pay InFocus a visit, but today he was practically hopping from foot to foot with excitement. The knowledge that he had introduced someone to the delights of photography, gave him such a boost.

Not wanting to pop into the shop in his uniform, Ashton ran home. Thankfully, he didn't live far from the depot, so he was home, showered, changed and back in town in less than half an hour. He had arranged to meet Carla at Rossi's Cafe near the town hall, and as he approached he worried that she might have gotten fed up with waiting and left.

His relief when he saw that she hadn't was greater than it should have been, considering he hardly knew her and they were only going shopping.

She hadn't spotted him yet – her eyes were on her phone – and he studied her through the cafe's window as he walked up to the door. She was smiling softly, and he was struck anew by how pretty she was. There was a sadness about her, though, and he wondered what her story was. For some reason, he suspected her visit to Dulcie wasn't just a catch-up with a friend.

Carla glanced up from her phone and saw him enter the cafe. When her smile widened into a beam, Ashton was gut-punched. Seeing it did something strange to his insides, and his heart stuttered.

What the hell was all that about?

Gathering himself, he made his way to her table, reining in his shock – he hadn't had such a reaction to a woman in a long time, and it wasn't welcome. He was barely out of a relationship, and now he was lusting after a woman who would be out of his life before he knew it. Or was that the attraction? Whatever it was, he had no intention of doing anything about it. It would soon pass. And even if he did want to pursue it, he highly doubted Carla would be interested.

'Hi. Ready?' he asked.

'Would you like a coffee or something before we go?'

'I'm fine.'

'Okay, then.' She picked up her bag and got to her feet. Out of the corner of his eye, he caught her biting her lip and he hoped he hadn't been too brusque.

'Do you know what camera you want?' he asked as they walked towards the shop.

'Not a clue.'

'What sort of things do you intend to photograph?'

'I'm not sure yet. Anything that catches my eye, I think.' She slowed and pointed to the cornice on one of the buildings. 'Like that, maybe. Or those.' This time, she was looking at an elderly couple who had paused outside a jewellery shop. Their hands were tightly clasped as they peered through the window, and the woman's lined face glowed when she turned her face towards her companion.

Carla asked, 'Apart from the ones you took around the farm, do you only take photos of wildlife?'

'I do photograph other things, but my favourite is wildlife in a more urban setting. Like a fox on a high street, or birds nesting in a warehouse. Here we are.' He stopped outside the shop and pushed the door, holding it open for her to enter first.

Barney looked surprised. 'Back again?'

She told Ashton, 'I was in here earlier checking out the cameras.' She turned to Barney. 'I bumped into Ashton, and he volunteered to help me choose.'

Barney nodded. 'Ashton will see you right. I'm here if you need me.'

Ashton was rather nervous at the weight of the responsibility. He wanted Carla to have the best camera she could afford but he didn't like to ask what her budget was, so he decided to start with the perfectly acceptable second-hand ones and go from there.

'This is a good one,' he said. The camera was little more than a body, but she didn't need a plethora of lenses to begin her photography journey. A couple of basic ones would do for the time being, and she could add to them later if she wished.

Twenty minutes later, they were leaving the shop, Carla clutching her purchases. She looked both eager, nervous, and slightly shell-shocked. He had to admit he was, too. She hadn't given him any indication yesterday that she intended to buy a camera, and he wondered whether she'd thought her purchase through or whether it had been an impulse buy.

'That's the hard part done,' she joked. 'Now all I have to do is learn how to use it.'

'You'll soon get the hang of it. Trial and error are the best teachers. Point, shoot, make a note of the settings, review the results.'

'I'll have to do some genning up.' Her eagerness was slipping away, and nervousness was gaining the upper hand.

'Would you like a couple of lessons?' he offered.

'Lessons?' Her eyes widened.

'Not formal ones. Just me, you, and our cameras.'

The smile was back. 'Yes, please.'

'Sunday?'

'Brilliant. Thank you so much.'

After arranging to pop up to the farm at ten o'clock on Sunday, Ashton said goodbye, and as he headed home he found he was looking forward to it. It would be nice to have some company, and he couldn't wait to see the photos she would take.

He ignored the growing suspicion that it was Carla herself that he couldn't wait to see.

CHAPTER SIX

Carla held her breath as she pressed the shutter button, then she checked the LCD and silently showed Ashton the screen. He had taken the same shot and he showed her his in return.

They weren't too dissimilar. Pleased, Carla grinned at him.

She and Ashton had been out on the hillside above the farm for the past couple of hours, taking pictures of the gorgeous scenery. Ashton had shown her how light and composition affected the outcome of an image, and she'd learnt a great deal already. But she had a feeling there was still a great deal more to learn.

She was so grateful to Ashton for accompanying her to the shop yesterday and helping her choose, because the number of cameras on display had been overwhelming. If she had been on her own, she would have probably been too confused to buy anything. Right now, she was having so much fun that she was glad she'd bought one, even if the purchase had been impulsive and not very wise under the circumstances.

The abrupt trilling of her phone shattered the peace, and Carla winced. She looked at the screen. It was Dulcie, and she wondered what she wanted. 'Sorry, I won't be a minute,' she said.

'No worries.' Ashton moved away to give her some privacy. His retreating back was broad-shouldered and slim-hipped, and as she answered the call, her eyes wandered south to his backside. Realising she was ogling him, she snatched her gaze away.

'Dulcie? What's up?'

'I've just had a thought.'

'Ooh, that's scary.'

'You're not as funny as you think you are, you know.' Dulcie's voice held a smile. 'Why don't you ask Ashton if he'd like to join us for lunch? I didn't think to mention it before you went out. I can give him his voucher at the same time.'

'Hang on. Ashton,' she called. 'Would you like to have lunch at the farm? I hear Otto does a mean Sunday roast.'

Ashton looked surprised. 'Um, that's kind, but I don't want to intrude.'

Dulcie yelled down the phone, 'Tell him he won't be!'

'Dulcie says you won't be, but if you've got other plans...?'

'My plan was a frozen pizza.'

'Tell him we're having beef with all the trimmings,' Dulcie said. 'Oh, poop, he's not vegetarian, is he?'

Carla didn't know. 'Are you a vegetarian?'

'No.'

'In that case, you're coming to lunch,' Carla told him. 'He's coming to lunch, Dulcie.'

'Great. I'll set another place. Forty-five minutes?'

'Fab.' Carla ended the call. 'We'd better get going.'

'Okay. Are you sure you don't mind?'

She gave him a sly look. 'Not at all. It means more time for lessons – unless you have to shoot off afterwards.'

When he informed her that he didn't, Carla was rather more pleased than the news warranted.

Aside from Ashton himself, there was Carla, Dulcie and Otto, Maisie and her fella Adam, as well as Beth (the girls' mother), Walter (who was Otto's dad and Beth's partner) and another sister, Nikki, plus her son Sammy, who appeared to be about twelve or thirteen. Ashton felt a little overwhelmed.

'No Gio today?' Beth asked.

Nikki shook her head. 'He's working.' She turned to Ashton. 'He's a copper.'

'I know him. He can usually be seen in a Panda car,' Ashton said.

'That's the guy,' Nikki confirmed. She and her sisters all had the same fair hair, blue eyes, and high cheekbones. They followed Beth in looks. Carla's dark hair and hazel eyes were a direct contrast, and his gaze kept drifting towards her.

Now and again, it also drifted towards Otto, and Ashton hoped the chef hadn't witnessed his debacle on the night he'd proposed to Lacey. The evening was a bit of a blur, but he could remember the way everyone in the restaurant had fallen silent as they waited for Lacey to say yes, and how the silence had stretched out uncomfortably when it became clear she wasn't going to.

Feeling overwhelmed, Ashton hung back, letting the conversation flow around him as he was invited to take a seat at the dining table.

'Before we start,' Dulcie said when everyone was seated. 'I want to give Ashton something.' She held out a small envelope.

'What is it?' he asked.

'Open it and see.'

He prised the flap open and sucked in a breath. 'What's this for?'

'Because you refused payment, and you deserve something for your time and expertise.'

'This is too much.'

'No,' Dulcie replied, her voice firm. 'It's not.'

'I don't know what to say.' He knew he was blushing, and he felt rather embarrassed.

'No need to say anything,' Otto told him. 'Right, tuck in before it gets cold.'

Relieved that everyone's attention turned to the food, Ashton slid the gift card into the back pocket of his jeans. When he saw Carla smirk, he understood why she had been in InFocus previously the day she'd bought her camera. He narrowed his eyes at her and shook his head in admonishment.

Her smirk grew wider, and his gaze was drawn to her lips. A sudden urge to kiss them took him by surprise, and he swiftly turned his attention to his plate and tried to think about something else.

'How's business?' Otto asked Adam, handing a platter of beef to Beth, who took a couple of slices of meat and passed it on.

'Ticking along. I've got more work than I can handle to be honest, although things will calm down once the house is completed.'

'When will that be?' Walter asked. 'Last time I was up your way, it looked almost done.'

Carla leant towards Ashton and murmured, 'Adam and Maisie have a place somewhere on the mountain. He runs a machinery repair business, and Maisie is opening a kennels. They've got some building work going on.'

Adam said, 'I reckon another week or so should do it. It won't be perfect, but it'll be habitable, so if that's okay with you Beth, we'll be moving out of the house in Picklewick shortly. It'll be better if we're on site.'

Carla offered Ashton another explanation. 'The house was a shell, so he and Maisie have been living in Beth's house in Picklewick while they do it up, because she's moved in with Walter. It's a bit like musical chairs but with houses and no music.'

Ashton had noticed. The names and addresses on letters were a giveaway, and he recalled that at one time Otto used to live in the cottage on the lane with his dad, before moving into the farmhouse with Dulcie. The musical chairs analogy was quite apt.

Beth cried, 'That's earlier than you expected. How exciting!' She turned to Carla. 'Have you been up to The Forever Home yet?'

'The what?'

'Adam and Maisie's place. That's what they've called it.'

Maisie said, 'You must! It's coming along a treat. I've got some photos of the way it looked before we started work on it.'

At the mention of photos, Carla sent Ashton a warm look, and he felt a corresponding glow in his chest. The Fairfaxes and the Yorks were a close-knit family, and he was acutely conscious that he was an outsider. Perhaps Carla also felt a little like that, he mused. They were two outsiders together (despite Carla's friendship with Dulcie) with the common bond of a love of photography to bind them together, however briefly. It suddenly struck him that he didn't know how long Carla would be staying at the farm. In fact, he knew hardly anything about her, and he realised he wanted to know more.

After the best Sunday lunch Ashton had ever eaten, he and Carla went outside to resume her lesson. Despite being secretly relieved, he felt rather guilty that his offer to help with the washing up had been turned down. Clearing up after all those people was a daunting prospect. Equally daunting was the thought of asking Carla about herself, and he didn't know why he wanted to know – he just did.

'So,' he began, as they perched on bales in the barn for Carla to practice taking shots in low-level light. 'How long will you be in Picklewick?'

Her expression clouded, and he wished he hadn't asked. 'Forever, if I have my way,' she said with a sigh.

'It is beautiful up here,' he agreed, but he had a feeling the scenery wasn't the sole reason for her reluctance to leave. 'I wouldn't want to go back to Birmingham after seeing this. Not that there's anything wrong with the city,' he added hastily, 'and I'm sure it's got some lovely parks and open spaces, but...' He trailed off, not wanting to dig his hole any deeper.

She sighed. 'It's complicated.'

Ah, he thought, his spirits sinking. That sounded like man trouble.

Placing her camera on the straw, she gazed at the rafters. 'I've got a thing going on at work, a not very nice thing, and I'm on extended leave. I suppose you could say I'm hiding out here and trying to forget about it. I'll have to go home at some point, of course, and I can't impose on Dulcie for much longer, but at the moment I'm happy to be her goat walker and general dogsbody. She's trying to get me to take it easy, but I'm not really cut out for relaxing. So, in answer to your question, I honestly don't know how long I'll be here. A few more days, a week. Who knows?'

Ashton was pleased she would be here for a while longer, yet rather deflated she had to go at all, as he'd found himself enjoying her company. She was funny and smart, and her eagerness to learn was a refreshing change to the complete disinterest Lacey had shown for his hobby. He appreciated that couples didn't often like the same things, and he hadn't expected her to pick up a camera and start snapping away. But her indifference had stung, especially since he'd always shown an interest in whatever she was doing.

He should have realised they weren't compatible, but he'd been in love, and love, as the saying goes, is blind.

Ashton felt a pang when he thought of his ex, and sadness swept over him. If only Lacey could have been a little more like Carla, maybe they would have still been together.

Was there a name for when you think of something and then that very thing happens, Carla wondered, as the loud beep of an incoming message made her jump. She checked the screen and saw Vicky's name flash up, followed by the message, *I've got news!!! Call me!!!*

Carla gasped. Surely she couldn't have had the baby already? If so, the little mite was about four weeks early.

'Do you mind if I make a quick call?' she said to Ashton, realising this was the second time today she'd been contacted whilst out shooting photos with him. At least he'd gotten a nice lunch as a result of the first one. The only thing he would get out of this call would be boredom.

'Go ahead.'

He made to rise from his bale, but she waved him back down. 'It's my friend, Vicky. She's pregnant and says she's got news, so if you don't mind loads of squealing, you're welcome to stay put. I'll only be a minute, just to get the bare bones, then I'll ring her later and have a proper chat.'

Vicky sounded breathless when she answered the phone.

Carla begged, 'Please don't tell me you're in labour.'

'*What?* God, no. Is that what you thought? My bump is still here.'

'What's the news, then?'

'You remember me telling you that I was going on a training course – though why they wanted to send me on it when I'll be on maternity leave for the next six months, I don't know. Anyway,' she took a breath. 'I met someone on the course who works in the

Leeds office, where Yale transferred from. Guess what she told me?'

'I've no idea.'

'She asked whether I knew him, and when I told her that he's my line manager, she wanted to know whether he was up to his old tricks yet. When I asked her what he meant, she said, *'sleeping with his staff.'* She didn't mean with *me* obviously, because I'm pregnant and the size of a small family hatchback, but with other women in the office. *Apparently,'* Vicky stressed the word, 'he had an affair with a girl in his department when he was there. Her name was Anita Campbell, and she was more into him than he was into her. She ended up resigning from her job. The woman I spoke to wasn't a hundred per cent sure what happened, but from what she could gather, he'd made life really difficult for Anita, wanting to transfer her to another department. So she left.'

Carla was silent as she absorbed the news.

Vicky said, 'Can't you see? He's got a track record.'

'But does he though? It's not a crime to have a relationship with someone you work with, even if the company frowns on it.'

'The woman reckons it was tantamount to constructive dismissal and that he was trying to distance himself from Anita because he was worried his girlfriend would find out.'

That sounded more promising. 'But it's still my word against his, and don't forget, his fiancée was a witness.'

'She only saw and heard what Yale wanted her to see and hear, and you could argue that as he's done this before, maybe his word shouldn't be taken at face value.'

'I dunno…'

'Do you want to keep your job?' Vicky demanded.

'Yes.'

'Well, then. But even if you didn't, you'll want a good reference.'

'There is that,' Carla agreed. 'It's all hearsay, though.'

'Speak to her.' Vicky urged.

'The woman on the course?'

'No, *Anita*. I've got her mobile number if you want it.'

'Um…'

'Look, I'll send it to you anyway. I haven't spoken to her myself, but the woman on the course has, so she's expecting your call. Think about it, yeah?'

'I will,' Carla promised.

After saying goodbye, the call ended, leaving her feeling dazed and confused. What should she do? Should she phone this Anita person? Or would she end up digging herself an even deeper hole?

Ashton cleared his throat.

'Oh, hell,' she muttered. She had forgotten he was there. 'How much of that did you hear?'

'Not much.'

She shot him a glance out of the corner of her eye. He was staring straight ahead.

'Okay, quite a bit,' he admitted.

'Yeah, I was afraid of that.'

'Do you want to talk about it or forget I was here?'

'Forget—' she began then paused. 'No, actually I'd like to talk about it.' Inhaling deeply, she blew out her cheeks. 'My line manager is called Yale, and we were dating for a few weeks but were keeping it quiet because the company we work for doesn't approve of line managers having romantic relationships with their staff, for obvious reasons. Anyway, one evening we went to this retirement bash and sneaked away for a quick kiss, and his fiancée caught us. Before you say anything, I had no idea he was engaged or seeing anyone else. He accused me of harassment and reported me to HR. I'm now on indefinite leave while they conduct an investigation.'

Ashton shook his head slowly. 'That's awful. I'm so sorry.'

'The thing is, Vicky says he's done something similar before,' she said, then went on to explain, ending with, 'I don't know whether I should contact this woman. Would it do any good?'

'Would it do any harm?'

'I don't know.'

'On the other hand, might it be of any use?'

'I don't know,' she repeated.

'From where I'm sitting, I don't think you've got anything to lose. But you're the one who has to make the decision and deal with whatever you discover.'

'I'll call her,' she said. Ashton was right, she didn't have anything to lose and possibly everything to gain. 'But not right now,' she added. 'I want to take some more photos.'

And neither did she want to waste any more of Ashton's time. She would contact Anita Campbell tomorrow, because she intended to enjoy the rest of the day.

The Black Horse was a typical village pub with horse brasses on the walls, beamed ceilings, and a landlord who seemed to know everyone by name.

Ashton had stepped through its doors many times, always with a letter or two in his hand and sometimes a parcel. However, he'd never visited the place for a drink, so this evening broke the trend.

After a very successful afternoon of photographing everything and anything on the hillside above the farm and in the fields around, he and Carla had made their way down the lane and into the village. And now they were sitting in the pub, examining each other's photos and contemplating an early supper. Ashton hadn't thought he would be hungry after the delicious Sunday lunch, but he had surprised himself, and was now rather peckish. He didn't want anything heavy, but a light snack would be most welcome.

Having ordered, they settled down with their drinks. 'Tell me about yourself,' he suggested.

Carla grimaced. 'Don't you know enough?'

'That's not you; that's something a turd of a bloke has done to you.' He saw her digesting this nugget of useless advice and cringed at how trite he sounded.

'I like that' she said. 'It's true.' She took a sip of her wine. 'What do you want to know?'

'How long have you and Dulcie been friends?'

'I've known her forever,' she began, and that was the start of him getting to know Carla Mason. In turn, he answered her questions, and by the time they'd eaten their meal, he felt he was beginning to understand her better.

'I've had a great day,' she said as they set off along Picklewick's main street, back towards the farm.

'So have I. We must do this again.' Even as the words left his mouth, Ashton guessed it was unlikely to happen. She could be gone tomorrow if she spoke to this Anita woman and decided her story was worth investigating.

'I'd like that. Perhaps you could show me the canal? And maybe we could have a bite to eat afterwards.'

If any other woman had made that suggestion, he would have assumed they were suggesting a date. But this was Carla, so he didn't, and he had no qualms agreeing as he said, 'We'll spot more wildlife early in the morning, rather than later in the day.'

'How early is early?'

'Five a.m.' He chuckled as her face blanched. 'Patience, the ability to stay still and quiet, and unsociable hours are often the minimum requirements for photographing wildlife.'

'Yeah, but five in the morning?' she protested.

'I'm usually up way before then,' he reminded her, 'So it's second nature to get up early on my days off.'

'Don't you ever have a lie in?'

'That's what cold and rainy winter mornings are for.'

'I wholeheartedly agree! There's nothing nicer than snuggling under the duvet when it's pitch black and belting down outside.'

Ashton had a vision of Carly's dark hair on his pillow, and he coughed. Where had *that* come from? It wasn't an unpleasant image, but it was hardly appropriate.

The image refused to go away though, lingering in the back of his mind as they negotiated Muddypuddle Lane, and he was more conscious of her than ever.

He could feel the heat of her skin as her bare arm brushed against his, and he was acutely aware of the light floral scent she wore and the way the evening sun illuminated the shine of her hair.

Ashton didn't need this reaction to her, but he couldn't seem to prevent it. Thankfully, she hadn't noticed, and when he realised that she was checking out her surroundings with her newly acquired photographer's eye, he smiled.

'Ooh, toadstools!' she cried, veering to the side of the lane and crouching down to peer into the hedgerow.

Ashton followed her and lowered himself onto his haunches. The fungi were beige-brown in colour, quite tall, and the shape reminded him of a witch's hat.

'Do you know what they are?' she asked.

'Afraid not. My speciality is animals.'

'I wonder if they're edible.' She stretched out a hand.

'Don't you dare!' he cried, nudging her aside.

Unbalanced, Carla wobbled and began to topple, but before she connected with the ground Ashton's arm shot out and he grabbed her around the waist. Her momentum nearly took him down, and he pulled her towards him. Then his legs gave way, his backside plonked onto the tarmac, with the result that Carla was now sitting in his lap.

Sorry.' Ashton was mortified. 'I didn't mean to—' He stalled. Her mouth was perilously close to his, and he had the strongest urge to kiss it.

His brain disconnected from his body as his gaze focused on her lips, pink and luscious as they parted to reveal her teeth. And when she ran her tongue over her bottom lip, he found himself leaning towards her, his heart hammering and every nerve ending tingling.

Without conscious thought, his eyelids drifted shut and their lips met, sending a bolt of desire through him. Then she was kissing him back, urgently, frantically, and he wrapped both arms around her, drawing her tight against him.

God, she felt so *good*.

His reaction was unmissable and instantaneous, and he let out a groan.

A blast of a car horn cruelly broke their connection, and Ashton dragged his mouth away. Looking around, he saw a hulking big truck slowing to a halt in the middle of the lane.

He leapt to his feet and held out a hand to Carla, who looked mortified. He guessed he did, too. He certainly felt it.

When he noticed who was behind the wheel, he groaned. Trust it to be someone he knew and not a random delivery driver.

Adam was grinning down at them.

Shamefaced, Ashton scooted into the side, almost burying himself in the hedge as he did so, wishing it would swallow him whole.

The truck's window glided down. 'Want a lift?'

It was Carla who answered. 'No thanks, we're fine.'

Laughter billowed out of the cab. 'I can see that. Don't do anything I wouldn't.'

Ashton began, 'We were— It's not what—' But it was too late. Adam was revving the engine and he tooted the horn as he drove past.

Ashton waited until the truck had rounded the bend and was out of sight, then said, 'I'm sorry, I shouldn't have—'

'Don't.' Carla's voice was strangled.

He winced. *Way to go, Ashton*, he thought sourly.

'I'm not,' she said.

'Pardon?'

'I'm not sorry.'

'You aren't?'

She shook her head.

'Actually, I'm not sorry, either.' He was shocked to discover it was true. He should be, but he wasn't. The kiss had been freaking marvellous, and he desperately wanted to do it again, but he held himself in check and they walked the rest of the way in silence.

When they reached the farm, Ashton asked, 'Will I see you again?'

'I hope so.'

'When?'

'Up to you.'

'Tomorrow?'

'Yes, tomorrow.'

'It's a date,' he said, and her face broke out into a most gorgeous smile as she replied, 'Yes, I believe it is.'

CHAPTER SEVEN

Carla flinched as the hinges of the back door creaked. She had just kissed Ashton goodbye, and was now trying to sneak into the farmhouse and shuffle off to bed before Dulcie saw her face and realised something had happened.

She could hear the sound of the television coming from the living room, and assumed Dulcie and Otto were snuggled on the sofa. Which was another reason to make herself scarce. They didn't need her doing a spare wheel impression, and they deserved to spend some time alone.

Tiptoeing through the dining room and into the tiny hall, she thought she'd got away with it, but as she put her foot on the bottom step, Dulcie called out, 'Carla, is that you?'

Sheepishly, Carla stuck her head around the door, trying to use it to hide some of her face.

'Did you have a nice time?' Dulcie asked.

'Er, yeah, it was okay.'

Dulcie's gaze sharpened. 'Just okay?'

With a sigh, Carla realised she might as well come clean. Dulcie would hear about it anyway because Adam was bound to tell Maisie what he'd seen.

'We kissed,' she said, stepping into the room. Otto grinned at her.

'You didn't!' Dulcie sounded incredulous, but the disbelief was tinged with satisfaction.

Glumly, Carla replied, 'We did. In the middle of the lane.' She wrinkled her nose. 'Do you think it's possible to get high from looking at toadstools?'

'*What?*'

'I saw a toadstool and crouched down to have a closer look, and so did Ashton. I'm not sure what happened, but he kind of fell over, pulling me with him, and then we were kissing.'

Dulcie smirked. 'Just like that?'

'Yes, just like that. Then Adam drove up the lane and caught us.'

'He *did?* Oh, my! What happened next?'

'Nothing.'

'Nothing at all?' Dulcie's eyebrows rose.

'No. Ashton went home.'

'Are you seeing him again?'

'Yes.'

'Then why so glum?'

'For one, I don't make a habit of sitting in the middle of a road, snogging. For another, I don't want to get involved with anyone. Not here, and definitely not now.'

'So why are you seeing him again?

Carla shrugged. Admittedly, she was attracted to him and enjoyed his company, but was that sufficient reason to go on a date?

Her inner voice let out a snide laugh, and she was forced to admit that she'd gone on dates for far less valid reasons.

'A bit of fun will do you good,' Dulcie continued.

'I didn't come here for fun. I came here to cry on your shoulder, not to get involved with some guy.'

'But you like him and he likes you, otherwise he wouldn't be helping you with your photography.'

There's no future in it,' Carla pointed out.

'Since when have you been bothered about the future? It's a date, not a marriage proposal.'

Carla decided to change the subject. 'I spoke to Vicky earlier,' she began and proceeded to recount the conversation, ending with, 'I'm going to call Anita Campbell in the morning.'

As Carla prepared for bed, she assumed she would lie awake mulling over the information Vicky had given her, and how, if it were true, it could affect the hearing.

However, it wasn't that which occupied her thoughts, it was Ashton – because as kisses went, it had been simply delicious.

Ashton's shift seemed to last forever. It was the longest shift he'd worked in his life, each minute feeling more like an hour, and he found himself hurrying through his round as though getting back to the depot earlier meant he could knock off earlier. It didn't, unfortunately.

He'd not had any post for the farm today and he couldn't decide whether he was disappointed, before coming down on the side of relief. He had a feeling that seeing Carla whilst he was at work might prove awkward.

But when he thought about their date later, his pulse quickened and there was a flutter in his chest, which was concerning. He was on a hiding to nothing, and he warned himself not to get carried away. Carla was gorgeous and he liked her immensely, but she would be out of his life soon, so he should enjoy this for what it was.

Unfortunately, he didn't know *what* it was. A confidence boost maybe? A reassurance that not every woman found him as boring as Lacey did. That he still had it, whatever *it* was. Actually, scrap that – he'd never been particularly popular with the girls. Too much of a nerd, he guessed. Not athletic, or edgy.

There was one thing you could say about him – his nan, bless her heart, often told him what a nice boy he was, but he suspected that was because he smuggled bottles of stout into the care home for her. His mum would have a fit if she knew.

He wondered whether he would have time to pay Nan a quick visit this morning, since he'd managed to get ahead with his round. She lived in Honeymead Care Home on the outskirts of Picklewick, which was on his round, and he tried to call in wherever he could.

Deciding he did, he popped into the off-licence in Picklewick's high street and bought her a couple of bottles and a multi-pack of spicy Nik Naks. That should see her right for a couple of days.

When he arrived at the care home, he was buzzed inside immediately and handed the stack of post to Rose on the reception desk.

'How's my grandmother today?' he asked.

'As chirpy as always. She's in the day room, waiting to have her hair done.'

Perfect. The day room took him past her bedroom, which meant he could smuggle in the bottles of stout and hide them at the back of her wardrobe behind her shoes.

He was in and out in a flash and striding into the day room with no one any the wiser.

His nan spotted him immediately, and her face lit up in a big smile. 'Ashton, my lovely boy. Come give your nana a kiss.' When he bent down to kiss her cheek, she hissed in his ear, 'Did you bring me any stout?'

'It's in the usual place.'

'You're a good boy.'

'I haven't got long,' he warned, sitting in the chair next to her.

'I guessed as much.' She fingered the sleeve of his Royal Mail tee shirt. 'How are you?'

'I'm good.' Her eyes narrowed, and she gave him a beady stare before her expression softened. 'You look better than the last time I saw you. Not as sad.' She pulled a face. 'I never did like Lacey. She didn't have any taste.'

'Because she turned me down?' He gave his grandmother a rueful smile.

'Partly. And because she thought her poop didn't smell.'

'Nan! That's not nice.'

'It's true,' his grandmother said. 'She thought she was too good for you.' A fierce light shone in her eyes. 'No one is good enough for my grandson.'

'You're biased.'

'I'm right. Now, what's your news?'

'I haven't got any.'

'Liar. I can see it in your face.'

Thankfully Ashton was saved from further questioning when his nan's attention was caught by one of the carers gesturing to her.

'It's my turn.' His nan patted her hair. 'I was thinking of having it coloured pink.'

'Go for it, Nan.'

'That's what I love about you,' she said, pinching his cheek as he helped her get to her feet and find her walking stick. 'Nothing ever rattles you. Not even that Lacey business. Right, I'm off for my pampering session. I was only joking about the colour, by the way.'

Ashton watched her shuffle down the corridor, his heart full of love, and as he left the care home, he idly wondered whether she would also think that Carla wasn't good enough for him.

The Golden Fleece in Thornbury was a trendy bar. Not really his scene (he preferred quieter, more traditional watering holes) but Ashton thought Carla might enjoy it. The food was supposed to be good, and the selection of gins was astounding. Not that he would sample any, as he couldn't stand the stuff, but he hoped Carla liked them.

He had collected her from the farm, conscious of a shadowy figure peering out of the kitchen window, and guessed it was Dulcie. There was an awkward moment when he wondered whether Carla expected a kiss, before they settled for a peck on the cheek and a brief hug.

And now they were sitting in the bar across the table from one another, debating whether to have a starter. He had the feeling Carla seemed reluctant, and guessed she might be worried about the price of the meal. This place wasn't cheap, although it wasn't as expensive as The Wild Side.

As though she'd read his mind, Carla said, 'Otto suggested we dine at The Wild Side, rather than drag you all the way to Picklewick to pick me up, then drive all the way here. I know Thornbury's not far, but…'

Ashton's mouth tightened and his jaw clenched. The Wild Side was the last place he wanted to eat at.

He thought he'd covered his reaction, but he clearly hadn't, as Carla said, 'I know it's pricey, but Otto wouldn't charge us the full amount.'

'It's not that—'

'Please don't tell me you've had a bad experience there,' she interrupted, then saw his expression. 'Oh, dear, you have.'

'Not in the way you think. The food was lovely, the occasion not so much.'

She was looking at him expectantly, and he realised he couldn't leave it there. He had to give her an explanation. He took a steadying breath. 'I proposed to my girlfriend there. She turned me down.'

Carla's expression was full of sympathy. 'It seems neither of us has been lucky in love.' She paused, and he could see her thinking. 'The Wild Side hasn't been open very long, so I assume this was fairly recent?'

'It was.' He drank some of his sparkling water, the pain of Lacey's rejection hitting him anew.

Carla said, 'I'm sorry.'

'I'll get over it.' He stared into space, his smile sad. 'It was probably for the best. We weren't compatible. Wanted different things out of life. And she didn't approve of my hobby. Said it was boring.' Then he added, 'She said *I* was boring, and that I lacked ambition.' He grimaced. 'She's right, I do, and I'm not going to apologise.'

'I don't think you're boring.'

'That's kind of you.'

'I'm being honest. I think you're fascinating.' Her eyes widened. 'I mean, photography is fascinating and you're a photographer, so…'

He chuckled. 'I know what you mean. But I'm the first to admit that I'm not the most exciting person in the world. I'm a postman, for goodness' sake, and I like my job. I don't want promotion or more responsibility.'

She giggled. 'I bet I can beat you in a 'who is the most boring' contest. I work in insurance for a start, and I still live at home.'

Oh, that's definitely a point for you. At least I've got my own place,' he teased.

'In my defence, my mum works for a travel company as a rep and she's away for months on end, so it's almost as good as having my own house, but without the mortgage.'

'No mortgage,' he said dreamily. 'I can't imagine what that's like.'

'I keep thinking I should move out and put a toe on the property ladder, but I can't afford it unless I do a flat-share thing, and I don't fancy that. I like my own space.'

'What would happen if your mum came back for good?'

'I'd have to move out, I think. The thought of bringing someone back when she's there...' Carla shuddered, then bit her lip. 'Not that I take men home very often.'

'You don't have to explain or justify anything.'

'But I don't want you to think—'

'I don't.' He hoped she could hear the sincerity in his voice. 'Shall we order? We've been nursing these menus for ages, and the waiter is hovering.'

With their orders given, Ashton remembered to ask her whether she had phoned Anita-what's-her-face today.

'I did,' Carla replied with a frown. 'But she wasn't prepared to discuss it over the phone. She wants to meet in person.'

'Is that a problem?'

'She might be a stalker or something. Besides, she lives in Leeds.'

'Will it help your case if you go?'

'I don't know until I talk to her. I discussed it with my union rep, and he said that depending on the information she gives me, it might help.'

'You should go.'

'I suppose.'

'Would you like me to come with you?'

Carla gasped. 'You'd do that?'

'Absolutely.'

'Why?'

'Because the guy is a jerk, and he shouldn't be allowed to get away with it. And I can see how much you're hurting.'

Her smile was warm. 'Has anyone told you that you're a very nice man?'

Ashton didn't say anything, and if Carla had been aware of the lustful thoughts that went through his mind when he kissed her good night later, she would have quickly changed her opinion of him.

Carla was seriously cheesed off that HR hadn't been in touch with her regarding a date for the meeting. How much longer was this going to go on? She was in limbo until it was resolved.

The silver lining, as Ashton pointed out on the journey to Leeds, was that at least the delay had given her time to speak to Anita Campbell.

Ashton, she'd discovered, usually looked on the bright side and his cheerfulness was rubbing off on her. In his company, she couldn't be morose. She was so glad he'd offered to accompany her today, and not just because it saved her from an arduous train journey. If it hadn't been for him, Carla might have been tempted to return to Birmingham and stay there, rather than travel back and forth to Picklewick, because she was conscious of not outstaying her welcome at the farm.

As soon as she returned to Muddypuddle Lane this evening, she really should have a discussion with Dulcie, because she honestly didn't know how long this situation would continue. It could be a matter of days, or weeks. God forbid, it might even be months, and there was no way she could stay with Dulcie for that length of time, no matter how useful she tried to be.

Unfortunately, Carla didn't want to return to Birmingham. She was quite settled at the farm, and neither did she want to leave Ashton. She would miss him more than was wise.

Over the past few days she had developed feelings for him, and that didn't sit well with her. She had got over Yale far too quickly for comfort (despite how he'd treated her), so what did that say about her?

Carla feared she couldn't trust herself to know how she felt anymore. Gone was the carefree woman who had been happy to have fun and not allow any man to touch her heart, and Carla missed her. She'd known where she was with that version of herself. She'd vaguely recognised the version who had thought she'd fallen in love with Yale, but this more sombre, serious Carla, who had developed a sneaking enjoyment of the countryside and a love of photography, was a complete stranger.

And she hadn't even begun to pick apart her growing feelings for Ashton.

She couldn't think about that now though, because they were nearing the outskirts of Leeds and heading for a place called Morley, just off the M62. After negotiating a tangled mess of a junction, Carla was glad to leave the motorway behind.

'Not far now,' Ashton said. The car's satnav was a godsend, and within a few minutes it had directed them to their destination.

Carla levered her stiff body out of the car. 'That was one hell of a journey. This had better be worth it. If Anita Campbell has led us on a wild goose chase, I won't be responsible for my actions.'

'I think I've aged ten years,' Ashton groaned. 'When I looked up the route online, it reckoned it should take around three and a half hours, not five. Thank goodness we set out in plenty of time, otherwise we would be late. I'm not looking forward to the drive back.'

'I bet you're wishing you hadn't offered.'

He looked her in the eye. 'Not at all.'

She met his gaze and held it, feeling a shiver travel down her back. Then she looked away. She'd unpick that later; right now, she needed to focus.

They were twenty minutes early, so Carla didn't expect Anita to be there yet. After making enquiries with a member of staff in the pub where they'd agreed to meet, Carla was directed to a table. A woman was already seated there, a glass of what looked like orange juice in front of her, alongside a cardboard document wallet.

Carla took a moment to study her. She was a pretty redhead, with curling locks, freckles, and the most gorgeous green eyes. Nothing like Carla, or Yale's fiancée. It appeared the man didn't have a type, unless *gullible* could be called a type.

'Anita?' Carla asked hesitantly.

'You must be Carla.' Anita gave Ashton a doubtful look, as though she hadn't expected Carla to have brought anyone with her.

'This is Ashton. He drove me here.'

Anita indicated they should sit, and once they were settled she pushed the document wallet across the table. 'This is why I wanted to speak to you in person,' she said.

'What is it?' Carla opened the envelope flap and slid out a sheaf of papers.

'Messages between me and Yale.' Anita spat out his name. 'He denied he sent them, and he even deleted his side of the conversation so there would be no record. But I'd taken screenshots.'

Carla was perplexed. 'Why did you do that?'

'I had a stalker a few years ago, and now I always screenshot anything that can disappear, just in case.' Her tone was matter-of-fact.

Carla flicked through them, scanning them quickly. Oh, my…

Anita said, 'I could have emailed them to you, but I wanted to meet you in person. I can't believe he did it again. I heard he took it further and reported you to HR. What a snake.'

Carla told her the full story, and Anita nodded along. When she'd finished speaking, Anita asked, 'What does his fiancée look like?'

'Tall, thin, dressed to the nines, with bouncy blonde hair. Expensive looking.'

'That's the woman he cheated on when he was with me, but she was his girlfriend then, not his fiancée. Her father is really well off. I mean, *really*. He's just started a new venture in Birmingham, something to do with luxury cars.'

'Is that why Yale transferred to the Birmingham office from Leeds?'

'I expect so.'

'He's a fool to be playing around,' Carla said.

'He's an arrogant so-and-so. I think he honestly believes he isn't going to get caught.'

'And even when he does, he comes out of it smelling of roses.' Carla was incensed.

Anita tapped the folder. 'I left the company of my own accord without a fuss, because I couldn't face the fallout.' Her eyes filled with tears. 'I loved him so much, and he broke my heart.' She blinked furiously.

'I wish I hadn't let him walk all over me. I wish I'd stayed and fought, but I didn't have it in me. Not then. I'm not sure I do now, to be honest. But I think you do.'

Carla nodded slowly. 'You're right, I do.' However, she wasn't sure whether the contents of this folder or what Anita had told her would be enough.

Anita said sombrely, 'Look at the last couple of printouts.'

Carla did. They weren't screenshots of messages and neither were they emails or photographs. They were transcripts of phone conversations. And what they said made Carla's blood boil. Yale really was a nasty piece of work.

'Are these verbatim?' she asked.

'They are.'

'You could have made all this up. I know you didn't,' she added hastily, 'but that's what they will say.'

'I expect they will, if that was all there is.' There was steel in Anita's eyes. 'I recorded both conversations. I know what he did to me isn't exactly the same as what he did to you, but it's close enough. He won't have a leg to stand on!'

Carla felt exhausted as she and Ashton returned to his car later that afternoon.

Anita had left shortly after her revelation, promising to keep in touch, so Carla and Ashton had decided to grab something to eat before tackling the long drive back to Picklewick. It had taken nearly five hours to get to Leeds, due to traffic and roadworks along several lengths of the motorways, and there was no reason to think the return journey would be any less fraught.

Carla was shattered, and she wasn't the one who would be doing the driving! Poor Ashton must be seriously regretting accompanying her today. It was a pity they couldn't break the journey—

She slapped a hand to her forehead. Of course! 'I've got an idea,' she said. 'We could come off the motorway at Birmingham and stay the night at my house.' Then she felt a fool for mentioning it, as she remembered something. 'Oh, but you can't – you've got work tomorrow.'

Ashton's smile was more of a smirk. 'Actually, I don't. I arranged to have tomorrow off because I knew today would be a long day.'

Carla was touched that he'd gone to all that trouble. 'I don't know what to say.'

'You don't have to say anything. You'd do the same for me.'

She was surprised to realise that she would. 'Does that mean you're happy to break the journey at mine?'

'I don't see why not. I must admit, I wasn't looking forward to driving back this afternoon. Anyway, I've never been to Birmingham.'

'Do you want to go out on the town this evening?' Carla hoped not. It was the last thing she was in the mood for.

'What? Not on your life! I was hoping to see an urban fox.'

Carla might have known, and she rolled her eyes good-naturedly. 'Pity you didn't bring your camera.'

'I know,' he sighed. 'I didn't think I'd need it.'

'I don't think you'll need it tonight, either. I've never seen a fox on my street.'

'Have you looked for one?'

'Not really.'

He gave her a 'well, then,' look.

She said, 'Are you sure I can't tempt you to go for a drink down my local?'

'Oh, go on then, you've twisted my arm.'

'Were you having me on about wanting to see a fox?'

His face creased into a smile, his profile showing her one of his gorgeous dimples. 'Only a bit. A pie and a pint will go down a treat.'

'You've just eaten,' she pointed out.

'And I'll want to eat again before I go to bed. My job means I'm on my feet for a lot of the day.' He tapped his flat stomach. 'I need the calories.'

Carla barely heard that last bit.

She'd zeroed in on the word 'bed' and it abruptly struck her that she would be alone in the house with a man she found seriously attractive and a thoroughly nice guy.

And he would be sleeping in the bedroom next to hers.

Maybe, given how fast her heart was beating at the thought and how dry her mouth had suddenly become, suggesting he stayed the night at her place wasn't the best idea she'd ever had.

By the time they'd exited the motorway at Birmingham, Ashton was more than ready to ditch the car and stretch his legs. He wasn't used to sitting in one position for this long, or being so sedentary, and his back was in half. To add to his woes, his neck was stiff, his shoulders were aching, and his eyes felt gritty from focusing so hard.

The return journey had been twice as bad, with even more traffic to contend with, and he'd seen more near misses in one day than he'd witnessed in a year in Thornbury.

Carla guided him through the unfamiliar one-way system, and when she finally instructed him to pull onto a driveway outside a semi-detached 1930s house in a leafy suburb, he sighed in relief.

Ashton got out of the car, groaning as his muscles protested, and looked around. 'Is there a shop nearby?' he asked, wishing he had suggested they push on, rather than agreeing to break the journey. He wasn't exactly prepared for an overnight stay. 'I need a toothbrush.'

Carla unlocked the front door, bending down to pick up a wad of post and giving him a view of her shapely behind. He swallowed and looked away.

'There are new toothbrushes in the bathroom,' she told him, flicking through the letters and flyers. She paused, and her face paled. Then she held up an envelope sporting a logo he recognised as belonging to a large insurance company. 'It's from work,' she said. 'And it sure as hell isn't a renewal quote.'

He followed her inside, noting her automatic actions as she draped her bag over the newel post and kicked off her shoes in the hall. He wondered whether he should follow suit but became distracted by her cute bare feet with their apricot-painted toenails.

She tore the envelope open. 'Would you like a cup of tea or coffee? Blast, there won't be any fresh milk.'

'Would you like me to pop out and fetch some?' he offered, thinking she might want some time alone to read the letter.

'Only if you want tea,' she replied absently, her eyes on the letter. 'There's creamer for coffee. Or wine. I'm deffo having wine.' She blew out her cheeks and waved the letter. 'I've got a date for my meeting with HR.'

'When?'

'Two weeks Friday.' She threw it onto the worktop and opened the fridge. Ashton saw there wasn't a lot in there, but there were two bottles of red. 'The glasses are in that cupboard,' she said, jerking her chin as she unscrewed the top of one of them.

He took two out and set them down. 'Isn't it good news that you have a date?'

She gulped her wine, drinking half of it in one go. 'I'm scared.'

'I expect you are. I would be, too. The prospect of being sacked can't be pleasant, but at least you'll know one way or the other. And from what Anita said, *you* probably won't be sacked, but *he* might. You'll be back at your desk in no time.'

Another gulp. Her glass was nearly empty.

Then Carla's chin wobbled, and her eyes filled with tears.

Ashton put down his drink and held out his arms. He couldn't do anything about her job situation, but he could give her his moral support. A cuddle mightn't make anything better, but it certainly wouldn't make it worse.

He held her for a long time, and the longer he held her the more reluctant he was to let her go. It felt so natural, so right to have her in his arms, her cheek against his shoulder, his face in her hair, and at that moment, Ashton realised he was in danger of losing his heart.

CHAPTER EIGHT

Dulcie was in the dining room on a call with a customer when Carla walked into the farmhouse the following morning. As she headed towards the stairs, her friend beckoned her over, then held up an index finger to signify that she wouldn't be long.

Carla sank into a chair while she waited, her thoughts flicking back to last night. No doubt Dulcie would give her the Spanish Inquisition treatment as soon as she got off the phone.

Dulcie's attention was on the screen but when she'd finished speaking to the customer, she tore off her headset and swivelled around in her seat. 'Did you spend the night together?' she demanded, her face alight with curiosity.

'Yes.'

'I knew it!' Dulcie punched the air. 'I said as much to Otto after you messaged me to say you were staying at yours. Thanks for that, by the way – I'd have been worried.' She fixed Carla with a piercing look. 'Did you get much sleep?'

'Not a lot.'

'Ooh. He looks like he might be a considerate lover. Was he?'

Carla smiled sweetly. 'I've no idea.' Then she burst out laughing at Dulcie's confusion. 'We spent the night at my place,' she confirmed, 'but not in the same bed. Ashton slept in the spare room.' She giggled. 'Your face was a picture.'

'But what about the 'not a lot of sleep' thing?'

'I didn't sleep well, but that had nothing to do with Ashton,' she fibbed, as her restlessness having been mostly because of him. Some of it had been due to worry over the forthcoming meeting with HR, mulling over the contents of the folder (there had even been a photo of Yale and Anita kissing, which was pure gold) and a feeling of complete and utter dislocation from her life in Birmingham.

She had spent half the night wondering how much she would miss Picklewick (and Ashton, *especially Ashton*) and fearing she would miss it far more than was good for her. What she couldn't decide was whether her reluctance to go home to Birmingham was the result of the usual post-holiday dismay at returning to real life that most people experienced, or whether there was more to it.

As she had lain in bed last night, the room illuminated by streetlights and the subdued noise of the city in the small hours reminding her of the rumbling of a sleeping giant, she had been shocked to discover that she didn't want this anymore. When she tried to imagine herself slotting back into this house, her job, and the social scene she had previously embraced with enthusiasm, she couldn't. It felt like a well-loved dress that had been worn all the time, but had now grown shabby and no longer fitted the way it once had.

When she closed her eyes, all she could envisage was the hillside above the farm, with the wind in the grass and the cry of birds overhead. All she could feel was the weight of a camera in her hand and the peace in her soul.

Dulcie was gazing at her in concern. 'How was your meeting? Was it useful?'

'It certainly was.' Carla pulled the document wallet from her bag and passed it over.

Dulcie flicked through it. 'Bloody hell, this is dynamite!'

'It is.' She wrinkled her nose.

'Don't you think this will be enough?' Dulcie asked.

'It should be.'

'What aren't you telling me?'

'I want to be exonerated – of course I do – but I don't believe I can work there after this.'

Dulcie's mouth fell open. 'But you love your job.' She scooted her chair closer, the wheels squeaking on the polished floorboards. 'Don't let this spoil things. You'll be back at your desk in no time and in an hour it'll be as though you'd never been away.'

'That's what worries me.'

'I don't understand.'

'I'm not sure I do, either.'

'What's going on, Carla? Has something happened?'

Carla got to her feet. 'Ignore me, I'm being silly. I'll feel better after I take a goat for a walk.'

'You don't have to. I think they're lead-trained by now. Why don't you have a quiet day? Read a book or something.'

Carla shook her head. 'I'd prefer to go for a walk.' She wanted a final look around before she left.

'Something *has* happened. Tell me. Is it Ashton?'

'Real life has happened. I had a letter from HR. The meeting is almost three weeks away. I can't stay here until then.'

'Why not?'

'Because I can't.'

'You *can*,' Dulcie insisted. 'I love having you here.'

'And I love being here.'

'What will you do in Birmingham? Mope, that's what.'

Dulcie was probably right, Carla thought. Then she brightened; at least she would have her newfound love of photography to keep her occupied.

'Have you spoken to your mum about this?' Dulcie demanded.

'Not yet.'

'Give her a call, see what she says.'

It was a good idea. Taking the folder with her, Carla went to her room. Dropping wearily onto the bed and narrowly missing Magic who was napping there, she messaged her mum. *Call me? I've got news.* It was still early in St Lucia, so hopefully she'd catch her mum before she began work.

Her phone rang a second later, and Carla felt some of the tension drain away when she heard her mother's voice.

'How are you, sweetheart? How was your trip to Leeds?'

Carla had been keeping her mum informed via messaging, but it wasn't the same as speaking to her in person. She relaxed into the pillows, the cat curling into her and Carla absently stroked its silky head.

'Interesting,' she replied and filled her mum in on everything that had happened. *Nearly* everything. Although she'd told Mum about Ashton and that he'd helped her with the camera purchase, she hadn't mentioned kissing him. Or that her feelings for him had gone beyond casual friendship. Actually, she wasn't entirely sure *what* her feelings were.

'It was weird being back home yesterday,' she said at the end of the explanation. 'It didn't feel like home anymore.'

'Good.'

'Excuse me?'

'I said, *good*. It's about time you thought about spreading your wings.'

'Are you trying to get rid of me?'

'Never. It will always be your home and you'll always be welcome, but you need your own space.'

'Hang on, Mum, I can't think about getting a place of my own when I don't know whether I'll have a job at the end of the month.'

'You will. And when all this is behind you, you can have a good think about what you want to do with your life.' There was a pause, then her mum blurted, 'I wish I could be there with you. I hate to think of you rattling around in that house on your own, miserable and lonely.'

She had a point. Carla *would* be miserable and lonely. 'Dulcie has asked me to stay on at the farm, but I don't want to intrude any more than I already have.'

'If Dulcie didn't want you, she wouldn't have suggested it.'

'True, but I do feel guilty. Everyone descends on her. Otto must be a bloody saint to put up with it.'

'I'd like to meet him. I've never met a celebrity chef.'

Carla laughed. 'Next time you're home, I'll see what I can do. But perhaps we'll stay in one of Picklewick's B & Bs rather than at the farm, otherwise Dulcie might get you cleaning out the chicken coop.'

'Ugh, no thanks! I'd better go, work calls. Let me know what you decide. Stay safe, sweetheart. I love you.'

'Love you too, Mum.'

When Carla went downstairs, Dulcie wasn't at her desk. She was in the kitchen, on her mobile phone. When she spied Carla, she ended the call and beamed at her.

'I've had a brilliant idea,' she announced. But when Carla wanted to know what it was, Dulcie refused to say anything further.

'If you think I'm walking up this hill, you can think again,' Dulcie told Carla a short time later, as her little hatchback groaned up the rutted track behind the farm which led to the top of the mountain. Carla hadn't been up this way, preferring to take the less arduous path around the side of the hill.

'Where are we going?' she asked.

'To Adam and Maisie's place.'

'Is it far?'

'Far enough, which is why we're not on foot.'

'Where is Maisie anyway? I didn't see her at the farm.'

'That's because she isn't there. She's at The Forever Home.'

Carla didn't bother asking any more questions, since Dulcie was being evasive, and stared out of the window instead.

The top of the mountain was a wilder place than its slopes, bleaker and windswept, with bracken and long grass stretching into the distance. There was no peak as such, just rolling grassland dotted with sheep, that seemed to go on forever.

When they finally reached a cluster of buildings, Maisie hurried out and the sisters greeted each other, then Maisie gave Carla a hug.

'It's looking good, Maisie,' Dulcie said, gazing at the house.

'Want to see inside?'

'Duh! Does a sheep poop in the heather? Lead the way!' Dulcie turned to Carla. 'I haven't been up here for a few weeks, and there wasn't any plaster on the walls last time I came.'

When they stepped inside, Dulcie let out a low whistle. 'Oh, wow. I can't believe this was once a shell with no roof and a tree growing in the middle of the living room.'

Neither could Carla. Maisie and Adam's house looked like something out of a magazine, with whitewashed walls, vaulted ceilings and polished hardwood floors. It was the ultimate in barn conversions.

Maisie said to Dulcie, 'As I told you on the phone, we're moving in on the weekend, so any help will be appreciated.'

'I'm sure Carla and I can hump a few boxes around. Especially since it will be in Carla's best interests.'

Carla was bemused. 'It will?' Despite Dulcie's offer and her mum's advice, she wasn't entirely sure she would still be here at the weekend. She had to go home at some point, and the jury was still out on when that would be.

Both Dulcie and Maisie were grinning at her.

'What?' she demanded, wondering if she was missing something obvious.

Maisie repeated, 'We are moving into this house on the weekend.'

'Yes, you said.'

'Which means, I'm moving *out* of the house in Picklewick.'

'Okay…'

'It's rented. There's a couple of months left on the lease.'

It dawned on Carla what Maisie was getting at. 'I can't afford it,' she stated flatly.

'You won't have to. Adam and I aren't paying any rent. My mum is. She's the one who's supposed to be renting it. When she came to Picklewick, she took out a six-month lease but ended up moving in with Walter, as you know. Me and Adam have been living in it while we renovated this place. She said you can move into her house until you're ready to return to Birmingham.'

Carla didn't know much about property rental, but she knew enough. 'Isn't that classed as subletting?' she pointed out.

Dulcie answered, 'It is, but both the estate agent who manages the property and the landlord are okay with it.'

'Blimey.' Carla didn't know what to say. It was a generous offer, but... 'I haven't got any furniture. Not a stick to my name.'

Maisie said, 'Mum has. It's her furniture in the house at the moment. Adam's is in storage.' She pulled a face. 'Mum's stuff is really old-fashioned, so we won't be bringing any of it with us to the new place. What do you say? Are you going to move in for the duration?'

'Yes – I think.'

To say she was shocked was an understatement, and she wasn't sure she was doing the right thing. Still, it was only for a couple of weeks, and it occurred to her that this was an opportunity to try living on her own. It would also allow her to find out what it would be like to live in Picklewick itself – because she knew, without a shadow of a doubt, that she didn't want to leave.

'We've got to stop eating out,' Carla protested as she and Ashton tucked into a sharing plate of Tex-Mex later that evening. They were dining in one of Ashton's favourite restaurants, one he didn't get to eat in often because Lacey didn't like the food.

'I know, but I thought we should mark the occasion,' he said, popping a taco in his mouth. Mmm, delicious!

'Me moving into Beth's house for a couple of weeks is hardly a cause for celebration.'

'I think it is.' He met her gaze solemnly, stretching a hand across the table to slip into hers.

It meant she wasn't leaving yet, and that was all he could think about – Carla leaving Picklewick and him never seeing her again. It was all he had been able to think about since yesterday, because seeing her in Birmingham had brought it home to him that she wouldn't be in Picklewick much longer. And it also reinforced the fact that he really didn't want her to go. A couple more weeks was definitely something to be celebrated as far as he was concerned.

She opened her mouth, then closed it again, and he wondered what she had been about to say. He considered asking but decided against it. He didn't know her well enough to pry into her thoughts. *What are you thinking,* was the kind of question lovers might ask one another. Although he wouldn't say no to taking her to bed (he was a red-blooded man with a healthy libido, after all), they weren't at that stage in their relationship and never would be. They were friends with kisses (not benefits), and he doubted they would be anything more than that. Which was a good thing, as he didn't want to fall for this woman any more than he already had.

But it didn't mean he couldn't kiss her, and he shuffled his chair around so he could do precisely that.

'Dulcie took me to see Beth's house this afternoon,' Carla said as they broke apart, the kiss too fleeting for his liking. 'It's perfect. You'll have to visit. I move in on Saturday.'

'I will,' he promised.

'What's your place like?'

'Small.'

'One bed or two?'

'Two, but the spare room is mostly filled with camera equipment.' Which reminded him – he hadn't yet spent the voucher Dulcie had given him. Maybe he would get Carla a new lens? It could be her going away present.

Shrugging off the thought of her leaving, he said, 'You'll have to pop over and see it. My camera stuff, I mean. Not the house. The house is nothing special.'

'At least it's yours,' she countered.

'There is that,' he agreed.

'And you promised to show me the canal.'

'So I did. Would you like to go on Sunday? I warn you, it'll be an early start.' He paused. 'Or will you be too busy unpacking?'

'I've got one suitcase. It's not going to take long.'

'Do you think you'll like living in Picklewick?'

She considered the question. 'I'm not sure. I love being at the farm, but I'm kind of in holiday mode at the moment. It's going to be a big jump to move from Birmingham to a little village. I'm worried it might be too sedate, if that's the right word.'

He laughed. 'I'm sure you'll be able to manage being sedate for a couple of weeks.'

'Yeah, I'm sure I will.' She laughed too, but it sounded strained, and he wondered whether she regretted her decision not to return to Birmingham immediately.

As he tried to figure it out, he felt a prickling on the back of his neck and glanced over his shoulder to see a familiar face staring at him. His heart sank. This was the last place he expected to see Lacey, considering she didn't like the food.

Her gaze drilled into him, and he squirmed uncomfortably. She was with one of her friends, and he couldn't help thinking how this must look, him being here with another woman barely two months since he'd proposed.

Ashton managed to tear his gaze away, and as he caught a waiter's eye, he tried to make it appear as though that was what he'd intended all along. 'Could we have some water for the table, please?'

'So, the canal,' Carla was saying, oblivious. 'Is it far from your house?'

'Nothing in Thornbury is far from anywhere else,' he joked weakly. 'It's bigger than Picklewick, but it's not city sized.'

'It's got everything you need though, right?'

'I suppose.' He could still feel the weight of Lacey's stare. She must think that he'd either got over her very quickly or Carla was a rebound relationship.

He swallowed hard and risked another glance. This was the first time he'd set eyes on her since he'd proposed. He'd phoned and he'd messaged, to no avail. She hadn't answered his calls or returned his messages, yet now there was a jealous expression on her face that had no right to be there.

Then it occurred to him that her expression mightn't have anything to do with him, and he scolded himself for thinking the world revolved around him. Clearly *her* world hadn't, because if it had, she wouldn't have dumped him. Right now, she was probably thinking he was a sad fecker and that she'd had a lucky escape. Maybe she was even feeling sorry for Carla.

Ashton had no appetite for dessert and was eager to leave. Despite it being early still, Carla didn't appear to want to linger either. They had been in the restaurant for one hour and fifteen minutes, tops. Some date this was turning out to be.

'Fancy a walk?' he asked impulsively. 'I thought we could stroll along the towpath.'

Carla glanced at her feet. 'I'm not really dressed for it.'

He followed the direction of her gaze. She was wearing strappy sandals with heels, so there was nothing for it but to take her home, unless... 'Want to pop back to my place?' he asked, as they made towards the car.

She was smiling. 'For coffee?'

'If you want, or I can open a bottle of wine.'

She raised her eyebrows and tilted her head. 'You really *do* mean coffee.'

'Why? What did you—? *Oh.*'

'You're blushing.'

'I'm not.'

'It's cute.'

'Cute?' He didn't want to be thought of as cute. He wanted to be thought of as rugged and handsome. 'I withdraw my offer,' he joked.

'Please don't. I want to see your equipment.' Realising what she'd said, she closed her eyes and let out a groan.

Her blush made him chuckle. 'You've gone red.' He was laughing aloud now, a proper belly laugh that left him gasping for breath. Carla glared at him for a moment before giggling, and very soon she had tears in her eyes and was holding her sides.

'I haven't laughed like that for ages,' she gasped.

And when he replied, 'I'm glad the thought of seeing my equipment amuses you,' it set her off again.

She leaned against him for support, and he slipped an arm around her waist. When she straightened up, it was perfectly natural for his mouth to seek hers and he simply didn't care that they were snogging in the street like teenagers.

When they broke apart, Ashton was breathless with desire.

'I think I'll have that glass of wine you mentioned,' she said.

He took hold of her hand, and they resumed their walk to the car.

'After *coffee*,' she added, leaning in to nibble on his ear.

Ashton stumbled, as what she said sank in; did she mean what he *thought* she meant?

The short journey from the restaurant to his house seemed to take forever. The tension between them was palpable, and the atmosphere in the car was charged with promise. Ashton's pulse throbbed, his palms were clammy on the steering wheel, and his thoughts were a confused mess. He wanted her so badly it hurt, but was what they were about to do wise?

Sod it. He was going into this with his eyes wide open.

He knew what he was letting himself in for – a relationship with Carla would never be a long-term thing – and as long as he kept that in mind, he should be fine.

Carla pushed her misgivings aside as desire surged through her veins. Ashton's smouldering look when he'd realised what she'd meant, and the way his eyes had darkened, the tension in his jaw and the hunger on his face, had melted her insides, searing its way through her body.

Dear lord, she hadn't felt this turned on since forever. And he hadn't even touched her yet. Not really – although the kiss they'd just shared had nearly made her burst into flames.

By the time they arrived at his house, her heart was skipping, missing beats and thudding to catch up with itself, and she was so weak with desire that she had trouble getting out of the car.

As soon as they were inside, he turned to her and she swallowed reflexively, wilting at the naked desire in his eyes.

'Wine?' His voice was gruff. It sent a shiver right through her.

'No.' Hers was barely more than a whisper.

With a low growl, he closed the distance between them, his arms snapping around her as he pulled her into his chest, a cage of bone and muscle locking her in place, pressing her to him.

She felt like a candle, consumed by the flame of his need as he kissed her, his mouth urgent and demanding, and she melted into him, wanting this as much as he.

When he broke the connection and bent to scoop her into his arms and carry her off to bed, all conscious thought fled, as Carla made love to him with her body, her heart, and her soul.

CHAPTER NINE

It was amazing how quickly one could get used to something, Carla thought as she stepped out of the house on Hazel Road and locked the door. In the two weeks since she'd moved into the house in Picklewick, she had become very used to it indeed, and she'd even begun to feel as though she'd lived there forever.

Slipping the keys into her bag, she walked swiftly down the road, her heels tapping on the pavement. The noise made her frown, and her feet didn't appreciate the unaccustomed court shoes either. They weren't used to wearing them. They were more used to being encased in trainers these days.

As she made her way to the bus stop, Carla tugged self-consciously at the hem of her newly acquired jacket. She also wasn't used to wearing office-type attire, having become accustomed to jeans, tee shirts and hoodies. They were the only items of clothing she had brought with her when she'd fled Birmingham for the farm on Muddypuddle Lane over a month ago – apart from two dresses in case she went somewhere nice (like Otto's restaurant, for instance) and a pair of shorts should the weather be nice enough to warrant getting her legs out. So in order to attend an interview with the temp service in Thornbury, she'd had to scour the rails of Picklewick's charity shop for something suitable to wear.

She had also become very used to living in Picklewick. However, it wasn't the ideal place to set down new roots. The village was too quiet, and despite not wanting to live in a city again, she would like somewhere a little livelier. Besides, rental properties in Picklewick were more expensive than those in Thornbury. She knew this, because she'd checked.

Carla hadn't mentioned any of this to Ashton, and Dulcie thought Carla was mad not to tell him, but Carla's reasons were valid. She didn't want their relationship and the fact that she had fallen for him, to colour her decision – because she wasn't doing this for him, or for *them*. She was doing it for herself.

Anyway, all this was purely speculative, a plan in place in case the meeting with HR didn't go in her favour. Charlie, her union rep, would be attending it with her, and he seemed to think the outcome was cut and dried. Carla had forwarded copies of the contents of Anita's folder to him, and he had almost crowed with glee, declaring that the 'other party' (which was how he referred to Yale) wouldn't know what had hit him.

Carla wished she had Charlie's level of confidence. Quietly optimistic was as far as she would go.

Arriving at the bus stop, she joined the queue of people standing in the bus shelter and attempted to prepare herself for her interview. The temp agency had called it an 'informal chat,' but she knew it was more than that. She had to look the part, sound the part, and play the part if she wanted to be considered for the more lucrative placements.

But try as she might, her mind kept drifting to Ashton and she wondered whether he was in Picklewick at this very moment on his rounds.

She caught a glimpse of a red van, and her heart gave a lurch before settling back into its normal rhythm when she realised it wasn't a Royal Mail one. She couldn't wait to see Ashton later, and she tingled at the thought. Since that fateful evening when they had made love for the first time, they'd hardly been able to keep their hands off each other, and Carla was most definitely in lust.

The man was freakin' gorgeous, and he knew what to do with a woman between the sheets. And on the couch. And on the carpet once, but it had made the skin on her back sore so she wouldn't be doing that again in a hurry.

In case he was in the village, she shrank back and hid behind an elderly couple and their pull-along shopping trolley, and only when she was on the bus, did some of her tension evaporate.

Staring out of the window, she told herself to focus. She would have plenty of time to think about Ashton on the return journey. She needed to stop daydreaming and concentrate on what she was in Thornbury to achieve. And whilst she was there, there was no harm in checking out what was available to rent.

'Got everything?' Ashton asked. He glanced at the suitcase by the bedroom door.

Carla scanned the room. 'I think so.'

He noticed she'd put fresh linen on the bed and he knew she wanted to leave Beth's rented house clean and tidy, but to him it felt like she was erasing every trace of herself, as though this was a hotel room and she was done with it. Done with *them*.

Yesterday had been bitter-sweet. They had spent her last day on the hill above the farm, taking photos, and when they'd spotted the stoat again, it had felt symbolic, her time in Picklewick bracketed by sightings of the little animal.

Last night he had held her until she'd drifted off to sleep. Unable to sleep himself, he'd lain beside her, listening to her soft breathing and trying not to think how lonely he would be without her.

Watching her pack this morning had been hard, so he'd sat in the garden with an untouched mug of coffee and waited until it was time to take her to the station.

With a heavy tread, Ashton carried her case out to the car while she did a final check, before locking up and posting the key through the letterbox. His heart squeezed painfully – far too soon they would be at the station, and he might never see her again.

She was subdued on the short journey to Thornbury, and he guessed she might be worried about her meeting tomorrow. She had tried to put it behind her for the most part over the past week or so, but he'd sensed it had been playing on her mind. He knew it would have played on his, if he had been in her position.

God, he would miss her.

Would she miss him?

In a way, he hoped not, because he didn't want Carla to experience the loneliness that he knew would be his lot after she was gone. He cared for her too much to think of her hurting.

Easing the car into a space in the station's car park, he switched the engine off and got out. 'Do you want me to wait with you until the train arrives?' he asked.

'Ashton....' Her expression was unreadable. She shook her head.

He sighed and opened his arms. Carla stepped into them, and he held her close for as long as he could, her head on his chest, his nose in her hair as he breathed in her scent.

Eventually, she pulled away to stare into his eyes, and he cupped her face with his hands.

'It'll be okay,' he said.

Then he kissed her one last time.

He hadn't fought for her. That was the only thing Carla could think of as she boarded the train. Ashton had let her go, had accepted that their relationship was over without so much as a murmur.

It hurt. A lot.

Did it alter her plans to return to Picklewick? Possibly.

The interview with the temp agency the other day had gone well, despite her honesty regarding the uncertainty around her current employment. Beth had told her that she could stay in the house in Picklewick until she sorted out more permanent accommodation in Thornbury, and her mum had insisted on gifting Carla her car, so she had everything lined up. All she had to do was make the decision.

She had tried so hard not to let it hinge on Ashton, but how could it not since she was in love with him? Ah, yes, the woman who had arrived in Muddypuddle Lane determined not to get entangled in another relationship, had well and truly lost her heart.

The journey to Birmingham seemed interminable, but eventually she trundled her case into the hall, the sound of her footsteps in the empty house echoing the emptiness inside her.

Can I come over? I need to see you.

Ashton read the message for a second time. Why did Lacey need to see him? What could they possibly have to talk about? He hadn't had any contact with her since she'd told him they were over, apart from seeing her in the Tex-Mex restaurant a couple of weeks ago, so why did she suddenly need to see him now?

His blood ran cold as a possible reason leapt into his mind. Could she be pregnant?

Ashton closed his eyes and breathed deeply, willing away the panic.

He would have been over the moon if she had told him this three months ago, but they weren't together any longer and the thought of being a single dad and estranged from his baby's mother, filled him with dread.

When? His response was terse.

Today?

I'm at home

20 mins ok?

It wasn't okay, but he had to know why Lacey wanted to see him.

Ashton snorted in derision. Be careful what you wish for, he thought. He had been scared of being lonely now that Carla had gone, but if Lacey was carrying his child, very soon he wouldn't have time to feel lonely.

What a bloody mess.

He went in search of something alcoholic, guessing they both might need some fortification, before remembering that pregnant women probably shouldn't drink.

He tried to recall what Lacey had been drinking in the restaurant, but all he could see was the look on her face. Had she known then that she was pregnant? If so, it would explain her odd expression.

When the doorbell rang, he flinched. Here goes, he thought, steeling himself. If she was indeed pregnant, he wanted to be part of his child's life and was fully prepared to fight for that.

Lacey was standing on the step, looking as lovely as always. A little tired perhaps, but if his suspicion was correct, it was to be expected.

'Can I come in?' she asked.

'Sure.' He held the door open, her familiar perfume wafting over him as she stepped inside. She appeared nervous, and he didn't blame her. He would be nervous, too.

Hell, he *was* nervous.

'Tea?' he asked.

'Can I have a glass of water?'

'Of course.' He poured one for her and one for himself, despite preferring something stronger, then sat down and gestured for her to sit.

She perched on the end of the sofa. 'I've, um… I don't know how to say this.'

Ashton waited.

'I think I've made a mistake.'

'You think… *What?*'

'Okay, I *know* I've made a mistake. I should never have broken up with you. I wasn't thinking straight.'

'Pardon?' He was struggling to get his head around what she was saying.

'I still love you, Ashton.'

'What?' he repeated incredulously. This wasn't what he'd expected her to say.

'Can we try again?'

'Me and you?'

She nodded, her head bowed.

'You want us to try again?' He couldn't believe he was hearing this.

'Yes.' Her voice was small.

'Why? You think I'm boring.'

'No, I don't. Honestly, I don't. I shouldn't have said it. I didn't mean it. Please Ash, I've made a terrible mistake. I've been so lonely without you, and I miss you so much. Please give us another chance. *Please.*'

Ashton closed his eyes. Not too long ago he would have given everything he had to hear those very words, but now there was Carla… Carla, who had walked out of his life, leaving a gaping hole of loss and loneliness.

'I saw you, Ash.' Lacey broke into his anguished thoughts. 'Outside the station earlier with that woman. You looked so sad. Do you love her? Am I too late?'

He *did* love her. With a stab to the chest, he finally admitted that he had fallen head over heels in love with Carla.

But Carla was no longer here. Lacey was, and he still cared for her.

Was it enough?

Carla was conscious that she didn't look her best for this meeting. She was wearing a suit and heels, but there were shadows under her eyes and her face was pale.

Nervously, her heart in her mouth, she entered the building and made for the lifts, hoping no one would see her as she slunk inside. And by 'no one', she meant Yale. He wouldn't be at this meeting, but he would probably be in his office, and she dreaded bumping into him.

It wasn't like a court of law, where the accuser and the accused would be in the same room. This was a disciplinary hearing, after which HR would make its decision as to her future with the company. She would have the right to appeal, and take it to an independent tribunal, but if this meeting didn't go in her favour, she didn't think she had the will to fight. Just like Anita Campbell, she would meekly accept her fate and walk away.

Her union rep was waiting for her, and they were shown into a small office for a private discussion before she was called. Although she'd met with Charlie online, she hadn't met him in person, and he looked younger in the flesh. He also looked confident. She wished she felt the same.

'Are you okay?' he asked.

Carla nodded. She felt sick and shaky, and her mouth was dry. She just wanted to get this over with.

The door opened.

'If you'd like to follow me,' a woman said. Carla recognised her as Mrs Bissett's assistant.

Three people sat around a large table, laptops open, pads and pens at the ready. Carla and Charlie took a seat, Carla barely listening to the preliminaries of why the meeting had been called.

Mrs Bissett had just launched into a spiel about the seriousness of the allegation against her, when Charlie interrupted. 'Can I stop you there?'

Mrs Bissett raised an eyebrow as he pushed a folder across the desk.

'You might want to take a look at this before you go any further,' he said. He got to his feet. Carla did the same. 'You'll need some time to peruse the contents, so we'll wait outside.'

To Carla, the wait was torture. However, the outcome of the meeting wasn't.

Ashton, Anita and Charlie had been right – Yale *hadn't* had a leg to stand on.

'That's wonderful news!'

Everyone Carla had spoken to – her mother, Vicky, Dulcie, Anita – had all said the same thing when she'd phoned them as soon as she'd got home. They were thrilled she had been reinstated, that the dark cloud hanging over her had been lifted, that her job was safe, and she would be returning to her desk tomorrow.

Or would she?

She hadn't decided what she was going to do. She knew what she *wanted* to do, but that wasn't the same as doing it.

Carla's hand hovered over the phone. There was one person who she had yet to call.

Ashton.

She checked the time. Ten minutes past one. He would still be doing his rounds. He might be in his van, driving. In fact, he probably was, so rather than phone, she would send him a message. It was safer. He could read it at his convenience.

God, that sounded so formal, and formal was the last thing she wanted.

She picked the phone up, then put it down again.

Was it too early for wine? A celebratory glass? This didn't feel like a celebration, though.

It felt flat. Meaningless. A hollow victory. And it was that realisation which was the deciding factor.

The phone was in her hand again – it was time to make another call.

Post redirected? *Tick.*
Fridge emptied? *Tick.*
Windows locked? *Tick.*
Everything turned off? *Tick.*
Carla had a final scout around the house, hoping she hadn't forgotten anything. The past couple of hours

had been a blur of frenetic activity, but once she'd made the decision there seemed little point in putting it off until tomorrow. By tonight she would be in Picklewick, and her new life could begin.

It felt strange to leave the house she'd lived in since she was a child, the house she would always refer to as home. For the time being, she was moving into Beth's rented house in the village until she found somewhere suitable in Thornbury. Living in the small market town was the perfect compromise. It wasn't as big as a city, yet neither was it too rural. And after speaking to the temp agency earlier, she already had a job lined up for Monday.

Carla wandered through every room, drinking each one in, before scolding herself for being silly. It wasn't as though she would never see this place again. As soon as her mum was back from the Caribbean, Carla would pay her a visit.

Locking up, she hurried to the car, now eager to be on her way. A new life beckoned, and she couldn't wait for it to begin. Whether Ashton would be in it remained to be seen.

She hoped with all her heart that he *would*.

It was late. Late for Ashton, but not late for most people. He had work in the morning and should be in bed, but unfortunately, he couldn't settle. Thoughts and images whirled through his mind, spinning like a merry-go-round. Except there was nothing merry about them.

He had been glad to see the back of yesterday (saying goodbye to Carla at the train station had been so hard), but today hadn't proved to be any better. He had waited in vain for a call from her, even if it was just to tell him the outcome of her meeting. However, his phone had remained silent: no call, no message.

Her lack of contact convinced him it was over. She was back in her old life, her time in Picklewick now nothing but a memory. And that hurt. He'd thought they had something special, but he'd clearly been kidding himself. And despite vowing not to let anyone else into his heart, he had fallen in love. The pain he'd felt when Lacey had dumped him was nothing compared to the heartache he felt now.

Wryly, he supposed he should be thankful to Carla for showing him what love truly was. He supposed he should also be thankful to Lacey for turning down his marriage proposal. If she hadn't, he would have spent his life not knowing how love really felt.

It was both beautiful and awful.

Right now, awful was winning hands down.

His mobile beeped, and he hoped it wasn't Lacey. She hadn't taken his rejection well yesterday, and her tears had tugged on his heartstrings, but he'd held firm. It wouldn't be fair on either of them if he settled for second best.

Ashton looked at his phone, and his heart lurched violently.

Carla. Finally.

Are you awake? she messaged.

Yes

He waited for a call, or even a reply. And he waited, and waited.

The ring of his doorbell made him jump. Who could this be at just gone nine on a Friday evening? It wouldn't be his parents, because they knew better. Anyway, they were still touring Scotland in their camper van and would be away for a few more weeks yet.

He heaved his weary body out of the chair and went to answer it.

Carla was outside.

Ashton blinked, then squinted. It *was* her; he wasn't imagining it. 'I didn't think you were coming back,' he said.

'I wasn't sure, either. Yet here I am.'

'How did the meeting go?' He wanted to scoop her into his arms and kiss her until she begged him to stop, but he couldn't move.

'Can I come in? If it's not too late?'

It would never be too late for Carla.

'Of course.' He stood aside for her to enter, then closed the door behind her.

She said, 'I was going to leave it until tomorrow to see you, but I couldn't wait.' She hesitated and he got the impression that she didn't intend to stay long.

The thought of her leaving when she'd only just got here, made his chest hurt.

'I've had a formal apology from HR,' she continued. 'And Yale has been suspended.'

'That's brilliant news. I told you, didn't I?'

'You did.'

'When do you start back?'

'I don't.'

Anger reared its head at the injustice of it. 'They can't do that!'

'*They* didn't. *I* did. I resigned.'

'You did what?' He was flabbergasted. Ashton sank into the armchair he hadn't long vacated. He didn't think he could take any more surprises today.

'That's not all,' she said. 'I'm moving to Picklewick.'

'For good?' Dear lord, he needed a stiff drink.

'Only until I find somewhere to rent in Thornbury.'

'But, what— I don't—' He inhaled deeply. His heart was racing, and he felt a little lightheaded.

'I've fallen in love with the place,' she said. 'Just like Dulcie. And just like Dulcie, I've fallen in love with a local chap. He's a bit boring, talks about image sensors and apertures quite a lot, and he's obsessed with taking photos—'

Ashton leapt to his feet and swept her into his arms, stopping her words with his mouth. Her lips parted, and she sank into his embrace with a whimper that sent him delirious with desire.

But before he whisked her off to bed and made love to her for the rest of the night, there was something he had to say.

'I love you,' he murmured gently.

Carla was more forthright. 'I bloody hope so! Now shut up and kiss me.'

And because Ashton was a thoroughly nice guy and he didn't like to disappoint a lady, he did just that!

Carla had never before reached the 'meet the parents' stage in a relationship, mainly because she'd never felt invested enough.

She was invested now alright, and she couldn't wait to meet Ashton's. They were away, but his grandmother lived in Picklewick's care home and that's where they were headed right now.

Her name was Nancy and Carla hoped they would get along.

An old lady with pink hair was seated in a wingback chair next to a large picture window with a view of the mountain above Muddypuddle Lane. Her lined face creased into a beautiful smile when she saw Ashton, and he bent to kiss her on the cheek.

She brushed him away, as eyes the same hue as Ashton's settled on Carla.

Carla squirmed under her scrutiny. 'Hi.'

'Come closer, let me look at you. So, you're the young lady who has stolen my grandson's heart. I hope you don't break it.'

Carla could feel Ashton's anxious gaze on her, but she didn't flinch. Nancy's directness was refreshing. 'I won't.'

'How do I know that?'

'Because he has mine.'

'Good answer.' Nancy patted the arm of the chair next to hers. 'Sit here. I want to know all about you. Ashton, fetch tea. I take it, you drink tea?'

'Of course,' Carla replied.

'Do you eat biscuits?'

'Loads of them.'

'What's your favourite?'

'Gosh, now you're asking. Something with chocolate on, I think.'

Nancy said, 'Ashton, bring a plate of biscuits while you're at it. This could take a while.'

The two women watched him leave, both of them with love in their eyes.

Then Nancy turned her attention back to Carla. 'He's such a nice boy. They don't make many like that these days. You want to keep hold of him.'

Carla leant towards the old lady and put her hand on Nancy's age-spotted one. 'Don't worry, I intend to.'

And she meant it!

WINTER WISHES

CHAPTER ONE

If Mark Stafford didn't get this damned book written soon, he was toast.

Throwing his pen down in exasperation, he leant back in his chair, put his hands behind his head, and stared out of the window of his small office, blowing out his cheeks. What was the deadline again? Oh, yes, the end of February.

He checked the calendar, praying it was a leap year so he would have an extra day. God knows, the way he was going, he would need it.

The house opposite flashed into life as their many Christmas decorations all lit up at once. It wasn't properly dark yet, but the November afternoon was overcast and gloomy. Unfortunately, the Santa waving at him from an illuminated ladder hanging from one of the bedroom windows did nothing for his lack of festive cheer. In fact, it made his grumpiness worse. Thank goodness neither his agent nor his editor could see him now; they'd think he was a proper Grinch, and that simply wouldn't do since he was supposed to be writing a Christmas book.

When the idea of writing a festive story had been pitched to him, he should have come clean and confessed that Christmas wasn't his cup of eggnog.

But he'd thought he could pull it off, so he'd agreed. Yet, five weeks into the project, he had nothing. No characters, no storyline and no inspiration. The situation was made even more annoying because this wasn't his first book, nor even his third. Mark had written eleven books in his career, so why was he finding this one so blimmin' difficult?

It wasn't as though he had to write a three-hundred-page novel. He was a children's author, whose target readers were four to seven years old. The book would be thirty-five to fifty pages maximum, *including* the illustrations.

Mark was the first to argue that writing children's books wasn't easy. The author had to appeal to both the child *and* the parent, and fewer words didn't mean less effort or dedication. It was different, that's all – a difference he'd thought he'd mastered.

Clearly not, if today's miserably disappointing effort was any indication.

It didn't help that the publisher wanted a title and the cover art in the next couple of weeks so they could begin the marketing process. But how could he give them that, when he had no idea what the story was going to be about?

His neighbour's manically waving Santa Claus was becoming irritating, so Mark lowered the blind. The afternoon had drawn in, and as much as he enjoyed taking a break from working by gazing into the street, he'd found himself doing considerably more gazing than working. Resting his eyes was one thing, but these past few days his peepers seemed to have taken a vacation.

He scowled, feeling hemmed in and claustrophobic. Maybe he should get some fresh air? It might clear his head.

Actually, there wasn't anything to clear. That was the problem – his head was empty. Perhaps filling it with Christmassy stuff might help? He could pay the city centre a visit and soak up some atmosphere. The festivities weren't in full swing yet, but there should be enough Christmas spirit around to get him in the mood.

Deciding this was as good a plan as any, he donned his padded jacket and plonked a knitted beanie on his head. It wasn't unduly cold out, but an annoyingly fine drizzle hung in the air.

The bus stop was a five-minute walk from his house, so rather than drive and try to grapple with Bristol's awful rush-hour traffic, he decided to hop on a bus. It would also mean he needn't worry about parking, which could be a nightmare. He would even have a bite to eat whilst he was out, because his fridge was rather empty and the freezer was equally as bad. He really should make more of an effort in the kitchen, but although he enjoyed cooking, he couldn't be bothered just for himself. Now and again he would have a frenzy and bulk cook lots of stuff, but that didn't happen regularly enough to keep his freezer stocked with home-made dishes. The only meals in there right now were of the ready variety, and none of them appealed.

His thoughts were still on food when the bus trundled into The Horsefair, and he hopped off at the next stop. The street was busy with people scurrying along the pavements, and shops were already belting out Christmas tunes, their window displays full of festive cheer. Overhead, twinkly lights were strung across the street and the lamp posts boasted flashing stars and snowflakes. Mark ducked into a store selling decorations, wandered aimlessly around it and then ducked out again, not having found what he was searching for.

He had yet to find it fifty minutes and numerous shops later, so he gave up and headed for a little place he knew on Philadelphia Street where the food was good.

As he ate, it suddenly came to him that he was trying to recapture the feeling that he used to have when he was a child. Christmas had been such a wonderful, magical time then, and the sheer excitement he'd felt had been overwhelming.

Mark stared at the pasta in the wide-rimmed bowl and shook his head. He was thirty-nine years old and hadn't been a child for a very long time, so how the hell did he think he could ever feel that way again? But his instinct – that gut feeling he always listened to when it came to his storytelling – was insistent that was what he needed to do. If he wanted to make this next book shine and sparkle, he needed to remember what it was like to be a child at Christmas.

Perhaps going on a writing retreat would help? He'd done something similar before; when he'd written the seaside series he had rented a house on the coast for three months to immerse himself in all things harbour and beach-related.

Mark realised he was looking for inspiration in the wrong place. Bristol wasn't it.

However, Picklewick, the small village where he'd grown up, might very well be.

Beatrice Webb let out yet another exasperated sigh. Getting her children ready for school was a daily battle and she didn't think she had the energy for another skirmish this week, but as today was only Thursday, she still had one more to go until the blessed weekend.

The murky mornings at this time of year didn't help, because Taya, at nine years old, was becoming a real lug-a-bed and was as grumpy as hell at being woken. Five-year-old Sadie was the opposite – up like a lark and raring to go. Unfortunately, Sadie's lark had risen at five-thirty, and by *raring to go,* Beatrice wasn't referring to school. Sadie tried everything to delay going, from hiding her school shoes to having a full-blown meltdown, and this morning she was insisting she had to write a letter to Santa and it had to be done before school so it could be posted on the way.

'Taya, please go brush your teeth,' Beatrice instructed, as she tried to wrestle her youngest daughter's hair into submission.

'I haven't finished my breakfast.' Taya had been reading instead of eating.

Although Beatrice had asked her not to read at the table, Taya had ignored her. She'd been tempted to snatch the book out of her daughter's hands but, for one, she didn't want to deal with the fallout, and secondly she knew how lucky she was that she didn't have to nag her child to read, the way many of her friends had to nag theirs.

'Please get a move on,' she urged. Turning to Sadie, she said, 'All done.'

Sadie patted the top of her head. 'I wanted plaits, not bunches.'

'You look lovely with bunches.'

'But I wanted plaits.'

'I haven't got time to do plaits. Sadie, get dressed. You too, Taya.'

Sadie smacked her pencil down on the table. 'I'm *not* going to school with my hair in bunches.'

Beatrice counted to five. 'When I asked you how you wanted your hair, you said you didn't know.'

'Well I do now, and I want plaits.'

She briefly considered fetching her scissors and snipping the offending bunches off. It would solve the problem – but in turn would generate a much bigger one.

'Taya, if you don't put your uniform on in the next five minutes, you'll be going to school in your pyjamas,' she warned.

Taya gave her a 'yeah, right' look and slowly got to her feet. Taking her book with her, she dawdled out of the kitchen.

With a sigh of relief that at least one of her children was doing as she was told, Beatrice turned her attention to her youngest daughter. 'Come on, it's time you got dressed too.'

Beatrice shot a look of longing at the toaster, but she knew she would be needed upstairs, despite Sadie being more than capable of dressing herself. If she wanted to get her kids to school on time, she would have to forgo breakfast. Telling herself that her waistline would thank her for it, she cleared away the breakfast things – and by *clearing away* she meant dumping them on the draining board to be dealt with later.

'Mummy, I'm going to ask Santa for a Wixset for Christmas,' Sadie announced.

Beatrice blinked. *What's a Wixset?* she wondered.

'And a talking puppy that wees and poops, because you won't let me have a real one. And a scooter. Not like my old scooter – I want one you plug in. It goes really fast. And I want a tiara. A proper one, not a plastic one.'

Ushering her reluctant daughter into the hall and up the stairs, Beatrice said faintly, 'I'm not sure Father Christmas can stretch to all that. It's rather a lot.'

'No, it isn't.' Sadie's reply was confident. 'Penelope had a scooter and a Wixset from her mummy for her birthday, and her granny and grandad got her a Poopy Puppy, and her dad bought her a tiara. It's got real diamonds. Penelope said so.'

Oh well, if *Penelope* said so, Beatrice grumbled silently to herself. Even without knowing what a Wixset was, she had a suspicion that that little lot would cost a fortune.

Sadie hadn't finished. 'And I want a head.'

Beatrice steered her into the bedroom and helped her remove her pyjamas. 'Just a head? No body?'

Sadie nodded. 'Just a head. I want to learn to do plaits, because the ones you do fall out.'

'Oh, right. Okay. A head with hair.' Beatrice used to have one of those when she was a girl.

'Duh! *Of course* with hair. Silly Mummy.'

The door to the bedroom bounced open as Taya stormed in. 'Mum!' she cried, 'I need a new school bag. The strap has broken.' She waved the offending item in Beatrice's face, and Beatrice's heart sank further when her daughter asked, 'Can I pick the next one?' because she simply knew it would be the one all her friends had and would be hideously expensive.

Not for the first time since her youngest had started school in September, Beatrice thought about getting a part-time job. But the problem was, finding one which fitted in around school times was as likely as the diamonds in Penelope's tiara being real.

'Mrs Webb, can I have a quick word?'

Beatrice saw Sadie's teacher beckoning her from the door of the classroom, and her heart sank for the second time that morning. A teacher *wanting a word* was never good, plus Beatrice had hoped to make a quick getaway, considering Sadie had walked into the classroom without any drama, but seeing Miss Barnes talking to her might evoke some.

Miss Barnes seemed equally as concerned, as she glanced over her shoulder. 'Nothing to worry about,' she said. 'I just wanted to inform you that Sadie is going to be Toadstool Number One in the Christmas play, and I know she wanted to be a fairy so she'll probably be a little disappointed when she finds out. But the fairies are all Year Three children as there's quite a lot of dancing, and…' She ground to a halt.

Beatrice said, 'Thanks for the heads up.' She was going to have to find some way of bigging up the toadstool role. Knowing her daughter's penchant for pink and silver, a sparkly pink number might do the trick. 'Can the toadstool be any colour?' she asked.

'Oh, yes. Just use whatever spare material you've got lying around.'

Bless her. From what Beatrice could gather, this was the teacher's first year in the classroom. She had an awful lot to learn about the competitive nature of certain mums. And although Beatrice didn't want to spend hours making a costume which would only be worn for a matter of hours, she wasn't going to let her daughter down by having her wear a substandard outfit. Maybe she could enlist some help in making it?

It was a good idea to strike while the iron was hot (in other words, before her enthusiasm waned or she forgot) so Beatrice decided to call in to see her mum on the way home. Thinking it best not to arrive empty handed, she popped into the bakery on the way and picked up a selection of cream cakes.

As she was passing the newsagents, being careful not to jostle the cake box, she automatically glanced at the window and the notices that were pinned there.

And stopped.

Frowning, she stepped closer and peered at a *Help Wanted* sign. The farm on Muddypuddle Lane was advertising for an assistant for their newly opened farm shop. Experience preferred, hours negotiable.

How negotiable? she wondered.

There was only one way to find out, but first she'd have to have a chat with her mum. There was no point in getting her hopes up if Mum didn't feel able to help out with childcare during the school holidays or at the weekends.

Her mum was delighted to see her, but that was probably more to do with the cream cake offering than with seeing Beatrice herself. Her mum mightn't be so delighted when she heard the favours Beatrice wanted to ask.

She decided to begin with the easiest first and said brightly, 'Sadie is going to be a toadstool in the Christmas play.'

Deborah was examining the cakes. 'Toadstools aren't particularly festive, are they?' She picked up a cream horn with her fingers. 'I'll leave the coffee puff for your dad.'

'You wouldn't leave it for Dad if *you* liked it,' Beatrice teased. Mum couldn't stand anything coffee flavoured, although she enjoyed a latte as much as the next person.

Deborah took a bite of her cake and said around the mouthful, 'I suppose you want some help making it?'

'You don't have to,' Beatrice assured her.

'I think I do if you don't want it to fall apart after five minutes.'

'Harsh.'

'But true,' her mum countered with a smile. 'I'll see what I can find. Put the kettle on, if you're staying.'

Beatrice couldn't leave yet, so she filled the kettle and switched it on. 'Mum, can I ask you something? Please say no, if you don't think you can. I know we've talked about it in the past, but you've had a taste of freedom and—'

'You've got a job?' Deborah beamed at her.

'Not yet. There's one going up at the farm on Muddypuddle Lane.'

'Doing what? You don't know anything about sheep or cows, and think of the dirt. Plus, you'll be out in all weathers.' Her mother shuddered.

'They want someone for the shop.'

Deborah's face cleared. 'Oh, yes. I'd forgotten about that. Phew, that's a relief. I had visions of you in overalls and wellies. Of course I'll look after the girls. I love having them.'

'I don't know the hours yet and they might want someone for the weekends,' Beatrice warned.

Her parents had retired earlier in the year and although Beatrice had discussed the possibility of going back to work with them, she didn't want them to feel obliged – after all, they deserved to enjoy their retirement, and although they adored their grandchildren, the kids weren't their responsibility.

'I'll phone the farm later and find out,' she said. 'Anyway, they mightn't want me.'

Her mum popped the last of her cake into her mouth and licked her fingers. 'How could they not want *you*, my darling girl?'

'You're biased,' Beatrice replied, but she hoped her mum was right. With Christmas approaching, she needed all the money she could get her hands on.

Picklewick was much the same as he remembered, Mark thought as he drove along the high street, heading towards the one and only pub where he would be staying for the next couple of weeks. After deciding yesterday that this was the place to be, he had wasted no time in throwing some clothes in a case this morning and setting off. After all, he didn't have anything keeping him in Bristol.

No, Picklewick hadn't changed – it was Mark himself who had.

Intrinsically, the village appeared the same as he remembered, but it felt new and strange, as though the past was a foreign land whose soil he now walked.

He hadn't been back to the area since his parents had moved to a bungalow in Bath, and that had been years ago. And even when they'd still lived in Picklewick, his visits had been fleeting, never for more than a long weekend, because his wife had found the village boring. Ex-wife, now; and the irony of her marrying a hotelier who lived in the wilds of Scotland still made him chuckle. He wondered how bored she was now.

The Black Horse came into view, and he smiled as he caught sight of the familiar sign hanging above the door. It swung in the stiff breeze, and when he got out of the car he could hear it creaking. The sound brought back memories, but he pushed them aside. He would have plenty of time to think about his misspent youth in this very establishment after he'd checked in and unpacked.

The landlord didn't recognise him at first. 'Here for work?' Dave asked as he showed him to his room.

'You could say that.'

'A couple of weeks, is it?'

'There or thereabouts.'

Dave unlocked a door. 'This is yours. Number three. You've got this floor all to yourself at the moment, so it'll be nice and quiet – apart from the noise from the bar of course, although it shouldn't be too bad as it never gets rowdy. Unless it's karaoke night, and then it can get a bit loud.' The landlord winced. 'Some of the singing leaves a lot to be desired. But Thursday is quiz night so it should be quiet enough this evening. Do you quiz?'

'Not really.'

The landlord was squinting at him, a puzzled expression on his face, then he slapped a palm to his forehead. '*Mark Stafford!* I should have realised, but it didn't twig. Long time, no see. How are you?'

'Good, thanks.'

'And your mum and dad?'

'They're living their best life in Bath.'

'I heard that's where they'd moved to. What about you? Do you live in Bath, too?'

Mark shook his head. 'Bristol.'

'Not too far from them, then. You're here for work, you say?'

Mark rarely broadcast what he did for a living, preferring to fly under the radar, but he decided to give the man a half-version of the truth.

'I'm an illustrator. Books,' he added, before Dave asked the inevitable question.

'Covers, like?'

'Sometimes.'

'Right. And you'll be working here?'

Mark guessed what the man was thinking. 'Don't worry, I won't splash paint everywhere. I'm a digital artist.'

'That's a relief. The missus would throw a fit if you got paint on her carpet.' He handed Mark an old-fashioned key. 'Breakfast between eight and nine?'

'Perfect.'

'Any special requirements?'

'None whatsoever.'

'Right, I'll leave you to it. If you need anything, just shout. We serve food in the bar from noon until nine p.m.'

'Thanks. I'll be down soon for a spot of lunch.'

Dave took his leave, but not before pointing to a slim folder on the dressing table. 'Local information,' he said, adding, 'Not that you'll need it.'

As Mark unpacked, he didn't think he would need it either, but when he gave its contents a cursory once-over, he was mildly surprised to be proved wrong. There was some kind of an event – a Christmas Wonderland – at the farm on Muddypuddle Lane on Saturday, and he intended to take a look.

'Pop up now, if you like.' That was what Dulcie Fairfax, the owner of the farm on Muddypuddle Lane had said when Beatrice rang to enquire about the job after she'd left her mum's house.

Concerned because she didn't have a CV prepared, and neither did she have anything smart enough to wear for an interview, Beatrice felt nervous and out of her depth as she drove into the farmyard later that morning.

She had managed to find a pair of black tailored trousers at the back of her wardrobe which hadn't seen the light of day for several years, and she teamed it with a cream blouse that gaped a bit around the boobs because she'd put on weight since having Sadie. So rather than look as though she was bursting out of it, she wore a black vest top underneath and left the buttons undone. Her black ankle boots were tidy enough, and when she stepped out of her car she was glad she'd worn them and not the high heels that she'd bought to go to a friend's wedding, as the farmyard was cobbled and uneven.

Beatrice looked around with interest. A huge tree sat in the centre of the yard, decorated but unlit; there was a kiosk with a chalkboard sign on it advertising The Grinch's Grotto, pony rides and various other activities; and there were several barn-type buildings, as well as the farmhouse.

A woman wearing scruffy jeans, wellies and an oversized hoodie emerged from one of the buildings, and Beatrice recognised her as the woman who'd won the farm in a raffle. The farm had originally belonged to Walter York and had been in his family for generations, but rumour was that he'd been in financial difficulties, with the result that the farm had been raffled off. Beatrice had bought a ticket, but it was Dulcie – a complete newbie when it came to farming – who had won it. She seemed to be coping alright now though.

'Beatrice? I'm Dulcie.' The woman hurried forward, holding out a hand.

Beatrice shook it nervously, suddenly feeling overdressed. She knew *of* her (how could she not, with Picklewick being so small?) but they'd never actually met, and she wasn't sure what to expect.

Dulcie said, 'Come through into the kitchen. I don't know about you, but I'm gasping for a cuppa.' She strode towards the farmhouse and Beatrice followed, picking her way carefully over the muddy cobbles.

'Tea or coffee?' she asked, after inviting Beatrice to take a seat at the chunky oak table in the kitchen.

'Nothing, thanks,' Beatrice replied, gazing around her in awe. This wasn't how she expected a farmhouse kitchen to look – this was something out of a cookery show on TV.

Dulcie noticed her interest. 'This is Otto's domain, not mine. He owns The Wild Side in the village.'

Beatrice knew who he was. *Everyone* in Picklewick knew that Otto York had been a renowned London chef. She also knew that he'd grown up in Picklewick and used to live on this very farm. But that was as far as it went – he had been a couple of years below her in school, so she hadn't had anything to do with him, and then he'd moved away and had made a name for himself. Like someone else she could mention, she thought, then gave herself a silent telling off – she was in the middle of a job interview, for Pete's sake! Now wasn't the time to be reminiscing about old boyfriends.

'It's nice,' she said, dragging her attention back to the present, her eyes roaming over the stainless-steel units.

'We've only just had it installed. You should have seen it before! Anyway, are you sure you don't want a drink? I'm having one, and I'm also going to have a red velvet crackle cookie. Otto's been experimenting with a festive version.'

'Okay then, thanks. Tea, please.'

Dulcie was really down to earth and as Beatrice sipped her tea and nibbled on her cookie (which really was rather moreish), Dulcie filled her in about the shop, which was also new, having only opened a couple of weeks ago.

'I can't manage everything by myself,' she explained. 'The business is really taking off, and I'm struggling. If you've finished your tea, let me show you around. We'll start with the shop first, since that's where you'll be working.' She led Beatrice outside and they walked back across the yard, towards one of the outbuildings. 'We sell fresh produce such as goat's milk, cheese, eggs and any fruit and veg that are in season and we've got a surplus of, so that can vary from week to week – day to day, even.' She came to a halt outside a door and pushed it open.

Beatrice scanned the room – a chiller, a counter, shelves… Everything looked clean and tidy. Festive bunting was draped around the walls and fairy lights twinkled behind the counter.

Dulcie said, 'We milk the goats every day, although the yield isn't great at this time of year and neither is egg production, but we're hoping the Christmas bits and pieces will make up for it. We've got handmade soap, lotions and potions, biscuits, pastries, savouries, milkshakes, soups… And we're hoping for a good turnout tomorrow for the first of our Christmas Wonderland events, and we've got lots of things planned. You might have noticed a sign for the Grinch's Grotto?'

Beatrice nodded, her eyes everywhere, and she felt a spark of excitement. She could really see herself working here.

'Come on, I'll show you the rest of it.'

The rest consisted of a barn with goats, a sheep, chickens (who were roaming free), a couple of Shetland ponies (borrowed from the stables down the lane), and rabbits. A fantastic grotto which was very in keeping with the Grinch's story, was in another building, along with a creative area where kids could make Christmas crafts, and a kitchen.

Dulcie said. 'We'll be selling mulled wine, soup, coffees, hot chocolate and anything else Otto dreams up.'

'You said the hours are negotiable?' Beatrice asked hesitantly, guessing they wouldn't be as negotiable as she would need them to be.

'What hours can you do?' Dulcie asked, and when Beatrice told her, she said, 'I'm sure we can work around that. When can you start?'

'Whenever you want.'

'How about tomorrow?'

'But you don't know anything about me!' Beatrice protested. Dulcie hadn't asked how she would deal with an awkward customer, or about her strengths and weaknesses, or any of the other questions she had anxiously expected.

'Walter, Otto's dad, does. He knows your father and he vouched for you. Besides, it's more important to me that we get on. I don't care about retail experience. What I care about is personality.' Dulcie beamed at her. 'So, *can* you start tomorrow?'

'Absolutely!'

'Fab. See you in the morning. By the way, you might want to dress down a bit.'

Beatrice glanced at her blouse and trousers, caught Dulcie's eye, and the two of them burst out laughing. She was going to like working here!

'Mummy has got some news,' Beatrice said to Sadie later that evening as she pulled back the covers for

468

her daughter to dive into bed. She had already told Taya, who hadn't expressed much interest.

'Story,' Sadie demanded.

'Don't you want to hear my news?' Beatrice pretended to pout.

Sadie sat up and folded her arms. 'What is it?' she sighed, rolling her eyes.

Beatrice saw herself in the gesture. 'I've got a job, so Nanny will fetch you from school tomorrow, okay?' Although her official hours were ten until three and she should be finished in time to collect the children, she didn't want to have to worry on her first day.

Sadie's expression didn't change.

'I'm going to be working in a shop,' Beatrice continued.

'A toy shop?' Sadie's eyes lit up.

'Not a toy shop. It's a—'

'Sweet shop!' She wriggled excitedly.

'No, not a sweet shop, either.'

Her daughter's face fell.

'It's a farm shop,' Beatrice said, then hastily added, 'Selling milk, cheese and fruit. Stuff like that,' in case Sadie thought she would be selling actual farms.

'Do they have animals?'

'They certainly do! Goats, chickens and rabbits. Dulcie, who owns the farm, said they have a cat, but I didn't see it.'

'Can I see the rabbits?'

'Yes, and you can see the goats, too.'

'Tomorrow?'

'Not tomorrow, but soon.' Dulcie had explained that the farm was organising activities on the run-up to Christmas and opening its doors to the public and when Beatrice heard what Dulcie was planning, she knew her daughters would love it.

'Enough questions,' Beatrice said. 'It's time for a story. What would you like?'

'That one!' Sadie pointed to a book on the top of the small pile on her bedside table.

'Not again,' Beatrice groaned.

'Yes again.'

'Okay, budge over.'

Sadie scooted across the bed and smuggled under the bedclothes, so her mum could sit next to her.

Beatrice reached for the book, and as she did so the author's name caught her eye and she winced.

It had been written by Mark Stafford – the man who had broken her heart.

CHAPTER TWO

Friday was one of those bright winter days where a weak sun shone out of a silvered sky and mist blanketed the valley floor. Dew-coated cobwebs were spider-strung over the bushes along Muddypuddle Lane, and the red berries of the hawthorn trees glistened like rubies in the morning light.

Beatrice parked her car in the farmyard and took a deep breath of autumn-chilled air. This was her first day in her new job and she couldn't imagine a more scenic location. At the moment, she felt incredibly blessed; whether she would still feel that way after a five-hour shift remained to be seen.

The tree in the centre of the yard was lit and it looked very festive, despite Christmas being five weeks away. But, as Dulcie had explained when Beatrice had come for the interview (which hadn't been much of an interview at all), the farm was gearing up to open its gates to visitors who would hopefully enjoy the Christmas experience.

Beatrice was rather looking forward to it and had happily agreed to work Saturdays on the run-up to the 'Big Day' because it meant more money to buy presents. However, she wasn't doing this *just* for the money. Beatrice was also doing it for herself. The pride she'd felt knowing she had a job, had made her glow all last night, and as soon as the children were tucked up in bed, she'd got straight on the phone to Lisa.

Lisa had been thrilled for her, and suggested they go out for a drink to celebrate but Beatrice had declined – she was already putting her mum out by asking her to collect the children from school. She could hardly ask her to babysit this evening as well, while she went out boozing with her best friend.

Dulcie was serving a customer when Beatrice entered the shop, so she quietly stowed her bag and coat underneath the counter and had a quick look at the chillers and shelves to see what was for sale today.

The farm's staples of milk, cheese, eggs, soaps and scented candles were well stocked, and she was also pleased to see a selection of festive-themed biscuits, milkshakes and chilled soups.

Dulcie greeted her warmly, looking frazzled. 'Am I glad to see you! I've got such a lot to do today. I've got a Grinch's grotto to finish, a seating area to set up, a—' She stopped. 'I could go on, but if I do I'll be jabbering away until lunchtime. Will you be alright in here on your own?'

'I'll be fine.'

'Shout if you need me. Oh, and do you think you could have a go at making up some festive hampers? I want to post photos on the website later.' Dulcie pointed to a box behind the counter. 'Here's one I made earlier,' she said. 'I'd like to offer different products and a couple of different sizes.'

'Is there anything else I can do to help?' Beatrice offered.

'You might regret saying that.' Dulcie pulled a face. 'I'd better get going. I've got smelly socks to fill. Actually, you don't happen to have any odd socks lying around at home, do you?'

Beatrice chuckled. Knowing that the farm had a Grinch theme going on, she realised immediately why Dulcie wanted them. 'I've got a drawer full. I'll bring them in tomorrow. How many do you need?'

'All of them? I'm scared we won't have enough, but I'm also worried that I've ordered too much, and we'll have loads of stuff left over.'

'What are you putting in them?'

'Grinch dust – you sprinkle it on your doorstep to stop the Grinch stealing your Christmas – bags of green sweets, a Grinch bauble for the tree, Grinch Stickers and a stretchy Grinch toy.'

'I sense a theme,' Beatrice laughed. 'It's also rather a lot, don't you think?'

'Is it?' Dulcie's expression was dubious.

'It must have cost a bit, and whenever my two visited Santa in his grotto, the gift was usually something inexpensive. How many children are you expecting? By the way, is it alright if my parents bring the girls to see the Grinch tomorrow?'

'Of course it is! As for how many kids – I honestly don't know.'

Beatrice had an idea, but she hadn't been here five minutes yet, so she wasn't sure how well it would be received. 'I've got a suggestion – and please tell me if I'm speaking out of turn because you know more about this than I do.'

'Don't bet on it,' Dulcie said.

'Why don't you keep some stuff back, and add a Grinch biscuit to the sock instead?' She looked at the iced snowflake biscuits as she spoke, thinking it would be easy to make a green version.

Dulcie was staring at her and shaking her head.

Oh dear, Beatrice thought, that didn't go down well.

'I could kiss you!' her new boss declared with a smile.

'You could?'

'That's a perfect solution. Otto can make an endless supply of Grinch cookies, and if we do have any non-food items left over, they'll keep until next year. The Grinch isn't going away – I'm determined to get my use out of the outfits I bought, and the grotto.'

Beatrice offered, 'If you want, I can fill the socks for you tomorrow.'

From the grateful expression on Dulcie's face, she *did* want.

Pleased that she'd already managed to make herself useful, Beatrice settled down to enjoy the day. She had a feeling that this job was going to be the best thing to have happened to her in a very long time.

For Mark, driving up Muddypuddle Lane on Saturday afternoon brought back boyhood memories of warm summer days playing in the ferns on the hillsides above Picklewick with his friends, making dens and building makeshift dams across the tumbling mountain streams.

It also brought back memories of when he was quite a bit older and had gone on long walks on this very hillside with his first love.

He wondered whether she still lived in Picklewick. The last he'd heard was that she was married with a baby, but that was ages ago.

Mark drove past the stables and continued up the lane until he came to the farm. A sign directed him to the rear of a large barn where there was a gravelled parking area. It was surprisingly busy for a dreary Saturday afternoon in November, and he felt a glimmer of hope that maybe the farm would kickstart his flagging creativity.

The place certainly looked festive. Fairy lights and lanterns were strung everywhere, a twenty-foot tree sat in the middle of the yard, and next to the entrance to the barn was a red post box with a sign above it urging children to "post your letter to Santa here".

Mark paused for a moment to admire the tree. Someone had gone to a lot of trouble to decorate it. But although it was very pretty, it failed to move the dial on his internal festive-ometer.

Glancing around, he saw signs for a shop, a Christmas kitchen, a craft barn and a Grinch's Grotto, and excited chatter and squealing filled the air as children queued with their parents.

Feeling self-conscious because he didn't have a small person with him, he thought it best to have a word with whoever was running the place, to let them know why he was here.

As he debated whether to wait in line to explain to the elderly lady selling the tickets or whether to go into the shop and ask, his attention was caught by a woman dancing across the yard. She was dressed as an elf and was beaming so widely that he couldn't help smiling as he made to intercept her.

'Excuse me?' he said.

'Don't you just love Christmas?' she smiled, coming to a stop.

'Not as much as some,' he replied, raising an eyebrow at her outfit. 'Can you point me in the direction of the manager or the owner?'

Her smile dimmed. 'May I ask why?'

'Don't worry, it's not a complaint or anything. I just need to have a word.'

'Are you from Environmental Health?' The smile had entirely gone.

'Not at all.'

She pursed her lips then nodded. 'Come into the house. Will this take long?'

'A couple of minutes, tops.'

'Good, because the Grinch needs a comfort break. He'll get grouchy if he has to cross his legs.'

Bemused, Mark followed her into the house, then blinked when she led him into a state-of-the-art kitchen. 'Wow.'

'Yeah, I know. I'm too scared to use it. My partner, Otto, had it installed. He owns The Wild Side in the village.'

'Ah, yes, the restaurant.' Mark hadn't eaten there yet, having taken his evening meals in The Black Horse, but he intended to give it a go at some point.

The woman leant against one of the stainless-steel units and folded her arms. 'I'm Dulcie Fairfax and this is my farm. What do you want to have a word with me about?'

'My name is Mark Stafford and I'm a children's author. I was born and bred in Picklewick, although I live in Bristol now, and I've come to the village to write my next book. Or to get ideas for it, at the very least.'

'What's that got to do with my farm?'

'I'm a bit low on festive spirit and it's a Christmas story, so I'm hoping your Christmas Wonderland might help.'

Dulcie's stern expression softened. 'A real-life Grinch, eh?'

He dredged up a smile. 'You could say that.'

'So, why did you need to speak with me?'

'Because I want to pay a visit to The Grinch's Grotto and as I haven't brought a child with me, I thought it might look a bit weird.'

'You're right, it may have done. Would you like me to see if I can find one for you to borrow?'

Mark was aghast. 'No, I—'

'Just joking,' she laughed. 'Go ahead and look all you want. Would you like me to show you around?'

'That's kind of you, if you can spare the time.' He would have felt very odd going in on his own.

'I was on my way to the Grotto anyway, so it's no bother.'

She led him back across the yard, and when they reached the entrance to the Grinch's Grotto where another elf was checking children and their parents in, Dulcie said in a low voice, 'Carla, can you put the rope across for five minutes? Walter needs a break.' Then she ushered him inside.

Mark hadn't known what to expect when he stepped into the barn, so he was pleasantly surprised to see it as exuberantly decorated as the yard. More lights, more bunting, and more lavishly decorated trees surrounded by mounds of fake snow, formed a

477

path which led deeper into the barn. It was quite magical, despite being over-the-top, but as they ventured further in and turned a corner, the lights became less twinkly, the bunting disappeared, and the trees lost their decorations.

It was a gradual thing, and Mark didn't notice at first, not until a structure that had been painted to look like a cave came into view. A *Santa Stop Here* sign was in front of the door, and someone had written '*Don't*' between *Santa* and *Stop*.

Three families were waiting to see the Grinch and as Mark and his guide approached, the door opened and a green face topped by a Santa hat, peered out.

'Bah! I hate Christmas!' it growled, then disappeared back inside and slammed the door shut. A second later, the door opened again, and the Grinch beckoned the nearest child forward. Mark caught a glimpse of a badly decorated and extremely bent Christmas tree, and a haphazard pile of presents stacked in the corner. Lying by the door and gnawing on a bone, was a black and white sheepdog wearing felt antlers.

The theme was green, red and white, and rather well done, but Mark's festive-ometer still didn't budge. The Grinch had originally been drawn in black, white and red. It wasn't supposed to be green, and *this* was why he was having so much trouble writing a Christmas book – because he couldn't get his head around the way everything about Christmas was so distorted. Take St. Nicolas, for instance…

Dulcie waited until the Grinch had seen all three children and the families had left the grotto, then said, 'Break time, Walter?'

The Grinch sagged a little. 'Thank God.' He pulled off the mask and took a deep breath, and Mark saw that underneath it was an elderly gentleman with grey hair and a lined face. He looked exhausted.

Dulcie helped him out of the costume. 'Are you okay to carry on, Walter, or would you like me to take over?'

'You have enough to do,' he said. 'How long have I got?'

'Ten minutes, but we can make it longer.'

He blew out his cheeks. 'Do you mind?'

'Of course not. I'll let Carla know.' She hurried towards the entrance, leaving Mark alone with Walter.

The elderly gent said, 'This is the first time she's done this. Just a couple of teething troubles, that's all. I'm sure everything will work out fine.'

Mark wasn't so sure; Walter didn't look too good and as Mark watched him leave, he wondered whether he should say anything to Dulcie or whether he should mind his own business.

But when Dulcie returned to the grotto, he could tell by her face that she already knew.

She picked up the discarded costume and sighed. 'I don't think it's a good idea for Walter to carry on. It's too much for him. Right, I'd better do it. Have you seen enough, or do you need more time to find your Christmas spirit?' Dulcie froze, her eyes widening. Then a smile spread across her face as she stared at him.

Mark guessed what was coming, and he shook his head as he backed away. 'Nuh-uh. Not a chance.'

'Aw, go on,' she pleaded. 'Just think of all those hopeful little faces – and you can indulge your inner

Grinch at the same time. I'll even pay you,' she added, and he realised she was serious.

'You'd trust me with this?' He waved an arm at the grotto.

'Yes.'

'You don't even know me.'

Dulcie fished around in the pocket of the pixie skirt and brought out a phone. 'I looked you up.'

'When?'

'Just now. You've made appearances in schools and libraries. You *like* kids.'

'I do, but I don't like Christmas. Anyway, I'm here to write,' he protested.

'Research is writing.'

'Who says?'

'You do.' She showed him the screen.

Mark groaned. On it was an interview where he had given advice to new authors. He remembered stressing how important research was when it came to writing.

'Just for today?' she pleaded. 'Three hours, at the most. Please?'

And that was how Mark Stafford, successful children's author, came to be dressed in a Grinch costume, trying his best to entertain small children on the farm on Muddypuddle Lane.

Beatrice was so busy she didn't know what to do with herself and was loving every minute of it. The hampers were flying off the shelves, as were the gift boxes of soaps, and every time the door opened she caught a whiff of mulled wine along with a blast of cold air, which made her thankful for her many layers and for the electric heater behind the counter that kept her legs and feet warm.

Things appeared to be going equally as well outside the shop. Although Beatrice didn't have a view of the barn, from the snippets she'd overheard from her customers, there was a queue to see the Grinch, the petting area was popular, and the food was going down a storm. In order to encourage repeat custom over the next few weeks, Dulcie and Otto were varying the food on the menu, hoping to tempt visitors back, and there was also a selection of today's offerings in the shop, so if people wanted they could purchase some to take home.

Beatrice didn't know how Dulcie and Otto managed to fit it all in, although they had some help in the form of Dulcie's mum Beth, and Otto's dad Walter, plus Nikki, one of Dulcie's sisters, and a couple of others. But it was still a lot of work, and whenever she glanced out the window she saw Dulcie dashing around in her pixie outfit.

Between serving customers, Beatrice filled the 'smelly socks,' and made up more hampers, and as she worked she kept an eye on the time.

Her parents were due to arrive shortly with the children, and she couldn't wait to see her girls' faces. Sadie had been so excited this morning at the prospect of meeting the Grinch, that she hadn't stopped talking. Mind you, she was also thrilled at the thought of stroking a goat, petting a rabbit and having a ride on a Shetland pony. Taya hadn't been quite as enthusiastic, but she was nearly ten, which was almost a grown-up as far as Taya was concerned, and such childish things were beneath her.

Beatrice was gift-wrapping a box of soaps when she noticed her dad peering through the window, waving to catch her attention.

'Two minutes?' she mouthed, and as soon as she'd served her customer, she sent a quick message to Dulcie to alert her.

Dulcie, bless her, arrived in seconds.

'I won't be long.' Beatrice assured her.

'Take as long as you need. You're due a break.'

Beatrice removed her apron. 'It looks busy out there.'

'It is!' Dulcie beamed. 'The Grinch is a big hit, and Otto can't keep up with the mince pies.'

'I've made up more socks,' Beatrice told her. 'Do you want me to take them to the grotto?'

'It's okay, I'll take them later,' Dulcie said. 'You'd better go, I think someone is getting impatient.'

Beatrice saw Sadie jumping up and down outside, tugging on her nana's hand.

'Mummy!' she cried, letting go of Deborah and barrelling towards Beatrice as soon as she stepped outside.

Sadie grabbed her around the waist and buried her face in Beatrice's stomach. Beatrice hugged her back. She would have liked to cuddle her eldest child too, but knew that Taya would hate it. Cuddles in public had become a no-no recently.

As the five of them headed towards the Grinch's Grotto, Beatrice took the opportunity to look around the yard. Several families were queuing at the kiosk for tickets, and more were waiting to enter the grotto itself. There was a steady trickle of people in and out of the petting area, and the tables in the makeshift cafe were all occupied.

No wonder Dulcie was pleased. This first Saturday was proving to be a runaway success, and Beatrice was thrilled for her.

Before long, Deborah was handing their tickets to the elf on the door and they went inside. Although Dulcie had shown Beatrice the entrance to the Grinch's Grotto when she'd come for the interview, none of the Christmas lights had been lit, and she gasped at how pretty it now looked.

Beatrice wasn't the only one who was impressed. Sadie was gazing around in awe, her cheeks glowing, her mouth open. Even Taya's eyes were wide, and Beatrice smiled: her little girl was still there, hidden beneath the urge to grow up as fast as she could.

They shuffled forward slowly, and Beatrice used the time to remind her daughters of the story of *The Grinch Who Stole Christmas*, even though it was a tradition that they watched the film every year, so they knew it inside out.

After ten minutes or so, the family in front of them were summoned into the cave by a cross face and a claw-like hand, and Beatrice's children were next in line.

'Mummy, look!' Sadie pointed to a black and white sheepdog lying next to the entrance to the Grinch's cave. It was happily gnawing on a chew, and there was a bowl of water beside it. But what made Beatrice smile were the felt antlers it wore, not on its head, but attached to a harness around its chest.

Sadie frowned. 'That isn't Max. Max is brown.' She was quite indignant.

Beatrice thought fast. The Grinch's dog *was* brown in the film. 'That's because this isn't Max. This dog's name is Rex, and he's keeping the Grinch company because Max is off practicing to be a reindeer, because he's not very good at it, is he?'

Sadie thought about it, then nodded, the explanation accepted.

Finally, it was Taya and Sadie's turn.

Beatrice watched the entrance to the cave expectantly and chuckled when the Grinch stuck his head out. He glanced at them, paused, then went back inside as though he couldn't stand the sight of them, and slammed the door shut.

The girls looked up at her. 'Is he coming back out?' Sadie asked.

'We'll have to wait and see,' Beatrice said.

A few seconds later, he shouted, 'What are you waiting for? Come in if you must.'

'Ooh, he's really grumpy, isn't he?' Beatrice said to the children, as she ushered them inside, then she said to her mum who was behind her, 'I don't think he's acting either. I reckon it's genuine.'

'Shh!' her mum hissed. 'He'll hear you.'

Beatrice giggled. 'Oops, for a minute I forgot I was working here.' Whoever the Grinch was, she didn't want to upset him, not if they had to work together. She didn't think she'd met him yet, although there was something about his voice that was familiar...

Abruptly her good mood dimmed.

How bizarre that someone wearing a Grinch outfit reminded her of a man she had tried so hard to forget.

And for the remainder of the brief visit to the Grinch's grotto, Beatrice kept her attention firmly on her girls.

The last person she wanted to think about right now was Mark Stafford.

'Don't bother telling me your names,' Mark said to the two children standing before him. 'I don't care. And I'm not interested in what you want for Christmas, either.' He scowled. 'Christmas shouldn't be allowed. How old are you anyway?' He aimed this comment at the younger one.

'Five.' She gazed at him confidently, not the least bit intimidated by his (or should he say *the Grinch's*) grumpiness.

'Pah! That's too old for Christmas. Or too young.'

'Why is your face green?'

'Why is yours *not green?*'

The child giggled. 'You're funny.'

'No, I'm not. I don't like funny. If I give you a smelly sock, will you go away and leave me alone?'

She nodded and he made a show of shoving a sock at them both. The eldest, a girl of about nine or ten he guessed, looked far less impressed with his performance than her sister.

The youngest one said, 'Mummy, can I give him a hug?'

'No!' he cried, louder than he meant to. 'I hate hugs, and I hate children who want to give them.' He didn't look at the mother. He daren't. But he did

485

notice her left hand. It was ringless. Did that mean she was no longer married?

His stomach fluttered for a second, before he told himself that it didn't matter.

Mark kept the scowl on his face until Beatrice and her family left the cave, then he slumped into his seat.

He'd recognised her instantly of course. How could he not?

His whole body tingled from the shock of seeing her, and it had taken all the strength he possessed not to react. She hadn't recognised him, and he was grateful for that. How embarrassing if her first sight of him in almost twenty years was when he was dressed from head to foot in lurid green fur and wearing a rubber mask.

She hadn't changed much – she still had the same eyes. Eyes that had once looked deep into his soul. Eyes he had run away from because he had begun to fall in love with her and she hadn't loved him back.

If he'd thought for one instant that seeing her again would make him react like this, he would never have returned to Picklewick.

It briefly occurred to him that he should leave, go back to Bristol. But being in the city hadn't worked out too well for him recently, and he was here now, so… Anyway, he had only reacted like that because he hadn't expected to see her here, that was all. It had been a bit of a surprise, but he was over it now. If he bumped into her again (which he probably would, considering Picklewick wasn't very big) he'd be more prepared. Not that he had anything to prepare for. They'd dated for a while, but it hadn't been serious. She was an old flame, nothing more. Or so he told himself.

Mark drew in a deep, calming breath, then let it out in a whoosh when he heard her voice coming from just outside the grotto.

She was saying, 'I'd better get back to work. Poor Dulcie is run off her feet, and she's got more important things to do than cover for me. Stop by the shop later? I'll treat you to some snowflake biscuits to take home.'

'We will,' Beatrice's mother said. 'But don't work too hard and make sure you take a proper break.'

Mark closed his eyes and counted to ten. Beatrice worked at *the farm?*

Oh, hell. All he hoped was that he could escape with his dignity intact.

'How did the rest of your day go?' Deborah asked when Beatrice walked into her mum's house later that evening to collect the children. 'They've had their tea,' she added.

Beatrice gave her a grateful hug, then stuck her head around the living room door and told the kids to collect their things, before she answered. 'I've been rushed off my feet. The time has flown by.'

She'd loved every minute of it, thoroughly enjoying the interaction with the customers, and she'd had so much fun bringing their attention to things they hadn't considered buying, such as a Christmas Eve Box or a gingerbread milkshake. She felt part of the team already, and she really wanted Dulcie to do well.

'Thank you for bringing the girls to see the Grinch,' she added.

Once again, her thoughts turned to the man in the green costume. She had been thinking about him on and off for the rest of the afternoon and hadn't been able to shake the feeling that he reminded her of someone. His voice had been achingly familiar, but it couldn't have been…

'It was a pleasure. We loved it, and you know your father – he's a big kid himself, so he was in his element.'

'I really do appreciate you looking after them.'

'I know, sweetheart. I'm just pleased you're doing something for yourself at last.'

Beatrice gave her an arch look. 'I'm doing this for the extra money,' she replied.

'That, too,' her mum agreed. 'But I can see how much you're enjoying it. You've got some of your sparkle back.'

'Just some?' Beatrice joked weakly. She was well aware that she'd lost her sparkle. It had disappeared around the time she'd discovered that Eric had been having an affair. Then he'd disappeared too, leaving her to bring up the children on her own. Mind you, even before he'd left, Eric hadn't been much of a husband or father. At least he was an *ex*-husband now, so that was something to be grateful for.

Her mum said, 'You've not had a full sparkle for years.'

'A full sparkle? Have you been on the gin?'

'Not yet. I'm serious, Bea, you haven't.'

'These past few years have been hard.'

'You lost it before you and Eric split up.'

Beatrice shrugged. 'Two small children can rub the sparkle off anyone,' she replied. However, she knew what her mother meant. Beatrice's sparkle had begun to dim after she'd had her heart broken at the tender age of twenty-one.

It had taken her a long time to learn to love again – and look how that had turned out. Beatrice would happily do without any sparkle if it meant not being hurt again.

But it was nice that her mum thought she'd regained some, even if it was merely a glimmer and not a full-on shine.

Anyway, what was all this talk about sparkles? She needed to take the kids home and sort them out, not prattle on about sparkles.

They were taking their time, so she went into the hall and shouted for them to hurry up, and when she strolled back to the kitchen, her mum was mashing a teabag against the side of a mug with a spoon.

'I've got some gossip,' Deborah announced. 'You remember that boy you used to go out with, Mark Stafford? Apparently, he's back. Staying at The Black Horse for a couple of weeks, so Monica says. I saw her this morning when I nipped out to fetch your dad's paper and a pint of milk. She was going into the butchers for a packet of their nice sausages, the ones with caramelised onions in them.'

Beatrice couldn't care less about the damned sausages, not when her heart was pounding and her legs felt weak at the mention of Mark's name. 'Why?' she managed. Monica ran the pub with her husband Dave, so it must be true.

Her mum looked bewildered for a moment. 'I expect there's sausage and mash on the menu today.'

'Mum, I don't care about the sausages. Why is Mark Stafford in Picklewick?'

'Work, Monica said. He's some kind of artist. She and Dave seem to think it's something to do with books, but she also said Dave might have got that wrong.'

Her mother's words washed over her, barely registering. Beatrice was too shocked to listen, because she knew *exactly* who had been hiding under that mask.

CHAPTER THREE

Beatrice climbed the stairs, a pile of ironing in her arms, and tried to ignore the squabbling coming from the living room. The girls could only entertain themselves for so long, and she sensed they'd reached their limit.

The chores had to be done though, and this morning she'd managed an impressive array of cleaning, tidying, washing and ironing. In fact, she'd got carried away and had done more than she'd intended. Whenever she thought she'd finished, she managed to find something else that needed doing. The house hadn't been this clean since she'd been forced to blitz it after hosting Sadie's fifth birthday party in the summer and sixteen children had rampaged through the place.

As she entered her youngest daughter's bedroom, her eye fell on Sadie's favourite story and her lips tightened. Its author was the reason she had been unable to keep still for more than five minutes today.

Placing the ironing on the bed, she picked up the book and scowled. Beatrice had to admit that Mark told a good yarn, one that appealed to kids and adults alike, and the illustrations were gorgeous. Taya had been given it a few years ago, and if Beatrice had realised who'd written it at the time, she might well have hidden it. Or thrown it away. But when she'd seen the name 'Mark Stafford' on the cover, she hadn't initially realised that the man she had entrusted with her heart and the children's author were one and the same. When she'd found out, she had been... not upset, exactly, but it had brought an unwelcome rush of buried feelings to the surface.

The book had become a firm favourite of Taya's and had eventually been passed on to Sadie, who loved it equally as much. Beatrice must have read the blasted thing at least a hundred times, and she was heartily sick of it – and not just of the story itself. The book was a constant reminder of a part of her life she would prefer to forget.

Unfortunately for her (not for the author) the book was extremely popular so there was no escaping it. Then the damn man had gone on to publish several more. So she now pretended that the books gracing her daughter's shelf had been written by some other Mark Stafford, a Mark Stafford who she had never met and had never loved. A Mark Stafford who hadn't chosen a career instead of her. And she had succeeded up to a point, her memories safely buried underneath those that had come after – marriage, babies, divorce. *Life*.

Then yesterday happened.

Why the hell had he come back? His parents had moved away years ago, so what reason could he possibly have to return to a backwater (his words) like Picklewick. "Something to do with his books" didn't sound at all believable.

And how had he ended up playing the Grinch at the farm? She was positive it had been him. Or was she?

Beatrice reached for her phone.

'Who was under the Grinch mask?' she asked Dulcie after the pleasantries were out of the way. 'I didn't think it was Walter.'

'It was originally, but this guy showed up, a children's author. He asked if he could take a look around because he's doing some research for a new book, and when we got to the grotto Walter wasn't feeling too good, so he stepped in.'

'What was his name?'

'Mark Stafford.'

'I knew it!' Beatrice muttered.

'Nikki has heard of him – his books are very popular, apparently – but I had to Google him. He was alright, wasn't he?' Dulcie sounded anxious.

'He was a brilliant Grinch,' Beatrice assured her. 'Very believable.'

'Thank goodness for that. You had me worried for a minute. He seemed really down to earth. I wanted to pay him, but he refused to take any money. That was nice of him, wasn't it?'

'It was.' Mark *was* a nice guy. Or he had been until he'd dumped her.

Her heart was thumping by the time she came off the phone, as something occurred to her. Something it shouldn't have taken this long to realise.

If *she* had recognised *him*, even with a green latex mask hiding his face, then *he* would have undoubtedly recognised *her*. And he hadn't said a word.

It wasn't working. This was Mark's third day in Picklewick and so far he had nothing, and his visit to the farm on Muddypuddle Lane on Saturday had produced zero results, despite the impromptu Grinch performance.

He still had trouble believing he'd actually agreed to it. With her powers of persuasion Dulcie would go far, he thought wryly. She'd failed to manage to talk him into a repeat performance next Saturday though. He hadn't minded helping out in an emergency, but he wasn't going to make a habit of it, especially since Beatrice worked at the farm.

It was no secret that he was back, so she was bound to get to hear of it, and there was also a possibility he might bump into her again, but he didn't want to be wearing a lurid green mask when he did.

He should go back to Bristol. It would be the sensible thing to do. If he was going to continue to suffer from writer's block, he may as well suffer from it in the comfort of his own home. He'd spent all of yesterday cooped up in this room, wracking his brains for ideas, without success, only emerging at mealtimes.

For Mark, his imagination was often sparked by an image or a scene; he would feel the urge to draw it, and from that a story would form. But nothing he'd seen in Picklewick so far had inspired him. And having Beatrice's face pop into his mind every ten seconds didn't help. She hadn't changed, she was as lovely as he remembered.

A thought drifted across his mind – what would have happened if he'd stayed in Picklewick? Might he and Beatrice have got married and had kids? A pang went through him, and he brushed it aside.

'What can I get you?' Dave asked when Mark ventured downstairs in search of a spot of lunch.

He wasn't hungry (the full English had been, well…. *full*) but he could do with a break. Staring into the distance with a blank sheet of paper in front of him, was rather demoralising.

'An Americano and a cheese and pickle sandwich, please.'

The landlord said, 'Coming right up,' but made no move to ensure that happened. Instead, he lingered, wiping a cloth across the already clean table. 'Someone called earlier, enquiring about you. A woman.'

Mark's pulse quickened. 'Who?'

'Nikki Warring. She teaches in Picklewick Primary.'

His disappointment was acute. 'What did she want?'

'She didn't say.' Dave fished a crumpled note out of his pocket. 'I was going to push this under your door, but since you're here…' He placed it on the table and Mark glanced at it.

Just a name and a mobile number, but he could guess what it was about. He'd visited many schools, nurseries and libraries since his first book was published.

The landlord hadn't moved, clearly hoping Mark would phone Nikki Warring at this very moment.

'Sandwich?' Mark reminded him.

'Yes. Right.' With a longing look at the note, Dave wandered off, leaving Mark alone with his thoughts.

The way his heart had leapt when he'd thought the caller might have been Beatrice, concerned him. His reaction to seeing her yesterday could be explained by the unexpectedness of the encounter. But today…?

He should definitely leave. Who was it who'd said that the past was a country one should never revisit? He couldn't remember, but the sentiment was spot on. Picklewick had been magical growing up. It wasn't quite as magical now that he was an adult and viewing it through adult eyes. It was still pretty and quaint, and still unspoilt, but it wasn't doing anything for him.

Not wanting to be rude, or offend his readership (the adult contingent, that is), after Mark finished his lunch he gave Nikki Warring a call.

'Mr Stafford! Thank you so much for getting back to me,' she said. 'I'm Dulcie's sister. I wish I'd known at the time that it was you who had stepped into the breach on Saturday – I would have loved to have met you. Actually, that's what I wanted to speak to you about. I teach at Picklewick Primary and I wondered whether you could be persuaded to visit our school? The children would be thrilled to bits if you did.' She paused for breath.

Seeing an opening, Mark leapt in. 'I'd love to, but I doubt I'm going to be in Picklewick long.'

'It won't take long. Just an hour of your time. Please? We don't often get many authors in this neck of the woods, and to think you went to this very school.'

And that was how Mark Stafford, successful children's author (hopefully dressed in his own clothes this time) agreed to visit Picklewick Primary School on Wednesday afternoon to entertain small children for the second time in less than a week.

Beatrice couldn't believe how quickly time could speed by. No sooner did she arrive at the farm shop, than it was time to leave to collect the girls from school. She was thoroughly enjoying every minute of her new job, and every day was different.

She assumed things would probably settle down after Christmas, but for now she was rushed off her feet. Today, for instance, she'd been taste-testing milkshakes (mince pie flavour had been her favourite) and putting together festive afternoon tea boxes. There had been a steady stream of customers, and she knew that as the weekend approached, it would get even busier.

It was only Wednesday but Beatrice was already looking forward to Saturday. If last week was anything to go by, this next one should be fun. She was secretly disappointed that Mark wouldn't be there, wearing the Grinch's outfit, but maybe that was a good thing because, despite how busy she was both during and outside of work, Mark had been a constant presence in her mind.

She was also looking forward to Sunday. Beatrice loved her girls with every cell in her body, but she rarely had a minute to herself, so she treasured the times when they were with their father. Eric didn't often have them for a whole day because he was a nurse in Thornton General, which meant he worked days, nights and weekends too. She was planning a pampering day, and she knew she was going to need it after the busy week.

Right now she was on her way to collect the girls from school and she just had enough time to drop the car off at home and walk the six minutes from her front door to the school gates.

A gaggle of people were gathered in the playground waiting for the doors to open and the children to pour out of their various classrooms, and Beatrice spotted her best friend Lisa making her way over.

Lisa was studying her. 'Have you heard? Mark's back.'

Quietly Beatrice replied, 'I heard.'

'How do you feel?' Lisa knew their history. How could she not, since she'd picked up the pieces. Beatrice had been a mess for a while.

She laughed, hoping it sounded natural. 'I'm fine. I've been over him for years. Mark Stafford is water under the bridge.'

'I heard a rumour that he was the farm's Grinch. That can't be right, can it?'

Airily Beatrice replied, 'I believe he was.'

'Have you seen him?'

'No.' It wasn't technically a lie. She hadn't seen *him* as such. She'd seen a green Grinchy mask.

'Do you think he'll have changed much?' Lisa asked.

Beatrice shrugged. 'No idea.'

'He looks the same in the photos of him online. Better, actually. More suave. Suaver.' Lisa flicked her wrist. 'You know what I mean.'

All Beatrice knew, was that she wished Lisa would change the subject. Mark had only been in Picklewick a few days and she was already heartily sick of hearing his name. She was certainly sick of thinking about him, especially since she suspected he hadn't given *her* a second thought since he'd left. And why would he? So what, if they'd dated once? It was a long time ago, and they'd hardly been in the same league as Romeo and Juliet. Well, *he* hadn't – she would have laid down her life for him. Once or twice she'd been tempted to tell him how she felt, but thankfully had been unable to find the courage – the devastation she'd felt when he ended their relationship had been bad enough, without adding the mortification of him knowing she was in love with him.

A bell rang and a second later children exploded from the various classroom doors, filling the playground with yells and screams, and a blur of movement.

Beatrice craned her neck to see Sadie, but the child was nowhere in sight. She caught a glimpse of Taya though, who was trying to play it cool by ignoring her.

'Oh, heck, what now?' she muttered, when she saw Miss Barnes signalling to her. 'Could you watch Taya for a minute?' she asked Lisa. 'I need to speak to Sadie's teacher.'

Lisa gave her a sympathetic smile.

'Can I have a quick word?' Miss Barnes asked.

Mutely, Beatrice nodded and followed the teacher into the classroom.

Sadie was sitting in one of the small chairs, her arms folded, her face mutinous.

Miss Barnes said, 'Sadie is a little upset today because she found out she's going to be a toadstool and not a fairy in the school play, and she's refusing to take part.'

Beatrice sighed. 'Leave it with me. She'll come around.' Maybe the pink sparkly fabric she had in mind would do the trick?

'Won't!' Sadie snapped. 'Toadstools are nasty.'

'Who says?'

'Everyone.'

Beatrice highly doubted that. 'Come on, let's get you home.' She held out a hand.

Sadie thrust her hands deeper into her armpits and stuck out her chin. 'No.'

'What do you mean *no*?'

'I'm not going until Miss says I can be a fairy.'

'In that case, you can stay here all night,' Beatrice said. Blackmail, even from a five-year-old, wasn't nice.

Miss Barnes said, 'We've had such a lovely afternoon, too. We've had a visit from an author, haven't we, Sadie? He spoke about your favourite book, didn't he? Look.' She pointed to the hallway. 'There he is. You don't want Mr Stafford to see you in a mood, do you?'

Beatrice froze, and her gaze was slowly drawn to the open classroom door and the hallway beyond. And she immediately locked eyes with him.

Recognition flared in his and a smile flitted across his face. He gave a small, awkward wave, then turned his attention back to Mrs Warring, Taya's teacher.

Irrationally, Beatrice wished she was wearing something more glamorous than jeans, boots and a padded jacket that made her look like a small hippo. The bobble hat with a red pompom on it wasn't her best look either, and neither was her make-up-free face. When all was said and done, she looked a mess.

Miss Barnes said, 'Excuse me a minute. I just want to say goodbye to Mr Stafford. He was so marvellous, and the children adored him.'

Beatrice dragged her gaze away and focused on her belligerent daughter. 'We're going,' she said, her tone brooking no argument.

'No.'

'If you don't do as you're told, you'll go straight to bed after tea, young lady.'

'Don't care.' Sadie settled herself more firmly in her chair.

'No TV and no games,' Beatrice warned.

Her daughter stared stubbornly straight ahead.

'No story,' Beatrice added, wondering what other sanctions she could impose.

Sadie shot her a glance, then hastily looked away.

Ah-ha! Leverage! 'In fact, I won't read you a bedtime story for the rest of the week, if you don't do as you're told.'

Sadie leapt to her feet and stamped her foot. 'I don't care! I won't be a toadstool. Toadstools are for boys.'

'Who says?'

Beatrice froze at the sound of Mark's voice. Great. Now he was a witness to her abysmal parenting skills as well as her frumpy, mumsy appearance.

Ignoring her, he walked up to Sadie. Sadie gazed up at him in awe, her defiance miraculously vanished.

Sitting in the chair next to the one Sadie had abruptly vacated, he reached into the inside of his coat and withdrew a small pad and a pencil.

Wordlessly he flipped the pad open and began to draw.

Sadie glanced at Beatrice, who shrugged. She had no idea what was going on, either.

Mark's head was bowed, his attention on whatever it was he was doing, and Beatrice grabbed the opportunity to look at him properly.

Taller than her five-foot-six by at least half a foot, he had always been athletic, but he had filled out over the years, his shoulders broader than she remembered, tapering to a lean waist. His long legs were encased in black jeans, and he struggled to fold them underneath the low table.

His short, dark brown hair was longer on top, and had flashes of silver at the temples, and crow's feet crinkled at the corners of his hazel eyes, those same eyes that had haunted her dreams for many months after he'd broken it off with her. A dusting of stubble shadowed his jaw, and her gaze lingered on his lips until she forced herself to look away.

His fingers gripped the pencil, guiding it across the page with firm, deft strokes and in less than a minute, he'd finished.

Sadie let out a gasp when he tore out the page and gave it to her. 'It's me, Mummy. He drawed *me!*'

So he had. He'd drawn her little face peering out from a toadstool and she had a wand in her hand, with stars issuing from its tip.

'See?' he said. 'Toadstools aren't for boys. They're for girls, because they're magic. Without toadstools, fairies wouldn't be able to fly.'

The logic of that passed Beatrice by, but Sadie grasped it immediately.

'Fairy dust!' she exclaimed.

'Exactly!'

Her eyes narrowed, then she said to Beatrice, in a tone remarkably like that of a queen bestowing a favour, 'I think I *will* be a toadstool. A pink one, with a wand. Can I show Miss?'

Without waiting for an answer, she trotted towards Miss Barnes's desk where the two teachers were examining some books.

As Beatrice watched her go, she felt Mark's eyes on her.

He said, 'She's cute.'

'She's a monster in little girl's clothing.'

He chuckled. 'She looks like you. They both do.'

'You make a good Grinch,' she countered.

'I'm not sure that's a compliment.'

Beatrice didn't say anything. He could take it whichever way he pleased.

Sadie appeared at her elbow. 'Can we go now? I'm hungry.'

'I think we'd better. Miss Barnes will want to go home.' She grabbed her daughter's hand and smiled at the teachers. 'Nice seeing you again, Mark,' she said, her voice cool and polite.

'Wait, have you got time for a coffee?'

Beatrice blinked. *He wanted to have coffee with her? Was this for old time's sake?*

'Can't. Sorry.' She gestured towards her daughter.

'Another time?'

'Another time,' she agreed.

'When?'

'Pardon?'

'When would be best for you?'

'Mummy, you could have coffee with Mr Stafford on Sunday, if you don't want to take me and Taya.'

Sadie's expression was hopeful. 'But I don't mind going now though. I could have a milkshake, and I promise to be quiet if you want to talk grown-up things. Taya will be good too.'

'No, I—' Beatrice began.

'Sunday?' Mark said.

Sadie announced, 'We're going to Daddy's house.'

Beatrice closed her eyes briefly. Thanks, Sadie. 'I'm busy on Sunday,' she said.

'She's going to have a bath with bubbles, but it won't take all day, will it, Mummy?'

Mark was staring at her, and Beatrice squirmed.

With a weak laugh, she said, 'I look forward to a relaxing soak in the tub without kids knocking on the door every few seconds. You know how it is.'

'Actually, I don't. No kids.'

'Oh.'

'Sunday?'

'I'm not sure.' She was so tempted that it was almost a physical ache. But seeing him again would be so unwise.

'It's just a coffee, Bea.'

Oh, bugger! Now he was thinking that she was reading more into it than he'd meant. 'Okay, eleven o'clock in Blake's Cafe on the main street.'

'See you there.' He began to walk away, then paused. 'Bea?'

'Yes?'

'Nice hat.'

Shit. Shit, shit, shit.

Beatrice sank onto the sofa, put her mobile on speaker, and reached for the glass of dry white wine on the side table next to her. She didn't make a habit of drinking on her own, and never on a weeknight, but this evening she felt the need to break her own rule.

'He asked me to go for a coffee with him,' she said, then winced as Lisa screeched, *'He asked you out?'*

'That's not what I said. He didn't ask me out. He asked me to go for a coffee.'

'Same thing.'

'It's not the same thing. It'll be a quick catch-up with an old friend – not a date.'

'Old friend, my peachy backside! He was your boyfriend.'

'Was being the operative word. That was years ago.'

'You were in love with him.'

'I might have been, but I'm not now.'

'Why do you think he asked you out?'

Beatrice didn't see the point in correcting Lisa again on the date front; instead, she said, 'For old time's sake.'

'Just be careful that old times don't become *new* times.'

'I'm not that daft. Anyway, I've heard he won't be in Picklewick long.'

'It doesn't take long,' Lisa pointed out, then her voice softened. 'I don't want to see you hurt, that's all.'

'I won't be. It's just a coffee with an old friend,' she reiterated.

'You keep telling yourself that.'

'Don't worry, I will. I'm not going to let Mark Stafford into my heart a second time.'

'That's the problem,' Lisa said. 'I don't think he ever left it.'

And although Beatrice scoffed at the idea, she had a suspicion her friend was right. He *had* been her first love, and did first love ever truly die…?

CHAPTER FOUR

Mark hesitated outside the cafe. It hadn't changed much and seeing it brought back a rush of memories. It whispered of summer afternoons after school, drinking ice-cold Cola, and winter ones sipping marshmallow-topped hot chocolates. And many of them had been with Bea by his side. This cafe was the embodiment of his youth, his salad days as Shakespeare had so eloquently put it. He had been green in judgement, indeed. But wasn't everyone at that age?

As the memories flooded back, Mark wondered how good an idea it was to invite Beatrice for a coffee. She'd clearly been reluctant, and to be honest, he wasn't entirely sure why he'd asked her. It had been a spur-of-the-moment thing, his mouth freewheeling down the road before his brain was in gear.

'Get over yourself,' he muttered. This was merely a chat and a coffee with an old friend. What was the harm in that?

With a deep breath, he pushed the door open and went inside. The bell above tinkled as the rich aroma of roasted beans filled his nose. The cafe was surprisingly busy, and although he was a few minutes early, Beatrice was already waiting for him.

She sat at a table in the corner, as though she was hiding away, and was fiddling with a packet of sugar, her eyes downcast. Behind him, the bell jangled again, but she didn't look up until he reached the table and paused.

'Hey,' he said.

'Hi.' She didn't smile. Her eyes were huge, her lashes long and dark, and he realised she was wearing make-up.

'Have you ordered?' he asked.

'Not yet.'

'What can I get you? A hot chocolate?'

She nodded. 'With marshmallows?'

'Absolutely! You can't have hot chocolate without marshmallows.'

'No...' She trailed off, her attention returning to the packet of sugar.

As he went to the counter to order their drinks, he wondered whether she still took two in her tea. And he wondered what she'd done in the intervening years while he'd been away. Got married, had two kids, got divorced... What else? Was she happy?

'I got you extra marshmallows,' he told her, placing the drinks on the table.

'Thanks.' She picked up a spoon and ladled some into her mouth, along with a generous dollop of cream, and he tried not to stare.

How many times had he kissed those lips?

She noticed the direction of his gaze and he hastily examined his own mug. 'So,' he began. 'How have you been?'

'Fine. Good. Great, actually.'

'Good, good.' He used his spoon to poke one of the marshmallows. It disappeared into the cream. He did the same to another, silence stretching between them.

Beatrice broke it. 'How about you?'

Mark opened his mouth to say 'good', then changed his mind. 'I've been better.'

'Are you ill?' A flicker of concern crossed her face, and he wondered what it meant.

'God, no, nothing like that,' he said. 'The only thing I'm suffering from is writer's block.' As soon as the words left his mouth, he regretted them. He had told no one, not even his agent or his editor. *Especially* not his editor.

'Writer's block? Is that where you can't think of anything to write?'

'Exactly.'

'I thought that was why you're here – to write one? Dulcie told me you're doing research.'

'I am. Kind of. I'm searching for inspiration.'

'Have you found any?'

'Not yet. I'm sure I will.' He took a sip of his drink, hoping he didn't have a cream moustache.

Beatrice said, 'You've got...' She touched her upper lip.

Dabbing his mouth with a serviette, he said, 'Anyway, enough about me. Tell me about you.'

'There's nothing to tell.'

'You've got children,' he pointed out.

'So I have.'

'You don't live with their father?'

'Thanks, Sadie,' she mumbled, then louder, 'We're divorced. How about you? Are you married?'

'Not anymore.'

'Oh. Sorry.'

'Me, too.'

'What happened?' Her eyes widened then she said, 'Forgive me, it's none of my business.'

'I don't mind talking about it. She didn't want kids. I did. I think the last straw was when I gave up the day job to become a full-time author.' It was more complicated than that, but the details weren't particularly pleasant.

Beatrice pursed her lips. 'That's tough.'

'Your turn.'

'I didn't realise we were swapping divorce stories.'

He made a face. 'You don't have to tell me, if you don't want to.'

'My ex is an arse. And before you ask why I married an arse, he wasn't one when we tied the knot. He became an arse later, after we'd had the kids.'

'Oh, right.' Her reply was cryptic and Mark wondered what the man had done. 'He still sees the kids, though?'

'He does, when it suits him. But he's still an arse.'

'Okay, I get it – he's an arse.'

'A lot of men are.' She looked him in the eye as she said it.

Although hoping she wasn't including him in that, he thought it prudent to change the subject. 'How long have you worked at Lilac Tree Farm?'

'Just over a week.'

'What made you decide to take a job on a farm?'

'Because Christmas is coming and my children want the earth – like every other kid on the planet.'

'I didn't mean that; I meant that I didn't think you were the mucking-out-the-cows type'

'Ah, okay.' She looked embarrassed, like she'd given too much away. 'I'm not. I only work in the shop. No cows. Or any other animal for that matter. Although the goats are rather sweet and the bunnies are very cute, the nearest I get to an animal, is selling their milk, or when Peg pays me a visit.'

'Peg?'

'Walter's dog. He persuaded her to sit outside the Grinch's cave, wearing antlers. It's costing him an arm and a leg in bones to keep her quiet.'

'Not his own, I hope?' Mark quipped and got a glare of disapproval for his efforts.

'I wish children were more like dogs,' she said. 'Happy with the simple things. You don't see them queuing up to see a Doggy Santa Claus and asking for diamante collars or gold-plated tennis balls. All they want is someone to love them, a comfy place to sleep, and a regular supply of dog biscuits.'

Mark grinned. 'But if there was a Santa *Paws* – see what I did? – pooches would still ask for things like squirrels to chase or squeaky toys.'

Sighing, she said, 'I suppose you're right. Whatever we've got, we always want more, even when we've got more than enough for our needs.' She blinked. 'Crumbs, that was a bit deep.' She finished her hot chocolate and licked her lips. 'I'd better go,' she said, getting to her feet. 'Thanks for the drink and the chat. It was nice catching up.'

'It was. I'm glad you're doing okay, Bea.'

'Why wouldn't I be?' she shot back.

'You know, divorce… two kids…'

Her face cleared. 'Yeah. You, too. I'm sure something will come to you soon.'

It already had. 'We should do this again,' he said.

'Next time you're in Picklewick,' she agreed.

'I mean, before then. Next week, maybe?'

'I thought you were leaving soon?' She seemed put out.

'I was thinking about it, but I've changed my mind. We could have dinner in The Black Horse. I'm fed up with eating on my own.'

'You forget I have children.'

'I haven't forgotten at all. Bring them with you. We can eat early; is five-thirty okay? My treat.'

'I can pay my own way.'

Mark was taken aback. 'I didn't for one minute think you couldn't.' An idea occurred to him, though why he was so anxious for her to agree, he had yet to determine. 'Call it a business meeting. I want to pick your children's brains.'

'Why?' Her suspicion was palpable. She clearly didn't believe a word he was saying.

'I have an idea for the new book and I'd like to run it past them, so dinner will be a legitimate expense.' It wouldn't, but she didn't need to know that.

'I thought you had writer's block?'

'I did, but I don't now.' He smiled warmly at her. 'It's amazing what a chat with an old friend can do.'

'Less of the old.' Her reply was automatic and lacked conviction. She sighed. 'Okay – when?'

'I'll fit in with you and your plans.'

'Friday,' she said. 'I don't want the kids worked up on a school night.'

'Friday, it is.' He'd hoped it could be sooner, but he supposed five days would give him time to hone his idea and produce some illustrations to show her children, and then he wouldn't be making himself out to be a liar.

Because the real reason he had asked her to dinner was that he simply wanted to see her again. But why that was, he wasn't prepared to think about too closely.

The front door banging open, accompanied by shouts of 'Mummy, why is it so dark?' jolted Beatrice out of her thoughts, and she leapt out of the chair and switched on the nearest lamp.

Sadie barrelled into her, smelling of Eric's cologne and bringing a blast of chilly air with her. 'I was scared you were out!'

'I'm not out, I'm here.'

'But it was dark. You don't like the dark.'

'*You* don't like the dark,' Beatrice corrected her youngest child. '*I* don't mind it. Where's your sister?'

Sadie's expression clouded. 'She told Daddy she hates him. She doesn't, does she?'

'Of course she doesn't. I expect she was cross with him, that's all.' Beatrice moved to the window and peered into the street. She could see Taya in the passenger seat of Eric's car. It was parked under the street light, illuminating her face. Taya looked remarkably like Sadie when she was annoyed about something.

Eventually she got out and slammed the door. The car rocked.

No doubt she would tell Beatrice about it later. For now, Beatrice wanted to make them some tea.

The front door banged open a second time as Taya stormed in, and Beatrice hurried to close it before it slammed shut. If this carried on, she would have to replace the damned thing, and she couldn't afford to do that. Did her kids *know* how much a new front door cost?

Beatrice scowled. Of course they didn't, and if they did, they wouldn't care.

Aware that she was being ridiculous (they were children for goodness' sake!) she peered into the street again, then gently closed the door, hoping Eric hadn't upset their eldest child too much.

Beatrice got the story out of Taya over tea. 'Have you fallen out with Dad?' she asked.

Taya narrowed her eyes at her sister. 'Tattletale.'

'I'm not!'

Beatrice hastened to soothe sibling angst. 'Don't blame Sadie. I could tell from the way you stormed into the house.'

When it came to her children, there was always some drama or another, most of it minor and fleeting in the grand scheme of things, but of gigantic importance at the time. Hopefully this was of the minor and fleeting variety.

'Dad has got a girlfriend,' Taya spat.

Beatrice frowned in irritation. 'Was she there? Did you meet her?'

'No, I heard them talking on the phone.'

'You shouldn't listen in on people's conversations,' Beatrice said absently, relieved that her children hadn't been subjected to yet another of Eric's girlfriends.

She wouldn't have any objection if there was a constant one, or even if he'd had two since they'd split up, but he seemed to have a different one every week. Where he found them was a mystery. In all that time, Beatrice had only managed one date. It hadn't been a great success. Maybe single eligible women were in greater abundance than single eligible men?

'She won't last,' Beatrice told her daughter confidently. 'They never do.'

Taya pouted. 'I told him *you* had a boyfriend.'

'You did *what?* Why?'

'You *said* he was your boyfriend.'

'Who?'

'That man who came to the school. The one who wrote those books.'

Beatrice couldn't believe what she was hearing. 'His name is Mark Stafford, but he's not my boyfriend. Whatever gave you that idea?'

'I heard you talking to Aunty Lisa.'

'What did I just tell you about listening to other people's conversations? The problem is, you get the wrong end of the stick, or only half a story. Mark used to be my boyfriend, years ago. Long before I met your dad.'

'Why did you go out with him today? Do you want him to be your boyfriend again?'

'It was a work thing.' Seeing Taya's confused expression, Beatrice explained, 'He's writing a new book and wanted to have a chat.'

'Why?'

'Because he wants to ask whether he could talk to you and Sadie about it.'

'Why?'

'Because he doesn't have any children of his own to ask. And before you ask why, I don't know.' She took a deep breath. 'I said we'd go out to tea with him on Friday.'

Sadie had been following the conversation closely. 'Me, too?'

'Yes, sweetie, you too.'

'Yay! Can I have a Big Mac?'

'We won't be going to McDonald's,' Beatrice told her. 'We're going to The Black Horse.'

Sadie's eyes were round, Taya's not so much. At nine, Taya was more worldly-wise than her sister.

'I like him,' Sadie announced. 'He draws good.'

'Draws well,' Beatrice corrected.

'That's what I said.'

Beatrice's gaze strayed to the fridge. The drawing that Mark had done of Sadie dressed as a toadstool had pride of place, alongside the artwork that Taya produced on a weekly basis. As well as being a reader, Taya was a budding artist.

It was time to change the subject. 'If you've finished your tea, scrape off your plates and clear the table, please.'

'Aww, do we—?'

'Yes. Please can we not do this every mealtime?'

'Dad lets us—'

'I'm not interested in what your father does,' Beatrice broke in. She *was,* but she wasn't going to sweat the small stuff. Arguing with him about little things like this, simply wasn't worth the aggro.

Taya said, 'He always asks me about *you.*'

The look on her eldest child's face squeezed her heart. 'Taya, sweetie, I know you'd love nothing more than for me and your dad to get back together, but it's not going to happen.'

'He's only got a girlfriend because he's lonely.'

Yeah, right, Beatrice scoffed silently. He must have been very sodding lonely when they were married, because he'd had two affairs that she knew of. How many more that she didn't?

One day her girls might discover the truth about their arse of a father, but they wouldn't hear it from her.

Taya continued. 'You've got us. He hasn't got anyone.'

Maybe Eric should have thought about that before he cheated on me, Beatrice thought. She'd forgiven him the first time, but not the second.

Telling him she wanted a divorce had been the second hardest thing she'd ever had to do. The hardest had been telling the children that their dad wouldn't be living with them anymore. Taya had been devastated. At not-quite-two years old, Sadie hadn't understood what was going on.

Now and again, Beatrice wondered whether she'd done the right thing, that maybe she should have turned a blind eye to his philandering for the sake of her girls. And although she'd done nothing wrong and nothing to be ashamed of, in the dark quiet hours guilt gnawed at her with sharp black teeth.

'Bugger, damn and blast!' The sodding car wouldn't start. Beatrice turned the key in the ignition again, hoping and praying the engine would turn over, but all she heard was a defiant click. Why did it have to break down when it was raining? Sod's bloody law, that's what it was. It hadn't been raining when she'd taken the girls to school, but as she'd trotted back to the house to pick up the car and drive to work, the heavens had opened.

Thankfully she'd had an umbrella in her bag so she hadn't got too soaked. It had been buried underneath the spare hair bobbles, the Calpol sachets, the plasters and everything else she carried around with her *just in case*, because, let's face it, if she didn't have it, she would wish she did (Mary Bloody Poppins, that's who she was). However, umbrella or not, she would soon be drenched if she had to walk all the way from the village to the farm at the top of Muddypuddle Lane.

She tried the key again. Nothing.

Initially, when she'd got in the car, the hem of her jeans wet, the umbrella dripping, the engine had kind of turned over, making a chugging sound as it tried to fire – or whatever it was that engines were supposed to do – but that quickly became an asthmatic wheeze, and now it was refusing to do anything other than click. She had a feeling it was giving her the finger.

Cross, she began phoning people in the hope that one of them would be able to give her a lift. First her mum, then her dad, then Lisa….

As she worked her way down her contact list, becoming more despondent with every unanswered call or 'sorry, I would but—' she finally realised that the only way she was going to get to work was if she walked.

Whilst she'd been cursing the car (although she had a feeling that the car not starting was all her own fault, because she'd left the headlights on yesterday), the rain had eased and the clouds were beginning to clear. Hopefully it would stay fine for the next half an hour. She'd have to get a move on though, if she didn't want to be late, and she knew she was cutting it fine.

As she walked along the high street, she tried Dulcie's number, wanting to make her aware that she might be a few minutes late, but the call went straight to answerphone. As did her next call, which was to the garage.

'Fiddlesticks! Isn't *anyone* going to answer the phone this morning?' she grumbled.

'Everything okay?'

Beatrice froze and her heart sank. Great, that was all she needed. 'Mark, hi.'

He was outside the odds-and-sods shop, about to go in. 'Are you alright?' he asked. 'You look flustered.'

Gee, thanks for the compliment. 'I'm fine. I haven't got time to chat, I'll be late for work.'

'Oh, okay. See you tomorrow.'

Her phone rang. It was her dad. 'Sorry, I need to take this,' she said to Mark as she walked away. 'Hi, Dad.'

'What's up?' Her father's voice was full of concern.

'Nothing's wrong, but I need a lift to work. My car won't start.'

'Sorry, Bea, but your mum and I are in Thornbury.'

Beatrice sighed. 'Never mind. I'll speak to you later. Thanks anyway, Dad.'

'I can give you a lift, if you like?' Mark said.

Beatrice knitted her brow. She hadn't realised he had fallen in step with her until he'd spoken. 'Haven't you got anything better to do?' she asked.

His expression was blank when he replied, 'Actually, I have,' and stopped, turning away.

Realising how rude she'd been, Beatrice caught hold of his arm. 'I'm sorry, that came out wrong. If you're not busy, I'd love a lift, please.'

He glanced at her hand. Beatrice hastily removed it from his arm and dug her nails into her palm. Touching him had unsettled her. Meeting his gaze, she felt herself blush, but she couldn't look away.

'My car is in the pub's car park,' he said. 'Come on.' He strode off and she had to hurry to keep up.

The short walk was conducted in silence, and when she got into his rather smart black car she felt distinctly awkward.

Mark broke the silence as he reversed out of the parking space. 'Have you got a garage you can call?'

'There's one on the outskirts of Picklewick, but I'll see if Dad's got some jump leads first. I've got a feeling I need a new battery, but if I can get it going, it'll save me having it towed.'

'How will you get home?'

'Walk, probably.'

He signalled to turn right, then pulled onto the main road. They should be at the farm in five minutes.

He said, 'I'll fetch you. What time do you finish?'

'There's no need, honestly,' she replied, then subsided when a gust of wind buffeted the car. The heavens opened once more and the windscreen wipers went into overdrive.

'Three o'clock,' she told him, gratefully.

But when he dropped her off in the farmyard, she feared she had made a mistake and that walking would be preferable after all – despite the risk of a good soaking. Because the risk of being hurt again by this man grew every time she clapped eyes on him.

Muddypuddle Lane was narrow, with room for only one vehicle at a time, apart from the two passing places. One of those was the entrance to the stables, the other was outside a pretty cottage halfway up.

Mark was on his way to fetch Beatrice from the farm, when he spied another vehicle coming down the lane, so he pulled in next to the cottage. And wished he hadn't when Dulcie pulled up alongside and waved at him.

It wasn't a 'hello' kind of wave: it was more of a 'can I have a word' kind of wave, and the word she wanted concerned a certain green costume and small children.

'Please,' she begged. 'Walter isn't up to it, and Gio – that's Nikki's other half – was supposed to be doing it, but he's having to work on Saturday. I hate to ask, but you were *such* a big hit. I'd do it myself, but I'm running a pinecone decorating session. It'll only be for a couple of hours. *Please?*'

He hesitated, and her face fell.

'I shouldn't have asked. Note to self – be more organised next year. This is my first year doing a Christmas Wonderland, so I didn't know what to expect. I can't believe how well it's taken off.' She brightened. 'I'm not complaining, you understand.'

Against his better judgement, he said, 'Okay, I'll do it.'

'You *will?* That's marvellous. Thank you!' She looked so pleased that Mark was glad he'd agreed.

What was a couple of hours out of his day?

Dulcie said, 'This time I insist on paying you,' and when he shook his head, she said, 'Dinner at The Wild Side, then? Just let me know when and for how many.'

'It'll just be me,' he said.

'Why not ask Beatrice if you don't want to dine on your own?' Dulcie's expression was devoid of guile, but he couldn't shake the feeling he was being set up. It occurred to him that her sister Nikki must have overheard him asking Beatrice to have a coffee with him when he was at the primary school the other day. Either that, or they had been spotted in the cafe — which was also quite likely.

Beatrice was waiting when Mark drove into the yard, and she hopped into the car. 'Thanks for this. I really appreciate it.'

'It's no bother,' he replied, trying not to stare at the silver glitter on her nose. 'You've got, um…' He touched his own nose, and she pulled down the sun visor and examined her face in the mirror.

Laughing, she said, 'I've been making up Christmas Eve boxes — or as much as can be done ahead of time. Can't add the perishables just yet. That'll be a last-minute job. Did you know that there's such a thing as edible glitter?' She rubbed her nose, transferring the glitter to her finger, then popped it into her mouth.

When she stuck out her tongue, it was sparkly.

'I didn't,' he replied. 'Thanks for enlightening me. That's one piece of knowledge I don't know how I've survived without.'

She beamed at him. 'Every day is a school day,' she sing-songed.

'I've got a present for you. It's on the back seat.'

Her smile dimmed, her expression becoming wary. 'What is it?'

'Take a look.' Mark watched her out of the corner of his eye as she wriggled around and reached behind her.

When she opened the bag and saw what was inside, she burst out laughing. 'Who says romance isn't dead!' she cried, holding a set of jump leads aloft. Then her eyes widened, her mouth became an 'O' of dismay, and she blushed furiously. 'I didn't— Oh, bugger!'

Mark barked out a laugh, quickly sobering when she glared at him. He wasn't entirely certain which of them had what end of the stick. He clearly hadn't meant the jump leads to be any kind of romantic overture – what bloke in his right mind would give a woman a garage-related gift if he was trying to woo her? But did she think that was what he was trying to do – woo her? Or had she been hoping that the bag had contained something a little less practical?

'Do you know how to jump-start a car?' he asked, thinking he'd better steer the conversation into less emotionally turbulent waters.

But his plan backfired when she rolled her eyes and gave an exasperated sigh. 'Yes, I *do* know how to jump-start a car. I'm not completely inept.'

Gritting his teeth, he asked, 'Where do you live?'

'Lavender Lane, number four, but do you mind dropping me at the school instead?'

'Not at all.' His voice was stiff and stilted, and without saying another word he drove along the high street, reaching the school a minute later.

'Thanks,' she said, unclipping her seat belt. Then she held up the bag. 'Thanks for these, too.' She got out.

Without thinking, he said, 'I'll wait for you.'

'Why?'

'I'll take you home, and you can use my car to start yours.'

'Oh, right, thanks. That's very kind of you. Can I meet you there? You don't have any booster seats, and I know it's not far, but….'

'No problem.' *Booster seats?* He clearly had a lot to learn when it came to kids.

Mark watched her walk through the school gates, then realised he was getting curious looks from some of the mums, so he hastily drove off.

Waiting outside Beatrice's house, it felt like ages before she appeared with the children in tow, but it couldn't have been more than ten minutes.

'I'll be with you in a sec,' she said, unlocking the door to number four, a neat, terraced house with an old banger of a car parked outside, which he assumed was hers.

She ushered the children inside, then hurried back out, looking flustered.

'Problem?' he asked, flipping the lever to open the bonnet, then getting out.

'Nosey children.'

Movement caught his eye, and he glanced at the window to see two small faces peering out. Tentatively he waved and Sadie, the youngest, waved back. The older one glowered and he assumed she wasn't a fan, too old for books aimed at four- to seven-year-olds.

Beatrice popped the bonnet on her car, but before she was able to connect the leads to the battery, Sadie came outside. 'I've got a tummy ache,' the child announced.

'Is it because you're hungry?' Beatrice asked. She said to him, 'I think she's been confusing hunger pangs for tummy ache lately.'

'Give me your keys,' he said. 'I know you're perfectly capable of jump-starting a car, but you're probably better off seeing to the girls while I get this going. It'll take a while to transfer enough charge, and then you'll have to take it for a drive.'

'Damn, I'd forgotten that. Oh, well, I could do with getting a few things, so we'll pop into Thornbury. The kids can have a McDonald's on the way back as a treat.'

Sadie's ears pricked up. 'McDonald's? Really?' She jumped up and down, flapping her arms. 'Yay! McDonald's!'

Beatrice said, 'Anyone would think I never fed them. Actually, they don't have fast food often, so maybe it is something to get excited about. For them, not me, you understand.' She handed him her keys and went back inside, her bouncy, excited daughter racing ahead of her.

After fifteen minutes or so of the car being on charge, he disconnected the leads then tried it again. Reluctantly, it coughed into life, so he left it running, just in case, and knocked on her door.

'All done,' he said, stepping back when Sadie shot out and threw herself at him.

'Thank you!' she cried. 'Mummy said we've got you to thank for going to McDonald's. So that's what I'm doing, saying thank you.'

Mark met Beatrice's gaze over the top of her daughter's head. 'Thanks from me, too,' she said.

'No problem.'

'Can Mr Stafford come with us, Mummy?' Sadie released him and looked hopefully up at her mother.

Seeing the alarm in Beatrice's eyes, Mark said, 'Sorry, Sadie, I'd love to but I can't.'

Beatrice didn't try to persuade him to change his mind but as he drove off, he wished she had. There was nothing Mark would have loved more right now, than to eat a burger and fries with Beatrice and her children.

CHAPTER FIVE

Beatrice held the pub door open for the girls and in they went, wide-eyed and shedding hats and scarves as the warmth hit them. It was only a short walk from their house to The Black Horse, but it was dark and cold outside, with a chill north-easterly wind, so she'd made sure they were dressed warmly – they would need the layers on the way home.

The children hesitated inside the door, the pub unfamiliar and overwhelming. Beatrice also paused as she took in the Christmas tree in the corner, the multicoloured lights strung around the windows, and the twinkling, flashing garland festooned across the mantlepiece. Flames leapt in the log burner, and along with the smell of food and hops, there was a hint of woodsmoke and pine in the air.

Scanning the tables, she spotted Mark and some of the tension she had been carrying eased.

From behind the bar, Dave waved at her and she gave him a fleeting smile as she shepherded the girls past, feeling awkward. She wasn't a weekly visitor to The Black Horse, but she drank there often enough not to feel discomforted that she was here to meet a man. This was her local, for goodness' sake – she'd had her first legal drink in this very pub (and her first illegal one, too), but this evening, she felt as though she'd walked into a strange bar and everyone was staring at her.

Actually, quite a few people *were*, and she knew all of them, including Dulcie and her younger sister Maisie, who had recently opened a boarding kennels on the mountain above the farm. When Dulcie saw whose table Beatrice was heading towards, she smirked and raised her eyebrows.

Beatrice stuck her nose in the air and fixed her gaze on Mark – which was a mistake, as she felt her cheeks pinking up, especially when he got to his feet and went in for a hug. The contact was brief, but it set her nerves jangling nevertheless as her body remembered what it was like to be held by him.

Heat flooded through her and she hastily shrugged out of her coat.

'Sit down, girls,' she instructed, folding it over her arm as she pulled out a chair for Sadie. Sadie ignored it and sat next to Mark. Taya sat next to her sister, leaving one unoccupied seat on Mark's other side.

Sadie shuffled her chair closer to him. Ironically Beatrice moved her own chair further away; not by much, but enough to give her a little more space to breathe. Right now, it felt as though there wasn't enough air in the room. Or was that due to the heat the log burner was spewing out?

Yes, that was it. Probably.

Sadie had begun chatting away as soon as she'd sat down, but Taya was more reserved and hadn't said a word, and Beatrice had the impression that her eldest child wasn't as keen on Mark as her youngest was.

It took a while to choose their meals, mainly because Sadie couldn't decide, but with the food eventually ordered, Mark settled down to business. Taking a digital tablet out of its fabric sleeve, he proceeded to discuss his idea with the girls, and both were fascinated with the artwork he'd done so far, Taya especially, who was emerging from her shell now that she had something electronic to focus on.

'I assumed you used paper and paint,' Beatrice said.

'I do, but digital art is less messy, and because digital lets me layer my work, if I want to change something, the colour of the dog let's say, then I can do so easily without having to repaint the whole thing.'

'Can I have a go?' Taya asked. She hadn't taken her eyes off the screen.

Mark said, 'You can, but on one condition – you give me your honest opinion about the story. I know it isn't aimed at someone your age, but your input is still valuable. Yours, too, Bea; as a parent.'

By the time their meals arrived, Mark's idea for his new book had been thoroughly discussed, and Taya had become totally enthralled with digital art.

'Can I have a tablet, Mum?' she asked.

Beatrice's heart sank; she'd been expecting her daughter to ask, but she was hoping she wouldn't. Tablets like this weren't cheap. Even with her new job at the farm, she was pretty sure she couldn't afford to buy one, especially with Christmas being only a few weeks away and she'd already begun buying gifts, not wanting to leave everything to the last minute.

Maybe if she had a word with their father? It was about time Eric pulled out his wallet.

'We'll see,' Beatrice told her.

'I won't ask for anything else ever again,' Taya promised earnestly.

Beatrice highly doubted that.

'Look what it can do, Mum.' Taya angled the screen so Beatrice could see.

Mark said, 'It's only a tool, Taya. *It* didn't create that – *you* did.'

Beatrice studied the image, pride swelling in her chest. Although she knew Taya was good at drawing and painting, until she saw what she'd created on Mark's tablet in a matter of minutes, Beatrice hadn't realised just how good. Taya appeared to have found her niche.

But was it just a fad? It was a lot of money to spend on something if it wasn't going to be used.

Mark put the tablet away while they ate and didn't bring it out again, which Beatrice was thankful for, and the conversation moved on from book writing and digital art. By the time they were ready to order dessert, they were discussing weird food combinations.

'Ice cream and chips!' Sadie cried.

Mark pretended to think about it. 'Do you know, I think that might be quite nice. How about popcorn and tomato sauce?'

'Gross!'

'Bacon and chocolate?'

'Ew!

'Pineapple and pizza?' he suggested.

Taya narrowed her eyes. 'Duh, that's a real thing.'

'No! It can't be!' Mark looked shocked, but Beatrice caught the twinkle in his eye.

'It's called a Hawaiian,' Taya said. '*Everyone* knows that.'

Sadie wrinkled her nose. 'It's yucky.'

Beatrice was inclined to agree with her, but ham and pineapple was Taya's favourite pizza topping.

'Haribo and porridge,' Sadie suggested.

Mark tapped his chin. 'Does your Mum make porridge in the microwave?' he asked, and when Sadie nodded he said, 'Would you put the Haribo in first, so they went all melty, or after the porridge is cooked?'

'*All melty?*' Beatrice laughed. 'Melty isn't a word.'

'It is. It's a made-up word. Us authors are allowed to make up words,' he replied loftily. 'Ask Lewis Carroll.'

'Who's Lewis Carroll?' Taya wanted to know.

Mark said, 'He wrote Alice's Adventures in Wonderland.'

'That's a film, not a book,' she told him.

'It was a book before it became a film. Lewis Carroll wrote it over a hundred and fifty years ago.'

'Is he dead?' Sadie asked.

'Very.'

'Then how can you ask him about made-up words?' Sadie looked confused.

'You can't, but he wrote a poem called The Jabberwocky and it's full of them.' And to Beatrice's astonishment, he recited the whole poem whilst the children ate their chocolate sundaes and she sipped her coffee.

The kids were enthralled, despite not understanding most of it and when he finished, she gave him a round of applause and he gave a mock bow.

'Bravo!' she cried, impressed.

In fact, she'd been impressed all evening by how good he was with the children, and she thought it such a pity he didn't have any of his own – he would make a great dad.

When Sadie started to yawn and Beatrice announced it was time to go, he insisted on walking them home, despite her protestations of it not being far.

As the girls trotted ahead, the adults followed at a more sedate pace. It felt surreal to Beatrice. How many times had she walked along this very street with him, their arms around each other's waists or holding hands? It was almost as though she'd gone back twenty years, and she had to stop herself reaching out to take his hand.

Beatrice shivered, but not from the cold. It was from a longing so intense that it stole her breath.

You can't turn back time, she told herself.

But it wasn't a longing for the girl she'd once been and the life she had yet to lead that was making her feel this way – it was *Mark*.

Sadie's giggle broke into her thoughts, and she brushed them away. It didn't do to dwell on the past and no good ever came of it. Anyway, it wasn't as though she could have changed anything. Even if she had told him she loved him, he still would have left, and she still would have been dumped. The only difference was that she would have had a generous dollop of humiliation to go with her heartbreak.

'I think they enjoyed themselves, judging by the amount of food they packed away,' she said, trying to rein in her wayward thoughts. 'Thank you for inviting us.'

'I did have an ulterior motive, if you remember.' His shoulder brushed against hers as he dodged around a lamp post with a flashing snowman at the top of it.

'I don't think Taya will allow me to forget. She was quite taken with your tablet.'

'There are cheaper options on the market, ones that will do roughly the same job,' he said quietly.

'That's good to know.'

'Do you want me to send you some links?'

'It wouldn't hurt to take a look,' she replied, thinking that Mark's version of cheap mightn't be the same as hers. Maybe if she and her parents clubbed together, they could buy Taya one between them?

Beatrice came to an awkward halt outside her house, wishing he hadn't insisted on walking her home. Even with the children present, it felt too much like a date, and she hoped he wasn't expecting to come in.

She said, 'I'd better get Sadie into her PJs. If I don't put her to bed, she'll be fit for nothing tomorrow.'

'Speaking of tomorrow, Dulcie has roped me into playing the Grinch again. I can't believe I let her do that.'

'Green suits you.'

'Why do I get the feeling that's not a compliment? See you at the farm tomorrow, Bea. Bye, girls.'

And with that he was off, striding back along the street, leaving Beatrice standing on her doorstep, wishing that she had asked him in after all.

The evening was still young so Mark had two options: sit in his room and watch TV, or return to the bar and people-watch. He chose the latter.

Perching on a stool, he ordered a pint and took out his mobile. After a bit of scrolling, he found what he was looking for and pinged off the promised links to Beatrice, then he leant against the counter and tried to marshal his thoughts.

He'd done what he'd set out to do in coming here; Picklewick had well and truly got his creative juices flowing, and although there was a great deal of flesh to be put on his new book, the bones of it were there. The artwork was rough and the story a ghost of what it would eventually be, but the hardest part, the premise – which was what he had been struggling with – was done.

He needn't stay in Picklewick any longer. He could return home, where it would be far more comfortable and much less expensive. Nothing was keeping him here, he had no reason to hang around.

However, an image of Beatrice flashed into his mind and it gave him pause. But only for a moment and then he pushed it away. Even if he did stand a chance with her, he wouldn't try. It wouldn't be fair on either of them. She was firmly rooted in Picklewick and he lived in Bristol.

He would keep his promise to Dulcie to play the Grinch tomorrow, then he'd head off home.

Decision made, he took a long draught of his beer, almost spilling it down himself when a woman bumped his elbow.

'Oops, sorry,' she began, then recognition flashed in her eyes and Mark realised he knew her. 'Mark

Stafford,' she said. 'Well I never! I'd heard you were in town.'

'Lisa Spencer, you haven't changed a bit.'

'Liar, but thank you anyway. And it's Lisa Edwards now.'

'How are you?'

'I've got three kids, a husband with a broken arm, two dogs, a hamster, and a full-time job, so I think 'frazzled' is a good description.'

'Wow! That's a handful. I still think of you as being, like, twenty. It's a shock to see you all grown up, a real responsible adult.'

'I'm faking it. I don't feel in the least bit responsible or adult. Bea and I were saying that very thing the other day. Now, there's a lady who *definitely* hasn't changed much, don't you think?'

'She hasn't,' he agreed. 'She hardly looks a day older than the last time I saw her.'

'Which was the day you dumped her.'

Ouch. 'It might have been. I honestly don't remember.'

'I do. So does Bea.'

Where was Lisa going with this? There had been a lifetime of water under that particular bridge.

'Why are you here, Mark?' she asked, and he frowned. It was none of her business.

She carried on, 'Bea told me that you're writing a book, but surely you can do that anywhere? It doesn't have to be in Picklewick.'

That was out of line, so he felt he could also be blunt. 'What's it to you?'

'I picked up the pieces last time. I don't want to see her hurt again.'

'What pieces? What do you mean?'

Her eyes widened and she bit her lip. 'Nothing. Ignore me. Honestly, I don't know what I'm talking about.'

He wasn't going to let it drop. 'Are you saying I hurt her? I didn't think she was that into me. I mean, we dated for a few months but we weren't in love, or anything.' Actually, maybe he had been – a little. But *she* hadn't.

'Ten months and three weeks,' Lisa shot back. 'And Bea *was* in love with you.'

Mark blew out his cheeks. 'I didn't know.' Bloody hell. Was Lisa telling the truth?'

'Would it have made any difference?' Lisa asked.

'No. Maybe.' He thought again. 'I honestly don't know. I was young, ambitious. Hungry.' Would love have been enough to keep him in Picklewick? He would never know.

Lisa said, 'What are you now? Are you still ambitious?'

'Not as much,' he admitted.

She pursed her lips. 'Look, forget I said anything. Bea will kill me if she found out I told you.'

'So why did you?'

She shrugged, as though she wasn't sure herself. 'She's been through a lot lately.'

'The ex-husband?'

Lisa nodded. 'He cheated on her – twice.'

Mark experienced a surge of anger on Beatrice's behalf. Beatrice was right, her ex *was* an arse. He said, 'I don't believe there's any chance of her being hurt again. I think she's well and truly over me by now, don't you?'

'Yes, you're right, of course she is. I'm being silly.'

'You're looking out for her, that's all. It's what good friends do. You two go back a long way.'

'We do.' She glanced over her shoulder. 'I'd better go. My husband will be wondering where I've got to. I only came to the bar for a packet of salt and vinegar crisps. Nice seeing you again, Mark.'

'You, too.' He noticed that she left without buying a packet. Had she decided she didn't want any after all? Or had the crisps merely been an excuse to speak to him?

He finished his pint and ordered another, and as he leant against the counter and sipped it, he thought about what Lisa said. If Beatrice had been in love with him and she had been hurt when he ended their relationship, it might explain her initial frostiness towards him, although she'd thawed somewhat since.

But why had Lisa felt the need to say anything now? It was ancient history.

Or was it?

Mark loved those moments of inspiration or insight when ideas sprang into his mind, whether they be for a story or an article. When he'd been a journalist, he used to be pretty good at joining the dots, at seeing connections. It was sometimes described as a lightbulb moment, and he was having one of those moments *right now*.

Beatrice hadn't just been in love with him back then – she still *was* in love with him. Or so Lisa believed. Mark wasn't entirely convinced he'd arrived at the correct conclusion, but if anyone knew Beatrice's heart, it would be Lisa.

She was warning him off because she didn't want Beatrice to be hurt again. And that could only happen if Beatrice still had feelings for him.

Mark straightened up in shock. This could change everything.

The mask wasn't the most pleasant thing to wear, and two hours was all Mark could manage in one go. Thankfully he didn't have to play the Grinch for longer than that, as Dulcie was taking over from him as soon as she was done decorating pinecones.

She arrived, flustered but looking happy, wearing her elf outfit and carrying another Grinch costume in a bag. 'The one you're wearing is too big for me,' she explained, pulling it out and stepping into it.

Mark took his mask off with relief. 'That's better. I can breathe again.' He held it aloft. 'What do you want me to do with it?'

'Can you turn it inside out and pop it in the bag? I'll clean it later, before the next poor sod has to wear it. I'm beginning to think I should have plumped for a regular Santa Claus costume, but the Grinch seemed like a good idea at the time.'

'He appears to be quite popular,' Mark said. 'The children love him.'

Dulcie beamed widely before putting on her own mask. 'They do, don't they? Right, time to get into character. Thanks again for helping out, and don't forget I owe you a meal at The Wild Side.'

Mark hadn't forgotten.

He left Dulcie to it and strolled across the yard, drawn towards "Otto's Christmas Kitchen" as the food area was called, by the tantalising smells issuing from it and his rumbling tummy.

The doors were open and framed by thick garlands which were dotted with red ribbons and gold-painted pinecones. Inside was equally as festive, with centrepieces of twinkling lanterns surrounded by a woven ring of holly and ivy on each of the picnic benches. Mark had come to expect fairy lights, and he wasn't disappointed because they were everywhere, strung from the rafters and draped around hay bales, and there was yet another Christmas tree just inside the door. The red and green plaid blankets were a lovely touch.

Dulcie had thought of everything.

Mark queued for a bowl of pumpkin soup topped with roasted chorizo, and a hunk of sourdough bread, and devoured it quickly. It was so good that he briefly considered going for seconds, but that would be greedy. Licking his fingers, he scrunched up the paper napkin and popped it in the bin, then blew out his cheeks.

As he was plucking up the courage to go see Beatrice to ask if she would have dinner at The Wild Side with him, he noticed a woman staring.

She smiled and walked towards him. 'Are you Mark Stafford? I'm Grace Daley.' She thrust out a hand. 'I'm a reporter with The Picklewick Paper.'

'Gosh! Is that still going?' He'd forgotten about that. Taking her hand, he shook it.

'It is, although we've had to change with the times. May I ask you a few questions?'

'It depends on what they are,' he replied warily. Reporters, as he was all too aware, needed to be treated with the same degree of caution as a microphone – always assume that anything you said could potentially appear in a tabloid somewhere, or in the case of a mic, be broadcast to all and sundry.

'Nothing controversial,' she assured him. 'Just about your books, where you get your inspiration, what you're working on now... That kind of thing. Can I buy you a coffee?'

Mark was used to interviews, having done several over the years and, as his agent kept stressing to him, getting his name out there was part and parcel of being an author. 'Books don't publicise themselves,' she was fond of saying.

'How about I buy *you* one?' he suggested, guiding her towards a free picnic table. 'They do some incredibly festive flavours.'

She chose a chestnut praline latte and although he was tempted by the chestnut syrup, whipped cream and caramel drizzle (it smelled divine), he opted for an orange espresso spiced with cinnamon, cloves and nutmeg.

When they had their drinks, Grace proceeded to ask him all the usual sorts of questions that he'd come to expect, and he answered them readily enough, even the ones about growing up in Picklewick, which were a little more personal than he liked. He tended not to respond to those, deeming that his private life should be, well, *private*.

But as they were about to wrap it up, the reporter asked a question that Mark didn't find as easy to answer, when she said, 'Where next after Picklewick?'

'Home,' he replied automatically.

But as the word passed his lips, he wondered where 'home' was, because for some reason Bristol no longer felt like it.

Beatrice was surprised to see him, and Mark wondered whether she'd forgotten he would be at the farm today.

She sent him a little smile, before turning her attention back to the customer she was serving, and while Mark waited for her to finish, he explored the shop. It wasn't very big, but it had a variety of items for sale, from foodstuff to soaps and candles. He was sorely tempted to buy a carton of that wonderful pumpkin soup, and if he had a way of reheating it, he would have done.

The place seemed to be doing a roaring trade and as more customers piled in, he wondered whether he would get a chance to speak to Beatrice in private.

Should he message her instead? If he did, the rejection he would invariably receive might be easier to deal with if she wasn't watching his face while she said it. Conversely though, she might be less inclined to say no if she *did* see his face, and by springing it on her now, she mightn't have a chance to think of an excuse.

It wasn't that he was desperate to take her out for a meal, but he *was* desperate to talk to her on her own, so doing it over a meal in a posh restaurant was better than having a drink in The Black Horse where every man and his dog might overhear.

Mark lingered for a while, picking things up and putting them down, and every so often when she'd finished serving one customer and before she started on the next, he'd try to have a conversation with her.

After several unsuccessful attempts, he realised that the only way he was going to speak to her was if he bought something, and even then he'd probably have to talk fast.

Mark looked longingly at the soup again, before picking up a gift box of handmade soaps. They looked like slices of cake, almost good enough to eat, and smelled lovely.

He took it to the counter. 'I thought my mother would like it,' he said, somewhat defensively in case she thought he was buying it for himself.

'Would you like it gift wrapped?'

'Yes, please.' Gift wrapping wouldn't take long, but he might need the additional time that the service would provide.

As she selected a length of pre-cut wrapping paper, he said, 'Dulcie isn't happy with me.'

She glanced up. 'Why is that?'

'I refused to take any payment for playing the Grinch.'

'That's kind of you.' She was frowning, and he hoped she didn't think he was telling her this just to show her what a nice guy he was.

'She feels really bad about it,' he added, watching her expertly fold the paper around the box. 'So I ended up accepting an offer of a meal in The Wild Side instead.'

'I've heard it's nice.' She used little gold stickers to keep the paper folds in place and reached for a ball of red string.

'You've not eaten there?'

She shook her head.

'The thing is,' he continued, 'I don't fancy going on my own. The meal is for two, so would you like to come with me?'

Beatrice was in the middle of tying the string into a bow, and she didn't look up.

He explained, 'I'm not going to go on my own. It's one thing eating a meal in The Black Horse on my tod, but in a posh place like The Wild Side, I'll look a real saddo.'

She popped the gift-wrapped parcel into a paper bag with the words Lilac Tree Farm written on it.

Mark held up his credit card, ready to pay. 'If you don't say yes, I'll tell Dulcie it's your fault that I won't be taking her up on her offer, and she can be cross with you instead.'

The look Beatrice gave him could have frozen mercury. 'When?'

'Whenever suits you.'

She rang his purchase up and handed him a receipt. 'I'll have to see if I can get a babysitter. Maybe Lisa could do it. You remember Lisa? We were best mates. We still are.'

He remembered Lisa all too well. 'What about your mum and dad?' he asked hurriedly. After his conversation with her last night, it might be better if Lisa didn't know about this – although he suspected she would get to hear of it at some point, whether Beatrice told her or via the local gossip mongers. But he hoped it would be after the meal, and not before it.

'I'll let you know,' she said, her attention already turning to the next customer. 'Thanks for the links, by the way.'

'Glad to help.' He smiled, but she didn't see it, and he left thinking that he mightn't hear from her again, or if he did it would be to tell him that she couldn't get a babysitter or that she'd changed her mind.

But he *did* hear from her, and when she suggested Tuesday, a huge grin spread across his face.

CHAPTER SIX

On Monday morning, Beatrice had her head in her wardrobe and was scrabbling around inside it hunting for her comfiest pair of jeans to wear to work, when Sadie appeared at her side.

'Mummy, I feel sick and I've got a tummy ache.' The plaintive note in her daughter's voice tugged at Beatrice's heartstrings.

Sadie's complaints of feeling sick were becoming a daily occurrence, usually when Beatrice was nagging the girls to get ready for school. She was beginning to fear that Sadie disliked school and was saying she felt ill in order to get out of going. However, she'd read somewhere that in young children mental distress could cause actual physical symptoms, so she wasn't about to accuse Sadie of making it up.

Sadie had loved nursery and she seemed to have settled into full-time school, but gradually, over the last few weeks – since October half term, in fact – she'd started to mention not feeling well. The usual culprits were feeling sick, and/or pain in her tummy. The symptoms didn't last long though, and Sadie more often than not perked up considerably by the time she arrived at school.

To Beatrice, it seemed as though Sadie disliked the *thought* of going to school, but didn't mind it when she was actually *there*.

Beatrice could sympathise with that. She used to feel the same about the exercise classes which she used to force herself to attend in the hope of staying slim and keeping fit. Maybe having a week off school at half term had disrupted Sadie and had made her decide she preferred being at home. Or perhaps something had happened at school that had upset her?

Beatrice crouched down beside her daughter, ignoring the nagging voice in her head reminding her that they were going to be late for school if she didn't get a move on. 'Where does it hurt?'

Sadie put a hand over her belly button. 'Here.'

'How sick do you feel?'

'Very.'

'Too sick to eat a biscuit?'

Sadie nodded.

Beatrice held out her arms and Sadie cuddled into her, saying, 'I won't be too sick for a biscuit in a minute.'

'Is that right?'

'Uh-huh. Has a minute passed yet?'

'No. How about you put your shoes on? That'll take a minute.' Beatrice didn't usually allow the girls biscuits this early in the day, but she was trying to gauge just how real the sicky tummy ache was.

'Do I have to go to school, Mummy? Can't I stay here with you?' Sadie asked, her face buried in Beatrice's neck. 'I promise I'll be good.'

'I won't be here, sweetie. I've got a job, remember? All the time you are in school, Mummy will be working in the shop at the farm.'

'I don't want you to.'

Bingo! *That* was it! It wasn't the change in routine brought about by the half term break that was the issue, it was Beatrice's new job. Maybe Sadie starting primary school and Beatrice going out to work for the first time in Sadie's young life, was proving to be too much too soon for her little daughter.

Reassured that there wasn't anything more serious troubling her child, and knowing that Sadie would soon get used to this new routine, Beatrice gave her a squeeze and stood up. 'Go put your shoes on and I'll get you a biscuit.'

'A Party Ring?' Sadie asked hopefully.

Beatrice had been thinking more along the lines of a plain Rich Tea, not a biscuit covered in lurid-coloured icing sugar.

'Don't push your luck,' she told her, relieved when Sadie bounced out of the bedroom, her tummy ache clearly gone.

Beatrice went back to her hunt for her jeans, and as she did so her attention was caught by the dress she'd bought in the sales last January and had never worn. Should she wear it to dinner with Mark? Black, figure-hugging to a certain degree, but not too much, and covered in a layer of black lace dotted with the occasional tiny diamante beads, it was both partyish and sophisticated – a typical LBD. But was it too over-the-top for a quiet dinner in a small restaurant with a man she shouldn't feel the need to impress?

This was *not* a date. She was doing him a favour and getting to enjoy a nice meal at the same time. As long as she didn't look like she'd just been cleaning out the chicken coop on the farm, did it matter what she wore? Mark wouldn't notice. So why did she feel this need to look her best?

'Mummy, I want my biscuit!' Sadie called, and Beatrice sighed.

She sighed again when Taya cried, 'Why does *she* get a biscuit and I don't? That's not fair!'

Grabbing the first pair of jeans she laid her hands on, Beatrice yanked them on, then went downstairs to distribute the biscuits before she had a full-blown mutiny on her hands.

'Mr Stafford? Mr Stafford!'

Mark halted in the middle of the pavement and glanced around. A plump middle-aged woman wearing a multicoloured voluminous coat and a pink knitted hat was waving frantically at him from the opposite side of the high street.

Mark had no idea who she was.

She darted across the road, and he winced when a car screeched to a halt as she stepped out in front of it. It missed her by a hair.

'It *is* Mark Stafford, isn't it?' she panted as she hurried towards him.

'It is,' he confirmed.

'Thank god. I'd feel awful accosting a total stranger.'

He didn't like to point out she was doing precisely that. 'Can I help you?'

'Oh, I do so hope you can. My class would love you.'

'I've already visited the school,' he said. Maybe she'd been off sick or on a course and had missed it.

'I know, that's why I wanted to talk to you. I hear you're a very amenable chap, very generous with your time.' She was trying to butter him up.

He said nothing and waited for her to continue, a polite smile on his face.

'I'm Melanie Parker and I run an art class at the community centre. We do all kinds, from watercolour to acrylic, landscapes to nudes, although it's probably best not to mention that, ha ha. Would you be kind enough to give a talk? A demonstration would be even better. I understand you do all your own illustrations.'

'I do, but I'm primarily a digital artist.'

'That's what I'd like you to talk about.' She leant in and lowered her voice. 'Some of them can't paint for toffee, bless them, so I was hoping they'd do better with an app.'

'Admittedly, it's a different skill set,' he replied, his voice guarded. App or not, he still had to draw the image, he still painted it: the only difference was the medium. Instead of paint and paper, he used a stylus and a screen. And he often perfected the initial drawing on paper first.

'I'm sure my students would be fascinated. They'll be interested to learn how you put a picture together.'

Mark wasn't sure what to say. He was used to giving interviews and talking about his books, and was used to going into schools and reading to the children. But this was the first time he had been asked to demonstrate the illustration side of his books.

He said, 'I'm not sure how it would work. I'd need an internet connection and an interactive whiteboard, so I can share my screen.'

Melanie Parker beamed at him. 'I'm sure we can cobble something together. Can you do tomorrow? We meet every Tuesday at two p.m. in the community centre. I'll be there from one thirty, setting up. Thanks ever so much. Toodle-oo.'

And that was how Mark Stafford, successful children's author, found himself trying to explain the ins and outs of digital art to a group of pensioners who thought the term 'graphic art' meant drawing people with no clothes on and appeared to be quite put out when they discovered it wasn't.

The coffee was mud-coloured and had a plasticky taste, but the Jammie Dodgers were nice. As biscuits went, it was one of his favourites. Mark helped himself to two.

Melanie said, 'I think that went well, don't you?'

'I'm not sure I've converted anyone.'

She laughed. 'Possibly not. The older you get, the more stuck in your ways you become. This lot – me included – grew up believing that drawing and painting involved pencils and paints. One or two might give it a go, though. But even so, I don't think I'm going to be out of a job any time soon. It's the next generation I worry about. Everything is electronic and digital these days – they won't know what a paintbrush is. Not when it comes to art. Houses still need to be painted. Although I wouldn't be surprised if somebody somewhere doesn't invent a way to digitally change the colour of your sitting room walls. Anyway, like I said, I think my students found it interesting. And thank you for signing my grandson's copy of *The Elephant Who Forgot*. I love the way all your books have a message. I think that's why they're so popular.' She paused for breath, and Mark took a deep one of his own.

Melanie was lovely, but she couldn't half talk!

She was off again. 'How is the new one coming along? I heard you'd come to Picklewick for a bit of peace and quiet to write it. I bet you haven't found the village as quiet as you'd like if that's the case, what with dressing up as the Grinch at the farm, visiting the school and now this.' She chuckled. 'I wonder what you'll get up to next? Helping with the nativity play at the stables? They have one every Christmas, you know. The old people love it.'

'Old people?' He had a worrying vision of a group of OAPs on horseback.

'Yes, the kids at the stables put on a play and the residents of Honeymead Care Home go every year to watch – the ones that can manage it, that is. They have a lovely time. And the ones that can't, are shown it via the internet, on the TV. The staff are ever so good. I should know because my mother is in there. Dementia. So sad. That's why *The Elephant Who Forgot* is so special. It helps Joey, that's my grandson, understand why his Gan-Gan doesn't know who he is sometimes.'

Mark smiled. 'Glad it's of help.' He hoped his next book would be as useful. They weren't just for entertainment: he wanted to help educate young minds, too.

'How are you enjoying being back in Picklewick?' she asked. 'I understand you grew up here. From what I can gather, it hasn't changed much. Mind you, villages like this don't, do they? That's their charm. I used to live in Thornbury, but I moved here a couple of years ago when I retired. You wouldn't believe it, but I'm busier now than I was when I was working. I've always loved art. Would have liked to do it full-time but it didn't pay the bills. Now I've retired, I can paint all day if I want. Apart from Tuesday afternoons, when I run this art class, and Mondays when I—'

'I'm sorry to interrupt but I've got to get back. A call with my editor.' Mark was fibbing, and he felt bad about that, especially when Melanie was so nice about it.

'Of course, I mustn't keep you. You're a busy man and you've been so generous with your time. Thank you, again.' She clasped her hands over her heart. 'We really appreciate it.'

Despite Melanie chewing his ear off at the end, Mark found he'd enjoyed giving the demonstration. They had been an enthusiastic and interested group, and had made him feel very welcome.

In fact, everyone he'd met in the village had been friendly and welcoming. He was beginning to wonder why he'd ever left!

Why was she so nervous? This was ridiculous. It was only a meal.

'You look nice, Mummy.'

'Thank you, sweetie.' Beatrice glanced at Sadie through the mirror and smiled.

'Are you going out with Aunty Lisa?'

'No, with Mark, the man who writes the books, the one who we had a meal with on Friday.'

'Is he your boyfriend?'

'No!' Realising she'd said that rather sharply, she smiled at her daughter again. 'He's not my boyfriend. I'm doing him a favour, that's all.'

'What kind of favour?'

'I'm having a meal with him in The Wild Side, that nice restaurant on the high street, because he doesn't want to eat dinner on his own.'

'Is he lonely?'

'Maybe.' Beatrice hadn't considered that.

'Doesn't he have any friends?'

'Not in Picklewick.'

'*We* can be his friends. He can eat dinner here, then he wouldn't have to eat on his own.'

'I don't think so.'

'Why not? Doesn't he like us?'

'He likes us fine. Get into your pyjamas before Nana and Grandad arrive.'

Her mother had raised her eyebrows when Beatrice told her the reason she was asking her to babysit. 'Is there something going on I should know about?' Deborah had asked.

'Definitely not,' Beatrice had replied, then went on to explain why she was going out to dinner with him, and that it was purely platonic.

Her mum hadn't been entirely convinced. But why should she be, when Beatrice wasn't entirely convinced herself? Her feelings for Mark Stafford hadn't been platonic back then, and they weren't platonic now.

She put the finishing touches to her make-up and sat back to check her appearance. She couldn't do anything about the fine lines around her eyes (whatever claims they made, no creams were able to reverse the effects of aging) but she looked okay. She'd done her best, and she just had to accept that she wasn't twenty anymore. Or even thirty. She'd be happy with thirty. Thirty wasn't even halfway. Forty, on the other hand, could very well be.

She'd already laid out her dress, and she shimmied into it, contorting herself into odd shapes as she struggled to do up the zip. With the addition of a clutch bag and a pair of heels, she was ready.

Hearing her parents let themselves in and Sadie's excited voice, she hurried downstairs, hanging onto the handrail, worried she might fall. Maybe she should change into her boots? The heel wasn't as high, but they didn't really go with the dress.

'Hello, darling, you look nice,' Deborah said, scanning her from head to toe.

'I said that!' Sadie cried.

'Thanks, Mum.' Beatrice turned to Sadie. 'Where's your sister?'

'Here.' Taya was slouching against the living room wall. She didn't look happy. Beatrice wanted to ask her what was wrong, but she didn't have time because the doorbell rang.

Mark was here.

Her heart leapt, missed a beat, then thudded as it caught up with itself, catching her by surprise and she coughed to cover it.

Lifting her coat off the hook in the hall, she hurried to open the door. Sadie was right behind her, and the child managed to squirm through it before it was fully open.

'Would you like to see my toadstool costume?' she cried, launching herself at Mark.

Mark gave her a hug, his eyes meeting Beatrice's. She shook her head. 'Your mum and I will be late if we don't get a move on. Another time,' he said.

'Promise?'

'I promise.'

'Anyway,' Deborah piped up, 'it's not finished yet, young lady.' She was gazing curiously at Mark.

Beatrice sighed. 'Mark, you remember my mum and dad?' Her dad was hovering in the background.

'I do. Nice to see you again.'

Deborah said, 'You too, Mark. How are your parents? Well, I hope?'

Beatrice stepped in, saying, 'We've got to go,' and she ushered him away from the door. 'Bye, girls. Bye Mum, Dad. I won't be late.' She pulled the door shut behind her and blew out her cheeks, wishing she had arranged to meet him at the restaurant.

They fell into step, their breath clouding in the cold air, and Beatrice hunted around for something to say. 'How did the art class go?'

He glanced at her. 'You heard?'

'It's all over the village.'

'Oh, god. Nothing bad, I hope?'

'The class loved it, but did *you?*'

'I did, actually. I've never really thought about the process before – not consciously – so I think I learnt something too.'

'Melanie is a hoot, isn't she? She's been singing your praises.'

'She's lovely.' He glanced at her again. 'So are you. I mean, you look lovely. Very nice.'

Beatrice spluttered and began to laugh. 'Very *nice?*'

'Beautiful. You look beautiful.'

'Okay, there's no need to overdo it.'

'I mean it. You do. You always did.'

What the hell was she supposed to say to that? She blushed furiously, and it made her cross. He wasn't supposed to compliment her: this wasn't how this evening was supposed to work.

They walked along the high street in silence, Beatrice feeling embarrassed. Mark didn't appear at all bothered. She concentrated on the festive displays in the windows and the lights twinkling overhead, and told herself that he was just being friendly. She also told herself that even if he wasn't, he would be gone before Christmas, his time in Picklewick fleeting.

Then she told herself for the second time that he was just being friendly.

Arriving at the restaurant, Mark held the door open for her. 'After you.'

She smiled politely and stepped inside, the warmth making her cheeks glow.

Otto came forward to greet them. He was wearing chef's whites, and Beatrice hoped their arrival hadn't taken him away from his kitchen duties.

'If you're out here, who is in there?' she asked, after he'd shown them to a table.

'Actually, I was hoping Mark could give us a hand,' Otto replied with a chuckle. 'The Wild Side appears to be the only place that hasn't nabbed him for one thing or another. I bet you never thought you'd end up being a Grinch?'

Mark shook his head. 'No, I didn't, and I can't believe I did it *twice*. Please don't tell me Dulcie is short-handed again?' he pleaded.

'Relax, you're safe. Let's get your drinks sorted and I'll send your server over with the menu. Enjoy your meal.'

'Thanks, I'm sure we will,' Beatrice said. She opened the menu and kept her eyes firmly on it. Everything sounded delicious, but she was having difficulty focusing. Her mind was stubbornly on the man sitting opposite. Did he really think she was beautiful, or had he just been saying that?

When their server arrived to take their order, Beatrice picked the first thing her eyes landed on. She was sure it would be delicious. Whatever it was.

With the menus whisked away and the starters yet to arrive, Beatrice was once again left with no idea what to say.

Luckily, Mark did – although after a while she began to wish he'd kept his mouth shut.

It began innocently enough. 'Being back in Picklewick, is like I've never left. I can't believe where all those years have gone,' he said.

'Me, neither. They've flown by.'

'Whenever I thought about the people I knew, Lisa, *you…*' He lingered on the word. 'I always thought of you as the way you were back then.'

'Sorry to disappoint,' she quipped, her heart fluttering.

'You don't disappoint. You never did.'

'You dumped me!' Oh, hell. Why was she bringing this up? What an idiotic thing to say.

'I did.' His voice was gentle. Regretful? Surely not. 'I hurt you,' he added, gazing at her intently.

Beatrice looked down and fiddled with the stem of her glass. 'Nah, it was fine. *I* was fine. I think. I can't really remember.'

'I think you can.'

'No, honestly, I can't. *Obviously* I remember you dumping me, but I don't remember how I felt.'

'Yeah, you do.'

'Are you on some kind of ego trip? Like, do you think that you're the one who got away, and I've been pining for you ever since? I'll have you know I've got two kids. They have a father. I slept with him. Twice. More than twice. A lot. So I haven't been pining for you.' She became aware that the gentle hum of conversation in the room had dimmed considerably. Oh god, had everyone heard?

'He was an arse,' Mark reminded her.

'I loved him.'

'But he turned into an arse. You said so yourself.'

'So were you.'

'I was not!' Mark looked affronted. 'Just because I ended our relationship doesn't mean I was an arse.'

Beatrice gritted her teeth. 'What are you playing at, Mark?'

'I'm not playing at anything.'

'Okay, I'll try again. Why are we here? You could have eaten here on your own – or not dined here at all. Dulcie wouldn't have minded. Why were you so insistent that I accompany you?'

'I wanted to talk to you, on your own.'

'What about?'

He huffed, and ran his hand through his hair, muttering, 'I don't know anymore.'

'I'll ask again; what are you playing at?'

'Bea, I—' He pulled a face. 'I don't know how it happened, but you've got under my skin.'

'Is that right?' Pull the other one, she wanted to add, but was interrupted by her starter being placed in front of her.

'Parmesan?' the server offered.

'Not for me, thanks.'

'Sir?'

'No. Thank you.' He stared at his food but made no move to eat it, his fork lying untouched. When the server moved away, he said, 'We were very young. Barely more than kids.'

'So?'

He shrugged, lifting one shoulder. 'We weren't ready for anything heavy.'

'*You* weren't.'

'No…' He chewed on his lip. 'I did care for you, Bea. More than you realised.'

'You had a strange way of showing it.'

'I didn't think you were into me as much as I was into you.'

Beatrice snorted. 'We spent ten months in each other's pockets. We were bloody inseparable. I'm surprised you didn't enlist the help of a surgeon to cut us apart. How could you not think I wasn't,' she quoted with her fingers, '*into you?*'

'And three weeks.'

'Excuse me?'

'Ten months and three weeks.'

That took the wind out of her sails. 'How—?' she began. 'You kept *count?*'

He shrugged again, looking away.

Could she have got it wrong? Had he ended the relationship because he'd thought she didn't care? Confusion pulsed through her, beating in time with her heart, rushing along her veins.

However, she refused to let it show.

'Why are we even discussing this?' she persisted. What was the point? The past was done and dusted. Whatever they once had, or might have had, was over. Long gone.

'Because since I've been back in Picklewick, I can't get you out of my mind.'

'But you... This can't... 'she stammered, then tried again. 'You're leaving soon.' She squeezed her eyes shut, opening them slowly.

'I can stay for as long as I want. As long as *you* want.'

Incredulous, she said, 'You're serious.'

'Do you ever wonder what would have happened if we'd stayed together?'

'Yes,' she breathed.

'Is everything alright with your meals?'

Beatrice jumped. 'Um, yes, fine, thanks.' She had yet to taste a single morsel.

Mark waited until the server was out of earshot. 'Shall we start afresh, see where it takes us? No promises, no recriminations.'

'I knew it,' she muttered.

'Knew what?'

'That this was a date. I thought you said it wasn't?'

'Do you want it to be?'

'Do *you?*' she countered.

'I do. Very much. Can I kiss you at the end of it?'

'Don't push your luck, buster,' Beatrice growled, but inside she was singing. This could be the start of something wonderful – for the second time.

Beatrice clung to Mark's arm, giggling as she tried to get the words out. Walking whilst laughing fit to burst wasn't easy, especially in these heels, even with him propping her up.

'What about that time…?' she began, then doubled over, tears running down her face.

Mark was laughing too, but she had a feeling he was laughing because *she* was. 'What time?' he asked.

'You know, when you— Oh god, I'm going to wet myself.'

'Please don't. You'll ruin your shoes.'

Beatrice crossed her legs, wheezing as she tried to breathe through her laughter. 'Stop, you've got to stop. I can't take any more.'

She blamed her state of silliness on the wine. Since having the kids she'd become a lightweight. Two glasses and she was anyone's.

They had begun reminiscing during the main course, and by the time they'd finished their coffees and were heading out of the door, they'd been laughing hysterically. It was a wonder Otto hadn't thrown them out: trust her to bring down the tone of the place.

And now she looked like a drunk who needed help to get home. Thankfully there weren't too many people strolling along Picklewick's high street this evening to witness her debauchery.

Gradually she regained control and straightened up, uncrossing her legs. The control was fragile though, and she was likely to lose it at any moment. She could feel the giggles bubbling away beneath the surface, waiting for a chink in her armour to explode into hysterical life again.

'I must look a mess,' she said, dabbing at the skin underneath her eyes with the pad of her ring finger. The mascara was probably all down her face by now, and she bet her nose was red.

'We used to have fun, didn't we?' Mark said softly.

'We did....'

'We still could.'

Her eyes flew to his face. He wasn't joking. His expression was serious.

He said, 'I meant it when I said we could start again.'

'I know.' She didn't. Not for certain. But she wanted to believe him.

He held her gaze. The atmosphere had abruptly changed. It was charged, electric, like the air before a storm. She couldn't breathe. He was close, coming closer, his eyes filling her vision, his breath warm on her face.

And then he kissed her.

CHAPTER SEVEN

Beatrice's eyes flew open. One second she'd been fast asleep, the next she was totally and utterly awake. *What had she done?*

'It was a kiss, just a kiss,' she muttered, but the dream she'd just woken from had been so much more.

Oh, boy…

Hot and flustered, she pushed the covers back and got out of bed, the soft darkness hiding her flaming cheeks. A cold shower might be in order before she woke the girls.

Padding quietly into the bathroom, she pulled the light cord and winced as she caught sight of herself in the mirror. From the glow on her face and the sparkle in her eyes, she looked like she'd done far more than kiss Mark. And in her dreams, she *had*.

She hoped she hadn't looked like this when she'd got in last night, because if so, her mother would be asking questions. Ones that Beatrice didn't have any answers to.

Despite her intention to have a cold shower, Beatrice wimped out and turned the dial up. It was bloody freezing in here: the temperature had dropped overnight and she'd forgotten to set the heating to come on, and as she waited for the water to warm up, she asked herself again, what had she done?

Filled with equal measures of dismay and excitement, she couldn't decide whether she'd been incredibly stupid or incredibly adventurous.

Maybe Lisa could enlighten her?

Shivering, Beatrice hurried to the bedroom to fetch her phone, the steamy warmth of the bathroom a welcome reprieve from the chill when she returned.

'Are you up?' she asked, when Lisa's sleepy voice answered.

'What time is it?'

'Hang on, I'm putting you on speaker.'

'What's that noise?'

She stepped into the shower, the hot water cascading over her head, the thought of a cold one long gone. 'I'm in the shower. It's six-thirty-five.'

'Why are you phoning me at half past six in the morn—? *Mark!* Did something happen?'

'I woke you, didn't I?'

'Yes, but I have to be up in ten minutes anyway, to get the kids ready for school. Go back to sleep Robin, it's only Bea,' she said to her husband, then to Beatrice, 'What happened last night?'

'Mark kissed me.'

'Bloody hell, Bea!'

'I *know*.' She lathered her hair, her eyes tight shut. 'He said I've got under his skin, and he wants us to start again.'

'Do you believe him? I don't want to rain on your parade, but he hurt you badly once before.'

'I think I do.'

'What are you going to do?'

'Give it another go.' She rinsed the suds out of her hair and reached for the conditioner. 'If I don't, I'll always wonder *what if.*'

'Just be careful.'

'I'll try. But Lisa?'

'Yeah?'

'I think it's too late for that.'

'That's what worries me,' Lisa said, before hanging up.

It worried Beatrice, too.

'You look like something the cat's dragged in,' Dave told Mark as he put a plate of bacon and scrambled eggs down in front of him.

'Thanks! That makes me feel a whole lot better.'

'Didn't you sleep well?'

'I didn't sleep at all.'

'Nothing wrong, I hope?'

'Not at all.'

'Is your room too cold? The temperature's dropped and there's an Arctic blast on the way. They reckon we're in for some snow. It's too early for snow, if you ask me. We don't usually get any this side of Christmas.'

'No, we don't,' Mark agreed.

Dave harrumphed. 'I keep forgetting you're from around here originally. Anyway, is your room warm enough?'

'It's fine, thanks.'

'You don't need a blanket?'

'No, honestly, I'm fine.' Mark realised that Dave wasn't going to leave him alone to enjoy his breakfast until he'd explained why he hadn't slept. 'I was working,' he said.

'All night?'

'It happens like that sometimes.' He'd been on a roll, finalising the drafts for the illustrations ready to send to his agent, and he'd also completed the cover art. After breakfast he intended to email everything off to Angela, and then he was going to have a well-earned nap.

Satisfied with Mark's reason for his sleepless night, Dave sloped off, leaving him free to reflect on the real reason he hadn't been able to sleep.

Beatrice.

My god, that kiss! It had blown him away.

Had her kisses been as wonderful all those years ago? He had a feeling they may have been, but he'd simply been too much of an idiot to realise it at the time. His lips still tingled, he could still taste her, smell her...

Every time he thought about her, it knocked the breath right out of him, and his heart stuttered before finding its rhythm again.

He felt more alive than he'd ever felt, every colour brighter, every sound more vivid. It was as though he'd been in a fog all these years but it had now cleared. And if he felt like this after just one kiss...?

Leaving the bacon and eggs to grow cold on the plate, he pushed his chair away from the table. Can't sleep, can't eat – he was a walking cliché.

Take it slow, he told himself as he climbed the stairs to his room. He and Beatrice needed time to get to know one another again, because neither were the same people they had been half a lifetime ago.

But, by god, was he looking forward to it!

The shrill ringing of his phone woke him, and Mark reached for it, blinking owlishly. 'Yeah?' he muttered, rubbing his free hand over his face.

'Is that any way to greet your favourite agent?'

He sat up, shuffling up the mattress so his back rested against the headboard. 'Angela.'

'You don't sound very happy. Is anything wrong?'

'What time is it?'

'You worked all night, didn't you?'

'Guilty as charged.'

'It's not good for you.'

'What are you – my mother?'

'I'm the woman who has just this second heard back from Estelle. She's thrilled with your new manuscript. So am I. The artwork for the cover is stunning. I defy any little boy or girl not to love it. Santa Paws,' she chuckled. 'She says there's talk at Pinkymoon of a cuddly toy franchise. They want a meeting.'

'For Santa Paws plushies?'

'Exactly! They've got to move fast, because of the design and the manufacturer's lead times. They want to do a special boxed edition: a book and cuddly toy. It'll make a fantastic Christmas present. Oh, and Estelle wants to have a chat about the possibility of more in the series.'

'More Santa Paws books?'

'No, the other characters. The market for Santa Paws is limited to Christmas, so can you change the focus? The main character could be—'

'Hang on,' Mark interrupted. 'You want me to change the whole story?'

'Not exactly. Just the focus. Take it off Santa Paws and put it on one of the other characters. Santa Paws works as a Christmas release, but if we run with the series idea, then—'

'Can I think about it?' For Pete's sake, it had taken him long enough to come up with *this* story, let alone change it now. 'How many books are they thinking of?'

'That's what we'll need to thrash out. I've gone ahead and set up a meeting for Friday. Does that sound good to you?'

Not really, he thought. 'So, to summarise, Pinkymoon Publishing loves my book but they want me to change the story and the main character?'

'In a nutshell.'

'And we're meeting with them on Friday?'

'That's right. I trust you can make it?'

'I'll be there.' There was more than a hint of resignation in his voice.

'Fabulous. I know it's short notice but you're only an hour and a half by train.'

'I'm not in Bristol.'

'Where are you?'

'A little place called Picklewick.'

'Picklewick… Picklewick…? Where have I heard that name before?'

'On my author bio. It's where I grew up.'

'I thought your parents lived in Bath?'

'They do.'

'So what are you doing in Picklewick?'

Falling in love, that's what he was doing. And he didn't know whether it was wonderful or terrifying.

Beatrice was making a casserole for tea. She'd ummed and ahhed over what to cook, wondering whether to stick to what she was good at (and what the kids would eat) or whether to pull out all the stops and make something fancy. She'd ended up deciding to play it down. This was Mark, a man who'd been known to eat baked beans out of a tin, and cold pizza left over from the evening before.

He might be a hot-shot children's author, but he was still the same bloke she once knew. She hoped. Anyway, he had two choices – like it or go hungry.

Beatrice was beginning to wish she hadn't given in to Sadie's insistence that she ask Mark to tea this evening, but at least if he saw first-hand the chaos that was her daily life, it would make him realise what he was letting himself in for, if he *was* serious about wanting them to start over. After this evening, he may well change his mind. It was one thing knowing that she and her children came as a job lot: it was quite another seeing it in action.

As Beatrice tidied up the kitchen, the most recent copy of The Picklewick Paper caught her eye. Her mum had brought it with her when she'd babysat on Tuesday and had forgotten to take it home. Or had she left it on purpose, because it had a piece about Mark in it?

Beatrice had read the article twice, and the part she kept going back to was the bit where Mark had said he would be going home after Picklewick. She knew his home was in Bristol, but what she didn't know was how long he intended to stay in Picklewick. And when he did leave – which he must – what would that mean for any future they might have?

Right now, Beatrice wasn't sure of anything, despite what Mark had said, despite the way he'd kissed her. She supposed she would just have to take it slow, and try not to get in too deep, too soon.

When the doorbell rang, even though she was expecting it, she jumped. 'Can you get that, please, Taya?'

'I'll go!' Sadie yelled, charging to the door before her sister could respond.

'Mark!' Beatrice heard Sadie squeal, then she heard him say something in return, but she couldn't make out the words.

When he entered the kitchen, he had a small child hanging onto him for dear life.

'Sadie, leave Mark alone, he doesn't need you clambering all over him. Taya, can you lay the table, please?'

'Why do *I* have to do it?'

'Taya…' The hint of warning in Beatrice's voice was enough to persuade her daughter to do as she was asked, but wasn't enough to wipe the sulky look off her face. Honestly, Taya was getting more teenagerish by the day. Goodness knows what she would be like when she actually *was* one. Beatrice dreaded to think.

Taya didn't perk up much throughout the meal, but Sadie was lively enough for them both. She didn't stop talking.

Right now, she was in the middle of telling Mark all about the toadstool costume that her nana was making for her. 'It's got sequins, and glittery thread, and it sparkles. I like sparkles.'

Beatrice laughed. 'I never would have guessed. This child should be called Princess Sparkle.'

Sadie ignored her. 'It'll be the bestest costume and I'll be the bestest toadstool. Even better than the fairies because I can do magic, can't I Mark? You said so.'

'Real toadstools can, but you aren't a real toadstool. You're a little girl.'

'I want to be a fairy.'

'I want to be an astronaut and fly into space.'

'In a spaceship?'

Mark nodded.

'Fairies can fly. Can you come watch the play? Mummy, can he?'

Beatrice saw Mark's eyes widen and she decided to rescue him. 'I expect Mark will be busy, so he won't be able to come.'

Taya finally spoke. 'Will Dad be there?'

'I don't know, sweetie. I'll ask him.'

'He never comes to anything,' she grumbled.

Taya was right, Eric rarely went to any school events. Sometimes she wished he would put his children first for once.

Beatrice decided to change the subject, steering the conversation into less fraught waters. 'Are you doing anything special for Christmas?' she asked Mark.

'I'm going to my parents in Bath,' he replied, 'but I'll be back in the New Year.' He sent her a look that made her shiver with anticipation.

Then she sobered. He might be coming back to Picklewick, but for how long? His home was in Bristol, after all.

After tea, whilst he helped her clean up, he told her about his trip to London tomorrow, and she listened with growing dismay.

'It sounds very glamorous,' she said. Picklewick was a far cry from meetings with agents and editors, book deals and cuddly toy franchises. Would he want to come back?

'Believe me, it isn't. Most of the time, I'm cooped up in my house, trying to get the images in my head onto paper. It can get rather lonely. I envy you.'

'You wouldn't say that if you had to deal with this pair day in, day out,' she replied, the sound of squabbling reaching her. The children were arguing over what to watch on TV.

'I love this, being here with you and the girls,' he said, and her heart fluttered.

He stepped closer and his gaze locked onto hers. The air grew thick as he reached out to brush his thumb against her cheek, his touch electric. 'I want to kiss you.'

Her breath hitched and a rush of warmth spread through her, but she was brought back to earth by a shriek. 'I'm sorry, I can't. I don't want them to see... There hasn't been anyone since their father.'

He drew back. 'You've nothing to be sorry for – it's me who should apologise. I wasn't thinking. I just wanted to... The children come first, I get that. But please can you stop being so damned sexy?' he whispered.

He looked deep into her eyes and for a moment the rest of the world faded as she saw his hunger. It sparked an answering longing in her.

But was desire enough to keep him here? Was *she* enough?

She hadn't been the last time...

Mark parked the car on the drive, his eyes scanning the house. It looked drab and unwelcoming compared to the other houses in the street. All of them, except his, were readily embracing the festive season. It was a shame to let the side down and be the only Grinch in the street, but it was pointless putting any decorations up when he would only be here long enough to do some much-needed laundry and repack his case.

His meeting was at one p.m. – a working lunch, which suited him fine, because it meant he didn't have to take time out of the day to eat. He'd only left Picklewick a couple of hours ago and he was already missing it. Or should he say, he was missing *Beatrice*.

After a check around the house to make sure everything was in order, he had a shower, opened the post, then flopped down on the sofa with a sigh of relief. It was great to be back in his own place, with a proper sitting room and a kitchen. Living in one room, as nice as The Black Horse was, had become somewhat claustrophobic. The space of a proper house around him felt totally luxurious and the thought of going back to the pub and his one-room existence didn't fill him with joy. But if he wanted to be in Picklewick what choice—

Mark slapped a palm to his forehead. He was an idiot. A moron, an utter numpty. *Of course* he had a choice. He could rent somewhere: a house, a flat or a caravan even, although a caravan would have to have bloody good heating to see him through the winter, because it was freezing out there.

Fired up with enthusiasm, Mark drove to the station at Temple Meads a short time later and spent the entire journey to London searching for properties to rent when he should have been concentrating on the impending meeting with his agent and publisher.

For Mark Stafford, successful children's author, his book didn't seem quite as important anymore.

Sadie and Taya dashed into the house as soon as Beatrice opened the door, in a flurry of discarded coats and flying hair, and from the smear of red sauce around her youngest daughter's mouth as she shot past, Beatrice guessed their father had taken them to McDonald's for their tea.

Trust him to fill them full of additives and leave her to deal with the fallout. It would be ages before they calmed down enough to go to bed. At least it was Friday, so she didn't have to worry about getting them up for school in the morning. She had to go to work, but Mum was coming here, rather than her having to bundle them out of the house and drive them to their grandparents.

A knock on the door caught her by surprise and she opened it again, assuming one of the kids must have left something in their father's car.

Eric's hands were empty. 'Have you got a minute?'

'What's wrong?' Beatrice glanced over her shoulder worriedly. The girls had seemed alright, and from the sound of them charging around upstairs and yelling like a pair of banshees, they appeared to be fine.

'Nothing's wrong,' Eric said, to her relief.

'Do you want to come in?'

His gaze flickered to the stairs. 'Can we do this outside? I don't want them to hear.'

Beatrice's spirits sank. Don't tell me he's got his latest girlfriend pregnant, she prayed, because if he had, he could bloody well break the news to his existing children himself. She wasn't going to smooth the way for him. On second thoughts, maybe she *should* tell them herself, because he'd only make a pig's ear of it and upset them.

Beatrice glowered and stepped outside, pulling the door shut behind her. Blimmin' heck it was cold! 'Well?' she demanded, crossing her arms and shivering.

Eric stuffed his hands into his coat pocket, and she almost growled in annoyance. He looked warm and cosy in a puffer jacket so thick that it could probably be worn up Everest, whilst she was freezing her ears off waiting for her ex to announce that he was going to be a father again for the third time.

'It's Taya,' he began. 'She isn't happy.'

'Excuse me?' If he'd told Taya already, Beatrice just might make sure he'd be incapable of having any more children, ever.

'This new chap of yours,' he continued. 'The author bloke. Taya doesn't want you to see him.'

Beatrice blinked as she struggled to get her head around what he was saying. 'Why? What has she told you?'

'That you've got a boyfriend and lied to her about it.'

'I didn't lie!' Beatrice retorted hotly. 'He wasn't my boyfriend.'

Eric picked up on her use of the past tense. 'But he is now?'

She pursed her lips and glowered. She had no idea what Mark was. Anyway, what gave Eric the right to comment on *her* love life? He had a different woman every week and Beatrice never uttered a peep, unless it concerned the kids.

As though he'd read her mind, he said, 'I know it's not my place to say anything – who you go out with is your business – but Taya seems really upset.'

'Too damn right it's none of your business and Taya's only upset because, unlike *you*, this is the first relationship I've had since you left.'

'Since you kicked me out, you mean.'

'You deserved it.' She crossed her arms tighter, hugging herself in an attempt to keep the cold out and her temper in. 'I'm not going over this again.'

'Bea, I'm sorry.'

'Yeah, so you said – about a thousand times.'

'It was a mistake.'

Her brows shot up. 'Which time? The first or the second?'

'Both. I was stupid.'

'You can say that again! You stupidly thought you wouldn't get caught, and you were even more stupid to think I'd forgive you a second time. Eric, you're an arse.'

'I know. I was a shit husband. I admit I treated you badly, but I still care about you, I don't want to see you hurt.'

'That's rich, coming from you.'

'I read the article in The Picklewick Paper. He might be from around here originally, but he'll be gone soon and—' His eyes widened. 'Did you used to know him? You went out with him, didn't you?' His tone was accusing.

'What if I did? It was long before I met you.'

'He's turned your head, coming back here, flashing his cash. Taya told me he took you to dinner in that restaurant run by that London chef, whatshisname... Otto York.'

Beatrice blew out her cheeks, not bothering to explain.

'Look,' he said, 'it's Taya and Sadie I'm worried about. I don't want them getting to know him, then him buggering off to wherever he came from. It'll upset them. Sadie already thinks the sun shines out of his backside.'

Beatrice was done with the conversation. To have Eric quote her own words back at her after she had asked him not to introduce yet another fly-by-night girlfriend to her children was the last straw. 'I'll take your concerns on board when I make my decision that it's none of your damn business who I date,' she growled.

Realising she was about to lose her temper big time, she snapped her mouth shut and without another word she turned on her heel and marched back inside, slamming the door so hard it made the windows rattle.

Bloody Eric! Who does he think he is? she ranted silently. It was alright for him to have a love life, but the minute she showed any interest in a man, he was warning her off? And to think he had the cheek to use Taya as a way to get to her. Obviously Taya was going to find it hard to adjust to her mother having another man in her life: it was only to be expected. And obviously Beatrice would put her children's happiness first. Her relationship with Mark was in the very early stages, despite their history, so it wasn't as though she was moving him in next week. She was going to take it one day at a time, and if it didn't work out, it didn't work out.

But even as she was thinking it, Beatrice knew she was already in too deep, and that if their relationship ended for a second time, she would be heartbroken all over again.

Mark was bone weary when he walked into The Black Horse on Friday evening, his suitcase in his hand. He'd been on the go all day and he was knackered. But after he'd unpacked and collapsed onto the bed, his brain decided it was time to give him a slideshow of everything he'd done, said and seen today, and within a few minutes his mind was whirling and he was becoming increasingly restless.

A glass of water didn't help, and neither did a long hot shower: he was still too wired to relax.

Maybe a walk would do the trick?

Dressing warmly, he slipped out the side door. It was only ten-fifteen, so the pub was still open, but he wasn't in the mood to speak to anyone, and especially not to Dave.

Letting his feet take him where they wanted, Mark re-ran the meeting in his head, but he simply couldn't pin anything down long enough to examine it properly. Every time he tried, his thoughts veered to Beatrice.

Should he tell her that he was planning on renting somewhere nearby? Was it too soon to be thinking along those lines? Would she even want him to make that kind of a commitment yet? Was he jumping the gun, and getting ahead of himself? Questions, questions… He had so many and he wanted to ask them, but he was too worried he would frighten her.

On the way to London, he'd pinged some enquiries off to a couple of estate agents in Thornbury, figuring that there was no harm in starting the ball rolling, and with less than two weeks to Christmas nothing much would get done beforehand. He knew it would take time to find a suitable property, and then there would be the rental agreement to sort out, the references and the finances, so he would probably be living out of a suitcase for a while longer.

There was also the Christmas period itself to contend with. He had promised to spend the festive season at his parents' house in Bath, and he was looking forward to seeing them, but part of him wished he didn't have to go.

Mark stopped outside a shop, the window softly lit by a twinkling tree, and as he imagined himself living in the village he was filled with a warm glow.

When his feet took him into Lavender Lane (of course they did: it had been inevitable), he noticed there was a light on in Beatrice's living room, which meant she was still awake. Dare he?

Mark dared, but instead of ringing the doorbell, he tapped gently on the window and waited. After ten seconds – which felt like an hour – he tapped again. A little harder this time.

He was rewarded by the twitch of a curtain as it was pulled aside, and Beatrice stared out. When their eyes met and she smiled, relief washed over him. He had been worried she might be cross.

And when she opened the door and gestured for him to go inside, he realised just how *not cross* she was when she stepped into his arms. Her lips parted, her chin tilted, and her eyes drifted shut as his mouth found hers. His hands were in her hair as he kissed her urgently, and she snaked her arms around his neck, pressing herself against him.

Mark groaned and she let out a sigh. His blood was aflame, desire scorching through his veins, heating him from the inside out. As the kiss deepened, his hands left her hair and skimmed down her back to grasp her bottom.

He wanted her so badly, so very, very badly, that when she drew back, breathing hard, her cheeks pink and her lips swollen, it took every ounce of self-control he could find to release her.

She glanced at the dark stairs behind. 'I can't,' she whispered, her voice husky.

'I know.'

'I want to. More than anything.'

'I think I should go, before we do something we regret.' He barely managed to get the words out.

The look in her eyes as she said, 'I wouldn't regret making love with you. Just not here, not now,' made his pulse roar.

How he managed to tear himself away he didn't know, and as he floated back to The Black Horse, there was one thing he was certain of – not having this woman in his life was unthinkable.

CHAPTER EIGHT

What do you do when you can't think of anything other than the woman you almost made love to last night?

Mark tried to write, but that didn't work and he ended up throwing down his pen in disgust. He tried to draw, but the stylus went the same way as the pen. Reading couldn't keep his mind off Beatrice for more than two sentences at a time, and the programme he tried to watch just became a background buzz to his daydreams of her.

She dominated his thoughts, and he couldn't think of anything else. His lips yearned to kiss her, his arms longed to hold her, his—

For pity's sake, if he carried on waxing lyrical like this, he should seriously consider writing romance. And if he carried on being unable to come up with a storyline for the character that Pinkymoon wanted him to write about, then he just might have to!

Packing it in for the day, he shoved his feet into his boots, his arms into his coat, and ventured outside. This was the last-but-one Saturday before Christmas, and Picklewick's main street was surprisingly busy. Mark assumed that Thornbury would hold greater appeal for shoppers than Picklewick, but apparently not, so he decided to have a proper look around the village. Despite having spent over three weeks here, he hadn't had a good mooch around, but if he was going to be living here, maybe he should. Besides, he wanted to see if he could find a gift or two for Beatrice and the girls. And not only them: he had his mum and dad to buy for, as well as his brother and family. And so far, he had been too preoccupied to buy anything other than the box of soaps when he was at the farm last Saturday.

Thinking of the farm made him think of Beatrice (to be fair, *everything* made him think of Beatrice) and he wondered what she was doing now. No doubt she would be busy serving customers, but was she thinking of him at all? In spite of the glaringly obvious physical attraction they had for each other, Mark wasn't sure how she felt about him. She might be in lust, but was she in *love*? Her best friend had told him that Beatrice used to be in love with him back then, and hinted that she still was, but did Lisa actually *know*?

Mark wished *he* did, but he wasn't prepared to risk damaging this fragile connection by asking Beatrice outright.

Picklewick had a decent selection of shops for its size and all the usual suspects: baker, butcher, chemist, greengrocer, florist, pet shop (could he get Sadie a hamster for Christmas? No, bad idea), but nothing caught his eye when it came to gift buying. It didn't help that he had no idea what to buy girls. His brother had boys, and even then Mark found his nephews difficult enough to find presents for. And as for Beatrice... Perfume seemed too impersonal, jewellery *too* personal. In fact, should he buy her anything at all? If he bought her a gift and she didn't get him one, would she be embarrassed? Feel awkward?

Bloody hell! Who knew Christmas could be so complicated? Maybe something small, just to show that he was thinking of her?

Eventually, after a trip to Thornbury, he settled on a safe option for everyone – books. You couldn't go wrong with books.

Why do radiators tick when they start to warm up, was Beatrice's first waking thought on Sunday morning, and this was because it was the heating coming on that woke her. The second was of Mark, which wasn't unusual considering she'd thought about him constantly since she'd discovered he was back.

But when she peeped out through the curtains to see what kind of a Sunday it was, she let out a gasp, and thoughts of Mark were driven from her mind.

Snow!

Oh, my goodness! And it was quite deep, too. Ten centimetres, she estimated, possibly deeper in places. It was only six-thirty a.m., but everywhere was white, the snow intensifying the light from the street lamps, and when she opened the window to feel the spiralling flakes on her warm skin, the world was still and hushed, holding its breath.

A feeling of peace stole over her as she gazed at the magical scene, then excitement started to build. The girls were going to love this! *She* was going to love this.

Beatrice threw on a dressing gown and hurried downstairs. A substantial breakfast was needed prior to going out to play, as well as warm, waterproof clothes. But first, a cup of coffee, which she would hopefully be able to drink in peace, before the whirlwind that was her youngest daughter got up.

It wasn't to be. No sooner had Beatrice raised a mug to her lips, than Sadie charged down the stairs, squealing so loudly that Beatrice feared most of Picklewick would hear.

'Snow, Mummy, snow!' Sadie thundered into the kitchen, her wellies in her hand. She skidded to a halt, dropped to the floor and began stuffing her left foot into the right Wellington boot.

Beatrice swooped in to intervene, grabbing the wellies. 'Oh no, you don't, young lady. Breakfast first. And did you honestly think I'd let you play in the snow in your pyjamas?'

Sadie pouted. 'I was going to put my coat on.'

Beatrice gave her The Look, and Sadie tried a different tack. 'I'm not hungry.'

'That's fine, but you're not going out to play on an empty stomach, so don't think you'll make it outside any sooner by not having breakfast.'

'Aww.' The pout turned into a scowl. 'I'm not hungry because I've got tummy ache.'

Beatrice narrowed her eyes. 'If you're not feeling well, maybe you should stay indoors until you feel better?'

'You're mean.'

Beatrice felt her daughter's forehead. It was cool to the touch, so she didn't think she had a temperature. 'Be honest,' she warned. 'Do you feel sick?'

Sadie leapt to her feet. 'I did, but I don't now. Can I have a biscuit for breakfast?'

Beatrice laughed. 'No, you most certainly cannot. I'm making porridge.'

'Yuck.'

'You *like* porridge.' Beatrice always made it with creamy milk and added a teaspoon of honey.

'Not today I don't.'

'Toast, then?'

Sadie shook her head, but before she could continue to plead for a biscuity breakfast, Taya bounced into the room, as excited as her sister at the sight of snow.

Sadie grumbled, '*She* said we have to have breakfast before we can go outside.'

Beatrice raised her eyebrows. '*She?*' Whilst she could appreciate that Sadie was excited, she didn't appreciate her daughter's disrespectful tone, or claiming to feel unwell in order to get her own way, especially when it came to trying to wriggle out of school.

However, there was only a week left, as school would break up for Christmas on Friday. This coming week would be an exciting one, what with the school play and all the other activities that the teachers had planned, so Beatrice would see what Sadie was like in January. But for now, she wanted to enjoy the day, and that meant having fun in the snow.

Beatrice was in the middle of a snowball fight and losing badly (two against one wasn't fair), when she heard her phone ringing.

Using it as an excuse not to be pummelled any more (Taya had a terrifyingly good aim), Beatrice retreated to the kitchen to see who was calling.

It was Lisa. 'Beatrice, lovely girl, how good are you with a shovel?'

Beatrice unwound her wet scarf from her neck with a grimace and glanced out of the window. The children were now heaping snow together to make a snowman. 'You can't be snowed in. It's not that deep.'

'Don't be silly, of course we aren't. But it's set to freeze tonight.'

'So?'

'If it does, and the paths aren't cleared, they'll be treacherous,'

'The gritters will be out. It'll be fine,' Beatrice said, as she noticed more fat flakes begin to fall.

'For the roads, yes, but I'm talking about the paths around the school. Do you remember the last time it snowed? The school was closed for two days because the paths were so treacherous. Nikki reckons the same thing could happen tomorrow. But if we clear them, the caretaker can put salt down so they won't freeze overnight. The school car park also needs to be cleared. Nikki's fine as she lives in the village and can walk to work, but none of the other teachers do.' Lisa lowered her voice and Beatrice guessed that one or more of her kids were in earshot. 'It's either that, or the kids stay home from school. I know which I'd prefer.'

'Give me half an hour. Mine are outside.' She winced as a blob of melting snow trickled down the back of her neck. 'I'll get them changed into dry clothes and meet you there.'

'Bring them round to mine. Robin can look after them.'

'Will do. See you in a bit.' Picking up her sodden scarf, Beatrice pulled a face. She'd better take a change of clothes for the girls, because no doubt they'd get wet again.

She was about to ask them to come inside, when she saw she had a message from Mark, and her tummy did a somersault.

Snow! Are you out in it?

Have been. Going 2 school 2 clear paths

Want any help?

Meet you there. 30 mins?

He responded with a happy smiley face and a snowman emoji.

Beatrice stared at her phone for a couple of seconds, her heart thudding, anticipation swooping through her as she remembered him turning up announced but oh-so welcome, late Friday evening. How she'd managed to stop before things went too far, she didn't know. Thinking about it made her feel weak and breathless. She would have given anything for an hour alone with him…

She hadn't seen him yesterday, and she felt giddy at the thought of seeing him now. As she got the children ready, she told herself she couldn't let her feelings show, not in front of so many people. And especially not in front of the other mums, who would be watching any and all interactions she had with him as intently as a flock of beady-eyed hawks.

Although it had been common knowledge at the time that Beatrice and Mark had been dating, only Lisa knew how Beatrice had felt about him, and Beatrice wanted to keep it that way. The problem was, Picklewick was small, and she didn't doubt that everyone in it knew that she and Mark had been out for a meal together – *twice*. She suspected that rumours were already rife, but she was determined she wasn't going to fan the gossipy flames any further today.

Bundling the children out of the door, Beatrice hurried them down the street. Her children loved going to Lisa's house and she knew they'd have a great time. They wouldn't miss her in the slightest, not with Lisa's kids to play with and a continual supply of snow to keep them entertained.

Flakes were still falling when she tried to kiss them goodbye at the front door, but both girls brushed her off, eager to get inside, and Beatrice sighed.

'Typical,' she grumbled. 'They don't want anything to do with me when there's something more exciting on offer.'

'Here.' Lisa handed her a shovel. 'Stop moaning. You'd complain if they were hanging onto your apron strings.'

'So I would,' she agreed, hoisting the shovel so it sat on her shoulder. 'Heigh-ho, heigh-ho, it's off to work we go,' she warbled.

'Blimey, you're in good spirits considering we're about to get backache and blisters. I'll be bloody annoyed if no one else turns up,' Lisa growled. 'If it's just me, you, Nikki and the caretaker, we're not going to get very far.'

Quietly, Beatrice said, 'And Mark.'

'What did you say? I didn't catch that.'

'And Mark.'

Lisa stopped dead. '*Mark* is going to be there?'

'Yes.'

Eyes wide, she muttered, 'I should have brought another shovel!'

'I hadn't thought of that.'

Lisa brightened. 'No problem. He can borrow mine. I'll supervise!' She resumed walking. 'I think you've got something to tell me.'

'I haven't.'

'Liar. Have you slept with him yet?'

'No!'

'You want to, though?'

'Duh!'

'Okay, stupid question. Obviously you do. But do you think it's a good idea?'

'Probably not.'

'But you're going to anyway?'

'Please don't judge me,' Beatrice begged.

'I'm not. I'm worried about you, that's all. But as you said, if you don't, you'll always be wondering.'

Beatrice's smile was crooked. 'I've seen him naked before, if you remember. I know what he looks like under his clothes.'

Lisa elbowed her. 'That's not what I meant, and you know it.'

It was Beatrice's turn to stop walking. 'I'm worried too. I still love him, Lisa. I never stopped.'

'I get that.' Lisa put an arm around her, gave her a hug, then propelled her onwards. 'I must admit, I would do the same in your shoes. Go get 'em, cowgirl!'

'Fat chance with the kids around.'

Lisa gave her a meaningful look. 'They're not around now, are they? They're at *my* house.'

'Are you suggesting that I…we…?'

'Why not?'

'It's eleven o'clock in the morning!'

'What's that got to do with it?'

'I can't just rock up to him with a shovel in my hand and say take me to bed right now.'

'I don't see why not, but if you insist on a build-up, do your bit at the school, then suggest he goes to yours for a spot of lunch. But instead of food, you could——'

'I get the idea. There's no need to spell it out.'

Lisa said, 'Me and Robin will look after the kids for as long as you need. Take your time.' She smirked and added, 'Don't I have the best ideas?'

'You do! I could kiss you!'

As they entered the school gate, Lisa whistled. 'Save your kisses for Mark. He's going to need them. Look at him go.'

Beatrice looked, and her mouth dropped open.

Mark, snow shovel in hand, was effortlessly clearing the path to the main entrance, his movements controlled and precise. He was coatless, and she could see the flex and bunch of the muscles in his shoulders and arms.

So could everyone else. A surprising number of parents had turned up, and Beatrice noticed several of the female contingent watching him out of the corners of their eyes. Mark seemed oblivious, as he concentrated on his path-clearing efforts. Beatrice, in turn, concentrated on *him*, Lisa's offer at the forefront of her mind. Trying to take desire out of the equation (which wasn't easy when the object of that desire was right in front of her), Beatrice attempted to be objective, but all she could think about was the way he made her feel.

And she realised there wasn't a decision to make – because *she'd already made it.*

Mark tensed as Beatrice's fingers stroked his chest, trailing through the fine hairs in slow circles. They were in her bed and she was curled against him, one leg over his thigh, his arm around her, and he was happier than he could ever remember being. For the first time in his life, he felt complete, his body satiated, his mind still, his heart full. So very, very full.

He didn't want this moment to end, though he knew it must. The afternoon was slipping inexorably into evening, and she would soon need to fetch the children from Lisa's.

With her hand still on his chest, her fingers continuing to stroke his skin, she said, 'I forgot to ask how your meeting on Friday went.'

'Not great,' he confessed. 'They want to turn Santa Paws into a series.'

She hesitated, her fingers ceasing their movement. 'Isn't that a *good* thing?'

'I've got to rewrite it, with the focus on one of the other characters. Poor Santa Paws is to take a back seat. They want to make him into a cuddly toy though, so there is that. And my publisher is talking about even more library visits and personal appearances. Apparently "my brand is robust enough to take it". Anyone would think I'm JK Rowling or David Walliams,' he huffed.

'But that's good, isn't it?'

'All I want to do is write my stories. I don't want to do the bits that go with it. But the market for children's books is tough, and my agent and publisher don't want me to lose any momentum.'

'Is that likely to happen?'

'Maybe.' Right now, he didn't care if it did. All he could think about was Beatrice.

Her phone rang, making him jump, and she sat up. 'I'd better get going. The girls will wonder where I am.'

Mark's gaze travelled down her bare back, lingering at her waist, before settling on the curve of her hip. She was beautiful.

He watched her hunt for her phone, her hand delving into the pocket of the jeans lying discarded on the bedroom floor, and when she looked at the screen, her mouth tightened.

'Hi,' she said, answering the call.

Mark got dressed and tried not to listen, but it was impossible not to.

'Fine, thanks… Yeah, a fair bit… No, it's stopped now… Sorry they're not here, they're at Lisa's. I'll get them to phone you when they get home.' She jammed the phone between her shoulder and her ear as she stepped into her jeans.

Mark looked away and pulled his shirt over his head. Was his fleece up here or downstairs? He couldn't even remember taking it off.

Beatrice said, 'Thursday at two o'clock… You will? Sadie will be delighted!' She glanced over at Mark then turned away, lowering her voice. 'I'll let you tell her yourself. See you Thursday… Bye, Eric.' Tossing the phone onto the bed, she said, 'That was my ex.'

Mark bowed his head. 'I guessed as much.'

'He didn't know whether he'd be able to make it to Sadie's school play, but he can now.'

'That's good.'

'Yeah, it is.'

He said, 'I hope you don't mind, but Nicki invited me as a guest of honour.'

Beatrice's smile was wry. 'Is that the kind of thing you meant when you said your publisher wanted you to do stuff?'

Mark took her in his arms. 'Yes, but they'll be cheesed off when they find out I'm not doing this for the publicity.' He kissed Beatrice on the nose.

'Why *are* you going?'

'To see Sadie in her toadstool costume, of course!'

Beatrice lifted her chin, offering him her mouth and he kissed her with renewed passion. When she ended it, his disappointment was acute.

'When can I see you next?' he asked, knowing he sounded needy but he couldn't help himself.

She lowered her head and murmured, 'I don't know. Soon, I hope, but with the kids…' She trailed off.

'I understand. They come first.'

Her head came up and she gazed into his face. 'They do. They have to.'

He kissed her again, this time a tender meeting of the lips. He knew they did, and he was okay with that, that's how it should be. Mark would fit in with whatever Beatrice wanted, because now that he'd found her again he had no intention of letting her go, and if that meant waiting until she felt able to welcome him into her family, he would wait for as long as it took.

Beatrice studied her youngest child as she shuffled into the living room, and thought she looked simply adorable dressed in her pink sparkly toadstool costume. Beatrice's mum had done a brilliant job: much better than Beatrice could have done.

But Sadie looked worried. Her little face was flushed and her eyes were huge. 'I don't feel well, Mummy.'

Beatrice had a flash of concern. 'Is it your tummy?' Sadie nodded.

'I thought you were looking forward to being the best toadstool in the world?' Maybe she had stage fright? After Sadie's initial reluctance on being told that she wouldn't be playing a fairy, she seemed to have come around to the idea of being a toadstool. But perhaps, with the play only a few hours away, she was becoming anxious?

Beatrice placed a hand on Sadie's forehead. She did feel rather hot, but then, it was probably quite warm in that costume. She'd only picked at her breakfast though, which hadn't bothered Beatrice at the time as Sadie and Taya had been in a heated discussion about Rudolf's nose, and Taya hadn't eaten much of hers either.

The kids were wound up like spinning tops already, and there were still six days to go until the big day. As far as Beatrice was concerned, Christmas couldn't come soon enough.

'Shall we get you out of this costume? You'll feel cooler with it off,' she suggested.

Sadie nodded, and Beatrice helped her take it off. 'Is that better?'

'Yes,' Sadie replied but she still sounded rather subdued.

'You don't have to take part in the play if you don't want to,' Beatrice told her. 'I'm sure Miss Barnes will understand if you don't feel up to it. Would you like me to have a word with her?'

'I *want* to be in the play.'

'But if you're not well…?'

'Please, Mummy, I want to.'

Beatrice checked her forehead again, but couldn't tell if Sadie was any cooler. 'I'm going to take your temperature,' she announced, getting to her feet.

'Nooo…' Sadie was starting to get fractious.

'If you've got a temperature, you can't go to school.'

'I haven't got a tempacher My tempacher is good.' Her chin wobbled. 'Please, Mummy, I want to go to school!'

Beatrice thought for a moment, then relented. 'Okay, but you've got to promise me you'll tell Miss Barnes if you don't feel well and I'll come get you.'

'I will.'

'Promise?'

'I promise. Thank you, Mummy. I love you.'

'I love you too, sweetie. Let's go brush your teeth and round up your sister.'

Beatrice would take the girls to school and when she handed over the toadstool costume to Sadie's teacher, she'd have a quick word with her. Beatrice's gut feeling was that Sadie probably *was* a bit off-colour today but not unwell enough to be kept off school, and that anxiety at being onstage wasn't helping. Even though Beatrice was looking forward to seeing Sadie in the school play this afternoon and she would feel immensely proud of her daughter, a part of her would be relieved when this was over.

Mark didn't relish being the guest of honour at Picklewick Primary's Christmas play, but he was quite looking forward to seeing Sadie in her costume. After persuading her to take part, he felt he had a vested interest; besides, it was kind of nice to feel part of the community he would soon be living in. He was quite excited to throw himself into village life, even if that involved helping to clear snowy paths.

As he sat next to the school's Chair of Governors in pride of place in the front row, Mark ran his thumb across the fading calluses on his palm, remembering the feel of the shovel in his hands. It had been a while since he'd done manual labour, but he hadn't minded it, not if it meant he'd got to spend time with Beatrice. Deciding it would be better not to dwell on what had happened afterwards (as wonderful as it had been, this was neither the time nor the place for thoughts like that) Mark focused his attention on his surroundings.

The hall was filling up with parents, grandparents and younger siblings – those little ones who had yet to start school – and the noise was steadily building. He glanced around, hoping to catch a glimpse of Beatrice, but caught Lisa's eye instead. Giving him a wide smile, she pointed to her right and mouthed, 'Over there.'

Nodding to show he understood, Mark looked over his shoulder.

There she was, three rows back and looking so beautiful that she took his breath away. Beatrice was sitting next to her parents, but there was an empty seat beside her and when a man tapped her on the shoulder and sat down in it, Mark guessed that the bloke was Eric.

He stared at him, consumed by curiosity, but looked away when he saw that Beatrice had noticed. The last thing he wanted was to make her feel awkward or to draw attention to her. Or himself, for that matter.

The chatter subsided when a line of children was ushered into the hall accompanied by a teacher, filing in one by one to sit cross-legged on the floor in front of the stage. Taya was amongst them, and he smiled. Her lips twitched in response, broadening into a wide beaming smile when she spotted her parents. Ruefully, Mark realised he had a while to go yet before he won Taya over. She was understandably wary of him, and he could fully respect that. He hoped that in time she would come to accept him.

The headteacher called for silence, and when she was happy that the audience was paying attention, a small boy walked self-consciously onto the stage and read out an introduction in a faltering voice.

Mark settled back in his seat to enjoy the show. There was something incredibly sweet about the way the children threw themselves into their parts, despite clearly being nervous. The lead fairy was adorable, and he could see Sadie watching her, a frown on her little face. It seemed to him that she hadn't fully embraced being a toadstool and was still coveting the fairy role.

The toadstools had just shuffled into position in a semi-circle around the fairies, who were singing a song at full volume and mostly out of tune, when Sadie fell over.

Expecting her to get back on her feet, it took Mark a moment to realise she wasn't moving.

There was an abrupt silence as the headteacher hurried forward and bent down to check on her, then straightened up, her face ashen.

The next few minutes were a blur, and Mark could only watch helplessly as Beatrice leapt onto the stage to scoop her small daughter into her arms. The terrified expression on her face pierced his heart and he made to go to her, but Lisa grabbed hold of his arm and he realised Eric was there.

He heard someone say, 'Call an ambulance,' but Eric shook his head.

Taking Sadie from Beatrice, he said, 'It'll be quicker by car.'

Mark watched him carry his limp and lifeless daughter out of the hall, Beatrice by his side, shouting, 'Mum, look after Taya!'

Then she was gone. And all Mark could do was pray.

CHAPTER NINE

'You should go home and rest, I'll stay with her,' Eric whispered, and Beatrice opened her eyes to see her ex-husband standing by Sadie's bed.

Her gaze flew to her sleeping daughter, tiny and pale, a needle in the back of her little hand, and she gulped back fresh tears. 'I'm not going anywhere. I'm staying here.' She kept her voice low, so as not to disturb the other patients on the ward.

'You'll be no good to her if you make yourself ill.'

'You've been here all night too,' she pointed out.

He shrugged. 'I'm used to it.'

'She will be alright, won't she?'

'She will, I promise.'

The tears spilled over. She'd done so much crying over the past twelve hours, she felt wrung out, but they kept coming. 'I should have known,' she said. She'd uttered the same thing over and over since Sadie had been rushed into theatre yesterday.

'Don't beat yourself up over it. I'm a nurse and *I* didn't realise.'

'You aren't with them all day, every day. How *could* you realise?'

'How could *you?* The symptoms of appendicitis can easily be mistaken for so many other things, and it's rare in children as young as Sadie.'

'I should have realised,' she repeated stubbornly.

Sadie's eyelids fluttered and Beatrice leapt to her feet, bending over the bed. 'I'm here, darling, Mummy is here.'

Eric said, 'She'll sleep for a while and when she does wake up she'll be groggy. Go home and rest.'

'Nuh-uh.' Beatrice shook her head, sitting down again when Sadie showed no further signs of stirring. 'I'm going to be here when she wakes up. I'm not going anywhere.'

'At least let me get you something to eat. The staff canteen is open 24 hours.'

'I'd love a coffee.'

'You've had nothing to eat since lunch yesterday,' he argued.

'I've got enough padding to keep me going for a while. Missing a meal or two isn't going to kill me. What time is it?' She'd lost track after the lights on the children's ward had been dimmed for the night.

'Four-forty.'

Too early to phone Taya. No doubt she was exhausted after the awful events of yesterday, but Beatrice had spoken to her last night to tell her that her sister was okay after her operation and was now sleeping. She'd done her best to sound reassuring, keeping her tone bright and cheerful, and she hoped she had put Taya's mind at rest. It was also too early to phone her mum, even though she desperately wanted to hear her mother's voice. She could do with a hug too, but she'd have to wait until later – if Sadie was allowed visitors.

However, Beatrice wouldn't be speaking to *anyone* if she didn't charge her phone. 'You wouldn't happen to have a charger handy, would you?' she asked.

'I'll see if I can borrow one, and I'll get you a coffee at the same time. Are you sure you don't want anything to eat?'

'I'm sure.' As he turned to leave, she said, 'Eric? Thank you.'

'For what?'

'For being here.'

'She's *my* daughter too.' He hesitated. 'I'd never forgive myself if anything happened to either of them. Or to you. I still love you, Bea.'

He left her with those words ringing in her ears, but she was too weary to think about them right now.

Her only focus was her daughter, and how badly she'd let her down.

Mark's finger hesitated over Beatrice's phone number. He was desperate to call her, anxious for news, but he didn't know whether she'd welcome it.

He'd had a single message from her late last night. It had been brief.

Appendicitis. She's had an operation. It went ok x

He'd read it several times, each time hoping it might reveal new information. So far, it hadn't.

Oh, sod it. At least if he messaged her, she would know she was in his thoughts. He assumed she was still at the hospital and had probably spent the night there, so even though it was early he sent it anyway. If she did happen to be asleep, it would be waiting for her when she woke up.

How is Sadie?

It seemed rather abrupt, so he sent another. Anything I can do? x

Then he waited in vain for a reply, checking his phone obsessively.

He'd showered and had just sat down for breakfast when his phone rang. His relief was immense when he heard Beatrice's voice.

She said, 'She's awake and hungry, and asking when she can go home.'

'Thank god. How are you?'

'Tired, waiting to speak to the doctor.'

'Do you need anything?'

'No, thanks. Mum will see to it. She's coming in this afternoon and bringing Taya.'

'Is Taya okay? It must have been frightening for her. And for you.'

'She's fine; worried, but she'll be okay when she sees Sadie for herself. Hang on…' Her voice faded and he heard her say, 'No, it's Mark.' Returning to normal, she said, 'Sorry, that was Eric; he thought I was on the phone to Taya.'

The memory of Eric's face as he strode out of the school hall with his daughter in his arms, leapt into Mark's mind. The man had looked distraught, and Mark could only imagine what he'd been feeling. No matter how badly Eric had treated Beatrice, he loved his children.

'It must have been a terrible shock, for all of you,' Mark said.

'I blame myself.'

'*Why?*'

'I should have realised—'

Mark heard a man's voice, then Beatrice said, 'I don't care, Eric, I *should have*. She'd been complaining of—' She stopped. 'Sorry Mark, Eric keeps telling me that it's not my fault.'

Mark didn't know much about appendicitis and what he did know had been gleaned from searching the internet last night, but Eric was right. 'It *isn't* your fault,' he said.

A weary sigh floated down the phone and he realised that nothing anyone said would make any difference: Beatrice was going to blame herself, regardless.

'Are you sure I can't do anything?'

'I'm sure, but thanks anyway. I'd better go.'

'Let me know what the doctor says?' he asked. 'And give Sadie a kiss from me.'

'I will.'

It was only when the call ended and there was no danger of her hearing, that Mark whispered, 'I love you, Bea.'

One day soon, he intended to tell her.

Deborah said, 'Do you think they'll let her come home tomorrow?'

'I hope so.' Beatrice plucked a grape from the fruit basket and popped it in her mouth.

Sadie pulled a face. She wasn't keen on grapes. 'I'm bored,' she announced loudly.

'I know you are.' Beatrice gave her mum a helpless look.

She was trying her best to keep Sadie entertained, but the child was sick of being in hospital. And so was Beatrice. She was astonished how she could go from being so terrified for her child that she couldn't breathe, to utter boredom in the space of three days. After the consultant had done his rounds on Friday and declared himself satisfied with how the operation went and with Sadie's recovery from the anaesthetic, Beatrice had hoped Sadie would be allowed home that day. But it wasn't to be. She had been kept in over the weekend, and for Sadie, by Sunday afternoon the novelty of being in hospital had well and truly worn off. There was only so much book-reading and colouring that she was prepared to do. And she was also fed up with watching TV, especially since the channels available were somewhat limited.

God help me if they keep her in for another day, Beatrice thought, although she couldn't see any reason why they would. The tiny wound on Sadie's tummy was healing well, she had been taken off the drip on Friday, and all her vital signs were excellent. In fact, apart from some discomfort at the site of the operation, Sadie was almost back to normal, and Beatrice marvelled at the ability of young children to bounce back from something that would take an adult a couple of weeks to recover from.

Hopefully, Sadie would only have to spend one more night in hospital, and she would be discharged in the morning. Apart from a quick dash home for a shower and a change of clothes, Beatrice hadn't left the hospital either, so she was almost swooning at the thought of sleeping in her own bed. Trying to catch forty winks in a hospital chair had aged her ten years, she reckoned.

Taya would also be glad when everything was back to normal, although the upside was that she'd seen more of her father these past three days than she'd seen for a long time. Both girls had. Working in Thornton General meant that Eric could pop onto the ward and spend a few minutes with Sadie during his shift. And he also visited her both before and after he started work. The rest of the time, if it was at all practical, he spent with Taya. And Beatrice could see how her daughter was flourishing now that she had so much of her father's attention.

To Beatrice's surprise, Eric had stepped up to the mark, and to her even greater surprise, he seemed to be enjoying it.

There he was now, hovering at the entrance to the ward.

He was looking at her parents, and Beatrice guessed that he was reluctant to intrude on their time with Sadie. But knowing he was on his break and that he didn't have long, Beatrice beckoned him in.

'Mum, Dad, why don't you take Taya to the shop and buy her and Sadie a treat?' Beatrice delved into her bag for some money but her mum brushed her aside.

'I'll get it,' Deborah said. 'Come on Taya, let your dad have a chat with Sadie. You'll see him later.' She whispered to Beatrice, 'He's taking her bowling this evening, but don't tell Sadie.'

'Gosh, no!' Beatrice agreed. Sadie would be furious if she knew they were going without her, and she made a mental note to suggest to Eric that he do something special with Sadie, just the two of them, when she was out of hospital.

Beatrice let Sadie and Eric have a few minutes alone, and she strolled over to the window. Yesterday had been the shortest day of the year, and today wasn't much longer. It would start to get dark soon, and Beatrice noticed that some of the nearby houses had already switched on their Christmas lights.

She frowned as she thought of everything she still had to do in preparation for Christmas Day. She'd not wrapped a single present yet, and she needed to do a big grocery shop. At least they were going to her parents for Christmas dinner, so she didn't have to worry about buying a turkey.

As she stood there contemplating Christmas, her thoughts drifted to Mark. She hadn't seen him since Sunday when they'd made love (the brief glimpse she'd had of him on Thursday during the play, didn't count) and she was missing him. He'd said he'd pop in to visit Sadie later, after her mum and dad had been, and she couldn't wait – though how she would stop herself kissing him, she didn't know. She hoped they could manage some time alone before he left Picklewick to go to his parents for Christmas, but with it being the twenty-second of December today, she wasn't sure whether they'd have the opportunity.

Sighing, she rested her forehead against the glass, then stifled a shriek when an arm crept around her waist.

Assuming it to be Mark, she squirmed around, only to be confronted by Eric.

Moving aside, she slipped out of his grasp. 'Don't,' she warned.

'Bea, listen to me, please. Seeing Sadie like this—' he gestured towards her bed and swallowed hard '—

has been a wake-up call. I thought we were going to lose her.'

Beatrice gulped. So had she.

'It made me realise how much I've lost and how much more I *could* lose. I don't want to miss any more of their lives.'

'You don't have to. You can be as involved as you want.'

'You don't understand – I want to tuck them into bed at night and be there when they wake in the mornings.'

'You work shifts.' Her response was dry. If he thought he could guilt her, he could think again.

'You know what I mean.'

'Hmph.' She'd heard it all before. He'd sung a version of the same song when she'd told him she wanted a divorce.

She began to walk away, back to Sadie who was busily colouring something and was thankfully not taking any notice of her parents' exchange, but Eric grabbed hold of her hand.

Caught off-guard, she was pulled towards him and she came up against his chest. She put up her hands, but before she could push him away, he cupped her face and kissed her.

Beatrice froze. She was sorely tempted to knee him in the goolies for his audacity, but she didn't want to make a scene. Instead, she tensed, her eyes open, her lips unyielding, as she waited for him to get the message.

Realising he wasn't getting anywhere, he released her. 'Just think about it,' he pleaded. 'We were good together once.'

She opened her mouth to utter a scathing retort, when she realised he was looking over her shoulder, an unreadable expression on his face. And when she whirled around, she saw Taya standing by her sister's bedside, wearing a delighted smile.

Oh, sodding bloody fiddlesticks!

Mark staggered back from the doorway to the ward, the bag with the fairy outfit dangling forgotten from his nerveless fingers. *Beatrice and Eric were kissing.*

He felt sick and pain flared in his chest. He thought his heart was going to shatter with the force of it.

Taya glanced around and when he saw the happiness on her face, he wanted to cry. She looked ecstatic.

Mark wanted to stay and fight, to tell Beatrice he loved her, but he had to walk away. She had decided to make another go of it with Eric for the sake of her children, and he couldn't do anything to jeopardise that.

A middle-aged couple were walking towards him and Mark recognised Beatrice's parents and he turned away, not wanting them to see the anguish in his eyes. He had let Beatrice go once before, not understanding what he was throwing away. He would let her go again, but this time he knew all too well.

As he walked out of the hospital and out of Beatrice's life, he was sure he was doing the right thing, no matter how much pain it caused him.

At least Mark hadn't dumped her by text. Beatrice supposed she ought to be grateful for that small mercy. But a letter wasn't much better. Just more old-fashioned.

Lisa handed it back to her after she'd read it, and Beatrice threw it on the coffee table. She grabbed a cushion, hugging it to her chest and hitched in a breath.

'He didn't even use proper paper,' she said, as though the news of his departure would hurt less if it was written on a sheet of Basildon Bond paper, rather than a leaf torn out of a drawing pad. 'Damn him!'

She sniffled and Lisa passed her a tissue. '"Doesn't think it will work",' she quoted. '"It's for the best". Yeah, best for *him*.'

'More wine?'

'How many bottles did you bring?'

'Just the one.' Lisa topped up Beatrice's glass and she knocked half of it back. 'Steady on, you don't want to get drunk.'

'Yes, I do,' she replied grimly. 'But I won't. I can't, not with Sadie like she is. I'll save getting blotto for when she's fully recovered.' This was her daughter's first night home since she'd collapsed at school. The letter, such as it was, had been waiting on the mat when Beatrice had got home. Thanks Mark, she thought bitterly.

'You mightn't want to get drunk by then,' Lisa soothed.

'Believe me, I will.' Beatrice dabbed at her eyes. It had taken a herculean effort not to fall apart in front of the girls, but they were in bed now and if she couldn't fall apart in front of her oldest and bestest friend, then who could she fall apart in front of? 'I should have listened to you,' she said.

'You had to try.'

'No, I honestly didn't. I could have kept him at arm's length, but I just had to fall in love with him again, didn't I?' She sounded as bitter as she felt.

'You never *stopped* loving him,' Lisa reminded her. 'That was the problem.'

'I never should have trusted him. What is it with me and men? Do I have a sign saying "treat me like dirt" on my forehead? God, I can bloody pick them, can't I? First Eric, now Mark. He got what he came here for, an idea for his sodding book – which *I* gave him – and he had a bit of fun at the same time. It was a win-win situation for him, wasn't it?' She drank the rest of her wine and held out her glass.

Lisa refilled it. 'That's your last,' she warned. 'You'll feel dreadful if Sadie wakes you in the night and you've got a hangover.'

'Stop being so bloody sensible!'

'No more wine.'

'It hurts, Lisa. It hurts so much. I thought we had something special.' She screwed up her face, the dam about to break. 'I guess the reality of a woman with two kids in tow was too much to handle.'

'He doesn't deserve you.'

'No, he doesn't. But that doesn't make it any easier. I wish he'd loved me back then. I wish he loved me now. But if wishes were horses, beggars would ride, and me and Eric would be back together. And we both know that's never going to happen.'

'You what?'

'It's a saying. It means— I don't know what it means. My nana used to say it.' Beatrice hugged the cushion closer.

'What about you and Eric?' Lisa was looking perplexed, and Beatrice realised she hadn't told her what had happened between her and Eric at the hospital.

'He wants us to get back together, to try again, for the sake of the girls. He says that Sadie's collapse was a wake-up call.'

'Are you going to?' She sounded aghast.

'No way. Eric and I are *not* getting back together. I did love him once, but he killed that when he was unfaithful. Taya's dearest wish is that we get back together, and to make it worse, she saw him kiss me.'

'Eric *kissed you?* When?'

'At the hospital. He caught me unawares. I didn't kiss him back, but Taya saw, and now she thinks there's a chance we'll get back together. I hate to disappoint her – it breaks my heart – but it's not going to happen. How can it, when my heart belongs to Mark?'

A creak sounded overhead, and Beatrice stiffened. Putting a finger to her lips, she shook her head, uncurled her legs and padded upstairs to check on the children, worried that Sadie had woken, but both girls were sound asleep.

Beatrice envied them. She had a feeling it would be a long time before *she* slept peacefully again.

The aroma of his mother's famous mulled wine permeated the house, filling Mark's nostrils with the scent of cloves and cinnamon. It was the epitome of Christmas, yet Mark couldn't remember a Christmas where he felt less festive. Today was Christmas Eve, but to him, it could have been any random Wednesday.

'I hope you're not going to mope around like a wet weekend, like you did yesterday,' his mother said. 'You've got a face that would turn milk sour.'

'I can't help the way my face looks.'

'Nonsense! Are you going to tell me what's wrong, or do I have to guess?'

'There's nothing wrong.' He dropped into a chair, wishing he'd gone to Bristol for Christmas. At least there he could be alone with his misery.

'Are you ill?'

'No, I'm fine.' Did being heartsick count as being ill?

'Are you having financial troubles? Because if you are, your father and I can help you out.'

'My finances are fine. But thank you anyway.'

'Problems with your book, your publisher, your Muse?'

'Not at all.'

'I didn't think so.'

'Why ask?'

'I wanted to be sure. What's her name?'

Mark tensed, then gave a small shake of his head and stared at the tinsel draped around the guilt-framed mirror above the fireplace.

'Have you fallen out, or is it unrequited love?' his mother persisted.

'You're not going to give up, are you?'

'I doubt it.' She opened her mouth to say something else but the shrill ring of the telephone in the hall interrupted her, and she bustled off to answer it.

Glad of the reprieve, Mark slumped back into the cushions and closed his eyes, the thought of trying to be jolly for the next few days filling him with dread.

His mother came back into the sitting room. 'It's for you.'

'What is?'

'The phone.'

'It can't be.'

'It is, if your name is Mark Stafford.' She gave him an arch look.

'Who is it?'

'Do I look like your secretary?' she demanded, then relented as he heaved himself out of his chair. 'She says she's your agent, Angela somebody-or-other. I didn't catch the surname.'

'Angela? Why is she calling me *here?*'

His mother tutted. 'Don't ask me – ask *her.*'

Mark sidled into the hall and picked up the handset. His parents had an old-fashioned phone with a curly cord. They called it retro; he called it archaic.

'Angela?'

'Thank god! I've been calling and messaging you for two days!'

'I switched my phone off.'

'Clearly. Is your computer off as well?'

'Pardon?'

'You're not answering your emails either.'

'It's Christmas Eve.'

'I sent it on Monday. And again yesterday.'

'How did you know I was here?'

614

'An educated guess.'

'How did you get this number?'

'Does it matter? Do me a favour and check your emails.'

'Why?'

'For god's sake Mark, just do it!'

'Wait there.' His phone was upstairs, so he went to fetch it, wondering what could possibly be so important, but not really caring. Surely whatever it was could wait until after Christmas.

He turned it on and went back downstairs while it caught up with itself, and when it did, he was assaulted by a barrage of notifications.

He said, 'Seven missed calls and nine messages? Really, Angela?'

'*Eight* messages.'

He looked again. She was right. She *had* only sent him eight.

The other was from Beatrice.

His heart clenched, a spasm of pain in the middle of his chest so acute that he gasped.

'I know, right?' Angela cried.

'What?'

'It's a tasty advance,' she continued and said something else, but Mark had stopped listening. He was trying to find the courage to read Beatrice's message.

Would there be any point? It would only make his heartbreak more acute. He'd suspected she might try to contact him, to apologise or to explain, and he hadn't wanted to hear it. He still didn't. Damn Angela for making him switch his phone back on.

'Mark? Are you there? *Mark!*'

'I'm here.' His reply was wooden.

'What do I tell Estelle?'

'About what?'

'The *advance*. Have you been on the eggnog already?'

'What do you suggest?' He didn't know what she was talking about and neither did he care: he simply wanted Angela to leave him alone so he could decide whether to read Beatrice's message or not.

He was leaning towards not.

'My advice would be to take it,' his agent said.

'Okay.'

'Great! I'll let her know and she can draw up the contract.'

'Fine.'

'You might sound a bit more enthusiastic.'

'Sorry… I'm thrilled. Honestly.'

'Good. A deal like that, isn't to be sniffed at. Right, that's me done. Have a lovely Christmas and I'll speak to you in the New Year.'

'You, too.'

He replaced the phone on its cradle and stared at his mobile's screen. 'Let's get this over with,' he muttered, knowing that he would end up reading it sooner or later.

But when he opened it, it was the best Christmas present he could have wished for.

The living room was warm and cosy; the lights on the tree twinkled, and Christmas songs played in the background, Beatrice having insisted that the TV be turned off for an hour.

Taya and Sadie were in the kitchen making a gingerbread house, but making a mess would be a more accurate description, as there were blobs and smears of brightly coloured icing all over the kitchen table and all over the girls as well.

She was glad to see Taya having fun though, so she would put up with a bit of mess. Considering it was Christmas Eve, her eldest child was oddly subdued, and the only explanation that Beatrice could come up with was that the events of the past few days had affected her more than she'd thought, and now that things were kind of back to normal, it was beginning to catch up with her.

That was something else Beatrice blamed herself for, but she'd had to focus on Sadie – Sadie had needed her more than Taya – but for a few days Beatrice had neglected her other child. And what really hurt, what she felt so incredibly guilty about, was the suspicion that she might have taken her eye off the ball when it came to her kids. She had been so wrapped up in her new job and her new (old) love affair, that she hadn't seen what was happening under her very nose.

No more. From now on, all of Beatrice's love, care and attention would be on her children. No distractions. And after Christmas she would have to have a serious think about whether she intended to carry on working. She loved her job, but if she hadn't been so worried about missing work and letting Dulcie down on Thursday, would she have listened to her instincts and kept Sadie home from school?

Rationally, she knew it wouldn't have made any difference – Sadie would still have needed her appendix removed. And by being in school and Eric being in the audience, Sadie had got to the hospital faster than if she had collapsed at home.

But all the rationalising and reasoning in the world couldn't prevent Beatrice from feeling as guilty as hell.

Lisa reckoned she was using the guilt to deflect from the misery of a broken heart, but Beatrice didn't think that was true, and even if it was, she'd take it, because anything was better than thinking about Mark.

The lights on the tree created a soft warm glow, but inside her, the chill of loneliness settled over her. She never should have let him into her heart again. The wound of his first abandonment had fleshed over, the scar on her heart still there, but buried deep. He had ripped it open again and it was now raw and bleeding, with a pain so acute she knew she would never risk loving anyone again.

Her heart ached, not just from his absence, but from the dreams she had woven in the quiet hours of her mind which were now lost. She had painted a future together in colours more vibrant than the pictures in his books. When she'd read his letter and understood that he didn't love her after all, her world had darkened, the colour leeched out of it. Hers was a story without a happy ending, and she hated herself for letting him write the first word on her heart.

Each day since he'd left had felt like a slow unravelling, a reminder of the love that had slipped through her fingers for a second time.

As she sat in the fading light, tears welled, but she refused to cry over him again. She'd shed enough tears, so with a shaky breath, she blinked them away and resolved to take it one day at a time. And if she never heard his name again, it would be too soon.

The doorbell rang.

With a deep sigh, she got to her feet. It was probably her parents. They'd taken to calling in most days to check on her and the girls. Sadie had scared them, too.

Sadie beat her to the door, thundering into the hall. 'Mummy! It's Mark!' she yelled.

Beatrice hurried after her. 'What have I told you about answering the door to strangers—' She stopped. It *was* Mark.

'Mark isn't a stranger,' Sadie said, grabbing his hand and trying to tug him inside.

Wasn't he? Beatrice had thought she knew him, but she hadn't. Not then, and certainly not now.

'Can I come in?' he asked.

'No.'

Confusion flitted across his face. 'I thought—'

'That you could rock up again and I'd welcome you with open arms?' She shook her head. 'I don't think so. Sadie, go to your room. You too, Taya,' she added, when she saw her in the kitchen doorway.

'Mum, let him in,' Taya said.

'Go to your room. Now!' She didn't want the children to witness this – whatever *this* was. Turning her attention back to Mark, she hissed, 'You'd better leave.'

'But you—'

'Go! Before I call the police.' She put her hands on her hips. She didn't know what game he was playing, but she wanted no part of it.

'Bea, don't do this to me,' he pleaded. 'You can't tell me you love me one minute, then tell me to go away the next.'

'I never said I love you.'

'You did!' He yanked his mobile out of his pocket. 'You sent me a message—' He stopped, the colour draining from his face. 'It wasn't meant for me, was it?'

'I don't know what you're talking about. I haven't sent any messages telling anyone I love them.'

He hung his head. 'Sorry, my mistake. I'll go.'

'Mum?'

'*Not now,* Taya. I thought I told you to go to your room.'

'*I* sent it.' Taya's voice was small. 'I borrowed your phone and sent it.'

'You did *what?*' Beatrice's gaze flew to Taya, appalled, and Taya began to cry. 'Why?' she demanded.

'Because I heard you talking to Aunty Lisa. When you got drunk.'

'I wasn't drunk,' she replied automatically. 'Taya, sweetie, what have I told you about listening to other people's conversations? Especially adult ones, when you don't understand what they're saying.'

'You said you didn't love Dad, but you love Mark. Is it true?'

Beatrice groaned. 'I care for your dad, but—' Oh hell, how do you explain something that complicated to a nine-year-old.

'You and Dad aren't getting back together, are you.'

Her eyes filling with tears again, Beatrice said, 'No, Taya, we're not. But that doesn't mean Mark and I are.'

'Why not? Mummy, you're so sad now.'

Mummy? Taya hadn't called her that in a while. 'I'm not sad,' she fibbed.

'You are. You were really happy when Mark was here, and now you keep crying.'

Blast, she didn't think the kids had noticed. She'd thought she'd hidden it well. 'Please Taya, go to your room, and take Sadie with you. I need to have a quick chat with Mark.'

But Taya wasn't done with her yet. 'Mark saw you kissing Dad.'

Beatrice's mouth dropped open. She looked at Mark. 'Is that why...?'

'Yes.'

'You left because you thought...?'

'Yes.'

'*You eejit.*' She glared at her daughters and waited until they had beaten a hasty retreat up the stairs. 'Why didn't you ask me?'

'How could I? What could I say – Bea, I saw you snogging your kids' dad, but do you have any feelings for me?'

'That's exactly what you should have said.'

'I'm going to be honest – I love you, Bea. I think I always have, but I was too stupid to realise it. I don't want to lose you again. Can you forgive me?'

Beatrice didn't have to think about it. She had forgiven him the moment she realised that he was willing to put her children's happiness before his own. He'd walked away to give her and Eric a chance – because that was the right thing to do. Mark Stafford *was* a nice guy. How could she *not* forgive him?

To think Taya had sent Mark that message! It made her heart melt. Beatrice owed her daughter a massive debt of gratitude, and she was so full of love that she thought she might burst.

She said, 'I think you'd better come in. We've got a lot of catching up to do.'

Mark gathered her into his arms and kissed her gently. 'The catching up can wait. It's Christmas Eve. I'll call you later.'

'You're not going anywhere. You're going to spend it with us,' she replied firmly.

But before she called the girls downstairs, she wanted a minute to kiss him properly, and as their lips met, Beatrice's heart – like the Grinch's – grew three sizes.

Mark loved her.

Wishes did come true, after all.

Mark inhaled deeply and his mouth watered. The turkey smelt divine. It looked it too: white meat, crispy skin, and surrounded by golden Yorkshire puddings.

Beatrice's father placed the serving platter in the centre of the table with reverence, saying, 'My wife cooks a mean Christmas dinner. Mind you, by the day after Boxing Day I'll be sick to death of turkey.' He leant in and whispered loudly, 'If I'm desperate for a change, I'll pop into The Black Horse and have lunch with you – no doubt the girls will want to go to the sales, so we can have a sneaky pint and get to know one another properly.'

'I heard that,' Deborah said, winking at Mark. 'Little does he know, but he'll be looking after our grandchildren. I'll be damned if we're dragging Taya and Sadie around the shops. Help yourself, Mark. Don't stand on ceremony.'

Beatrice passed him a tureen of glazed carrots. The children were already spooning food onto their plates. Sadie, he noticed, was paying particular attention to the pigs in blankets, a determined expression on her face.

'They're her favourite,' Beatrice said. 'That's why Mum cooked so many, because she knew Sadie would eat the lot if I let her.'

'Thank you again for inviting me.'

'I was hardly going to let you starve.'

He chuckled. 'I'm sure Dave and Monica would have taken pity on me and made me up a plate.'

She squeezed his leg. 'And you would have ended up eating it on your own in your room. Not a chance.'

Mark had talked Dave into giving him his old room back, on the understanding that there wouldn't be any food served on Christmas Day – although normal service would be resumed on Boxing Day – so having not had any breakfast, apart from the complimentary biscuits in his room, Mark had been starving by the time he arrived at Beatrice's house shortly after noon this morning. They had agreed that he wouldn't arrive before then, so Eric could spend the morning with his daughters.

By the time Mark got to Beatrice's, he had found her sitting on the sofa with a Baileys Irish Cream in one hand, a Terry's Chocolate Orange in the other, and surrounded by toys and wrapping paper. The girls had been glassy eyed with excitement, their mother glassy eyed with exhaustion, having been woken several times in the early hours by Sadie asking whether Santa had been yet and worrying that the

Grinch had stolen her Christmas, despite the green Grinch dust that had been sprinkled on the doorstep.

The children were happy to see him (probably because he came bearing gifts, and the books were enthusiastically received), and he had spent the next hour or so playing games with Sadie and showing Taya how to set up her new tablet, before accompanying them to Beatrice's parents' house for Christmas lunch.

He had no idea what Beatrice had said to her mum and dad, but they had welcomed him with open arms, so Mark assumed it hadn't been anything too awful.

'So,' Deborah said to him, 'are you back in Picklewick for good?'

Mark shot an anxious glance at Beatrice. 'I hope so. If Beatrice is okay with that.'

Beatrice rolled her eyes. 'Why do men need things spelling out? I'm most definitely okay with that. But where are you going to live? You can't stay at The Black Horse indefinitely.'

'I don't intend to. I've already put feelers out with a couple of estate agents.' His original intention had been to rent somewhere, but if he sold his house in Bristol he could buy a place in Picklewick instead. And with the advance from Pinkymoon Publishers, he could afford to buy somewhere very nice indeed – somewhere with plenty of room for a wife and two little girls… When the time was right, he would ask Beatrice to marry him.

After a lovely Christmas Day spent with Beatrice's family, it was eventually time for the tired children to go home, and Mark walked Beatrice and the girls back.

He hadn't intended to come in. He'd intended to say good night on the doorstep, but Sadie had other plans and had grumpily insisted that Mark read her a bedtime story. He obliged by reading her favourite book, the one he had written and illustrated himself.

It had been the best Christmas ever, and when Beatrice took him to her bed much, much later; it was the perfect end to a perfect day.

And that was how Marc Stafford, renowned children's author, began the rest of his life with a woman he had loved for most of it, if only he had realised.

Not ready to let go of Muddypuddle Lane yet?

The Forever Home on Muddypuddle Lane

is a brand new series filled with wonderful new characters – and a few you already know and love...

One little dog. Two broken hearts. A chance for love...

Cat-lover Gretta Lavern has never been fond of dogs, so when she unexpectedly becomes responsible for a little Frenchie named Bertie, she is far from happy. With her well-ordered life now in disarray and her pampered Persian cat at war with the newcomer, Gretta is soon at her wit's end. There is only one thing for it – the dog has to go.

Surly Jakob Darrow prefers the company of pups over people, but when Gretta enlists his help to find Bertie a forever home, he feels a spark reignite within him—one he thought had long faded.

And while Gretta is also inexplicably drawn to Jakob, they are total opposites and neither of them is looking for love.

But Bertie has other plans...

As Gretta faces her fear of vulnerability and Jakob confronts his deep loneliness, can the love of a small dog heal their hearts and bring them together, or will their differences tear them apart?

Acknowledgements

My family deserves a great deal of thanks, mainly for putting up with my incessant daydreaming. Love you to the moon and back xxx

Thanks to my lovely editor and friend, Catherine Mills, for her support and advice.

My friends also get a huge hug for all the love and encouragement, even if they don't understand all the wittering on about story arcs!

Finally, I can't go without sharing my heartfelt gratitude to you, my readers.
You make the writing worthwhile xxx

About Etti

Etti Summers is the author of wonderfully romantic fiction with happy ever afters guaranteed.
She is also a wife, a mum, a pink gin enthusiast, a veggie grower and a keen reader.

Printed in Dunstable, United Kingdom